KU-175-220

Trouble at the Little Village School

Also by Gervase Phinn

The Little Village School

Out of the Woods But Not Over the Hill

THE DALES SERIES
The Other Side of the Dale
Over Hill and Dale
Head Over Heels in the Dales
Up and Down in the Dales
The Heart of the Dales

A Wayne in a Manger
Twinkle, Twinkle, Little Stars
A Load of Old Tripe

POETRY
It Takes One to Know One
The Day Our Teacher Went Batty
Family Phantoms
Don't Tell the Teacher

GERVASE PHINN

Trouble at the
Little Village School

HODDER

First published in Great Britain in 2012 by Hodder & Stoughton
An Hachette UK company

First published in paperback in 2013

3

Copyright © Gervase Phinn 2012

The right of Gervase Phinn to be identified as the Author
of the Work has been asserted by him in accordance with
the Copyright, Designs and Patents Act 1988.

All rights reserved. No part of this publication may be reproduced,
stored in a retrieval system, or transmitted, in any form or by any
means without the prior written permission of the publisher, nor be
otherwise circulated in any form of binding or cover other than that
in which it is published and without a similar condition being
imposed on the subsequent purchaser.

All characters in this publication are fictitious and any resemblance to
real persons, living or dead is purely coincidental.

A CIP catalogue record for this title is available from the British Library

ISBN 9781444705607

Typeset in Plantin Light by Hewer Text UK Ltd, Edinburgh
Printed and bound by Clays Ltd, St Ives plc

Hodder & Stoughton policy is to use papers that are natural, renewable
and recyclable products and made from wood grown in sustainable forests.
The logging and manufacturing processes are expected to conform
to the environmental regulations of the country of origin.

Hodder & Stoughton Ltd
338 Euston Road
London NW1 3BH

www.hodder.co.uk

For my sister Christine Charlesworth, with
love and tremendous gratitude

I

'So, what do you reckon then?' asked the caretaker as he leaned idly against the doorframe, jangling the bunch of heavy keys in his overall pocket. He was a gangly, gaunt individual with sandy thinning hair, a hard beak of a nose and the staring eyes of a deep-sea fish.

It was the start of the spring term at Barton-in-the-Dale Primary School and he and Mrs Scrimshaw, the school secretary, were in the small office.

'What do I reckon to what?' she asked, peering over the top of her unfashionable horn-rimmed spectacles and brushing a stray strand of mouse-coloured hair from her forehead.

The caretaker moved into the room, perched himself on the corner of her desk and leaned closer. The school secretary caught a whiff of floor polish and disinfectant and wrinkled her nose.

'Come on Mrs Scrimshaw,' he chuckled. 'You've got eyes in your head. You must have noticed.'

The secretary removed her glasses and placed them carefully on the desk. She looked up at the caretaker. 'Noticed what?' she said, feigning ignorance.

'About our head teacher and the local GP.'

'I really don't know to what you are referring, Mr Gribbon,' she said stiffly. She replaced her glasses and looked down at the letters before her.

'Oh, come along, Mrs Scrimshaw, don't play the innocent with me,' said the caretaker jovially. She winced. 'It can't have escaped your notice. It's as plain as a pikestaff. You know as well as I do that there's something going on between them.'

'Mr Gribbon,' replied the school secretary sharply, 'what Mrs Devine and Dr Stirling do in their own time is of no concern of mine – nor yours for that matter.' She shuffled in her chair and picked up a paperknife. 'As you well know, I'm not a one for gossip and rumour-mongering,' she added.

'Well, I reckon there's something going on,' he persisted, rubbing his chin thoughtfully. 'I mean, when he's in school she can't take her eyes off of him and it's clear to me that he's got the hots for *her*. Why, when he was in last term doing that session on sex education—'

'Mr Gribbon,' interrupted the school secretary, 'it is none of anyone's business what Mrs Devine and Dr Stirling might be getting up to.'

'So, you do think they are getting up to something then?' He smiled conspiratorially.

'I didn't say that,' she objected.

'I mean,' said the caretaker, sucking in his breath and blowing out noisily, 'he couldn't stand the sight of her when she started here and now they're as thick as thieves.'

'Couldn't stand the sight of her?' repeated Mrs Scrimshaw, placing the paperknife back down on the desk. 'I think that's something of an exaggeration. I admit that Dr Stirling, like a lot of other people, I might add, didn't take to Mrs Devine when she took over as head teacher here, and some didn't entirely see eye to eye with her, but once people in the village got to know her and saw how she started improving everything in the school, they soon changed their minds. And I for one think she's been like a breath of fresh air since her arrival.'

The school secretary's observations were accurate. When Elisabeth Devine had been called for interview for the post of head teacher at the small village school, dressed in startling bright red shoes with silver heels and black lacy stockings, she had caused quite a stir. She was so very different from the present incumbent of the post, the formidable Miss Hilda Sowerbutts, she of the pleated tweeds, heavy brogues, bullet-proof stockings, sour face and sharp tongue.

With Elisabeth's appointment the school had undergone a dramatic change. A moribund place under the management of Miss Sowerbutts, it had begun to flourish under Elisabeth's firm and decisive leadership. The once dark and neglected premises had been transformed into a bright, cheerful and welcoming environment.

Of course, it had not all been plain sailing. Soon after her appointment a bombshell had been dropped on the school. Elisabeth had learned that those on the Education Committee had it in mind to close Barton-in-the-Dale. There had been a concerted and ultimately successful campaign and the future of the school now seemed assured.

'How long is it since the doctor's wife fell off of her horse and broke her neck?' asked the caretaker now.

Mrs Scrimshaw pursed her lips and looked at him reproach-fully. 'You do have such a way of putting things,' she sighed. 'Talk about being blunt.'

'Well, it's been a while, hasn't it?' continued the caretaker, sliding off the desk and jangling his keys noisily.

'She had that dreadful accident two years ago,' Mrs Scrimshaw informed him.

Mr Gribbon sniffed noisily. 'So the good doctor will be on the lookout for another wife,' he observed, 'and Mrs Devine being divorced and all, it seems to me she'll be in the running. They make a good couple, don't you think?'

'I wouldn't know about that,' said the school secretary, look-ing down at the letters on her desk and picking up the paperknife again. The caretaker could sense her irritation. 'And as for being divorced, that is sheer speculation.' She sliced open an envelope.

'Well, there's no man on the scene,' observed the caretaker.

'She could be a widow,' said the secretary, 'or separated. Anyway, as I've said, Mrs Devine's private life is no concern of mine – or yours for that matter.'

'Yes, well, if you ask me—' began the caretaker.

'I'm not asking you, Mr Gribbon,' interrupted Mrs Scrimshaw. 'Now if you don't mind, I have a great deal to do this morning and I guess you have jobs to do.' She tapped the pile of letters on her desk. 'Being the start of the new term there's this little lot to deal with, for a start.'

The caretaker made no effort to move. He stretched and scratched his scalp. 'Well, I suppose I'd better finish off buffing my floors before the hordes arrive,' he grumbled.

'Good idea,' muttered the school secretary, not looking up.

'Excuse me, Mr Gribbon, I'm sorry to interrupt your conversation but may I have a quick word with Mrs Scrimshaw?'

The caretaker turned as a small boy, about eight or nine years old, came into the office. He was a rosy-faced child with fox-coloured hair and was dressed in curiously old-fashioned clothes – white shirt and tie, long grey shorts, grey knee-length stockings, knitted cardigan, and substantial black shoes. His way of speaking was also curiously old-fashioned. He was like a throwback to the 1950s. The caretaker rolled his eyes and shook his head tetchily.

'You're here bright and early, Oscar,' remarked the school secretary, looking up and peering over her glasses.

'Oh, I like to get here early on the first day of term, Mrs Scrimshaw,' the boy replied cheerfully. 'Actually I'm quite keen to be back. I've been rather bored over the holidays.'

'Well, what is it you want?' she asked.

'I was wondering, Mrs Scrimshaw, if you have managed to go through the post this morning?'

'No, not yet. Why?'

'Well, there may be a letter there for me,' the child informed her, approaching the desk.

'And who's sending you letters to the school?' barked the caretaker.

'Well, you see, Mr Gribbon,' the boy explained, 'this term we're doing a project on our favourite writers, and over the Christmas break our teacher asked all the children in the class to pick a book to read. We will have to do a book review and say whether we like it or not and then write to the poets and authors. Mrs Robertshaw's going to put up a display in the corridor about all the writers whom we have read, with pictures of them, book jackets and posters, and any letters we receive. I think it's a really super idea.'

'And?' asked the caretaker.

'Pardon?' replied the boy.

'Why are you receiving letters here at the school?'

'Well, it occurred to me,' said the child, 'that it would be really good to send a letter to my favourite writer straight away so I dropped him a line over Christmas. I have a new laptop computer and thought I'd get a bit of practice in with the word-processing, so I wrote to the poet Peter Dixon. He's really very good at rhymes and rhythms and his poems are very amusing. I sometimes laugh out loud.'

'Really?' said the caretaker disbelievingly.

'I thought I'd put the school address on my letter since it is a school project,' the child told him.

Mrs Scrimshaw, who had been looking through the pile of letters on her desk while the boy was speaking, shook her head. 'No, there's nothing, Oscar,' she said.

'Could I have a quick look,' asked the boy, 'just to make sure?'

'There's no need for that,' said the secretary. 'There is no letter here for you.'

'So take yourself off,' the caretaker told him, 'and don't go walking on the hall floor. I've not buffed it up yet.'

'Actually I'm glad I've seen you, Mr Gribbon,' said the boy, ignoring the instruction. 'I noticed that the boys' toilets were very smelly last term. They could have done with a good clean. I'm afraid they were not very hygienic.'

'You don't say?' The caretaker grimaced.

'And the floor was quite wet. I nearly slipped and could have hurt myself,' continued the boy.

'Well, you should look where you're going then, shouldn't you?' said the caretaker, a vein in his temple standing out and beating angrily.

'I've just called in now,' continued the boy, undeterred by the caretaker's angry tone of voice, 'and I have to say they are still rather smelly.'

'If you boys aimed where you're supposed to aim,' snapped Mr Gribbon, 'then there wouldn't be wet floors and the toilets wouldn't be smelly.'

'But there's nobody been in the toilets this morning except me,' replied Oscar.

'Look here—' began the caretaker, stabbing the air with a finger in the boy's direction.

'Perhaps,' continued Oscar, 'you could put a ping-pong ball down each of the toilet bowls for the boys to aim at. It might solve the problem. I've done an experiment and when the toilet is flushed the ping-pong ball floats and—'

'Look—' began the caretaker again, spots of angry red appearing on his cheekbones.

'And you might use an air freshener.'

The caretaker opened his mouth to reply but the boy smiled widely and said, 'Well, I think I'll get on with my book in the library. I'll call back again at break, Mrs Scrimshaw, and see if my letter has arrived in this morning's post.'

'Goodbye Oscar,' said the school secretary, giving a fleeting smile as she caught sight of the caretaker's angry red face.

As Mrs Scrimshaw busied herself opening the letters in the school office, the caretaker departed grumbling to buff up his floor and young Oscar headed for the small school library to read his book, Miss Brakespeare, deputy head teacher at Barton-in-the-Dale village school, stood at the front of her classroom, hands clasped before her, and examined the room with pride. She looked approvingly at the vivid displays, the bright new tables and chairs, the neatly stacked books, the colourful drapes at the windows and the bookcase full of glossy-backed paperbacks. So wide was her smile that had she been wearing lipstick that morning she could very well have left red traces on the lobes of her ears.

The deputy head teacher had spent several days over the holidays in readiness for the new term, sorting out her store-room, sharpening pencils, tidying the books, mounting pictures and posters on the walls and preparing her lessons. She had never felt quite as content at the start of a new school term as she did on that crisp January morning, with bright sunshine lighting up her room, and she looked forward to welcoming back the children in her class.

Miss Brakespeare took a deep breath. Yes, she thought, as she surveyed her classroom now, she was very happy with how things had turned out.

A head appeared around her classroom door. 'Your class-room looks nice, Miriam.' The speaker was a broad woman with a wide, friendly face and steely-grey hair gathered up untidily on her head.

'Thank you, Elsie,' Miss Brakespeare replied, clearly pleased with the compliment. 'One tries one's best.'

'You haven't forgotten the staff meeting at eight-fifteen, have you?'

'No, no, I'm just coming.'

Mrs Devine and the teachers met in the staffroom, formerly the head teacher's room in the time of Miss Sowerbutts. Elsie Robertshaw, teacher of the lower juniors, and Rebecca Wilson, teacher of the infants, sat with Marcia Atticus, the vicar's wife, who was training to be a teacher at the school. Elisabeth smiled as she saw Miss Brakespeare bustle through the door in a stylish grey suit, pink silk blouse, black stockings and patent leather shoes. What a change had taken place in her deputy, she thought, and not just in her appearance. When Elisabeth had first met her at the interviews for the headship, she had not formed a very positive picture of her future colleague. The mousy little woman with the round face and the staring eyes, dressed in an ill-fitting cotton suit, dark stockings and sandals, had appeared dowdy and dull. Her hair had been scraped back in a style that was a good twenty years out of date, and there had not been a trace of any make-up. She had smiled a great deal, sighed a great deal and nodded a great deal but had said very little. But over the term she had blossomed, and the school inspector who had given her such a poor report noted, on his return visit, that she had made a vast improvement.

'Good morning, everyone,' said Elisabeth cheerily, 'and a very happy new year.' There were smiles and good-humoured murmurs in response. 'I won't keep you long, because I am sure there are things you need to get on with and the children will be arriving soon. I just wanted to welcome you back and say I am really looking forward to working with you all again this term. We travelled through some pretty stormy waters last year, didn't we, with the proposed closure of the school and all the uncertainty?'

'We did indeed,' agreed Miss Brakespeare, nodding like one of those toy dogs seen in the backs of cars.

'But thankfully that is all behind us now,' continued Elisabeth, 'and we can look forward to some stability. We start off with some really good news. Firstly, as you were aware, Mrs Robertshaw and Miss Wilson were on temporary contracts last term. I heard from the Local Education Authority over the holidays that their contracts have now been made permanent.' There were claps and congratulations. 'Secondly, I am delighted to say that Mrs Atticus, who as you know has been accepted for teacher-training at St John's College, will continue her teaching practice here at Barton-in-the-Dale.' There were more murmurs of approval. 'We have a bright, refurbished school and six new pupils starting with us this morning, so the future looks more than rosy.'

The school secretary poked her head around the staffroom door.

'You asked me to let you know, Mrs Devine, when the pupils start to arrive,' she said.

'Thank you, Mrs Scrimshaw,' replied Elisabeth, rising and smoothing out the creases in her skirt.

'And you want to get well wrapped up before you venture out there,' said the secretary. 'It's started snowing again and it's freezing cold. And watch your step, the path's like a skating rink. I've had a word with Mr Gribbon and he's putting some salt and grit down.'

Outside, Elisabeth found the caretaker throwing sand and salt on the path like a farmer sowing seeds. 'Bloody weather,' he grumbled to himself.

Since starting as the head teacher it had been Elisabeth's practice to stand at the school gate each Monday morning to greet the children and speak to the parents, something which the former incumbent had never condescended to do. By doing this, Elisabeth found that she met parents she otherwise would rarely see and that those too reserved to call into school over a problem were more willing to talk to her at the gate than inside the building.

Being the start of the new term, it was an unusually large turnout of mothers and fathers that morning. Elisabeth smiled and greeted each parent with a friendly 'Good morning.' Most nodded and smiled and some came over to have a word. Elisabeth noticed Dr Stirling talking to Mrs Stubbins, a round, shapeless woman with bright, frizzy, dyed ginger hair, an impressive set of double chins and immense hips. She was wrapped in a voluminous coat and wore a multicoloured woollen hat with a bobble on the top. She was probably recounting the catalogue of ailments she had. Dr Stirling caught sight of Elisabeth and his face brightened. He finally managed to extricate himself and came over to join her.

'Good morning,' he said.

'Hello, Michael,' she replied.

They stood for a moment in silence.

Michael Stirling was a tall, not unattractive man, aged about forty, with a firm jawline and a full head of dark hair, greying at the temples and parted untidily. What was most striking was his pale blue eyes, the first thing Elisabeth had noticed about him. Their relationship at first had been fraught. When she had first met him she had found him stubborn and pig-headed. He was a man of few words, but when he did speak to her he seemed to find fault with everything she did. She had soon discovered she was wrong about him. Underneath that seemingly distant and sombre exterior was a shy and compassionate man. She recalled his first tentative kiss in a darkened classroom under the sprig of mistletoe after the Christmas concert. It was just a small, tender kiss, not one of those fiery unbidden kinds described in romantic fiction. It was really little more than a brief brush of the lips. But she had not forgotten it. She felt something greater than the close friendship that had developed, and perhaps wanted more from the relationship, but she was wary. She could tell that he felt the same.

'I thought, being the first morning of the new term and my surgery not starting until later this morning,' he said now, 'I'd walk the boys to school.'

'I see.'

He rubbed his hands and exhaled, his breath causing a

cloud of steam in the cold air. 'I think I'm in for a busy day ahead,' he said, making an effort at conversation. 'I get a lot of patients in this weather, colds and flu, that sort of thing.' He stopped and stared.

'Was there something else?' asked Elisabeth.

'Well, yes, there was, I mean there is, actually,' he said.

'Which is?' asked Elisabeth after a long pause.

He came closer and lowered his voice so as not to be over-heard. A faint odour of sandalwood soap and aftershave clung to him. 'Would you care to have a meal with me tonight?' he asked. 'There's a little French restaurant in Clayton which comes highly recommended. I thought we might—' His voice tailed off.

'I'd love to,' Elisabeth replied.

His face broke into a smile. 'You would? That's splendid. Well, shall I collect you about seven?'

She nodded. 'That's fine. I look forward to it.'

'That's good,' he said, nodding. He made no effort to move. The snow had settled on his hair.

'I had better go,' said Elisabeth. 'I'll see you tonight.'

The caretaker, who had stopped dispensing the salt and grit to observe the two of them, spoke out loud to himself. 'Now you tell me,' he said smugly, 'that there's nothing going on between them two.'

At morning break, as Elisabeth patrolled the school, the caretaker appeared jangling his keys. 'It's a cold one today, Mrs Devine,' he said, 'and no mistake.'

'It is that, Mr Gribbon,' replied Elisabeth, 'and I realise it makes more work for you. Thank you for gritting the paths and clearing the snow so promptly.'

'No problem,' he said.

'I was meaning to have a word with you today on another matter.'

'Oh yes?' he said, looking troubled. 'Nothing untoward, I hope.'

'No, nothing untoward,' Elisabeth repeated. 'I wanted to thank you for getting the school so clean and bright over the Christmas break.'

'A pleasure, I'm sure, Mrs Devine,' he said grinning and rubbing his jaw, clearly pleased with the praise.

'I guess it was quite a job,' continued the head teacher, 'having to move all the old desks and replace them with the new tables and chairs and then giving the school a thorough clean.'

The caretaker decided not to mention that the replacement of the desks had been done by two removal men and that a team of industrial cleaners and decorators had been employed by the Local Education Authority to undertake the renovations.

'Well, I try my best, Mrs Devine,' said the caretaker, jangling the keys in his overall pocket.

As they turned the corner of the corridor they came upon a small boy sitting in the corner of the school library, poring over a thick tome. He looked up, caught sight of them, snapped the book shut and stood up.

'Hello, Oscar,' said Elisabeth.

'Oh, hello, Mrs Devine,' said the boy in a cheery, sing-song tone of voice. 'Happy new year.'

'And the same to you,' replied Elisabeth, smiling.

'Hello, Mr Gribbon,' said the boy.

The caretaker grunted. His glance was like the sweep of a scythe.

The boy produced four ping-pong balls from his pocket. 'Look what I found in the games box, Mr Gribbon,' he said. The caretaker breathed in noisily and gripped his keys tightly. 'I think you know what to do with them.'

Le Bon Viveur at Clayton was a small restaurant tucked away discreetly in the shadow of the great cathedral. It was a most elegant place, everything sparkling and stylish. Elisabeth and Dr Stirling were greeted at the entrance by a slim, dark-complexioned individual with shiny boot-black hair scraped back on his scalp and large expressive eyes. He was immaculately dressed in a dinner jacket and smelled of expensive cologne.

'Good evening,' said Dr Stirling. 'We have a reservation for eight o'clock.'

'*Ah, oui.* Dr Stirling?'

'That's right.'

'May I welcome you both to Le Bon Viveur,' said the man, smiling and displaying a set of perfectly even and impressively white teeth. There was a trace of a French accent. 'Your first time here, I think?'

'Yes,' said Elisabeth.

'I sincerely hope that this will not be the last visit for you,' he continued, bowing slightly. 'Should there be anything you require, please ask. I am at your disposal. I am Bernard Richeux, the owner.' He bowed again. 'Now, *monsieur, madame,* if you would care to follow me . . .'

The diners were shown to a corner table covered with a spotless and stiff white cloth and set out with delicate china plates, starched napkins and heavy silver cutlery. In the centre was a single red rose in a small cut-glass vase.

'I imagine you would both enjoy an *apéritif*?' observed the Frenchman.

'What a welcome,' said Elisabeth, as the owner departed to get the drinks. 'I feel like royalty.'

'He was a bit over the top, don't you think?' asked Dr Stirling.

'Not at all,' disagreed Elisabeth. 'I thought he was charming. It's nice to be treated with such consideration.' She looked around. 'I say, it's frightfully posh here, isn't it?'

Dr Stirling grunted in agreement before glancing at the

menu. 'It's all in French,' he whispered, 'and there are no prices. I can see this is going to cost me an arm and a leg.'

'There speaks the true-blue Yorkshireman, thrifty as ever,' said Elisabeth, smiling. 'Who was it who said "the Yorkshireman knows the price of everything and the value of nothing"?'

'It was Oscar Wilde, for your information,' retorted Dr Stirling, good-humouredly, 'and he was referring to the cynic and not the Yorkshireman. Yorkshire folk are the most generous, good-hearted and friendly people in the country but we are prudent and want value for money, and there is nothing wrong with that.'

'Well, don't worry your head, Michael,' said Elisabeth, patting his hand, 'we'll go Dutch.'

'No, no, I wasn't suggesting—' he started, suddenly becoming serious and colouring up. 'I was just making an observation and—'

Elisabeth laughed. 'I was teasing you,' she told him.

'I'm afraid I do have a tendency to say the wrong thing, don't I?' he said. 'I never meant that I—'

'I know you didn't,' interrupted Elisabeth.

Dr Stirling recalled for a moment the first occasion he had spoken to Elisabeth Devine following her appointment as head teacher. He had crossed swords with her about the education of his son and had later regretted what he had said. 'I'm afraid I'm not that good with words,' he conceded. 'Never have been.'

'Well, what about your French?' asked Elisabeth, looking at the menu.

'Non-existent,' he replied, shaking his head. 'I've not the slightest idea what all these dishes are.'

'Don't worry,' Elisabeth told him. 'I'll tell you what we can have.'

'You speak French?' he exclaimed.

'*Ah, oui*, Dr Stirling. Every year when I was a child we used to camp for a month in the Vendée. My brother Giles and I got pretty good at the language. Then I spent a year in Arcachon when I was at university, and before coming to live in Barton I taught a French conversation class.'

'What a dark horse you are, Mrs Devine,' said the doctor. 'I had no idea.'

'Ah, there are many things about me that you don't know,' she replied with a mischievous little grin.

'I'm looking forward to finding out,' he said smiling shyly. He glanced at the menu. 'What's *frisée avec lardons*?'

'Lettuce and bits of bacon,' Elisabeth told him.

'And *sole aux épinards*?'

'Fish.'

'*Cailles flambées*?'

'Quails with cherries.'

'This one sounds quite exotic,' said Dr Stirling. '*Lentilles – saucisses à l'ancienne.*'

'Sausage casserole,' Elisabeth explained.

'It sounds so much better in French, doesn't it?' he observed. 'I think I'll settle for the *soupe aux cerises*. You can't go wrong with soup. What sort is it?'

Elisabeth laughed. 'No, Michael. *Soupe aux cerises* is cherries on toast.'

'Show-off,' he said good-naturedly.

The owner returned with the drinks and the wine list. 'Now perhaps you would like me to take you through what is on the menu this evening,' he said.

'No need,' said Dr Stirling, 'I have received a very full translation from my dining companion, thank you.'

'You speak French!' exclaimed the owner, turning to Elisabeth and displaying his shining teeth.

'*Pas tellement bien,*' she replied.

Then the owner and Elisabeth spent the next five minutes chattering away in French.

'Pardon, *monsieur*,' Dr Stirling butted in. 'Much as I dislike breaking up this interesting little tête-à-tête, perhaps we might order something to eat?'

'But of course,' said the owner. 'The chef's special tonight is *Madame Poisson's poule au pot*, which is an irresistible chicken dish, a favourite so we are told of the famous Madame de Pompadour.'

'That sounds good,' said Elisabeth. 'I'll think I'll go for the chicken.'

'Me too,' said Dr Stirling.

'And the salad to start.'

'Me as well,' added Dr Stirling.

'And the *gláce au chocolat*,' said Elisabeth. 'Chocolate ice cream,' she mouthed across the table.

'Same for me,' said Dr Stirling.

'And might I suggest the wine to complement the meal?' asked the owner. 'La Révélation du Baron is very palatable. It has been coolly fermented to capture the bright tropical fruit flavours, an opulent wine with an elegant peach and honey-suckle note and a hint of spice.'

'That sounds fine,' replied Dr Stirling.

The food and the wine were excellent, as was the service. The owner seemed to spend more time at Dr Stirling's and Elisabeth's table than any other. Over coffee and a compli-mentary *digestif* they sat for a minute in contented silence. Then Dr Stirling reached across the table and took Elisabeth's hand in his.

'You look lovely tonight,' he said.

'Thank you, kind sir,' replied Elisabeth, 'and you've made quite an effort yourself. You look very well-groomed.'

'I sound like a horse,' he replied laughing.

When she had first met him Elisabeth had been less than impressed with Michael Stirling's appearance, and 'well-groomed' had been the last words that came to mind. She recalled for a moment that first meeting when she had been called for interview for the headship of the village school. He was the governor who scowled and said little, and although he was not unattractive it was clear he cared little about his appearance. Elisabeth noticed that his suit was shiny and unfashionable and had seen better days, that his shirt was frayed around the collar, his tie crumpled and that his shoes could do with a good polish. She smiled to see him now. Quite a transformation.

'That's the influence of a good woman,' he said, interrupting her thoughts.

'Pardon?'

He smiled. 'You were miles away. I was saying that I just needed someone, a good woman, to take me in hand.' He looked down and thought for a moment. 'After my wife died, looking after my appearance was the last thing on my mind.'

This was the first time he had mentioned his wife, who had been killed and had left him and his young son devastated. Elisabeth let him talk. 'I threw myself into my work,' he continued, 'and became so very tetchy and depressed. I lived for each day and was no company for anyone. That's why I was offhand with you and said things I very much regret.' He looked up. 'But you've brought me out of myself, Elisabeth, you really have. You've made me feel there is a future, that life is worth living again.'

Elisabeth felt tears in her eyes. 'Well, it's been a super evening,' she said. 'Thank you so much for inviting me, Michael. It was a really nice thought.'

He looked earnestly at her, then cleared his throat and swallowed hard. His eyes glistened. 'I wanted to tell you that over the last few months my feelings towards you—'

'Now then!'

A broad individual with an exceptionally thick neck, vast florid face and small darting eyes approached the table. It was

Councillor Cyril Smout, former governor at the village school in Barton and the only dissenting voice when the governors had voted against the proposal to close the school the previous year. When the Education Department had rescinded its decision and the school had remained open, he had tendered his resignation. There had been questions asked at County Hall about his excessive expenses, but nothing had been proved conclusively and he continued to be the loud, bullish and blunt member on the Education Committee he had been since winning the seat.

'Good evening, councillor,' sighed the doctor.

'Mrs Devine,' said Councillor Smout, a broad smile on his fat face.

'Councillor,' replied Elisabeth.

'You two look nice an' snug 'ere tucked away in t'corner. I saw you when I come in but din't want to spoil yer little chinwag.' A smile still suffused his face. 'I should 'ave thought that you'd 'ave a lot on yer plate, Mrs Devine, what wi' it bein' t'start o' t'term an' all, to find t'time for winin' and dinin' at t'Bon Voyeur.'

'And I should have thought that you would be far too busy with council business,' retorted the doctor pointedly. 'It's surprising *you* have found the time to wine and dine.'

The sharp comment was lost on the councillor. 'Oh, I'm 'ere on hofficial council business. I'm entertainin' t'mayor of our twin town in France. 'E's not that fluid in English an' I don't speak a word of 'is lingo, so it's not been easy. P'raps you'd like to come ovver an' meet 'im?'

'No, thank you,' replied Dr Stirling. 'We are just about to go.'

'Suit yerself.'

The owner appeared.

'Has everything been to your satisfaction, doctor?' he asked.

'Excellent, thank you,' replied Dr Stirling.

'I hope that we may see you again at Le Bon Viveur,' began the owner, 'and if I might say—'

'Well, if *I* might say,' interrupted Councillor Smout, thrusting out his jaw and addressing Monsieur Richeux, 'I can't say as 'ow things 'ave bin to *my* satisfaction.'

The owner turned slowly to the speaker. The smile had left his face and his mouth drooped in distaste. 'Really?' he said.

'I can't say as 'ow I found t'food to my likin',' continued Councillor Smout. 'Far too fancy an' not my cup o' tea at all. I din't know what I was eatin' 'alf o' t'time an' I 'ave to say that t'portions were not over-generous and, I might add—'

'Please do,' said the owner. 'I cannot wait to hear.'

'That we was sat there for a long time before we was served.'

'You know, sir,' the owner said, a wry smile on his face, 'were I to challenge you to a duel, I should choose English grammar as my weapon.' With that he departed.

'T'thing is wi' foreigners,' the councillor confided, bending down to speak into Elisabeth's ear, 'foreigners allus 'ave problems gerrin their 'eads around our language, don't they?'

Dr Stirling and Elisabeth looked at each other and then burst out laughing.

2

'Does anyone know who the father is?' asked Mrs Sloughthwaite, proprietor of the Barton-in-the-Dale village store and post office, leaning over the counter with her great bay window of a bust supported comfortably on the top. She was a round, red-faced woman with a large fleshy nose, pouchy cheeks and bright inquisitive eyes resting in small hammocks of flesh. It was surprising that she was ignorant as to the parentage of the child in question, for there was no one in the village with such an extensive knowledge as she had of all the goings-on. The shopkeeper and postmistress made it her business to know about everything and everybody, and no customer left her premises without being subjected to a thorough interrogation. Once gleaned, the information was quickly circulated throughout the village.

There were two customers in the shop that Monday morning: Mrs Pocock, a tall, thin woman with a pale, melancholy, beaked face, and Mrs O'Connor, the local GP's housekeeper, a dumpy, smiling individual with tightly permed hair the colour of copper-beech leaves and the huge, liquid brown eyes of a cow.

'Well, it could be anyone's,' observed Mrs Pocock, her lips twisting into a sardonic smile. 'I mean, without putting too fine a point on it, she puts it about a bit that Bianca. No morals at all if you ask me – like a lot of young people these days. Mrs Widowson who lives next door to the family is forever seeing the girl at the gate to her house, skirt barely covering her backside, kissing and carrying on with no end of boys. She attracts them like wasps around a jam dish. I mean, it was bound to happen.'

'It's like history repeating itself,' observed the shopkeeper.

'In what way?' asked Mrs O'Connor, patting her hair.

'Well, young Danny Stainthorpe's mother had him when she was barely out of school uniform,' continued Mrs Sloughthwaite, leaning over the counter. 'She was a tearaway, was young Tricia, and no mistake. It's amazing how well the lad has turned out.'

'And she was another unmarried mother,' added Mrs Pocock sanctimoniously, 'and not a father in sight. It astonishes me how these youngsters get pregnant at the drop of a hat and other women try for years to have children and then have to resort to this VHF treatment.'

''Course, Tricia's own mother was no better than she should be,' observed the shopkeeper. 'Do you remember her, Mrs Pocock, that big brassy blonde who served behind the counter at the Blacksmith's Arms in a skirt as short as a drunken man's memory?'

The customer shook her head and gave a bleak smile. 'Maisie Proctor,' she said.

'Who could forget that madam? All kid gloves and no knickers, as my mother would say. You recall her, don't you, Mrs O'Connor? Set her cap for Les Stainthorpe, who, as you know, was a good few years older than her, spent all his money and then ran off.'

'With that brush salesman from Rotherham,' added the shopkeeper, 'leaving the husband to bring up the daughter.'

'And a lot of people think the baby wasn't Les Stainthorpe's,' added Mrs Pocock.

'Then the lass goes and gets herself killed and he has to bring up her child,' said the shopkeeper.

'But fancy pushing a pram with a kiddie in it down a dark

country road,' said Mrs Pocock. 'I mean, she was asking to get knocked down and killed.'

'The boy's grandfather did a good job bringing up young Danny.'

'He did,' said Mrs O'Connor. 'He's a lovely wee fella, so he is, and as happy as Larry since he's come to stay at the doctor's.'

'It was very good of Dr Stirling to foster the boy after the lad's grandfather died,' said Mrs Pocock. 'He could have ended up in a children's home. I certainly wouldn't want to look after another adolescent. I have enough trouble with my Ernest.'

Knowing the Pocock boy as she did, Mrs Sloughthwaite was not going to argue with that observation, but she kept her thoughts to herself.

'And I hear Dr Stirling is thinking of adopting the lad,' continued the customer.

'He is,' said Mrs O'Connor. 'Just needs to sort the paper-work out.'

'Well, good luck to him,' said the shopkeeper. 'He's a nice lad, is Danny, and he deserves a good home.'

'What surprises me is that she didn't have a termination,' remarked Mrs Pocock.

'Who?' asked the shopkeeper.

'Bianca. You would have thought—'

'I don't hold with that sort of thing,' interrupted Mrs O'Connor, giving a small shiver. 'A life is precious, that's what my owld grandmother Mullarkey used to say. "Every child is a gift from God and should be treasured".'

'Well, you want to see some of them "gifts from God" hanging about the war memorial of an evening, making a racket and up to no good,' said Mrs Pocock. 'I'd "treasure" them and no mistake.'

Mrs Sloughthwaite rested a dimpled elbow on the counter

and placed her fleshy chin on a hand. She's a one to talk, the shopkeeper reflected. Mrs Pocock wants to put her own house in order before she starts commenting on the behaviour of others. Take her son Ernest, for example, that most disagreeable and sullen-faced boy. Give him a few more years and he'll be in the centre of the gang of unruly teenagers congregating around the war memorial. Mrs Sloughthwaite smiled to herself but said nothing.

'It's still wrong to take a life,' the doctor's housekeeper was saying. 'And you can give it all the fancy words you want, in my books it's murder.'

'Each to their own views, Mrs O'Connor,' retorted Mrs Pocock, 'but in my opinion it would have been best for the lass not to have had it. There're too many children being born to irresponsible parents. I mean, what sort of life can that child expect? Teenage mother with not much up top, feckless grandfather who's never done a day's work in his life, looseliving grandmother who spends most of her time playing bingo or in the pub, and all crammed into that small terraced house with I don't know how many children and you can bet that the lot of them are on state benefits.'

''Course, nobody knew she was having it, you know,' added Mrs Sloughthwaite, divulging a juicy titbit. 'She kept it a secret right until the very end.'

'No!' gasped Mrs Pocock.

'Mind you,' said the shopkeeper, 'knowing Bianca, she probably didn't know herself until it arrived. She's not the brightest button in the box.'

'Nobody knew she was expecting!' exclaimed Mrs Pocock. 'I find that hard to believe.'

'Well, that's what I've heard,' said the shopkeeper. 'Fred Massey was in here yesterday and he was told it in the Blacksmith's Arms by the girl's father. She's a big girl is that Bianca, and lately she's been wearing all those baggy pants, loose tops and that big grey overcoat. I mean she's come in here looking like the Abdominal Snowman. She didn't say a thing to anybody, by all accounts. It wasn't until she went into labour and her younger sister, that Chardonnay, went to fetch Mrs Lloyd and then phoned for the ambulance, that anyone knew anything about it. Her parents were at the pub at the time.'

'Well, that figures,' said Mrs Pocock, shaking her head and sniffing self-righteously.

'And by the time they got back,' continued Mrs Sloughthwaite, 'they were told Bianca had been taken to Clayton Royal Infirmary with a baby. Mrs Lloyd called in the shop yesterday and she said their faces were a picture. I wish I could have been a fly on the wall.'

'Her parents got a Christmas present they weren't bargaining for and no mistake,' remarked Mrs Pocock, giving another small cynical smile.

'Christmas afternoon it was,' continued Mrs Sloughthwaite. 'It's a blessing that the girl's sister had the good sense to fetch Mrs Lloyd. She arrived when the baby was well on its way.'

'I blame all this on that sex education they get in school nowadays,' remarked Mrs Pocock, screwing up her face as if the room was filled with an unpleasant odour. 'It gives them ideas. Keep them in the dark as long as you can or they'll be up to all sorts of hanky-panky.'

'I knew nothing about that sort of thing when I was at the Notre Dame Convent,' mused Mrs O'Connor wistfully. Mrs Pocock rolled her eyes and exchanged a glance with the shop-keeper. 'The thought of Sister Pauline Thérèse talking to us about such things would never be countenanced. The only thing she ever mentioned regarding the opposite sex, as I recall, was when she told us if ever we went to a dance, never to sit on a boy's knee unless there was a telephone directory between us, and never to wear black patent leather shoes because they reflected your underwear.'

'It was all the same in those days,' agreed Mrs Sloughthwaite. 'We knew nothing. When I was a lass, Brenda Merton once told me in the playground that her next-door neighbour was having a baby just through having a bath after the lodger and I believed her. Then I remember hearing at school that some other girl who worked in the pickle factory on Tennyson Street was in the pudding club. I had no idea what she really meant. I went home and asked my mother if I could join this pudding club, having a partiality as I did for jam roly-poly and spotted dick. My mother washed my mouth out with carbolic soap. But I beg to differ with you there, Mrs Pocock. I think it's a very good idea for youngsters to have sex education lessons. If Bianca had have had them she might not be in the predicament she now finds herself in.'

'Well, I don't agree,' replied her customer, holding her body stiffly upright. 'When Mrs Devine said at the governors' meeting that she'd invited Dr Stirling into school to talk to the children about such matters, I was none too pleased and I told her so, not that any of the other governors agreed with me.'

'How is Dr Stirling by the way, Mrs O'Connor?' quizzed the shopkeeper, deftly changing the subject so she could begin her interrogation.

'Oh, he's fine,' replied Mrs O'Connor, being deliberately evasive. She knew Mrs Sloughthwaite's tactics of old and only told her what she wanted her to hear.

'So he spent Christmas alone then, did he?'

'There were the two boys,' Mrs O'Connor told her.

'I would have thought Mrs Devine might have joined him, her being by herself as well.'

'I wouldn't be knowing anything about that,' lied the housekeeper. 'And, as you know, I spent Christmas over in Galway with my sister Peggy.' She knew that Dr Stirling and Mrs Devine had indeed spent most of Christmas Day together, but she was not going to divulge this to the shopkeeper.

'They seem to be getting on like a house on fire these days,' observed Mrs Sloughthwaite casually.

'They're very good friends, so they are.'

'Nothing more?'

'I wouldn't be knowing.'

'They seem to see a lot of each other.'

'It's a small village.'

''Course, if it had been up to Dr Stirling,' Mrs Pocock said suddenly and much to the shopkeeper's annoyance, interrupting the cross-examination, 'Mrs Devine would never have been appointed. He was dead set against her at the interviews for the headship at the school.'

'That's all water under the bridge now,' said Mrs O'Connor.

Before Mrs Sloughthwaite could resume her questioning, the bell above the door of the shop tinkled and a customer entered.

Major Cedric Neville-Gravitas, late of the Royal Engineers and Chairman of Governors at the village school, strode purposefully to the counter, smiling widely. He was a striking-looking man of military bearing with a carefully trimmed moustache and short cropped hair which shot up from a square head. He was dressed in a bright, tailored Harris tweed suit and matching waistcoat and sported a colourful bow tie.

'When shall we three meet again? In thunder, lightning, or in rain?' he said jovially.

This greeting was met with three blank faces.

'From *Macbeth*,' he explained.

'I am aware of that, major,' said Mrs Pocock. 'Was it intended to be amusing?'

'Beg pardon?' asked the major, the smile leaving his face.

'Comparing us to the three witches?'

'Just being whimsical, my dear Mrs Pocock,' replied the major. 'No offence intended.' He rubbed his hands vigorously and tried a conciliatory smile.

'Well, it's about as whimsical as a slipped disc,' said Mrs Pocock.

'What a lovely bright January day it is,' continued the major, attempting to defuse the tension by quickly changing the subject. 'Quite mild for the time of year, don't you think?'

'What can I get you, major?' asked Mrs Sloughthwaite, rising from the counter and clearly unwilling to be infected by his cheery goodwill. She disliked the man. In her opinion he was shallow and two-faced and she wouldn't trust him as far as she could throw him.

'I would like a loaf of your excellent crusty bread, Mrs Sloughthwaite,' said the major cheerily, 'and four of those delicious-looking scones and a jar of your special raspberry preserve. I have a visitor for tea.'

The shopkeeper resisted the urge to enquire who this visitor might be. She would no doubt find this out later from another source. She busied herself with the major's order.

'I trust I shall see you at the next governors' meeting at the village school on Friday, Mrs Pocock?' said the major.

'Yes,' she replied brusquely. 'You will. I've not missed one yet.'

'I should have thought,' began Mrs Sloughthwaite, placing the various items in a plastic bag, 'that you would have done the right thing, major, and resigned as Chairman of Governors after the hoo-ha over the closure of the school.' She enjoyed being provocative.

'Done the right thing?' repeated the major sharply. 'I don't follow your drift.'

'Well, you were all for closing the school, weren't you?' remarked the shopkeeper nonchalantly.

'I most certainly was not!' he replied, rather taken aback. 'I exercised discretion. As I have explained to countless people in the village, I felt it appropriate in the first instance to abstain from the vote.' He shifted uncomfortably from foot to foot and twisted his moustache.

'Yes, well, if you had joined the rest of us governors when we voted against the closure,' Mrs Pocock told him with a hard, stern expression on her pale face, 'instead of sitting on the fence, we would have had a much stronger case.'

'My dear Mrs Pocock!' exclaimed the major, 'I did not sit on the fence, as you term it! As Chairman of Governors I took a neutral position, and having assessed the situation and seen how successful the village school had become and how well-regarded its head teacher was, I campaigned vigorously in favour of keeping the school open.' He breathed through his nose like a horse.

'Well, you were last in the village to do so,' said Mrs Sloughthwaite, resting her substantial bosom back on the counter.

The major tugged angrily at his moustache and an unfortunate twitch appeared in his right eye. 'I shall collect my provisions later on, Mrs Sloughthwaite,' he said, the jovial smile gone from his face, 'since I am in rather a hurry. But before I go, I should just like to say that I resent such slurs circulating about me around the village. They are quite unfounded and not a little hurtful, and I should like to add that Mrs Devine was very insistent that I remain as chairman of the governing body. With that, I shall depart.'

The major strode for the door, leaving his purchases on the counter.

'He's a dark horse, is that one,' observed Mrs Pocock.

'I wouldn't be surprised if he was the father of Bianca's baby,' remarked Mrs Sloughthwaite, chuckling. 'Wandering hands he has, and I've seen him ogling anything in a skirt.'

'You must be joking,' Mrs Pocock told her. 'Him, the baby's father? He's old enough be the girl's grandfather.'

'Well, as my owld grandmother was wont to say,' observed Mrs O'Connor, '"there's a dreadful sting in a dying bee".'

Her two companions stared at her blankly but didn't say a word.

As the three women in the village store considered other possibilities with regard to Bianca's unexpected Christmas present, Mrs Devine, head teacher of Barton-in-the-Dale village school, surveyed the bright-faced pupils who sat before her in the classroom that morning. She recalled when she had first met these children on the day of the interviews for the headship, and how she had thought to herself what a motley group it was: large gangly boys, lean bespectacled boys, dark-skinned boys, pale-faced boys, boys with freckles and spiky hair, girls with long plaits, girls with frizzy bunches of ginger hair, girls thin and tall, dumpy and small, and all forty plus of them sitting uncomfortably at old-fashioned hard, wooden desks. The class had filled the hot stuffy room on that summer day, serious and silent and regarding her with not a little suspicion. Now the children looked very different: bright-eyed and happy and chattering away excitedly.

Elisabeth felt a great sense of satisfaction at what she and the teachers had achieved in the short time since she had taken over as head teacher. The appearance of the building, the morale of the staff and the behaviour of the children had improved beyond measure. She had invited visitors into the school and organised sports teams, after-school clubs, lunch-time activities and trips out of school. She had stemmed the declining numbers and had fought a vigorous and ultimately successful campaign to keep the school from closing.

Miss Brakespeare accounted the success to the fact that the new head teacher, when she was not teaching, spent most of her time around the school, unlike her predecessor, who had kept herself closeted in her room all day. Morning and after-noon breaks saw Elisabeth walking through the building, strolling around the playground or sitting in the hall at lunchtime getting to know the children. Her commitment and enthusiasm began rubbing off on the teachers, who, like her, started arriving at school early, leaving later and spending little time in the staffroom. Yes, Elisabeth thought to herself as she looked at the smiling faces before her now, she had achieved a great deal.

The class was full of characters. There was Chardonnay, a large cheerful girl with bright ginger hair and a round saucer face, and her friend Chantelle, who sported huge bunches of mousy brown hair which stuck out like giant earmuffs. On the front table, where she could keep her eye on him, was Malcolm Stubbins, potential troublemaker, a large-boned individual with an olive brown face, tightly curled hair and very prominent front teeth. Also on a front table sat Ernest Pocock, another pupil who could be troublesome. Behind him were Darren Holgate, a moon-faced child with a shock of curly black hair and a face as freckled as a hen's egg, and little Eddie Lake, who seemed to have a permanent smile etched on his face. On the back table were Danny Stainthorpe and his best friend James Stirling. Elisabeth had got to know these two boys better than any other of her pupils.

She had met Danny prior to taking up the position of head teacher. With a view to moving into the village, Elisabeth had been looking at a potential property and had come upon a rather dilapidated pale stone cottage which stood alone at the end of a track of beaten mud overgrown with nettles. The building looked neglected and sad, with its sagging roof, broken guttering and peeling paint. A small boy with large low-set ears, a mop of dusty blond hair and the bright brown eyes of a fox had climbed over the gate in the paddock to speak to her. This was Danny. He was a lively and confident boy of ten or eleven, and Elisabeth had immediately taken a liking to him. She discovered that he lived with his grandfather in a caravan parked in the neighbouring field. Soon after she had started at the school the boy's grandfather had become ill and died, leaving Danny alone and inconsolable. However, things had improved when Danny had been fostered by Dr Stirling, who was now in the process of adopting the boy and rearing him along with his own son. So things had worked out very well.

James Stirling had had a difficult time too. Following his mother's death as a result of a riding accident some two years before, this small, pale-faced child with curly blond hair had withdrawn into himself, speaking only to his father and his friend. After an altercation between Elisabeth and James's father, Dr Stirling had decided to take his son away from Barton-in-the-Dale school and send him to the preparatory school at Ruston. The boy, distressed and frightened at the thought of leaving his only friend and starting a new school, had run away, to be discovered by Elisabeth late at night curled up in her garden. Since then, with sensitive handling and encouragement and specialist help from the educational psychologist, the boy was gaining in confidence and had begun to speak more. Here was another success story.

Elisabeth looked at the two boys now and smiled. Happy and chatty and full of life, they looked as if they hadn't a care in the world.

She clapped her hands to gain the children's attention and the chatter ceased immediately. 'I hope you all had a really lovely Christmas,' she said.

'Yes, miss,' they chorused.

'And that you are all bright-eyed and bushy-tailed and ready for a lot of hard work this term.'

There were good-humoured groans.

'And what sort of Christmas did you have, Eddie?' she asked.

'Great. We went to Center Parcs, miss. It's a holiday village in the middle of a forest and we had a really good time. This fat woman in a gold bathing suit got stuck in the water chute.'

The children laughed. 'Oh dear,' chuckled Elisabeth.

'She climbed up the ladder and clung on to this silver bar at the top. Then she let go and shot down the chute like a big bullet, then she slowed down and stopped in one of the bends. She got stuck. The man that was behind her didn't see her, so he set off and bashed into her and they came out together at the bottom all knotted and tangled up and spluttering and gasping and spitting water. It was really funny. The attendant shouted at them and told them to stop messing about.'

'This has the makings of a really good story, Eddie,' said Elisabeth. 'And what about you, Malcolm?'

'What about me?' Then as an afterthought he added, 'Miss.'

'Did you have a pleasant Christmas?'

He shrugged and sighed. 'It was all right,' he said glumly. 'We had all these relations round and they did my head in. All these aunties giving me slobbering kisses. Then my mum had an argument with my Auntie Doreen and Uncle Phil and they went home.' He brightened a little. 'Anyway, I got a new pair of football boots.'

'So we can expect some winning goals from you this term,' said Elisabeth.

'Hope so, miss.'

When Elisabeth had started at the school she had found the boy to be truculent and disobedient, but she had dealt with pupils like this before and with firm and determined handling his behaviour had improved greatly. She accounted football to have been partly responsible for the change. When a football team had been established, Malcolm had become the star player. He knew now that should he step out of line he would not be allowed to play.

'Ernest,' said Elisabeth now.

'Yes, miss?'

'Would you like to tell us what you did over Christmas?'

'Not much, miss. My mum dropped the turkey, the dog was sick and my dad got drunk.'

'Quite eventful then?'

'Yes, miss.'

Elisabeth smiled. 'Did you get the presents you hoped for?'

'I got an easel and some paints,' he replied.

Ernest Pocock seemed a very different boy from the uninterested pupil she had first met. Mrs Atticus, who had been invited into the school to run an art class at lunchtime, had discovered that this boy had a real gift for painting.

'Well, I look forward to more of your successes this term in the County Art Competition, Ernest,' said Elisabeth. 'You did really well last year, didn't you?'

The boy nodded and gave a small smile. 'Yes, miss.'

'Miss, miss!' Chardonnay shouted out, waving her hand in the air like a daffodil in a strong wind, impatient to relate what had happened in her house over the holiday. 'We had a right time at Christmas.'

'Really?' said Elisabeth.

'Our Bianca had a baby on Christmas Day.'

'Your sister had a baby?' said Elisabeth, startled.

'Yes, miss. It were a little boy,' the girl told her, jumping to her feet.

'Well, how old is your sister?'

'Seventeen, miss,' said Chardonnay. 'She didn't know she was having it and nobody else did either. Mam and Dad had gone to the pub in the afternoon and I had to stay in with Bianca because she wasn't feeling too well. Anyway, when my mam and dad had gone out our Bianca said she felt funny and the next thing what happened was she flopped on the settee and all this water come out over the floor and she started moaning and groaning.'

The rest of the class sat in stunned silence during what could only be described as a performance, as the girl related the facts in graphic detail and at great speed, illustrating her account with facial expressions and actions. There wasn't a sound. Some children shuffled in embarrassment, others stared at her uncomprehendingly, some pulled faces and others sat open-mouthed. Chardonnay rattled on regardless, with ruthless directness and in a voice strong and determined.

'Anyway, I thought she was really ill,' the girl told her audience. 'She kept holding her stomach like this. "Oh!" she went. "I feel awful." Then she told me to go and fetch Dr Stirling but he wasn't in so I went to get Nurse Lloyd who lives on Common Lane. She was a middlewife and used to deliver babies. Anyway, she weren't happy having to leave her Christmas tea and told me to go for the doctor and I told her I had done but he was out. Then she phoned for an ambulance but they said it would be ages coming because of the snow and the roads being icy and all, and it being Christmas Day as well, so she said she'd come with me. When we got home Bianca was stretched out on the living-room floor moaning and groaning and saying she was going to die. Nurse Lloyd looked at her and told me to get some towels and boil some hot water, and then she told me to hold Bianca's hand to calm her down because she was moaning and groaning something rotten. Then the baby just popped out. There was lots of blood.' Chantelle gave an involuntary shudder and there were several sharp intakes of breath. 'I think Mrs Lloyd was mad with the baby because she slapped it on its bum and it started roaring its eyes out. Then this play centre come out.'

'Play centre?' repeated Elisabeth.

'It's all this gooey stuff what comes out after the baby.'

'Ah, the placenta,' whispered Elisabeth.

'And it was fastened to a long sort of cord.'

'What, the play centre?' asked Chantelle, saucer-eyed.

'No, it was fastened to the baby. It's called the umbrella

cord and Mrs Lloyd had to cut it. She knew what she was doing because she was a middlewife. Mrs Lloyd wrapped the baby in a towel and gave it to our Bianca. Then the ambulance come and I went to fetch my mam and dad from the pub and we all went to the hospital to see the baby. It was put in an incinerator.' Chardonnay turned to the class. 'If anyone has any questions, I'll answer them.' There was a bewildered silence in the classroom.

'I don't think we'll have questions, thank you, Chardonnay,' said Elisabeth, quite at a loss for what else to say.

'Miss,' said Eddie Lake, 'I got a play centre for Christmas.'

3

Mrs Holgate twisted the ring on her finger nervously. 'So you think my Darren does have a problem then, Mrs Devine?' she asked.

'I do,' replied Elisabeth, 'but first of all, may I say what a pleasure it is to teach him.'

'Really?'

'Really. He's a well-behaved, good-natured and hard-working young man, but he does have a problem.'

'With his reading and writing,' sighed the boy's mother.

'With his reading and writing,' agreed Elisabeth. 'But we can help him. I think your son has a form of dyslexia or word blindness called dysgraphia, which means he finds writing in particular difficult. A lot of dyslexic people have problems with language, and Darren tries very hard but it does cause him some problems. The content of his written work is of a good standard, it's lively and interesting, but it's the spelling and handwriting that causes him problems.'

'My husband thought Darren might be dyslexic,' said Mrs Holgate. 'He'd seen this programme on the television and there were children like my Darren who couldn't spell, but when we spoke to Miss Sowerbutts on parents' evening she said he was just slow and that some children are good spellers and others are not. She said you can't teach spelling. You've either got it or you haven't. She said he needed to concentrate more and take greater care with his writing.'

'Did she?'

'She said dyslexia was just a fancy label parents say about their children who can't spell.'

'Well, I don't agree with Miss Sowerbutts,' Elisabeth replied. 'There *is* a condition called dyslexia. It has been quite clearly proved and I feel sure this is Darren's problem. With some specialist help his work will improve.'

Listening to the parent's words, Elisabeth recalled the occasion when she had first broached the subject of James's special needs with Dr Stirling. She had received a similar response to the one the parent had got from the former head teacher. 'James has no condition, disorder or problem,' he had told her dismissively. 'He is just a quiet, under-confident little boy who is still grieving for his mother. I am weary of hearing and reading about all these so-called children's disorders and syndromes.'

'I first met Darren when I came for the interview for the head teacher's position,' Elisabeth told the parent, 'and I looked at his work. It was imaginative and well-expressed, but his spelling and handwriting were below average for a child of his age. At first your son was reticent in letting me see his exercise book and told me his writing was not very good. He tried hard, he said, and liked writing but found words really difficult. I think he was of the opinion that he was not very clever.'

'That's true,' agreed the mother. 'He's always saying he's rubbish at writing and that he can't seem to do anything right. He gets so upset and angry with himself. He's not a lad to push himself forward and he lacks confidence.'

'It's not unusual for children with dyslexia to have low self-esteem and lack confidence in themselves, but I am telling you, Mrs Holgate, that your son is a bright, creative boy. Dyslexia affects a lot of people, some say over ten per cent of the population, and it is no reflection of a person's intelligence.'

'I see.'

'At the beginning of the term, Mrs Goldstein, the educational psychologist, came into school and I asked her to speak to Darren, look at his work and give him a couple of tests. His verbal reasoning skills are high, he has a good visual memory, his number work is excellent and he has an above average IQ. The test on vocabulary, comprehension and spelling did, however, show that Darren does have a problem with some aspects of his writing.'

'Yes, he told me he'd been doing tests,' said the parent. 'I thought all the children were doing them, though.'

'What I am suggesting, Mrs Holgate, is that we put Darren on a personalised programme where he will receive some specialist support to help him reach his potential. It will be tailored to his needs and will only involve one lunchtime tuition a week and some work for him to do at home. Does that sound acceptable to you?'

'Oh yes, Mrs Devine,' said the parent. There was a tremble in her voice. 'I only want what's best for Darren. He gets so frustrated and unhappy at times with his writing and he's always telling me he's not as good as the other children in the class.' She suddenly started to cry. 'Oh, I'm sorry. It's just that I feel a great weight has been lifted off my shoulders.'

'So if you would have a word with Darren and see how he feels about it . . .' said Elisabeth. 'He has to be willing to do it.'

'I will, Mrs Devine,' said the parent. 'I'll speak to him tonight.'

The following day at lunchtime the subject of the discussion approached Elisabeth hesitantly as she walked around the playground.

'My mum said you would like a word with me, miss,' he said. He looked on the verge of tears.

'Don't look so worried, Darren,' his teacher reassured him. 'You are not in any trouble.'

'My mum said you want me to do some special course, miss.'

'That's right.'

'Will I have to go to another school?' His bottom lip began to tremble.

'Of course you won't have to go to another school. All it means is that you will spend one lunchtime a week with me and maybe with one of the other teachers, and you will be given some work to do at home to help you with your spellings and handwriting. How does that sound?'

The boy sniffed and wiped his nose on a finger. Elisabeth reached into her pocket and passed him a tissue. He blew his nose loudly. 'I'm rubbish at spelling,' the boy told her. 'I always have been.'

'But you won't be for long. Not if you work hard and try your best. Will you do that?'

'I'll try, miss.'

'We can start next week if you like,' said Elisabeth. 'You know, Darren, what I said to you when I first met you was right. I don't tell children something just to make them feel better. I meant what I said to you when I told you I liked your story about your dog and that it was well written and very amusing.'

The boy nodded, sniffed and smiled. 'Miss, you know how you said that if you really want to say how you feel then the best way is through poetry?'

'Yes, I do. A very famous poet once said that poetry is the shortest way of saying things and that it looks nicer on the page than prose. It gives you room to think and dream. You have to write down what you want to say at first and deal with the punctuation and spelling later on.'

'I've written some poems, miss,' the boy informed her. 'Sometimes when I've not got a lot to do at home I write a poem. You don't have to get everything right with poetry, do you?'

'Will you let me see some of your poems?' asked Elisabeth.

'I haven't shown them to anybody, miss,' he said. 'I just do them for myself.'

'Well, that's all right. There are things I write that I don't want anybody else to see.'

At the end of the day Elisabeth found a piece of paper on her desk, folded neatly into a square. She opened it up. It was from Darren. The writing was spidery, the spelling poor, but the content took her breath away with its honesty and emotion.

The Trubble with Words

Words spel trubble.
They trip you up,
Trap you,
Trick you,
They dont folow the rules.

Words spel trubble.
They cofnuse you,
Snare you,
Scare you,
Make you seem a fool.

Words spel trubble.
They ambush you,
Buly you,
Hurt you,
Make you feel unhappy inisde.

Words spell trubble
They decieve you, Supprise you,
Worry you,
They make you cry.

Miss Brakespeare was tidying up her classroom when Elisabeth put her head around the door.

'First couple of weeks nearly over,' she said brightly, catching sight of the head teacher.

'And things seem to be going well,' said Elisabeth.

'Very well, actually. I cannot tell you what a difference it has made having a smaller class,' replied her colleague, 'more space and all these new tables.'

'I haven't had much of a chance to see you since the term started,' said Elisabeth. 'It's been so busy and gone so quickly. How was your Christmas?'

Miss Brakespeare shook her head and gave a small smile. 'Not what you would call a barrel of laughs,' she replied.

'Oh dear,' said Elisabeth.

'I am afraid Mother seemed to delight in playing the martyr more than ever. I know she's not been well but she could put a bit of a brave face on it, especially when it's Christmas, a time of supposed peace and goodwill. I'm afraid she's a dedicated hypochondriac. When Father was ill he rarely complained. Right up to his death he remained cheerful and made the best of the time he had left. My mother, I'm afraid, is one of the world's grumpy old women. Nothing anyone does for her seems to be right. Her presents didn't suit, there was nothing on the television, the house was too cold and nobody bothered to come and see her. The turkey wasn't cooked enough, the sprouts were too hard, the stuffing dry and the potatoes overcooked. I tried to persuade her to go with me to the carol concert at the chapel but she wouldn't. She went to bed early on Christmas Eve feeling sorry for herself and grumbling that this would be the last Christmas she would be having. "I won't be here next year, Miriam. I'm on my way out," she told me.'

'You went to the carol service then?' asked Elisabeth.

'I did,' replied Miss Brakespeare. 'Mr Tomlinson asked

me to turn the pages while he was playing the organ. I do it most Sundays for him.' She reddened a little. 'It gets me out of the house.'

'He's such a nice man, isn't he?' said Elisabeth.

'He is, yes,' replied the deputy head teacher coyly.

Elisabeth was aware that her deputy head teacher had been seeing quite a bit of the chapel organist of late and thought that this might very well have contributed to Miss Brakespeare's constant, cheerful good humour and to the fact that she was making a real effort with her appearance. She smiled but resisted making a comment. 'Did Chardonnay sing?' she asked.

'She did, and beautifully too,' replied Miss Brakespeare. 'The minister looked quite overcome. George – Mr Tomlinson that is – said it was like listening to an angel. He said it was amazing that she has such a clear and powerful voice and she's never had any voice coaching.'

Elisabeth had discovered quite a deal of hidden talent when she arrived at Barton-in-the-Dale. In an effort to widen the children's experience and offer them greater opportunities, she had invited a number of people into the school to work with the children. As well as Mrs Atticus, the lunchtime art teacher, there was the Reverend Atticus, who frequently called in to take the morning assembly. Mr Parkinson, the scout leader, came in to run a football team, in which Malcolm Stubbins had proved to be such a skilful player, and Mr Tomlinson had started a school choir, in which Chardonnay amazed everyone with her singing.

'So to be honest,' Miss Brakespeare confided, 'I'm glad to be back at school. Oh, here I am nattering on about myself. Did you have a nice Christmas?'

'Very pleasant,' replied Elisabeth. 'I had Christmas morning at Forest View with the staff and children.' She failed to mention to her colleague that the afternoon and evening had been spent with Dr Stirling and the two boys at her cottage.

It had been quite a mystery to the governors at her interview why Elisabeth should want to leave her last position as head teacher of a large and very successful primary school in the city to take on the small village school, which had received such a poor report from the school inspectors. Apart from her deputy and the staff she had never divulged the reason for wanting to leave her last post, this being so that she could be nearer to her son. John was a pupil at Forest View, a special school for autistic children and a stone's throw from Barton-in-the-Dale.

'How is your son?' asked Miss Brakespeare now.

'He's very much the same,' Elisabeth told her. 'Improvement tends to be slow. John's very settled and likes his teacher, and the routine suits him well, which is the main thing. It's a very good school and I'm so pleased he managed to get a place there. I go to see him every Saturday and, touch wood, I've not missed a visit yet.'

'Well, I'm glad you decided to come. You've been a real tonic and made such a difference.'

'That's kind of you to say, Miriam,' said Elisabeth. 'Anyway, come along, you shouldn't be here at this time. You should be getting off home.'

'I think I'll stay another half-hour,' the deputy head teacher told her. 'It's Mother's weekly visit from Dr Stirling today – he calls in on her every other Thursday – so I need to brace myself to prepare for the blow-by-blow account of her many ailments.'

Elisabeth left the school to find Miss Sowerbutts at the gate. The former head teacher must have been waiting quite some time, for it was getting on for five o'clock.

'May I have a word with you, Mrs Devine?' said Miss Sowerbutts. Her face was pinched with cold and irritation.

'Yes, of course, Miss Sowerbutts,' replied Elisabeth, meeting her eyes. 'Would you care to come into the school?'

'No, thank you,' Miss Sowerbutts said in the petulant tone of the aggrieved. 'What I have to say can be said here. I wanted to tell you that I am most displeased.'

'About what?' Elisabeth asked calmly.

'About your blatant unprofessionalism.' The woman's face was rigid.

'I'm afraid I really don't know to what you are referring,' Elisabeth told her.

'It has come to my ears that in speaking to a parent you have pooh-poohed the advice which I gave her.'

What an odd word to use, thought Elisabeth. 'Pooh-poohed?' she repeated.

'I believe that you have told Mrs Holgate, who works in Farringdon's hardware shop, that you disparaged the advice I gave to her about her son? She informed me, when I called in to buy various items, *and* with some perverse pleasure *and* in front of another customer, that her son is on some fanciful course or other and that what I had told her about him when I was head teacher was wrong.'

'If you mean that I disagreed with your assessment of Darren's problem, then I readily admit that I did,' Elisabeth told her.

'The boy has no problem!' snapped Miss Sowerbutts. 'He just can't spell. There are people in the world, you know, who cannot spell, Mrs Devine. We don't need to put some fancy label on it. Disobedient children are not naughty any more, they now have "attention deficit disorder" or some such twaddle, and children who are unable to spell now have dyslexia. All nonsense in my view.'

'I told Mrs Holgate that I felt her son does have a form of dyslexia, and this was borne out by Mrs Goldstein, the educational psychologist.'

'Huh,' grunted the former head teacher.

'Darren requires some help and support with his writing,' continued Elisabeth, 'which he is now getting.' She resisted the temptation to tell the former head teacher that the boy should have received such help and support a long time ago, and remained silent.

Miss Sowerbutts's eyes narrowed and she gave a small disparaging smile. 'I might have guessed there would be a psychologist lurking in the background making work for herself. The term "dyslexia" in my book is nothing more than an excuse parents propound for having a less able child who cannot write.'

'I don't think Darren is less able,' retorted Elisabeth, wearying of this bossy, self-important woman. 'Actually I think quite the reverse. He is a bright and articulate young man and the content of his writing is very good.'

'Nonsense!'

'But then you have never taught him, Miss Sowerbutts, have you,' Elisabeth told her with mounting anger, 'so how would you know?'

'Huh!' the former head teacher huffed. 'I said to Miss Brakespeare when the governors had appointed you that you would bring in all these modern approaches and trendy initiatives. She'll bring in a whole raft of progressive teaching methods that will be full of educational jargon and be keen on fashionable fads and fancy schemes, I said. I've been proved right. Let me tell you this, Mrs Devine, I've been in the business of educating children for a great many more years than you and—'

'But no longer, Miss Sowerbutts,' interrupted Elisabeth, 'and whatever you think is no concern of mine. You are not the head teacher of Barton-in-the-Dale. I am, and I will introduce anything I feel is appropriate and for the benefit of the children.'

The former head teacher clutched her canvas bag tightly. 'I never took to you when we first met,' she spluttered. 'I found you full of yourself.'

'And the feeling was mutual,' answered Elisabeth. 'I never took to you either. To be honest, I found you discourteous and uncooperative when I came to visit.'

'I have been a head teacher in this county for twenty years, Mrs Devine,' Miss Sowerbutts told her angrily, 'and spent all my teaching career in the village school, so I pride myself on having a deal of influence in educational circles. I shall be contacting your Chairman of Governors, the Director of Education and the Chairman of the Education Committee to lodge a formal complaint about your unprofessional behaviour. This will not be the end of the matter, I can assure you of that.'

'What you do is up to you, Miss Sowerbutts,' said Elisabeth. 'Now, if you will excuse me.'

As Elisabeth made a move to go, Mr Gribbon appeared at the door of the school. 'Hello there, Miss Sowerbutts!' he shouted down the path. 'Have you come to look around and see what changes we've made to the school? I think you'll be very impressed.' The stare she gave him would have stunned a charging rhinoceros at fifty yards.

The governors convened in the staffroom of the school the following Friday evening: the Chairman, Major C. J. Neville-Gravitas, R. E. (Retd); the Reverend Atticus, Rector of Barton and soon to be elevated to be Archdeacon of Clayton; Ms Tricklebank, a senior education officer from County Hall; Dr Stirling, the local GP; Mrs Pocock, the parent governor, and Councillor Cooper, the newly appointed Local Education Authority representative.

Mrs Pocock wore her sour expression like a comfortable old coat and sat in silence, arms folded tightly over her chest.

Dr Stirling, who sat next to her, was in earnest conversation with the Reverend Atticus. The senior education officer sat next to the major, discussing the evening's agenda. Elisabeth placed a tea tray on the table and arranged some chocolate biscuits on a plate. The major looked up and chuckled at the sight of the confection.

'I trust those are not from a box of what Mrs Sloughthwaite calls her "Venetian selection", Mrs Devine,' he said jovially. 'You know, I think everyone in the village must have a box tucked away somewhere. I would check on the sell-by date if I were you.'

'There's nothing the matter with the chocolate biscuits!' snapped Mrs Pocock. 'They're very nice actually, and if you've any complaints then I suggest you take it up with Mrs Sloughthwaite.'

The major closed his eyes briefly as if pained. When he opened them again a twitch had appeared in the right eye. This was going to be a difficult meeting, he predicted. 'Well, shall we make a start?' he said, raising a small smile. 'Firstly I would like to introduce Ms Tricklebank, a senior education officer representing the Director of Education, who will act as clerk this evening and give us the benefit of her advice.' He turned to the woman of indeterminate age with thinning grey hair tied back tightly on her scalp, and who wore a rather intense expression on her face. She sat on the chairman's right, clutching a sheaf of papers. 'And another new face,' continued Major Gravitas, 'is Councillor Wayne Cooper, who replaces Councillor Smout as the Local Education Authority representative.' He smiled at a nervous, thin individual who sported a shock of frizzy ginger hair. The senior education officer was dressed in a crisp white blouse and shapeless navy blue jacket, the young councillor in a pinstriped suit. They were quite a contrast; she looked to be near retirement, he as if he had just finished school.

Mrs Pocock looked in the direction of the two newcomers with cold mechanical interest before speaking. 'Well, I hope you are both better than the last education officer and councillor what we had on the governing body,' she said, glaring at them. 'They were both a waste of space.'

'Good evening,' said the woman seriously. 'I shall endeavour to be helpful.'

The young man looked uneasy, shuffled in his chair and gave a weak smile.

'That Mr Nettles, your predecessor,' the parent governor told the woman, 'was about as much use as a chocolate teapot.'

'Mr Nettles is now dealing with school meals,' she was told.

'Well, God help the children if they let that man loose on food,' Mrs Pocock remarked with a contemptuous little sniff. 'He'll like as not poison them.' The major opened his mouth to speak, but Mrs Pocock had not finished. 'What I would like to know is what exactly is your function?'

'I beg your pardon?' asked Ms Tricklebank stiffly.

'What exactly do you do?'

'I support schools, advise head teachers and school governors, represent the Director of Education on interviews and working parties and at meetings, write reports for the Education Committee, liaise with the Department for Education, am involved in curriculum developments and a whole lot more.'

The major sighed. 'Mrs Pocock, Ms Tricklebank is not on interview. She is here to offer guidance and she has been asked to oversee . . .' He stopped to think for a moment. '. . . Oversee various initiatives. Now if I may proceed? The other piece of information I wish to impart prior to starting the meeting proper,' he said, 'is that Mrs Bullock, the foundation governor, has tendered her resignation.'

'Unlike some I could mention,' muttered Mrs Pocock, drawing her mouth together in a tight little line. The major drew in a long breath through his teeth but decided to ignore the pointed remark.

'I think she found it difficult hearing much of what we were saying,' said the vicar. 'Perhaps we might send her a letter of appreciation for all her hard work and dedication?'

'Yes. Of course,' said the major. 'Should we do the same for Councillor Smout?'

'Certainly not!' exclaimed Mrs Pocock. 'We've got nothing to appreciate him for! He was the one who wanted to close the school.' Then she glanced at the chairman. 'Like others I could mention.'

'I never felt Councillor Smout was committed to the school,' added the Reverend Atticus, his head on one side. He pressed his long fingertips together.

'Not committed, vicar!' she exclaimed. 'He wanted to close the place, that's what he wanted to do. Good riddance to him, that's what I say. Anyway, from what I've heard he's been fiddling his expenses and got suspended.'

'No, no,' Councillor Cooper replied. 'Councillor Smout was fully exonerated. It appears it was merely an oversight on his part.'

'Huh,' Mrs Pocock grunted, 'if you believe that, you'll believe pigs will fly.'

'Mr Chairman, could we get on please?' asked Dr Stirling.

The major, his voice deliberately steady, turned to Elisabeth. 'I should just like to say before we address the agenda how very pleased I am, and I am sure my fellow governors will concur, with the management and leadership of the school. I think you have done a magnificent job, Mrs Devine, in the short time you have been with us, and we look forward to another very successful term.'

'Hear, hear!' said Mrs Pocock and the vicar in unison.

'Perhaps, Mr Chairman,' said the Reverend Atticus, 'we might have our appreciation of Mrs Devine minuted.'

Major Neville-Gravitas nodded. 'Of course,' he said.

'Now the first item on the agenda is the replacement on the governing body of Mrs Bullock,' said the major. 'Are there any suggestions for someone we might consider co-opting?'

'We want someone who is committed to the school,' said the vicar.

'And who will play an active role,' added Dr Stirling.

'And who can hear what's going off,' added Mrs Pocock.

'Perhaps Mrs Devine has somebody in mind?' said the Reverend Atticus.

'Indeed I do,' Elisabeth replied. She had been deliberately very quiet until this moment. 'It is someone who was wonderfully supportive and proactive when the school was threatened with closure.'

'Unlike some,' said Mrs Pocock under her breath.

'This person I am thinking of,' continued Elisabeth, 'lives in the village. She is someone who has very close associations with the school, for it was her grandfather who endowed the building, which was originally intended for the children of his estate workers, and she has donated a sum of money for the new school library. I am referring, of course, to Lady Wadsworth.'

'An excellent suggestion,' agreed the Reverend Atticus. 'She is ideal as a foundation governor, since her grandfather founded the school. I second that heartily.'

'I agree,' said Dr Stirling.

'And I've no objection,' said Mrs Pocock. 'It would be nice to have an aristocratical person on the governing body. Adds a bit of class. I just hope her hearing is all that it should be. I used to have to repeat everything loudly for Mrs Bullock.'

'Councillor Cooper?' asked the major. 'Are you happy with this?'

'Yes, of course,' the councillor replied.

'And I take it you have no objection, Ms Tricklebank?' the chairman asked.

'No,' the senior education officer replied. 'It seems a very sensible suggestion.'

'Well,' said the major, 'that seems to be settled most satisfactorily and by a unanimous decision. I shall leave it to you, Mrs Devine, to ask Lady Wadsworth if she would consider joining our governing body.'

'I am sure she will be delighted,' Elisabeth told him.

The major coughed and tugged nervously at his moustache. The twitch appeared again in his right eye. Having been briefed beforehand by Ms Tricklebank, he knew that the next topic for discussion would doubtless prove controversial. 'Now we come to the main item on the agenda. Perhaps I might hand over to Ms Tricklebank at this juncture?'

'It concerns the future of the Education Service,' the senior education officer told the governors.

Mrs Pocock jolted up in her chair as if she had been bitten. 'You are not trying to have another go at closing this school, I hope, Miss Tickleback,' she said.

'Tricklebank.'

'What?'

'My name is Tricklebank, Mrs Peacock.'

'And mine's Pocock.'

'Well, now we've got that sorted,' said the major, sounding irritated, 'perhaps we might continue. You were saying, Ms Tricklebank?'

'Sadly, it may be necessary for us to close some of the less viable schools,' said the senior education officer, 'but I should stress that for the moment there is no intention to close this particular school; I can assure you all of that.'

'That is good to hear,' said the Reverend Atticus.

'As I said,' she continued, 'this school is not threatened with closure. The changes envisaged concern the future of the whole of the Education Service and it involves some of the small schools in the county.'

'In what way?' demanded Mrs Pocock.

'If I might be allowed to finish,' replied Ms Tricklebank sharply.

Mrs Pocock scowled. The major drew a deep exasperated breath.

'You will be aware that cuts have to be made in the education budget as a result of the declining numbers of children in the county, and that—'

'They're not declining in this school,' interrupted Mrs Pocock. 'If anything they are on the increase. Isn't that right, Mrs Devine?'

'Yes, it is,' she replied. 'In fact six new pupils started at the beginning of the term.'

'Of course, from your point of view this is very good news,' said Ms Tricklebank, 'but in other schools the numbers are dropping and in some cases quite dramatically.'

'Well, what happens in other schools is no concern of ours,' said Mrs Pocock.

'Well, it is, actually,' the senior education officer told her. 'There needs to be some reorganisation, with a number of smaller schools combining to make the most effective use of resources.'

'So this school might be amalgamated with another one?' asked the vicar.

'It is likely,' Ms Tricklebank replied. 'They would form part of a grouping or consortium.'

'And when might these amalgamations take place?' asked the vicar.

'Not until there has been a full consultation with all the affected parties – governors, parents and local interest groups.

I should think, if it does happen, it would be at the start of the new academic year.'

'Next September,' said the Reverend Atticus.

'I should think so,' replied Ms Tricklebank.

'And were we to enter into this consortium, the school we would amalgamate with would be the nearest one to Barton-in-the-Dale?' observed Dr Stirling.

'Possibly, yes,' replied Ms Tricklebank.

'Which is at Urebank.' said Elisabeth.

'Well, I don't like the sound of that for a start!' exclaimed Mrs Pocock.

'Nothing has yet been decided,' said the senior education officer, 'but that could be an option. This meeting is just to acquaint you with the situation. There will be further discussions and consultations in due course.'

'Well, I don't want us to join up with Urebank,' said Mrs Pocock.

'You may not have a choice,' replied Ms Tricklebank.

4

Elisabeth had a sleepless night. She lay in bed listening to the wind tugging fretfully at the window frames and a thin rain pattering on the glass. The term had started so well, she thought, and now there was this bolt from the blue. The idea of Barton-in-the-Dale school combining with Urebank and her having to work with Robin Richardson, the headmaster there, filled her with a deep dismay.

She had crossed swords with the man in question soon after she had started in her new post. Now it appeared they might very well be working together – in what capacity she just did not know.

The following morning Elisabeth looked out of the kitchen window. The weather reflected her mood. It was a dull, cold, overcast Saturday, the sky a blanket of gloomy grey clouds. Danny was in her garden, busy digging in the borders, his elbows moving up and down like pistons. He was dressed in his grandfather's old waxed jacket and substantial rubber boots, and wore a flat cap a size too large pulled down over his forehead. It was good to see him so happy. It had been hard for the boy the previous year.

She put on her outdoor coat and joined him.

'Hello, Danny,' she said, coming up behind him, her hands dug deep in her coat pockets.

The boy jumped as if touched with a cattle prod and dropped the spade. 'By 'eck, Mrs Devine, tha med me jump.'

'Sorry about creeping up on you like that,' said Elisabeth. 'You looked as if you were in a world of your own.'

'I were just thinkin' about mi granddad,' the boy told her. 'He allus 'ated this time o' year. He used to stick 'is 'ead out o' caravan dooer and say, "Nowt growin', nowt movin' and so cowld you can 'ear yer bones a-clickin."'

'It's a bit chilly for doing this sort of work, isn't it?' Elisabeth asked. 'Perhaps you ought to wait until it gets warmer.'

'Nay miss. I was stuck in t'house. I likes to be out and about, and yer garden needs fettlin'. Now I've left them pile o' leaves ovver theer behind yon tree 'cos you'll like as not 'ave some 'edgehogs in there.'

'Yes, I think I have,' said Elisabeth. 'Last summer I saw them on the lawn at dusk.'

'They'd 'ave been snuffling for food,' Danny told her. ''Edehogs won't be out at this time o'year. They'll be wrapped up in balls under them leaves. Yer need to look after yer 'edgehogs, Mrs Devine, 'cos they eat slugs and snails what can kill yer plants. They're t'oldest mammals in t'world, tha knaas, but pesticides what kill yer beetles and caterpillars mean they go 'ungry, so they need feedin'. Yer 'edgehogs that is, not yer beetles and caterpillars. What they really like are chopped peanuts, peanut butter and meat scraps, but don't put any out now 'cos you'll attract yer rats.'

'I'll remember that,' said Elisabeth.

'And t'branch o' yon sycamore tree, one what got split oppen wi' lightning, that wants cutting off. It might come down on yer cottage in a strong wind and end up through yer roof.'

'Yes, I've been meaning to get that seen to,' said Elisabeth. 'Don't you go trying to do it.'

'Nay miss, I don't like 'eights,' Danny told her. The boy patted his pocket. 'I'll put some food out for t'birds afore I go, an' all.'

'So you're the mystery bird-feeder are you? I guessed it might be you. That's very kind of you, Danny.'

'You gets all sooarts o' birds in this garden an' t'kestrel knows it an' all. I've seen 'im 'overing up theer in t'sky watchin' an' waitin'. 'E got a pigeon last week. I don't mind 'im gerrin' pigeons because they're a blasted nuisance – tree rats, mi granddad used to call 'em – but I don't like it when 'e teks a blackbird or a linnet. Mind you, they're offen too quick for 'im.' He pointed to the chattering sparrows in the large syca-more tree. 'Just listen to 'em. Yer blue tits and great tits are partial to nuts, but yer goldfinch and greenfinch and siskins, they likes them nyjer seeds.'

'Whatever is a siskin?' asked Elisabeth.

The boy chuckled. 'Yer might be t'ead teacher o' t'school, miss, but tha dunt know much abaat birds, do ya?'

'Not really,' replied Elisabeth smiling. 'I'm what you village folk call an "off-comed-un". I've a lot to learn about the countryside.'

'Well, a siskin is like yer greenfinch but smaller and with a streaked belly and forked tail. You can tell t'males 'cos they 'ave a black cap on their 'eads and they're reight show-offs. Mi granddad liked siskins. Ya don't see much of 'em in summer but you see lots in winter if ya keep your eyes oppen. "There's nowt like t'sound o' t'sweet twittering of a flock of siskins feed-ing among the trees in the wintertime." That's what mi granddad used to say.' The boy became suddenly pensive and looked up at the sky. Then he rubbed his eyes.

Elisabeth put a hand on Danny's shoulder and squeezed it gently. 'You think a lot about your grandfather, don't you?' she said.

'Aye, I do. I do miss 'im,' said the boy. 'This were fust Christmas I've 'ad wi'out 'im.'

Neither spoke for a moment but looked beyond the garden to a vast and silent landscape of fields and hills, criss-crossed by thin white walls which rose like veins impossibly high to the craggy fells.

'You shouldn't be spending all your money on food for my birds, Danny,' said Elisabeth. 'I'll give you some money for the nuts before you go.'

'Yer all reight, miss,' said the boy, sniffing. 'I get pocket money and don't 'ave much else to spend it on after I've bought t'food for mi ferret.'

'Where is your ferret, by the way?' asked Elisabeth.

Danny reached into the pocket of his jacket and produced the little sandy-coloured, pointed-faced creature with small bright black eyes. He held the animal under its chest, his thumb under one leg towards the ferret's spine, and using the other hand he gently stroked the creature down the full length of its body. 'I never go anywhere without Ferdy,' he told her. Then he recalled the time he had taken the creature to school and it had bitten Malcolm Stubbins and landed him in trouble. 'Except, of course, tekkin' 'im to school.' He returned the animal to the warmth of his pocket.

Elisabeth smiled. 'You're happy with Dr Stirling, aren't you, Danny?'

'"Like a pig in the proverbial," as mi granddad used to say. It's champion, miss, it really is. 'E's a proper gent is Dr Stirling. That's summat else mi granddad used to say.' He thought for a moment. 'Mrs Devine,' he said.

'Yes?'

'Can I asks you summat?'

'Of course you can.'

'When I'm adopted like, I'll be sort of like Dr Stirling's son, won't I?'

'You won't be *sort of* like Dr Stirling's son, Danny, you will be his son. It will be all legal.'

'I don't want to change mi name,' said the boy, his forehead furrowing. 'I want to still be called Danny Stainthorpe.'

'I don't think there will be a problem with that.'

'Mrs Devine?'

'Yes?'

'Do ya reckon Dr Stirling will let me call 'im Dad, like James does?'

'I should think that he will insist on it,' replied Elisabeth.

The boy's face broke into a great beaming smile. 'I don't know what it's like to 'ave a dad. I never knew mi real dad and I don't remember mi mum.' He thought for a moment. 'Mrs Devine?'

'Yes, Danny?'

'Thanks for all you've done for me. After mi granddad went into t'hospital, I just din't know what to do. I were frightened and I just couldn't think straight. If it 'adn't 'ave bin for you and Dr Stirling . . .' His voice trailed off.

'I know,' Elisabeth said gently. 'Now come along, young man, I think you've done enough in my garden for today.'

The boy touched her arm with the tips of his fingers. 'I just wanted to tell you that,' he said.

Elisabeth felt tears pricking the corners of her eyes. She changed the subject. 'Do you think things might brighten up?' she asked.

The boy stared up at the leaden sky. Then he took off his cap and ran a hand through his dusty hair, wrinkled his forehead again and broke into a frown. 'I reckon not,' he said sagely.

'By the way, I meant to have a word with you,' said Elisabeth.

The boy pulled a face. 'Nowt up, I 'opes?'

'Well, I think there may be.' The boy looked worried. 'Should Mr Massey's sheep grazing in my paddock be lambing at this time of year?'

Danny shook his head and laughed. 'No, they shouldn't. It's wrong time for lambing. It were Clarence, 'is nephew, what did it. 'E let t'jock gerrin in 'mongst yows.' He saw the quizzical expression on Elisabeth's face. 'Jock's yer ram and 'e should 'ave been kept away from yows at this time o'year. It's not reight time for tuppin'. 'E allus seems to get things wrong, does Clarence. Can't seem to do owt reight. 'Is Uncle Fred went barmy. It's not reight time for lambs is January, what wi' cold an' all.'

'No,' agreed Elisabeth. 'I don't suppose it is.'

'Ya see,' continued Danny, 'ya usually puts yer jock in wi' yows around Bonfire Neet, then ya gets yer lambs in early April. Ya keeps 'im away at other times o' year or if tha does purrim in t'same field 'e wears 'is winter clouts.'

'You've lost me there, Danny,' said Elisabeth.

'Yer winter clout is a sort of triangle o' tweed cloth what's fastened underneath yer jock and coverin' 'is you-know-what. That stops 'im doin' what comes natural. If 'e's wearin' 'is winter clout he can't—'

'I think I've got the idea, Danny,' interrupted Elisabeth, colouring a little. 'Thank you for explaining that to me.'

'No problem, miss,' said the boy. He thought for a moment and then put his cap back on the back on his head and chuckled. 'It's funny though, in't it, miss?

'What is?' asked Elisabeth.

''Ere I am, teaching t'teacher,' he said, shaking his head.

Later that morning Elisabeth visited Forest View Special School. John had been a pupil there for just over a term. He was an easy-going, contented boy who had settled in remarkably well in this peaceful, spacious and secure environment, surrounded by beautiful rolling green countryside. The walls were in pale restful colours, the lighting was soft and there were no strident bells sounding every hour.

When John was born Elisabeth, like every mother with her newborn child, had thought her baby to be the most beautiful little miracle in the world, with his great blue eyes, soft skin and tiny fingers and toes. Simon, the proud father, had held the baby high in the air and told him he would be a son in a million. Then as the weeks passed Elisabeth had begun to feel that there was something not quite right. At first the baby had seemed a model child; he had smiled early, fed easily and slept soundly, but when he had made no effort to walk like other children of his age or to speak, and had begun increasingly to reject any physical contact, she had begun to feel more and more anxious. The doctor had reassured her that there was nothing to worry about. She could tell he thought her to be just another overanxious parent. Her husband at first had been unsympathetic when she shared her misgivings with him, and had told his wife to listen to the doctor and not to fuss, that everything would be fine. He had realised with a shock, after a visit to the specialist which Elisabeth had insisted upon, that things were not right with his son.

'John has a condition known as autism,' they were told. 'It is a strange, complex and often upsetting condition often manifested in people who are unable to form social relationships. I am afraid your son appears to have a severe form of autism. It means that human behaviour will be perplexing for him. He will probably cope quite well with the physical world because it is more predictable, but unexplained changes will disturb him. Autistic people often become locked inside themselves and are obsessed with precision and order. Everything has to be exact and in its place. Sadly they can be unaware of those who love them and show little affection.'

Cracks soon began to appear in their marriage. They stopped seeing their friends, going out to the theatre, even having a holiday, and soon the simmering silences and arguments became part of their everyday life. While Elisabeth wanted to find out more about their son's condition, Simon was reluctant even to talk about it. He was bitter and angry, he told her, that with all the children born into the world John had to be like this. He had expected his son would be a bright, articulate, clever boy whom he could read to, take to football matches and help with his homework – all the things most fathers did. It soon became clear that he just could not cope with this silent little boy who lived in his own closed world and would be dependent upon them all his life. When John was five, Simon had packed his things and left. Following the divorce, Elisabeth heard that he had remarried some high-flying young accountant in the office where he was a senior partner. She had telephoned him just the once to tell him how John was getting on, and was told it would be for the best if she didn't get in contact again. It distressed his new wife. Since then Elisabeth had heard nothing from him.

Mr Williams, head teacher of Forest View, was in the school entrance waiting to meet her when Elisabeth arrived. He was a small, dark-complexioned, silver-haired Welshman with shining eyes, and usually greeted her with a broad smile. That morning he looked solemn.

'Hello,' Elisabeth said. She sensed something was wrong from his expression. 'Is everything all right?'

'Could you just pop into my office for a moment?' he said. 'I need to have a word with you before you see John.'

'Has something happened?' she asked anxiously as she followed him into his room.

'Do sit down,' said Mr Williams, pointing to a chair. He sat behind his desk. 'John had a bit of an outburst yesterday. He got into quite a state and has not quite got over things yet.'

'What happened?' asked Elisabeth.

'He was arranging some coloured beads, sorting them out and putting them in order of size and colour, which, as you know, he likes to do. One of the other children touched them and then moved them around and John got into quite a state and lashed out. He's never done this before. Fortunately the other child wasn't badly hurt, but she became very distressed too.'

Elisabeth remained silent and stared at the floor. 'It's so out of character for John to do this, isn't it?' she said finally.

'It is,' agreed Mr Williams. 'He's usually such a placid, easy-going and good-humoured boy, but you see when someone invaded his space and disrupted his routine he became confused and annoyed. This is not unusual with autistic people. They take things very seriously. Of course several of the other children do suddenly become angry if something or somebody upsets them but it has never happened before with John, so let's hope this is a one-off.'

'Yes,' murmured Elisabeth. 'Let's hope.'

'As I mentioned to you when John first came here,' continued the head teacher, 'there is no disorder as confusing to comprehend or as complex to diagnose as autism. John displays many of the symptoms of this condition: repetitive actions, rigidity of thinking, oversensitivity to noise and touch and getting upset if his routine is broken. I really don't think this spat is something to get overly worried about, but I thought you needed to know before you see him today. He might seem a bit different.'

'Why do you think he's started to be like this now?' she asked.

'I'm afraid I cannot say,' replied Mr Williams. 'Maybe he's growing up and hormones are kicking in. You know what some youngsters can be like when they reach adolescence. There are all the changes taking place in their bodies. I know my own nephew went through that moody, "you can't tell me anything, you're always getting at me" stage and flying into tantrums, arguing with his parents and storming out of the house. John of course can't shout or tell you what troubles him. Perhaps this is a way of expressing his feelings.' Elisabeth looked so dejected the head teacher reached out across the desk and touched her hand. 'Elisabeth, your son has made really good progress since he has been here. He can dress himself, go to the toilet and clean his teeth, which many children here cannot do. He can express his needs calmly and has started to respond to light demands placed upon him. He is coping well with distractions that might have previously annoyed or made him anxious. All these are positives. Anyway, I just thought you needed to know about his small outburst – and that's what it was, a small outburst – before you see him this morning. We will of course keep a close eye on him, as we do with all the children. I hope that perhaps this behaviour turns out to be just a temporary thing.'

'I hope so too,' replied Elisabeth.

John was sitting by the window in the classroom gently rocking back and forth. She noticed that the other children were keeping well away from him.

'They are giving him a bit of a wide berth this morning,' explained the teacher. Mr Campsmount, a young man with a ready smile and bright eyes, clearly loved his job. He had started teaching at the school the year before and had been described by the inspectors in their report as an outstanding practitioner – well organised, enthusiastic, highly committed and relating well to his pupils.

'So I hear,' sighed Elisabeth.

'It's not like John to get into a paddy,' the teacher told her. 'He's always such a pleasant lad. He's a bit upset at the moment but I wouldn't worry too much. I am sure he'll soon be back to his usual self.'

'I hope so.'

'After all, we all get angry at times, don't we? I remember I went ballistic when my younger brother smashed up my bike when I was John's age. Lost it completely. Why should these children be any different?'

'I suppose not,' she replied.

'You might like to take John for a short walk in the grounds when he's calmed down a bit – perhaps when you next visit. As you know, when he came here he found trips out of the school stressful but he quite enjoys them now, especially the puddles.

He's also become fascinated with insects. He never hurts them, but he loves to watch them and have them on his hand. Anyway, I'll leave you with him. He always enjoys your visits.'

If only I could be sure of that, thought Elisabeth.

She went to John's favourite table by the window and sat beside her son. He stiffened when she touched his hand, avoided eye contact and stopped rocking. The beads were in front of him on the table but remained untouched. As a small child he had always been happiest when left alone sitting on the carpet sorting out shapes and bricks, spending hours meticulously arranging them. Sometimes he would take all the pans out of the cupboard in the kitchen and put them in order of size. He became quite obsessive about neatness and routine.

'Hello, John,' said Elisabeth.

The boy started rocking again, moving rhythmically to and fro, his brow furrowed as if something troubled him.

'Well, young man,' she said, trying to sound cheerful. 'I hear you've had a bit of a do?' John continued to rock and stare before him. 'Well, it's all over now.' She squeezed his hand.

Elisabeth spent an hour with her son, sometimes chattering on about the school and things she had done, at other times just sitting there in silence holding his hand and staring through the classroom window at the panorama of pale green fields and limestone walls and distant peaks. When she had done this on previous visits, she had often wondered if John understood anything, but on the odd occasion when she mentioned a memory there would be a reaction – a slight turn of the head, a small change of expression, a rapid blink of an eye. That morning John continued his slow rocking seemingly oblivious to all that she said.

'I wouldn't worry your head too much about it, Mr Gribbon,' said Mrs Scrimshaw casually as she tidied her desk before departing for home.

'It's all well and good you saying that,' the caretaker told the school secretary, 'but if they're getting rid of some teachers, downscaling as they like to call it—'

'Downsizing,' corrected the school secretary.

'Whatever. It means they'll be redeploying and sacking other people as well, and it might be you and me what has to go.'

'When, and indeed if, this proposed amalgamation does take place,' said Mrs Scrimshaw, 'and nothing has been decided yet, there will be two premises to manage, one here and one at Urebank, so that means they will need to have a secretary here and one over there to answer all the calls and deal with all the paperwork. I have no worries on my account. In fact, I've been assured by Mrs Devine that my position looks pretty secure.'

'Aye, well, I'm very pleased for you, I'm sure, but what about me?' whinged the caretaker. 'She's said nothing to me. Has she said anything to you?'

'About what?'

'About me,' he said, thrusting out his jaw.

'Why should Mrs Devine discuss your future with me?' asked Mrs Scrimshaw. 'I suggest you ask her about your position yourself.'

'I will do,' replied the caretaker.

'Of course they may just have the one caretaker,' added the school secretary mischievously.

'What?'

'A peripatetic.'

'Somebody what's disabled?' exclaimed the caretaker. 'How can he do the job? He won't be able to get up a ladder.'

'Peripatetic – someone who moves from one premises to the other,' explained the secretary, shaking her head.

'Moves from one premises to the other?' the caretaker repeated. 'I don't like the sound of that. I can't be going backwards and forwards to two schools like a fiddler's elbow. I have enough on dealing with this place. I couldn't manage two, not with my back. Anyway, I'm supposed to be getting a part-time cleaner to help out here. Mrs Devine promised me.'

'Well, the situation might have changed,' the secretary told him. 'I don't imagine they'll be taking on any more staff at this time. As I said, it may be that they appoint one caretaker to look after both schools.'

'Well, it's not something I want to take on,' grumbled Mr Gribbon. 'I can tell you that for nothing.'

'Well, you might not have to.'

'How do you mean?'

'The caretaker at Urebank might do it,' she told him.

Mr Gribbon went suddenly quiet. 'Yes, I suppose they might,' he said under his breath.

'They'll probably appoint a site manager,' said the secretary, 'to oversee both places, and a team of cleaners at each school.'

'You think?'

'Well, it's a possibility.'

'I don't like the sound of that either,' grumbled the caretaker.

'I suppose when the governors consider who to appoint they'll look at the track records of you and the caretaker at Urebank.'

'Meaning what?'

'Meaning they'll consider who does the better job.' Then she added impishly, 'I'm sure you have no worries on that account, but if I were you I'd keep your bad back to yourself. They might not think you are up to the job.'

'Not up to the job!' he exclaimed. 'Who says I'm not up to the job?'

'Nobody here,' said the school secretary, 'but when it comes to appointments you know what school governors can be like.'

'I shall have to have a word with Mrs Devine,' said Mr Gribbon, looking distinctly uneasy.

'I think that's a good idea,' agreed the secretary. 'Now I must make tracks. I have a Women's Institute meeting this evening. Mr Lilywhite is talking about "The Amusing Side of Waste Management" and I'm in the chair.'

Chantelle appeared at the door of the school office.

'Mr Gribbon,' she said, 'can you come? One of the infants has been sick right down the corridor on her way home and the tap won't turn off in the girls' toilets and the handle's come loose on the outside door and—'

'Don't bring me no more bad news,' he told the girl loudly before stomping past her on his way to see the head teacher.

The girl rolled her eyes and shrugged. 'What's got into him?' she asked. 'He's like a bear with a sore bum, as my nan would say.'

Mrs Scrimshaw could not contain a smile.

'Might I have a word, Mrs Devine?' Mr Gribbon was waiting for the head teacher outside her classroom the following morning, jangling his keys and looking uneasy.

'Of course,' Elisabeth replied. 'I was meaning to have a word with you anyway.'

'You were?' He looked worried.

'Yes, but you go first. What is it that you wished to see me about?'

'It's just that I'm a bit concerned about my position, Mrs Devine,' said the caretaker.

'Your position?' she repeated.

'With this amalgamation. Will it mean that I might lose my job?'

'No, I think your position is pretty secure,' Elisabeth reassured him. 'Schools need to be cleaned and cared for, and good caretakers are hard to come by. I am sure you have nothing to worry about.'

'So I won't be made redundant, then?' he asked.

'No, I can allay any fears you have in that direction.'

'You can what?' he asked.

'Assure you that it is not likely to happen.'

'And I won't be one of these pyrotechnics?'

'Pyrotechnics?'

'Them that travel between the schools.'

'Ah, peripatetic. No, I can't see that happening either.'

'It's just that Mrs Scrimshaw seems to think that they might appoint some site manager what looks after both schools and that I might have to travel.'

'Mrs Scrimshaw only knows as much as anyone else, and we are all in the dark as to what may or may not happen, Mr Gribbon, but I am sure things will remain pretty much the same as far as you are concerned.'

The caretaker looked mollified. 'Well, that's good to hear,' he said, raising a smile.

'I was meaning to speak to you about the part-time cleaner we have been trying to employ here,' Elisabeth told him.

'I suppose they've put the kibosh on that now,' observed the caretaker. 'Mrs Scrimshaw said that they'll not likely be employing new staff until this amalgamation takes place.'

'Mrs Scrimshaw seems to be privy to a great deal about the proposed amalgamation,' said Elisabeth good-humouredly. 'In actual fact they have agreed at County Hall at long last for a part-time cleaner to start here. Just two mornings a week. She will be on a temporary contract for the time being, but hopefully, if she proves satisfactory, she can be made permanent when they have sorted out the staffing for the amalgamated schools.'

'Oh, well, that's good news,' said Mr Gribbon.

'She will be calling in at school later this week. Her name is

Mrs Pugh. Perhaps I might leave you to look after her and show her the ropes? I have an education officer coming in for the morning on Thursday and then Mrs Atticus's college tutor and the school nurse visiting on the Friday, so I will be pretty much tied up.'

'No problem, Mrs Devine,' replied the caretaker. He strode off down the corridor with a spring in his step, keen to enlighten the school secretary with the good news about the part-time cleaner and his assured future.

5

On Thursday Ms Tricklebank arrived to spend a morning in the school. She had spoken to Elisabeth following the governors' meeting and asked if she might visit Barton-in-the Dale to get to know the staff and pupils and learn something about the school. Of course, Elisabeth realised that there was another agenda for the visit, namely to assess the quality of the education. The senior education officer would no doubt be visiting Urebank as well, to judge that school and make comparisons. It was therefore important, as Elisabeth told the teachers at the staff meeting and the children in the school assembly, that the visitor gained a favourable impression. At the staff meeting the teachers looked anxious.

'What is she like?' asked Mrs Robertshaw.

'Well, I've only met her once at the governors' meeting,' replied Elisabeth, 'and to be frank she is a bit of an unknown quantity. She said very little at the meeting and kept things pretty close to her chest. She's not a person given to much smiling. Rather a stern and forbidding woman if first impressions are anything to go by.'

'Sounds frightening,' observed Miss Brakespeare, giving a slight shudder.

'I'm sure that when she sees what we have achieved here, meets the children and looks at the work they are doing,' said Elisabeth, 'she will leave very impressed.'

It was Mr Gribbon who first saw Ms Tricklebank on the Thursday morning. He observed a dumpy, red-faced woman with a rather intense expression on her face standing by the school gate watching the children as they filed up the path.

'Morning,' he said, approaching her.

'Good morning,' she replied.

'Are you from County Hall?' he asked.

'Yes,' she replied. 'I think I am expected.'

'I'm Mr Gribbon, the caretaker.'

'I see.'

'Well, come along,' he said. 'Don't stand out here in the cold. I'll show you what's what.'

'Perhaps I might see the head teacher first,' said the senior education officer.

'Oh, she'll see you later,' he told her. 'That's if she can fit you in. She's very busy this morning. She teaches during the day and has important visitors to see at lunchtime. She's asked me to look after you.'

'Really?'

As Ms Tricklebank followed the caretaker up the school path, he continued to talk non-stop. ''Course, it's an old school as you can see and it takes a lot of cleaning, I can tell you. Dust gets everywhere and we have a problem with cockroaches. They come out from under the skirting boards at night. You get used to them. They're bloody difficult to kill are cockroaches, I can tell you. They can live for a month without food. 'Course in a school they've got plenty to go at what with the kiddies dropping crisps and sweets and I don't know what, and the teachers are as bad. I put this poison powder down the corridors every night then sweep up the bodies before school.' He chuckled. 'For the cockroaches that is, not the teachers.'

'If I might—' began Ms Tricklebank.

'You're not allergical to cockroaches are you?' the caretaker asked.

'Interesting as this is,' started Ms Tricklebank, 'I think I really must—'

The caretaker continued obliviously. 'You're all right up ladders, are you? Because some of the shelves are high up. I deal with the floors and the boiler of course. You'll be responsible for the toilets, amongst other things. You'll find Mrs Devine the head teacher nice enough but she's a real stickler for cleanliness, not like the last one, and she watches you like a hawk. She misses nothing. Now, the children's toilets will need a good going-over when you're in and—'

'Excuse me,' interrupted Ms Tricklebank, 'I think we are at cross-purposes here. Whom do you imagine you are speaking to?'

'You're Mrs Pugh, the new part-time cleaner, aren't you?' the caretaker replied.

'No, I am not,' replied Ms Tricklebank. 'I am the senior education officer.'

'Oh,' gasped Mr Gribbon, stopping in his tracks and hoping that the floor would open and swallow him up.

The first lesson Ms Tricklebank joined was with Miss Brakespeare and the top juniors. The deputy head teacher was rather unnerved by the serious-faced woman who wandered from desk to desk, talking to the children and scrutinising their exercise books.

'And what would you say is the best thing about your school?' she asked a large boy with a round moon of a face and great dimpled elbows. He stared at her suspiciously. 'The best thing about Barton-in-the-Dale?'

'Dunno,' he replied.

'Is it the lessons, the various activities, the school trips?' she prompted.

'Dunno.'

'Well, if there was anything you could change what would it be?'

'Dunno,' repeated the boy.

'There must be something,' she persisted.

'I've got to gerron wi' mi work,' he told her crossly, looking down at his book.

Ms Tricklebank left the classroom with a cursory 'Thank you' to Miss Brakespeare.

In the infant classroom the senior education officer sat stony-faced in the corner, listening as the teacher began to read from *The Tale of Benjamin Bunny*. As the children filed out of the classroom later for playtime, Ms Tricklebank tackled Miss Wilson on the choice of story.

'Don't you think Beatrix Potter's stories are rather dated?' she asked, as if challenging the teacher to disagree. 'There is so much bright, interesting and perhaps more appropriate reading material available for young children these days.'

Miss Wilson was taken aback. Then colour suffused her face. 'If you would care to look in the reading corner,' she said sharply, 'you will find plenty of bright, interesting and modern books. I believe children should be exposed to a wide variety of literature, including some which might be considered dated. In my opinion Beatrix Potter is one of the finest writers for young children. If we only presented children with up-to-date material they would never come across fairy stories and fables and classics like *The Wind in the Willows*, *Alice Through the Looking Glass* and *The Water Babies*.'

Ms Tricklebank held up a hand and gave a small smile. 'I take your point, Miss Wilson,' she said, as calm as a nun. 'I was merely interested in your opinion.'

After morning break, which Ms Tricklebank spent in the playground talking to the children and watched by the teachers from the staffroom window, she joined Mrs Robertshaw with the lower juniors. The children sat in a semicircle around the teacher.

'Now, children,' said Mrs Robertshaw, 'we have with us this morning a visitor.' All heads turned in the direction of the senior education officer, who sat by the window straight-backed and expressionless. 'This is Ms Tricklebank and she may wish to speak to you. I am sure you will make her feel very much at home. We are very friendly in this school, aren't we, children?'

'Yes, miss,' the class chorused.

The senior education officer gave a small nod of the head.

The teacher turned her attention back to her class. 'Last week Jeremy asked me which was my very favourite story when I was a girl. Well, I am going to read it to you this morning. It's called 'The Selfish Giant'.'

Oscar waved his hand in the air. 'It's by Oscar Wilde, miss,' he volunteered.

'Yes it is,' agreed the teacher. 'And—'

'He's my mother's favourite writer,' said Oscar. 'I was named after him. My father says he was a very colourful character and led a very interesting life.'

The teacher raised an eyebrow. 'Yes, I think it could be said he was most colourful and led a very interesting life,' she replied. 'I wouldn't disagree with your father about that, Oscar. Now this is the tale—'

'Miss, I've heard this story before,' the boy told her.

'Really?'

'It's very sad.'

'Yes, it is,' replied the teacher.

'It's a sort of a parable, isn't it, Mrs Robertshaw?' he said.

The teacher put on a forced smile. 'Yes, I think you could say that it is.'

'What's a parable, miss?' asked a small girl with long blonde plaits.

'It's a simple story with a—'

'A moral,' said Oscar.

'What's a moral?' asked the girl.

'Well—' began the boy.

'Oscar,' snapped the teacher, 'we can talk about the story later on. Before that I have to read it. Now no more interruptions please, otherwise I shall never finish the story and we won't find out what happens.'

'But I do know what happens, miss,' said Oscar.

'Well, you are going to hear what happens again,' said the teacher somewhat brusquely. 'Now, children,' she continued, 'I read a good many books when I was your age but the one story which I loved the most, the one which brings back so many happy memories of my childhood and the one which I wish I had written myself, is 'The Selfish Giant' by Oscar Wilde.'

'He was gay, wasn't he, miss,' said Oscar.

Mrs Robertshaw sighed.

'What does that mean, miss?' asked the girl with the blonde plaits.

'Happy and light-hearted,' said the teacher quickly.

'No, I meant he was—' began the boy, waving his hand in the air again.

'Oscar!' exclaimed the teacher. 'I said no more interruptions. Now let's get on with the story. It is about a very mean and bad-tempered giant who prevents the little children from playing in his beautiful garden.'

The children listened intently as the teacher recounted the tale.

'"My own garden is my own garden",' she told the children, '"and I will not allow anyone to play in it but myself." When spring comes the Giant's garden remains cold and barren and a great white cloak of snow buries everything. The Giant cannot understand why the spring passes his garden by. Summer doesn't come and neither does autumn and the garden stays perpetually cold and empty of life. One morning the Giant sees a most wonderful sight. Through a little hole in the wall the children have crept into his garden and every tree has a little child sitting in the branches amongst the blossoms. They have brought life back to his garden and the Giant's heart melts. He creeps into the garden but when the children see him they are frightened and run away. One small boy doesn't see the Giant, for his eyes are full of tears. The Giant steals up behind the child and gently takes his little hand in his. Many years pass and the little boy never comes back to play in the garden. Now very old and feeble, the giant longs to see his first little friend again. One day the small child returns.'

The teacher read from the book:

"'Downstairs ran the Giant in great joy and out into the garden. He hastened across the grass, and came near to the child. And when he came quite close his face grew red with anger, and he said, "Who hath dared to wound thee?" For on the palms of the child's hands were the prints of two nails, and the prints of the two nails were on the little feet.

"Who hath dared to wound thee?" cried the Giant; "tell me, that I may take my big sword and slay him."

"Nay!" answered the child: "but these are the wounds of Love".'

At this point the teacher stopped reading and she stared at the page. Then her eyes began to fill with tears. 'Oh dear,' she said, sniffing, 'I'm sorry, children. I shall have to stop for a moment.' There was a tremble in her voice. 'This part always makes me want to cry.' She reached in her handbag and took out a handkerchief and blew her nose noisily. Many of the children looked moved to tears too and some began rubbing their eyes.

Oscar came out to the front of the class, took the book from the teacher's hand and said, 'I'll finish it, miss.' And like a seasoned actor taking centre stage, the boy read the story in a clear, animated and confident voice and the class listened in rapt silence.

"'Who art thou?" said the Giant, and a strange awe fell on

him, and he knelt before the little child. And the child smiled on the Giant, and said to him, "You let me play once in your garden, today you shall come with me to my garden, which is Paradise."

And when the children ran in that afternoon, they found the Giant lying dead under the tree, all covered with white blossoms.'

No one spoke when the boy had finished reading. The only noise was from the teacher snuffling into her tissue. Then the small girl with the long blonde plaits spoke. There was a tremble in *her* voice. 'This Oscar Wilde doesn't sound very gay to me, miss,' she said.

The last classroom Ms Tricklebank visited was Elisabeth's. The visitor spent a few minutes looking at the displays on the wall and then through a selection of the children's folders, making notes in a small black book. Elisabeth's heart sank when, of all the pupils in the class to speak to, the senior education officer selected the two most likely to give the worst impression: Ernest Pocock and Malcolm Stubbins.

Ernest knew all about Ms Tricklebank, for his mother had returned from the governors' meeting and spent the entire evening describing the proceedings to the boy's father. She had been highly critical of the new representative of the Education Department, describing her as 'a hard-faced, sharp-tongued madam' with 'a droopy mouth like last month's rhubarb'. Three words had come to her husband's mind as he listened to the diatribe – 'pan', 'kettle' and 'black' – but he had said nothing.

'Can you spell your name?' Ms Tricklebank asked the boy.

Ernest looked up scowling. ''Course I can,' he replied. 'I'm not stupid, you know.'

The senior education officer sighed. 'What are you called?'

'Ernest Pocock.'

The name registered with Ms Tricklebank. This would be the son of that disagreeable governor. 'May I look at your exercise book?' she asked.

The boy slid the book across the table and eyed the visitor suspiciously.

'And how do you think you are getting on?' she asked, looking at a page of writing in the middle of the book, entitled 'Bonfire Night'.

'With what?' he asked.

'Your work.'

'Well, you can see,' the boy replied, tapping the page with a grubby finger. 'I think I'm doing OK.'

Ms Tricklebank scrutinised the writing. Then she looked up. 'What advice would you give to someone handling dangerous fireworks?'

'To be careful,' he replied.

She continued to read. 'This is quite an interesting account,' she said, 'and I can see that there's been a big improvement in your spelling. However, your grammar is not too good.'

'She were all right when I saw her last Sunday,' replied the boy.

The response might have amused another visitor but Ms Tricklebank's face remained set. 'No, not your grandmother,' she said, 'your grammar – the way that sentences are put together.'

'I don't know what you're on about,' said Ernest.

'No, I don't suppose you do,' said Ms Tricklebank under her breath. She moved to the next table, where a surly-faced boy observed her.

'What is your name?' she asked.

'Malcolm Stubbins.'

'And what are you doing this morning, Malcolm?' she asked.

'Fractions.'

'And how are you coping with fractions?'

'Coping?' he repeated.

'Do you think that you have got to grips with them?'

'Yeah.'

'And if I were to give you a problem involving fractions, do you think you might try and solve it for me?'

'I suppose.'

'Well then, if a mother had three children but only four potatoes, how could she divide the potatoes so that each child got an equal share?'

'Make 'em into chips,' replied the boy.

'Would you like to speak to any of the other children?' Elisabeth asked the visitor when she saw Ms Tricklebank making for the door.

'No thank you, Mrs Devine,' she replied. 'I've seen quite enough.'

On her way out that lunchtime, Ms Tricklebank discovered Oscar in the small school library, poring over a large book. 'May I ask you what you are reading?' she asked.

'Of course,' he replied, removing his glasses and staring up at her. 'It's about great British military heroes. I've got up to Baden-Powell. He was a general in the Boer War.'

'And do you know what he is connected with?' the senior education officer asked.

'A hyphen,' replied the boy.

Ms Tricklebank raised an eyebrow and shook her head. There was for the first time that morning an imperceptible smile on her lips. 'Well, young man,' she said, 'I shall let you get on with your reading. By the way, that was a very thoughtful thing for you to do, helping your teacher out like that.'

'Well, she was upset,' replied Oscar, replacing his glasses.

'Yes, I could see that,' replied the important visitor. 'It was most considerate of you to do what you did.'

'Oh,' replied the boy casually, 'I often have to do it with Mrs Robertshaw.'

Mr Richardson, headmaster of Urebank Primary School, was a dour, exceptionally thin and sallow-complexioned man, with the smile of a martyr about to be burnt at the stake. He sat at his desk, his hands clenched before him.

Councillor Smout was seated opposite him in an easy chair. He looked like a toby jug, legs apart and his plump hands resting on his considerable paunch. The councillor was a broad individual with an exceptionally thick neck, vast florid face and small darting eyes. A former governor at the village school in Barton, his had been the only dissenting voice when the governors had voted against the proposal to close the school the previous term, and when the Education Department had rescinded its decision and the school had remained open, he had tendered his resignation. There had been questions asked at County Hall about his excessive expenses, but nothing could be proved conclusively and he continued to be the loud, bullish and blunt member of the Education Committee he had been since winning the seat. He also retained his position as Chairman of Governors at Urebank School.

'I can't see as 'ow there'll be a problem,' said the councillor now.

'You think not,' replied Mr Richardson, leaning forward and staring intently at his Chairman of Governors. 'As I explained to you, I assumed that with this amalgamation of the two schools I, as the longer of the two serving heads in the county and with a proven track record, would be appointed as the new head teacher, but it now appears to be in some doubt. I had this call from the new senior education officer, a Ms Tricklebank . . .'

'Yes, she's tekken ovver from Mester Nettles,' the

councillor told him. "'E's been moved to school meals. She's quite a character, is Ms Tricklebank, an' 'as a reputation for being summat of a troubleshooter. She's been tipped to tek ovver as t'Director of Education from Mester Preston when 'e leaves at t'end o' March. She's been purrin charge of this amalgamation.'

'She intends to visit the school next week to meet the staff and look around,' Mr Richardson told him.

'She'll be sussing out t'place,' said the councillor, 'so you 'ad best put your stall out and mek t'right impression.'

'I got the distinct feeling, when she phoned me up to make the appointment and I broached the matter of the amalgamation, that things are not that certain about the headship and that—'

The councillor held up a fat hand as if stopping traffic. 'Robin,' he interrupted, 'it's a formality. Everything's got to be done above board. There's procedures what we 'ave to follow. Don't you worry your 'ead. I've 'ad a word with t'Director of Education.'

'And he gave you the impression I would be offered the post?' asked Mr Richardson. There was a searching look in his eyes.

'Well, no, not in so many words,' replied the councillor, scratching his double chin. 'What he said was that you and Mrs Devine would both be called for interview and t'likelihood is that one of you would be appointed.'

'With respect, councillor,' said Mr Richardson, 'it doesn't sound like a formality to me.'

'Men are much better at handlin' difficult lads than women,' said the councillor. 'They'll want a man for t'job.'

'I'm not so sure they will,' murmured Mr Richardson.

'Anyway, in t'long run it's not up to Mester Preston, is it? Or Ms Tricklebank, for that matter. It'll be up to t'newly constitu-ated Board o' Governors what will decide who gets t'job.'

The headmaster of Urebank School looked down at his hands and sighed.

'Let me put mi cards on t'table 'ere, Robin. I wants you for t'job. This new governing body will be made up of some o' them what are at Barton and some o' them what are 'ere at Urebank.'

'But I—'

'Let me finish,' said Councillor Smout. 'Now on this new governing body they will 'ave four of those from Barton-in-the-Dale: old Major Neville-Gravitas, who 'appens to be a pal of mine and is in my golf club, t'vicar, some lady of t'manor who they intend co-opting, and Councillor Cooper, who has just been appointed to replace a Mrs Bullock who was well past it and as deaf as a post. I've 'ad words with Councillor Cooper and he knows on what side 'is bread is buttered. T'parent governors what are at Barton now, a loud-mouthed woman called Mrs Pocock and t'local GP, won't be illegible because their kids will 'ave left Barton for t'secondary school by t'time t'schools are amalgamated. So we won't 'ave them to contend with.' He counted on his fat fingers. 'So that's four governors from Barton. Now then, ovver 'ere at Urebank we'll 'ave four governors an' all and that's not countin' t'chairman who will 'ave t'casting vote should there be a tie in t'voting.'

'I see this, councillor, but—'

''Old on! 'Old on! So, there'll be four o' them and five of us. I reckon I'll be asked to be t'chairman of t'new governing body. I don't reckon Major Neville-Gravitas will want to tek it on. 'E 'ad 'is fingers burnt when t' Barton village school were up for closure.'

'I see.'

'And I will therefore 'ave t'castin' vote, not that I shall need to use it because Councillor Cooper will vote with t'Urebank governors, who will all vote for you.'

'Are you sure of that?'

'As sure as I can be. Councillor Cooper is a nice enough young chap, a bit wet behind t'ears but keen to get involved in things, and I've bin showin' 'im t'ropes. I've 'ad a word with 'im and 'e'll vote for you.'

'He said so, did he?'

'No, not in so many words, but I'm sure 'e will when push comes to shove, and I wouldn't be surprised if Major Neville-Gravitas casts 'is lot in wi' us an' all.' He tapped his fat nose. 'He owes me a favour.'

'Well, that does make me feel somewhat better,' said Mr Richardson. 'I have to say I couldn't work with Mrs Devine. She is far too assertive and ambitious for my liking and full of her own importance.'

'Yes, I find 'er far too pushy as well,' agreed Councillor Smout. 'But that's by-the-by. I reckon she'll be 'appy enough to be redeployed to another part o' t'county when she dunt get t'job. Anyroad, from what I gather she couldn't work wi' you either.' Mr Richardson gave a weak smile. 'So, as I said, I can't see as there'll be a problem.'

Mr Richardson felt satisfied that the visit of Ms Tricklebank the following week had gone well. The weekend before the senior education officer's visitation, attractive displays had been mounted in the corridors and in the classrooms, exercise books had been marked carefully, shelves and storerooms tidied, floors polished, toilets cleaned and potted plants arranged strategically around the building. The teachers, having been impressed upon by the headmaster as to just how important this visit was, had practised their lessons and warned the pupils to be on their very best behaviour. The most articulate pupil in the school, a confident and bright-eyed girl from the juniors, had met Ms Tricklebank at the entrance, presented her with a small posy of flowers and conducted her to the headmaster's room, giving, on the way, a rehearsed little speech in which she said how happy she was at Urebank and how well she was doing in her work.

Mr Richardson's only disappointment was how very little the senior education officer had said. She hadn't commented on anything she saw or the lessons she had observed, and had been non-committal when he raised the question of the amalgamation.

'Nothing has been decided yet,' she had told him. 'The Director of Education will, in good time, be seeing you and the head teacher at Barton-in-the-Dale.'

Still, all in all, thought the headmaster of Urebank School, no visitor could be anything other than impressed with his school.

Ms Tricklebank's office was at the end of the County Hall annexe. The austere room was dominated by an old square desk the colour of dried mud, on which were neatly stacked papers, reports and booklets, a plain black telephone, an empty in tray, a full out tray and a box of sharp pencils. There had been no effort to make the room warm and comfortable, for the walls, the colour of sour cream, were devoid of pictures or prints, the floor was covered in a dark green laminate and the two chairs were of the hard wooden straight-backed variety. There wasn't a potted plant in sight. A row of gunmetal grey filing cabinets had been placed by the small window, the view through which was of a shiny red brick wall. The place, cold and stark, resembled the sort of interrogation room that featured in old black and white war films.

The senior education officer looked up when Councillor Smout, without knocking, walked in. 'Mornin', Ms Tricklebank,' he said.

'Good morning, councillor,' she replied.

Without being asked, her visitor plonked himself down on

a small chair which creaked ominously beneath his considerable weight.

'I'm in County 'All this mornin' for this 'ere meeting about
the amalgamation,' he told her.

'Yes, I was aware that the Education Committee is discussing the proposals today,' she replied.

'An' I thought I'd pop in an' 'ave a word wi' you. I believe
that you will be takin' t'lead on this one, spear'eadin' it as
they say?'

'That's correct. How may I help you, councillor?' She
surveyed him unblinkingly.

'Well, t'thing is, Ms Tricklebank,' he said, leaning back and
placing his hands on his paunch, 'it strikes me that t'headship
of t'new set-up should go to t'one what's got a proven track
record an' 'as been in t'county t'longest.'

'Mr Richardson,' she said.

'Not to put too fine a point on it an' lay mi cards on t'table,
aye. As you know, I'm t'Chairman o' Governors at Urebank
an' 'ave known Robin Richardson for donkey's years. I think
'e's right for this post. 'E's been an' ead teacher a long time,
runs a tight ship, keeps good order an' knows what 'e's about.
I mean, you've been into t'school an' you must 'ave been right
impressed wi' what you've seen. I think it's only right an'
proper Robin Richardson should get t'job. 'E's better suited.'

'Than Mrs Devine?' added Ms Tricklebank.

'She's a capable woman, I won't deny that, but she's not bin
in t'county above two minutes. Anyway, Barton was in line for
closure an' 'ers was to be a temporary post. I 'ave to say that
some o' t'councillors, me included, were not best pleased
when t'planned closure o' t'school 'ad to be scrapped, largely,
I may add, because of t'campaign what Mrs Devine organised. It's not as if she'll end up wi'out a job anyway. She'll be
redeployed an' offered a post somewhere else.'

'I see,' said Ms Tricklebank, resting her hands on the

desktop. 'And have you spoken to the Director of Education about this?'

'I 'ave mentioned it,' the councillor replied, 'but as you well know Mr Preston is off to pastures new at t'end o' this term an' won't be 'ere when this hamalgamation takes place. You will be 'ere, an' as I've said he's left things in your 'ands to deal wi'.'

'You are quite right, councillor,' replied the senior education officer. 'I am dealing with it, but you must understand that it is not my decision who will be appointed. The decision rests with the newly constituted governing body. I don't even have a vote.'

'I know that, Ms Tricklebank, but you 'ave influence,' said the councillor. 'You'll be advisin', tellin' us what's what, who you think is t'best candidate. You'll be recommendin' who should be offered t'post.'

The senior education officer on this occasion kept her counsel.

Councillor Smout smiled, sat up, then leaned over the desk. 'Changin' t'subject, I shouldn't be surprised if you'll be throwin' your 'at in t'ring for t'Director o' Education's job,' he said casually.

'I beg your pardon?'

'You're thought very 'ighly of in t'county, Ms Tricklebank, and I 'ave to say your name 'as bin mentioned by quite a few people as Mr Preston's possible successor.'

'Really?'

'Oh yes. When t'post is hadvertised I think quite a lot o' those on t'shortlisting panel will welcome an application from you.' The smile had not left his face. ''Course, I shall no doubt be asked to be on t'panel an', even if I do say so myself, I do 'ave quite a bit of influence wi' t'other councillors.'

The senior education officer didn't reply.

'So,' continued Councillor Smout, rising from his chair,

'I'm askin' you, Ms Tricklebank, to give this matter some serious thought.'

'Concerning the headship of the amalgamated schools or the director's post?' she asked.

'Both,' replied Councillor Smout before striding to the door. He turned. 'I'll wish you good day,' he said.

When he had gone Ms Tricklebank stood and stared out of the window at the brick wall. Then she closed her eyes briefly as if pained, and mulled over what he had said.

6

Lady Helen Wadsworth sat behind a small gilt desk with gold tasselled drawers, in the library at Limebeck House. It was too ostentatious and colourful a room for a library, with its heavy burgundy velvet drapes, huge patterned Persian silk carpet, deep plum-red armchairs and inlaid tables, but then her grandfather, the second Viscount, had liked things showy. He had been a man with more money than taste. Two walls, panelled in ornate, highly polished mahogany shelving, were crammed with never-read, leather-bound books; the others were covered in a soft green patterned Chinese paper, now faded in places and showing signs of damp. Above the impressive carved marble fireplace, bearing the Wadsworth coat of arms, a huge Chippendale-style mirror caught the light from the dusty chandeliers.

Lady Wadsworth drummed her fingers on the papers before her and looked up through small gold-rimmed spectacles at an enormous portrait in oils of her grandfather. He gazed portentously back at her. A rotund man with heavy-lidded eyes and surprisingly spindly legs, he posed awkwardly, one hand on his hip, in a tight-fitting Prussian-blue jacket and white silk waistcoat, stockings and breeches, a scarlet robe draped around his shoulders. At his feet were two lazy-looking liver-and-white German pointers. The lady of the house bore an unnerving resemblance to the man in the portrait. She was a large, rather ungainly woman, too tall and stark to be considered handsome, with coarse hair the colour of brown boot polish, and she had inherited the same heavy-lidded eyes and thin legs. She rang a small brass bell on her desk and a moment later the butler arrived.

'You rang, your ladyship?' he said languidly.

'I did, Watson,' she replied. 'I've been going through the accounts.' The butler rolled his eyes. 'I am afraid that things are not too good, not too good at all.'

There's an understatement if ever I heard one, thought the butler, but he merely nodded.

'There is so much that needs doing,' continued Lady Wadsworth, sighing. 'One doesn't know where to start.'

The butler could have ventured to suggest that she might start with a complete overhaul of his bedroom, that cold, damp, draughty room in the east wing with the peeling wallpaper, threadbare carpet and noisy pipes, but he remained silent.

'Yes,' she sighed again, 'so much to do.' She peered at a sheet of paper. 'What is the state of the lodge?' she asked.

'Derelict, your ladyship,' he replied.

'And the damp?'

'Still rising, your ladyship.'

'The stonework?'

'Still crumbling, your ladyship .'

'The paintwork?'

'Still peeling, your ladyship.'

'And the roof?'

'Still leaking, your ladyship.'

'The windows?'

'Still rotting, your ladyship.'

'Is there anything to feel happy about?' she asked tetchily.

'We had a particularly good crop of mushrooms from the cellar this year, your ladyship,' he replied.

'Really, Watson,' she tut-tutted, before looking back at the papers on her desk. 'This is not a time to be flippant. I have all these bills to pay. This one, for the plaque I commissioned to commemorate the opening of the village school library which I endowed, is outrageously expensive. I never appreciated how much it would cost.'

'Well, it was, as I recall mentioning to you at the time, your ladyship,' remarked the butler, 'a trifle excessive, and a simpler wooden tablet might have sufficed rather than the brass.'

'And I recall saying to you that if a thing is worth doing, it is worth doing properly,' she retorted. 'Excessive indeed! Since I have endowed the library I think it was only right and fitting to have a tasteful brass plaque put up on the wall stating as much. What I want from you, Watson, are not comments and criticisms and frivolous remarks but suggestions on how I might get out of this financial mess that I have found myself in.'

'I am not an accountant, your ladyship,' he replied. 'Perhaps you need to consult a financial adviser.'

'Fiddlesticks!' she exclaimed. 'They take a massive commission for telling one very little.'

'I take it the idea of selling Limebeck House to the big hotel chain is not an option?' he remarked.

'Out of the question!' snapped his mistress.

'Then the only other alternative, your ladyship, is for you to sell something.'

'Yes, I have thought along the same lines. But what?'

'Perhaps the Stubbs painting in the drawing-room?'

'Oh, I couldn't sell the Stubbs,' she told him. 'I've grown up with those horses. It would break my heart to part with it.'

'The Chinese porcelain?'

'No, no. That was my mother's.'

'The Chippendale chairs?'

'And where do you suggest I sit?' she retorted. 'No, I couldn't part with the chairs. Anyway, they are not authentic.'

'Might I suggest, your ladyship, that were you to sell the Stubbs you could commission a copy. I believe there are artists who can produce a reproduction so very like the original that only an expert could tell the difference.'

Lady Wadsworth looked up at the portrait. 'If only you could advise me, Grandpapa,' she said. The second Viscount Wadsworth gazed down self-importantly.

'Is there anything the matter, Charles?' asked the vicar's wife.

Her husband, the Reverend Atticus, surveyed his dinner: a circle of cold, insipid-looking pork edged in fat and surrounded by several undercooked bullet-like potatoes, a lump of pale watery cabbage, a mound of hard peas and a ball of crusted stuffing. It looked deeply unappetising, but he said nothing.

'No, no, my dear, I was just thinking,' he replied, giving a watery smile. He speared a potato and ate it slowly. It was, as he could have guessed, hard and tasteless.

'About what?' she enquired. A forkful of fatty meat hovered before her mouth.

'I beg your pardon, my dear?'

'You were thinking about what?' she asked.

The vicar placed his knife and fork down carefully and stroked his high forehead with pale, slender fingers.

'Whether or not this is the most opportune time for me to broach a matter which has given me not a little unease over the festive season,' he told her.

'This sounds ominous,' said his wife. She placed her own knife and fork down upon the table and folded her hands in front of her. 'Do tell.'

The vicar had thought long and hard about what he would say to his wife and he had put it off. Before Christmas the bishop had telephoned to enquire if he might be interested in the position of Archdeacon of Clayton. The Reverend Atticus had been offered preferment in the past, when the dean's position had arisen, but, without discussing the matter with his wife, he had declined. A gentle-natured, contemplative and easy-going man, he was quite content as a country parson and neither desired nor sought promotion, despite his wife's persistent pestering of him to be more assertive and ambitious. Her constant complaints about life in the village and her frequent reminders of how her sainted father, a former bishop, had risen up the ranks of the Church of England had become wearisome. So when the senior post of archdeacon had been offered the Reverend Atticus had immediately accepted, thinking his wife would be delighted that at long last he had been promoted and they could move to the city and live in the shadow of the great cathedral. However, a fly had appeared in the ointment. Soon after agreeing to the bishop's offer and before he had told Mrs Atticus, he learned that his wife had been accepted to train as a teacher and would be based at the village school, a few hundred yards away from the rectory. He had never seen her quite so happy and, perhaps more importantly, occupied. She now seemed very content to stay where she was and would not take too kindly to having to uproot.

'Well, my dear,' said the vicar, looking up into his wife's eyes, 'for some time now you have been pestering me—'

'Pestering!' snapped Mrs Atticus. 'Really, Charles, I never pester.'

'Well, perhaps that is a little too strong a word to use,' said the vicar. 'Let me rephrase it. You have been at great pains to point out to me on many occasions how I have been, as you term it, "passed over" for preferment within the Church, that I have remained a mere country parson while others have climbed the ecclesiastical ladder leaving me, as it were, on the bottom rung.'

'Really Charles, you do tend to go around the houses,' said his wife. 'What exactly are you trying to say?'

'Many has been the time, Marcia,' continued the vicar, 'when you have reminded me of the fact that I have not been promoted, although deserving of it, and that your late and revered father, the former Bishop of Clayton, was an arch-deacon by the time he reached thirty-five and a bishop when he was forty-six.'

'Well, that is true,' agreed the vicar's wife. 'Furthermore—'

The vicar held up his hand. 'My dear, if I may be allowed to continue. I have given what I am about to tell you some considerable thought. If I might proceed . . .'

His wife raised an eyebrow and the corners of her mouth twitched. She was about to say something sharp by way of reply but held her tongue.

The vicar pressed on with barely a pause between words. 'As I have said, you have frequently mentioned to me how you hoped I might get preferment within the Church and become a dean or an archdeacon, and maybe a bishop like your esteemed father, how you were unhappy as a country parson's wife, that you have no privacy and people tend to put upon your good nature. You have told me many times how you constantly get stopped by my parishioners asking about church functions and services, and that you are always the vicar's wife and not a person in your own right.'

'Well, that is very true,' began his wife.

'Furthermore,' continued the Reverend Atticus, 'you have told me how you hoped that one day we might live in the cathedral precinct and be at the centre of the city, meet differ-ent and interesting people and have something of a life.'

'I'm sorry, Charles!' snapped his wife, at last managing to get in a word, 'but this is becoming wearisome. It sounds like one of your sermons. Will you stop beating about the bush and tell me exactly what is on your mind? You have been—'

'Please, Marcia,' interrupted the vicar, 'do allow me to finish.'

Mrs Atticus gave a great heaving sigh, pursed her lips and shook her head. The vicar could sense her irritation but was determined to complete what he wished to say.

'As I have said, I know how unhappy you have been in Barton-in-the-Dale.' He took a deep breath. 'So, when I was offered the position of Archdeacon of Clayton—'

His wife gasped. 'Offered the post of archdeacon!' she exclaimed.

'So when I was offered the post of archdeacon by the bishop before Christmas,' her husband continued, 'I naturally assumed you would be delighted.'

'But that was before I started to train as a teacher and—'

'And so I accepted,' the vicar told her bluntly.

'You did what?' gasped his wife.

'I accepted the position,' said the vicar. 'I told the bishop I should be honoured to accept.'

'Without discussing it with me?'

'I assumed you would be very pleased.'

'Well, I am not pleased, Charles. In fact, I am very displeased. It will mean moving to Clayton and I do not wish to move to Clayton. It is true that I did want you to be promoted and I did consider it was very short-sighted of the Church to pass you over for the dean's position in favour of that sanctimonious little Dr Peacock with the wire-rimmed spectacles and the strident voice, but that was before I started going in to help out with the art in the school. I felt liberated, valued and more fulfilled, a person in my own right and not just the wife of the vicar. Then when I gained a place at St John's College to train as a teacher and could do my teaching practice here at the village school—'

'I know that, Marcia,' said her husband quietly. He briefly closed his eyes.

'I love teaching and I think I'm very good at it,' she told him.

'Of course you are, my dear,' sighed the vicar.

'I also realised,' she continued, 'that being a country parson is your vocation and it is something at which you are very good. You're a people person, Charles. You would be like a fish out of water as archdeacon, dealing with all the tiresome administration and with disputes about one thing and another.'

'One of the required qualities of an archdeacon, my dear, is that he needs to be a people person,' said the vicar, 'and I do feel—'

'I remember how the pressures and tensions of being the archdeacon took their toll on my poor father,' continued his wife, not listening. 'He had to implement all these unpalatable diocesan policies, sort out the buildings, inspect the churches and deal with all the problems the bishop pushed his way. It was most stressful for him.'

This was the first occasion his wife had raised the matter of her father's pressures and tensions. She had always held him up as the very model of a senior cleric. 'Well, I am not so sure I couldn't make a success of it,' her husband told her. 'The role does involve the welfare of the clergy and as *oculus episcope*—'

'As what?'

'Being the bishop's eye,' explained the vicar, 'I feel I could be very useful.'

'I see,' said his wife coldly, her lips pressed together.

'So having given the matter some considerable thought,' continued her husband, 'I feel I could rise to the challenge and be influential as archdeacon and, without sounding arrogant, bring something positive to the position. The more I have thought about it the more it has appealed to me.'

'Well, you seem to have made up your mind,' said Mrs Atticus, 'so there is really little more to discuss.'

'Nothing precludes you from training at the college in Clayton and doing your teaching practice in a school near there,' said the vicar patiently.

His wife shook her head. 'That is not a possibility. As you are well aware, I have just started at the village school on the graduate training programme. I am happy there, I get on well with the teachers and head teacher, the children know me and the school is a stone's throw from the rectory. I really do not wish to train at some new school with colleagues I have never met.'

'Well, perhaps you could stay at Barton-in-the-Dale school?' suggested the vicar.

'What, and travel out here from Clayton every day? You know how unpredictable the buses are, and what about in winter when the roads are virtually impassable?'

'But next winter, my dear,' said the Reverend Atticus, 'your teaching practice will presumably be over.'

'Yes, I am aware of that,' replied his wife, 'but I have every hope that I will be offered a post at the village school when I qualify. Anyway, while I am on teaching practice there I would have all the books and materials and equipment to carry. It is out of the question.'

'Perhaps you could learn to drive?' suggested her husband, 'and we could get a small car.'

'Oh, Charles, this is just too much to take in.' Her voice quavered with emotion and tears welled in her eyes. 'Too much,' she repeated. 'If you will excuse me, I shall have to have a lie-down. I can feel a migraine coming on.'

'Marcia,' said the vicar, rising from the table. 'I little appreciated how much working at the school meant to you.'

'Well, it does, Charles,' she replied, her eyes blurred with tears. 'It means a great deal to me.'

'Then I shall speak to the bishop,' her husband told her.

'And?' asked his wife, dabbing away her tears.

'And tell him I have changed my mind,' he replied, giving her a small resigned smile.

Mrs Sloughthwaite, the fount of all village information and gossip, folded her dimpled arms under her substantial bosom.

'It's not often we see you in here, vicar,' she said, watching the Reverend Atticus as he ran a long finger along the canned goods on the shelf.

'No, Mrs Sloughthwaite,' he replied, 'and I have to say it's not often I see you in St Christopher's. I was delighted to see you there yesterday.'

'I don't like to miss a wedding, vicar,' she told him. Mrs Sloughthwaite didn't like to miss anything that occurred in Barton-in-the-Dale. She had closed the village store especially to attend.

'Well, maybe I will see more of you in future.'

'Maybe,' she said. 'That must be the last of Joyce Fish's granddaughters to get wed then?'

'I believe so. She's a pleasant young woman, is Tracey.'

'She was a bit of a handful at school, by all accounts, and I reckon her new husband will have his hands full as well.' Then she added under her breath, 'In more ways than one.'

The vicar gave a weak smile and turned his attention back to the tinned goods on the shelf.

'I thought she looked a picture,' remarked the shopkeeper, 'though I did think for somebody with her build she'd have been better off not wearing such a tight-fitting gown. Mind you, all the Fish family are big-boned. I was told that they had to have a special coffin made for her great-grandmother when she passed on. Took eight men to carry her.'

The vicar looked at the formidable bulk of the shopkeeper but said nothing.

'She must have been frozen to death, the bride, in that

low-cut dress, and as I said to Mrs Lloyd, the bridesmaids were blue with cold, shivering down the aisle.'

'It was indeed a rather bitter day,' said the vicar, examining a tin of stewed steak.

'I've never seen such multicoloured outfits in all my life,' the shopkeeper rattled on. 'Every colour under the rainbow but not a hat in sight. They were all wearing those fornicators, or whatever they're called.'

'I believe they are called fascinators,' corrected the vicar amiably.

'Well, they don't fascinate me – a couple of coloured feathers glued to an Alice band. I wouldn't give them house room.'

The vicar selected a tin of beans with pork sausages and an individual fruit pie from the shelf and placed them on the counter.

'I should have thought you've have been sitting down to roast beef and Yorkshire pudding this Sunday lunchtime, Reverend,' she observed, placing the items in a plastic bag.

Chance would be a fine thing, thought the vicar. 'No, I have been left to my own devices today.' Marcia had informed him that morning that she had far too much preparation and lesson planning to do for the coming week and that she hadn't the time to make him any lunch. The vicar was not unduly perturbed. Beans on toast would be a welcome change from the usual unappetising fare his wife served up.

'And how is she liking it at the village school?' asked the shopkeeper.

'I beg your pardon?'

'Mrs Atticus. How is she getting on at the village school?'

'Oh, very well indeed,' replied the vicar. 'She has taken to teaching like a duck to water.'

'I hear from Mrs Pocock that she's a dab hand with a paintbrush.'

'Indeed,' said the vicar. 'How much do I owe you for the—'

'She was telling me that her Ernest had come on by leaps and bounds in Mrs Atticus's art class. Very artificated, she said he is.'

'Yes, I believe so.'

'She's not a proper teacher, is she?'

'Pardon?'

'Your wife, she's not fully matriculated?'

'No, she's training at the school,' the vicar told her. 'She has been very fortunate to have a placement there. It's a new scheme called graduate training.'

'On the job.'

'I beg your pardon?'

'She's learning how to do it on the job.'

'Quite.'

'Well, I take my hat off to teachers having to cope with some of the youngsters these days. They don't know what discipline is, some of them. And as for morals. You've no doubt heard about that Bianca?'

The vicar hadn't heard about Bianca but decided not to give the shopkeeper the prompt to relate one of her long accounts, so he just smiled.

Mrs Sloughthwaite shook her head. 'They leave a lot to be desired, young people these days. He can be a difficult lad, can Ernest Pocock. I hope your wife doesn't have trouble with him.' Mrs Sloughthwaite left the door open for the vicar to comment. She was adept at that.

The Reverend Atticus smiled again but remained silent, knowing that any comments he might make would be relayed around the village in quick time. His cheeks were beginning to ache with the set expression.

The shopkeeper was not one to give up. 'So the lad's no trouble?' she asked.

'No,' replied the vicar, 'the young man seems biddable enough.' He could have revealed that his wife found the sullen-faced boy a bit of a handful at times but she recognised he had a talent and, from what she had been told, he was certainly better behaved than he had been in the past, when he spent a deal of his time standing outside Miss Sowerbutts's room. 'How much do I owe you for the beans and the pie?' he asked, desirous of escaping from the grilling.

'The beans are on special offer,' he was told. 'Three tins for the price of two.'

'I'll just have the one tin, thank you,' said the vicar. 'One can have a surfeit of beans.'

The door opened and a woman with a hard, stern expression on her face entered. She was wearing a shapeless grey knitted hat, matching scarf and gloves and a heavy black coat. A battered canvas shopping bag hung loosely over her arm.

The vicar sighed inwardly. There was little chance now of him getting away to his beans on toast.

'Good morning, Miss Sowerbutts,' he said brightly.

'Good morning, Reverend,' she replied.

'It's a lovely bright day, isn't it?'

'If you like the cold,' she replied.

'I trust you had a pleasant Christmas?' he enquired.

'Not really, but I don't wish to go into that.'

'I see that your cottage is up for sale,' remarked the cleric.

'Yes, it is,' she told him. 'I shall be moving before Easter. There is nothing for me in the village these days and I find the many changes not to my liking, added to the fact that I find my garden far too big for me to manage.'

The vicar was tempted to tell her that she would be missed but resisted the temptation, for he knew it would have been disingenuous of him to do so. 'Well, I hope you will be very happy,' he said. 'And are you to stay in the area?'

'I have bought a luxury apartment in Clayton, one of a select development – De Courcey Apartments – overlooking the river and the cathedral. It has everything I require.'

Mrs Sloughthwaite, in common with most others in the village, disliked the former head teacher of the village school with her brusque manner, preening self-satisfaction and permanent scowl. The woman never had a good word for anybody and felt she should give everyone the full benefit of her opinions. She rarely called into the shop, and when she did she complained about the produce and bought few items. She was one person the shopkeeper would not miss if the woman took her custom elsewhere. Mrs Sloughthwaite, who had been ignored, drew herself up and folded her arms across her bosom. 'Good morning, Miss Sowerbutts,' she said loudly.

Miss Sowerbutts swivelled around. 'Oh, good morning,' she replied curtly, before turning her attention back to the vicar. 'Anyway, Reverend,' she said, 'I am glad I have met you. It will save me calling at the rectory. There is something I would like you to do for me.'

'Of course,' said the vicar unenthusiastically. He managed a small smile.

'Now, my cat has gone missing, Reverend.'

'Oh dear,' said the vicar in his most sympathetic of voices, which he had perfected over the years when responding to a distressed parishioner.

'Yes. Tabitha is a very superior breed: a Lilac Point Siamese. She has a special diet of fish and chicken. I disposed of an empty salmon tin but she must have found it in the waste bin and pushed her head into it and the silly cat got her head stuck.'

'Oh dear,' repeated the cleric.

'I tried to extricate her but she ran off.'

'With a salmon tin stuck on her head?' said Mrs Sloughthwaite, making no attempt to suppress a smile.

'Yes,' said Miss Sowerbutts crossly.

'And what colour is your cat?' asked the vicar.

'Reverend Atticus, the colour of my cat is of no consequence.

I am sure if anyone sees a cat running around the village with its head in a salmon tin they will know it is mine.'

'It might have come off by now,' ventured the shopkeeper.

'Yes, well, it may have, though she had her head firmly wedged and I fear for her. She is cream in colour with a black face, glossy coat and large pricked ears, and she is very sensitive.'

'So, how may I be of help?' asked the vicar, hoping she would not suggest that he join a hunt for the animal.

Miss Sowerbutts plucked a card from her bag. 'I should like you to place this notice in a prominent position in the church porch. You might also put a piece in the parish magazine. Someone may have seen her.' Then, turning to the shopkeeper, she placed a similar card on the counter. 'And I should be obliged if you would do the same and display this in the shop window.'

The shopkeeper left the card on the counter and stared at it for a moment. 'And I should be obliged if you would occasionally buy something from the village store rather than doing your shopping elsewhere,' she said.

The woman bristled. 'Where I do my shopping is my concern,' she replied sharply.

'And what I put in my shop window is mine,' retorted the shopkeeper.

Miss Sowerbutts snatched up the card and thrust it back in her bag. 'Very well. You can be assured that I shall never patronise this shop again,' she said.

'Well, I can't say that I shall lose any sleep over that,' the shopkeeper told her, 'and I should imagine you'll find there are plenty of other places to patronise.'

Miss Sowerbutts stiffened and fixed Mrs Sloughthwaite with a piercing stare. 'And what do you mean by that?'

'What I mean—' Mrs Sloughthwaite began.

'I am sorry to hear about your cat, Miss Sowerbutts,'

interrupted the vicar, attempting to defuse the situation. 'I should be happy to display the card for you. I'm sure the animal will turn up.'

'Well, I hope so.' Then with an icy stare at the shop-keeper she departed, banging the door and clanking the bell behind her.

'Not a happy woman,' sighed the vicar.

'I wish she'd get a salmon tin stuck on her head,' said Mrs Sloughthwaite, 'and leave it there.'

7

Mr Preston sat behind the large mahogany desk in his office contemplating what he would say to the visitors, the first of whom he was keeping waiting outside. He was a shrewd man, the Director of Education, clever with words and with that plausible, friendly persona able to win people over to his way of thinking. He would need all his skills, he imagined, to deal with the two head teachers he was about to see. He gazed out of the window, which gave an uninterrupted view over the busy and bustling high street, and considered how best to approach what could prove to be a tricky and troublesome business. His one consolation, he thought, would be that by the time the village schools had been reorganised into the consortiums, which had been agreed at the last meeting of the Education Committee, he would be well out of it. He had been appointed as chief executive for a city in the Midlands and would be moving to his new post at the end of term, leaving it to his successor to pick up the pieces.

He stood, adjusted his expensive silk tie, buttoned his expensive dark blue suit, stroked his hair and walked to the door, which he opened widely and with a flourish. He put on his professional smile and gestured for his first visitor to enter.

'Do come in, Mrs Devine,' he said. He pressed Elisabeth's hand warmly. 'I am delighted to meet you again and I do appreciate your coming in to County Hall to see me.' He touched the back of a small leather chair with the tips of his fingers. 'Do please take a seat.' He was perfectly courteous but his voice was slightly flat. 'May I offer you a cup of tea?'

'No, thank you, Mr Preston,' Elisabeth replied, returning his smile. As he went to sit down, she looked around the room. It was plush, with its large mahogany desk, great glass-fronted bookcase full of leather-bound tomes lining one wall, and framed pictures and prints drawn and painted by the county's children and students displayed on the other. Opposite the bookcase a huge window looked out over the main street.

'I gather congratulations are in order,' she said.

'Ah, you mean my move to the Midlands,' he replied. 'Yes, I am looking forward to the challenge. I gather there is much to do. I shall, of course, be sorry to leave the county.'

'I see you have a piece of my pupil's work on your wall,' Elisabeth told him.

The Director of Education glanced around, the better to see the paintings. 'Really? These were the winners in the County Art Competition,' he told her.

'Yes, I guessed as much,' she said. 'Ernest came second. His is the watercolour with the stone barn and the millpond.'

'It's very good,' said Mr Preston, giving another disarming smile. He rested his elbows on the desktop and steepled his fingers. 'And how are things going at Barton-in-the-Dale?'

'I think they are going very well,' replied Elisabeth. 'Ms Tricklebank will no doubt have told you about her visit. I hope she was satisfied with what she saw?'

'Ms Tricklebank was most interested,' said the Director of Education, clearly not wishing to give anything away.

'She didn't say a great deal,' Elisabeth told him.

'She is admittedly a woman of few words, but she is extremely capable and has a great deal of experience.'

He was a very clever and persuasive individual was Mr Preston, thought Elisabeth, confident, good-humoured and very adept at charming an audience, but she didn't quite trust the man.

'I guess you know why I have asked for this meeting?' said Mr Preston.

'I think so,' replied Elisabeth. 'I should imagine it's about the reorganisation of the schools in the county and in particular Barton-in-the-Dale.'

'Mrs Devine,' said the Director of Education, leaning forward, uncoupling his hands and folding them over before resting them on the desktop, 'you will of course be aware of the situation regarding the education budget and how we have to make stringent savings. I think Ms Tricklebank outlined to you and your governors what has been suggested and the difficult decisions we have to make.' He paused.

Elisabeth decided not to respond for the present and wait to hear what he had to say.

'The thing is, Mrs Devine,' he continued, 'pupil numbers are declining and we have to look to the best ways of using the limited resources that we have. As you know, I am not in favour of closing schools and—'

'I am sorry to interrupt, Mr Preston,' said Elisabeth, sitting up straight in the chair, 'but could I remind you that you did give me an assurance when you visited the school last term that Barton-in-the-Dale would not be closing. Indeed Ms Tricklebank at the governors' meeting did say that—'

The Director of Education held up his hand and smiled. 'Indeed, and I can assure you again that this will not happen, certainly not in the foreseeable future anyway.'

Elisabeth relaxed. 'That's good to hear,' she said.

'As I said, I am not in favour of closing village schools, but what it does mean is that in certain parts of the county where pupil numbers are in decline we have to consolidate. In other words, some of the smaller schools will have to merge into consortiums.'

'Yes, I appreciate that, and I realise that Barton-in-the-Dale is one such school,' said Elisabeth.

'Yes, it is.'

'And I assume it will merge with its nearest primary school.'

'Indeed.'

'Which is Urebank.'

'Yes.'

Elisabeth sighed. 'I see. You will be aware that the head teacher at Urebank and I do not see eye to eye?'

'I *am* aware of that, yes. Mr Richardson did request a meeting with me last term when pupils from Urebank were leaving to go to Barton-in-the-Dale.'

'Yes, he mentioned that he would be contacting the Education Office.'

'I explained to him that parents have a perfect right to send their children to whichever school they wish, providing, of course, there is room for them. He was not happy about the situation.'

'Then you will appreciate that working with Mr Richardson could be very difficult for the both of us?'

'I do, Mrs Devine, and I can see a possible solution to this predicament. Now, you might recall that when I came out to see you after the matter of the school closure had been settled, I mentioned that the post of head teacher was coming up in a large purpose-built school in the north of the county. It comes with an excellent salary. I would like you to consider applying. Obviously I cannot promise you the post but I feel you would be a strong candidate.'

'And I told you, Mr Preston, that I wasn't interested,' replied Elisabeth. 'Perhaps I should explain why. I have a son, John, who has severe autism and is at Forest View Special School, where he is very happy. It is an excellent school and very near to where I live, which is very convenient. I wish him to remain there. The reason for my moving to Barton-in-the-Dale was so I could be nearer to him and visit him regularly. That is why I don't wish to move.'

'I wasn't aware of that,' said the Director of Education. He drummed his fingers on the desktop, thought for a moment and looked out of the window. 'Well, in that case you will appreciate the situation this puts you in with regard to the headship of the newly amalgamated schools?'

'Not entirely.'

'In the first instance the position of head teacher will be open to yourself and Mr Richardson at Urebank to apply for. Like you he is an experienced and well-respected head teacher, and he has worked in the county for his entire teaching career. It could be that he is offered the post and you the deputy head teacher's position. Of course, it could be the other way around.'

'I see. So we will be in competition for the head teacher's post?'

'Indeed,' replied Mr Preston, 'and, following interviews, it will be for the governors to decide whom to appoint. The unsuccessful candidate, as I said, will be offered the position of deputy head teacher in the consortium or, if he or she so wishes, be redeployed to another school in the county.'

'I see,' said Elisabeth.

'Of course if neither of you are deemed to be suitable by the governors then the post will be advertised nationally. To be frank, I can't see that happening, but one never knows. Some interviews can be something of a lottery.' He smiled and steepled his fingers again. 'I just wanted to see you and clarify matters and to assure you that I have your interests and those of your staff very much at heart.'

'Thank you, Mr Preston,' she said, 'I appreciate you explaining things.'

'I think we will leave it there for the time being, Mrs Devine,' he said standing and extending a hand. 'Thank you for coming in to see me. I shall be in touch.'

Elisabeth walked slowly down the long, echoey corridor, her high heels clacking on the polished tiled floor. The interior of County Hall was like a museum, hushed and cool, with high ornate ceilings, marble figures and walls full of gilt-framed portraits of former councillors, mayors, aldermen, leaders of the Council, high sheriffs, lord lieutenants, members of parliament and other dignitaries. It was a dark and daunting place, devoid of colour. The meeting had depressed her and she needed to think what she would do now. There was no way she could work with that patronising man at Urebank. She would be glad to get back to school. This very building depressed her. As she made her way down the wide curving staircase the man who was uppermost in her mind was making his way up. Mr Richardson saw her, looked away and continued up the steps without a word.

Mr Preston's meeting with the headmaster of Urebank School did not go quite as smoothly.

'The intention, Mr Richardson, as you are aware,' the Director of Education told him, 'is to merge some of the small village schools within the county.'

'It seems a very sensible idea, if I may say so, Mr Preston,' said Mr Richardson, giving an unctuous smile. 'It means that the village schools which are so much a part of the communities will not close.'

'Some sadly may have to close,' the Director of Education told him, 'but Urebank is, at the moment, quite safe. Of course one cannot predict what might happen in the long term. Ms Tricklebank and I have been looking at the various options—'

'Yes, I had the pleasure of meeting Ms Tricklebank recently when she visited my school.'

'Indeed.'

'I hope she enjoyed her visit and found everything satisfactory?'

'Yes, she was most interested in what she saw,' said Mr Preston. 'Now, it is our intention that Urebank will merge with

Barton-in-the-Dale. Our proposal is that we will have two sites, the infants housed at one school and the juniors at the other. Of course we will hold consultation meetings with the interested parties but it is very likely that from next September the schools will be amalgamated.'

'And there would be the one head teacher?' asked Mr Richardson.

'Yes, based at one of the sites, and the deputy head teacher at the other. Generous packages will be offered to those members of staff at both schools if they wish to take early retirement, and others will be offered posts in the new set-up or redeployed. I hope we will avoid the necessity of having to make some teachers redundant.'

'So, as I understand it,' said Mr Richardson, 'should I be appointed the head teacher of the amalgamated schools, Mrs Devine would be offered the position of my deputy?'

'If you were appointed, yes,' said the Director of Education.

'And we would not be working together in the same building?'

'No.'

'Well, that doesn't sound quite as bad as I thought,' he conceded. 'As you know, Mrs Devine and I do not get on. I did write to you, if you remember, about what I considered to be her unprofessional conduct. I have to say—'

'I do recall,' said the Director of Education, cutting him short.

'I have to say that I would find it quite impossible,' continued Mr Richardson, 'to work with her in the same building on a day-to-day basis, but if she were based on another site I guess it would not be too bad. The juniors could be based at Urebank and the infants at Barton.'

'Possibly,' said Mr Preston, 'but we were thinking the other way round.'

'I should prefer to stay with the juniors at Urebank,' said Mr Richardson.

'Looking at the demographic of the two villages,' Mr Preston told him, ignoring his remark, 'there are more new houses and apartments in Urebank, and more families with young children than there are in Barton, which tends to have more of an ageing population. Should we base the infants at Urebank then the very youngest children would not have to travel quite such a distance to school.'

'Well, loath as I am to leave my present school,' said Mr Richardson, 'I suppose I could move to Barton and Mrs Devine could take charge of the infants in Urebank. I do feel the head teacher should be with the older pupils. They tend to be more difficult to handle and some need a firm hand.'

'One moment, Mr Richardson,' said the Director of Education, the perfected smile appearing on his face. 'The position of head teacher has yet to be decided.'

'No, no, of course not,' Mr Richardson said quickly. 'I mean yes, I see that.'

'It will be decided by the newly convened governing body,' he was told.

'Yes, of course, but I assumed, having spoken to Councillor Smout, that I am the front-runner. Having been in the county longer than Mrs Devine and at a larger school I thought that naturally I would be—'

'The procedure will be to interview you both for the position of head teacher in the first instance,' Mr Preston told him, 'and if neither is successful then it will go to national advert.'

The headmaster of Urebank was too disappointed to speak.

'So you see, my lord, I consider that under the circumstances it is with great regret that I feel I have to decline your most generous offer for me to become the Archdeacon of Clayton.'

The Reverend Atticus, his eyebrows knitted together in

concern, was sitting opposite the bishop in the office at the Bishop's Palace.

'No, no, no, Charles,' said his lordship, waving a finger back and forth. 'I won't hear of it.' The bishop, a round, jolly-looking individual with abundant grey crinkly hair and kindly eyes, shook his head. 'You will be excellent in the position, and what is more, I need you. There is no one more suitable. You will be the oil to help things run smoothly, the very glue to hold together the churches in the diocese. Your advice and wisdom on a host of matters spiritual, legal and practical will be invaluable. The Dean and the canons, indeed all the clergy to whom I have spoken, are unanimous in endorsing my decision.'

'But my lord, were I to accept the position it would mean moving. I appreciate that I could not stay in my present parish. An archdeacon, on his appointment, is obliged to leave the church where he is the vicar. Is that not the case?'

The Reverend Atticus peered at the bishop with the searching, worried eyes of a rabbit caught in the headlights' glare. 'As I explained, my lord, Marcia has secured a place to train at the village school. She will, I am certain, make a very good teacher and there has been such a positive change in her since she started there. She's more content, more settled. Were we to move to the cathedral precinct here in Clayton it would mean she would have to travel back and forth to Barton. She doesn't drive and would have to rely on public transport, which is notoriously unpredictable, and she would have to carry all manner of equipment and books. I am, of course deeply honoured, my lord, to have been offered—'

The bishop held up his palm to silence him. 'Charles,' he interrupted. 'Listen to me for a moment.'

The vicar took a little breath as if he was about to speak, but he didn't say anything and then looked down at his hands.

'God moves in a mysterious way, his wonders to perform,' said the bishop.

'I beg your pardon, my lord?' said the vicar, looking up.

'God has found a solution to our predicament.'

'He has?'

'Indeed He has.'

'In what way, my lord?'

'You are quite correct when you say that it is generally the case that a priest appointed as archdeacon will have to move from his or her present parish, but it is not chiselled in tablets of stone. As the bishop, I do have some leeway. Now the present archdeacon, the Venerable Dr Bentley, as you are no doubt aware, is not a well man and is getting on in years and ready to retire. He has become increasingly anxious of late about moving from the archdeaconry premises here at Cathedral House. He has lived here for many years and has amassed a most extensive library. I did feel it would be unchristian of me at the moment to request that he vacate his present residence for you and your wife to move in. We have looked around for another suitable location near the cathedral for you both but without success.'

'May I ask how this solves the predicament, my lord?'

'Don't you see, Charles?' said the Bishop, 'You can remain at the rectory in Barton for the time being, continue as the rector there and drive to Clayton each day. Your wife could then continue at the village school and I shall arrange for you to have an assistant priest to help out with the duties at Barton. I should not expect you to take on the many responsibilities and duties of the archdeacon and still remain as active in the village church. A curate can take the load off your shoulders. Now how does that sound?'

'It sounds very generous of you, my lord,' said the Reverend Atticus.

'Then it is settled. And as to the curate, I have the person in mind, an Oxford scholar and very personable. I shall arrange for the Reverend Dr Ashley Underwood to call out and see you after you have talked it over with your wife, and I shall expect you at your desk here Monday next.' The bishop stood, leaned over his desk and shook the vicar's hand warmly. 'Good day to you, Archdeacon,' he said.

Marcia Atticus was staring out of the window in the drawing-room when the new archdeacon arrived back at the rectory.

'Good afternoon, my dear,' he said cheerily, rubbing his hands.

'You sound in a good mood, Charles,' she remarked coolly.

'I am, my dear Marcia, I am.' He went over to a tray on a side table and poured two large glasses of sherry.

'Charles!' his wife said sharply. 'It's a little early for drinks, isn't it?'

A glass was thrust into her hand.

'I think a small celebratory libation is in order,' he said, his countenance wreathed in a great smile.

'So I take it the meeting with the bishop went well?' she asked.

'Very well,' he replied. 'Very well indeed.'

'And how did he react when you told him you no longer wished to be archdeacon?'

'He refused to accept it.'

His wife placed the sherry glass down on a small table so heavily that half of it spilt. 'He refused to accept it?' she repeated. 'And what did you say?'

'I said I would bow to his decision and become the new archdeacon if that was his desire.'

'You said what?'

'I said I would become the new Archdeacon of Clayton.'

'After what you had said to me?'

'Indeed.' He smirked.

'Oh, Charles,' she sighed. 'You promised.'

The vicar placed his arm around his wife's shoulder. 'My

dear, I said I would become the new archdeacon when the bishop agreed that I could stay here at the rectory in Barton, travel into Clayton each day and that he would secure for me an assistant priest to help out with the work here in the parish. It appears he already has a man in mind, a Reverend Dr Ashley Underwood, who, I believe, is very highly qualified and most capable. This means, of course, that we will not be moving and that you will be able to continue your training at the village school. As one of the younger members of our congregation might ask, how does that grab you?'

Mrs Atticus thought for a moment to take in what she had been told. Then a flash of pure pleasure lit up her face and her green eyes sparkled. She reached for the glass and held it up. 'Your very good health, Archdeacon Atticus,' she said.

The great black door to Limebeck House, flanked by elegant but eroded pale stone pillars, was opened by the butler. The visitor, a lean, pallid man with a Roman-nosed face and short, carefully combed silver hair, walked into a spacious entrance hall painted in pale yellow and blue. He gazed up at the jungle of decorative plasterwork on the ceiling, the intricate twisting designs standing out from the darker background, and noted that it was in need of urgent renovation. The retainer pushed shut the heavy door and rearranged the draught-excluder in front of it.

'May I have your name, sir?' asked the butler, straightening up. He spoke in a hushed voice and his face was entirely expressionless.

'Crispin De'Ath,' replied the visitor. He continued to stare up at the lofty-ceilinged hall with the flaking plasterwork, gloomily lit by tarnished gilt chandeliers.

'Her ladyship is expecting you, sir,' said the butler. 'If you would care to come this way.'

The visitor followed the slow, measured steps of the butler

down a long corridor, passing a succession of vast, high-ceilinged rooms with dark portraits on the walls and porcelain arranged on the dusty antique furniture. Their unhurried progress ended at two mock-marble columns. The retainer opened the door and the visitor was ushered through it.

'If you would care to wait here in the library for a moment, sir,' said the butler. 'I shall inform her ladyship that you have arrived.'

Mr De'Ath, senior partner and art historian in the firm of Dawkins, Deakin & De'Ath, Auctioneers and Fine Art Valuers, glanced around the room appraising all he saw. Far too flamboyant and cluttered for a library, he thought, but then he questioned whether the dusty, leather-bound tomes displayed in the bookcases were ever taken out. He stroked the small gilt desk with gold tasselled drawers. A nice piece, he thought, but of no real value. The patterned Persian silk carpet was interesting but not in the best condition, and the two inlaid tables by the window would need a deal of restorative work. The huge Chippendale-style mirror over the fireplace, however, might fetch a reasonable price at auction.

Presently Lady Wadsworth made her grand entrance. She had dressed for the meeting in her brightest tweeds and heaviest brogues and had decorated herself with a variety of expensive-looking jewellery. With her wave of bright russet-coloured hair and her lipstick as thick and red as congealed blood, she looked wonderfully impressive and every bit the lady of the manor.

'Lady Wadsworth,' said Mr De'Ath, bowing low.

'Thank you for coming, Mr De'Ath,' she replied, extending a hand, which her visitor shook.

'It is a great pleasure,' he said.

'Do take a seat,' she told him, gesturing to a plum-red armchair.

'What a remarkable house this is,' he said, sitting and

crossing one leg over the other. She noticed his handmade shoes, gleaming with polish, and the red socks. He rested his folded hands on his lap.

'I like it,' she replied, 'though it is a cold draughty place at the best of times.'

The butler arrived with a silver tray on which had been arranged a fluted china teapot, two delicate china cups and saucers, a milk jug, sugar bowl, tongs and spoons. Mr De'Ath noticed that the cups were chipped around the edges and the jug had a hairline crack. 'Rockingham,' he said.

'I beg your pardon?'

'Rockingham china,' he told her, tapping a cup.

'Yes,' replied Lady Wadsworth. 'Sadly the last of the tea service, I'm afraid.'

The butler poured the insipid-looking liquid, bowed and departed.

'So,' said Mr De'Ath, reaching for a cup, 'you have a Stubbs?'

'Indeed,' replied Lady Wadsworth. 'I believe it was purchased by Sir William Wadsworth, my great-great-grand-father, around the 1760s. It's been in the family for many years and, of course, I am very loath to part with it.'

'I quite understand,' said Mr De'Ath, in the sympathetic tone of voice he had perfected over the years when arranging the auction of a treasured heirloom. 'It is distressing for one to part with something which has been in one's family for so long, but sometimes it does become necessary.'

'I believe,' continued Lady Wadsworth, plopping two sugar lumps into her tea, 'that in his day George Stubbs was considered a mere horse painter and overlooked as a serious artist, but Sir William must have had an eye for quality. He owned horses himself, of course, and had a winner in the St Leger. I suppose he paid just a hundred or so guineas for the picture. It's a very beautiful portrait called *Mares and Foals in a Landscape*.'

'Indeed, Lady Wadsworth, you are quite correct,' agreed Mr De'Ath, placing his cup down carefully on the table. 'George Stubbs, like many famous painters, was not considered of any great consequence in his own lifetime, but as they say, time stops all prejudice. Now he is regarded by many as the greatest equine painter of all time, quite unsurpassed.' He suddenly uncrossed his legs and leaned forward, becoming quite animated. His eyes shone. 'No one can paint horses so flawlessly,' he said. 'The perfectly executed sinews and veins, the intense observation, the realistic detail, the symmetry and arrangements of his subjects. I am so looking forward to seeing your picture.'

'That is very good to hear, Mr De'Ath,' said Lady Wadsworth, 'because I guess it will fetch a good price.'

'Oh yes, indeed,' nodded the visitor. 'A very considerable sum. I have an American client who will be most interested indeed.'

'I should not like it to go to America, Mr De'Ath,' said Lady Wadsworth sharply. 'The picture is quintessentially English and should stay in this country.'

'I am afraid, Lady Wadsworth,' he replied, 'that we are not in a position to preclude any prospective buyer, should you place it for auction.'

'A pity,' she replied. 'Of course I am greatly saddened to have to sell the Stubbs. It has, as I have said, been such a part of this family for generations. I used to stand and stare at it as a small child. It seemed to draw me into the scene. I could almost smell the horses and feel their breath on my cheeks.'

'I do understand it will be a great loss to you,' said her visitor, giving her the benefit of his most sympathetic expression. 'So, shall we look at the picture?'

8

'Today, children, I thought we might write a poem,' Elisabeth told her class.

Malcolm Stubbins pouted moodily.

'And please don't pull that awful face, Malcolm,' said Elisabeth. 'As my mother would say, if I had an expression like that when I was young, "One day the wind will change and your face will stay like that".'

'I don't like poetry,' grumbled the boy. 'It's all la-di-da and blood—' – he paused momentarily in time to correct himself – 'and flipping daffodils.'

'Well, clearly your knowledge of poetry is very limited, Malcolm,' said the teacher good-humouredly, 'and perhaps by the end of the lesson I will have persuaded you that poetry can be about anything and that sometimes it is the very best way of expressing your feelings.'

The boy shrugged and grimaced.

'Now one of the reasons we are going to write a poem today,' continued Elisabeth, 'is that the School Library Service has organised a poetry competition for schools and will award prizes for the winners.'

'What sort of prizes, miss?' asked Malcolm.

'I suppose they will be book tokens,' replied the teacher.

The boy scowled. 'I've already got a book at home,' he said.

'Well, I don't think you can have too many books,' said Elisabeth, 'and if you read a bit more, Malcolm, your school-work would improve.'

'But I want to be a professional footballer, miss,' said the boy. 'You don't see footballers reading books.'

'I'm sure some of them do,' said the teacher.

'Well, I've never—' began the boy.

'Malcolm,' interrupted Elisabeth, 'I think this discussion has gone on long enough. I would like you to listen. Now, it is intended that an anthology of the best entries will be published by the School Library Service. All schools in this part of the county have been asked to submit some poems. We have some excellent poets in this school and I think we are in with a good chance of winning a prize.'

'Miss, can I write about our Bianca's baby?' asked Chardonnay.

'I don't see why not,' replied the teacher. 'I can see you still pulling that face, Malcolm. You can write a poem about football if you like.' His face brightened a little.

'Danny could write about his ferret,' said Chardonnay.

'Yes, he could,' said Elisabeth.

'Or he could write about living in a caravan.'

'Yes, that might be a possibility.'

'Or about some of the animals and birds he's seen in the countryside.'

'I think we've heard enough about what Danny should write about for one morning, Chardonnay,' said Elisabeth.

'Yea, you gerron wi' yer own poem, Chardonnay,' blustered Danny, embarrassed at being the centre of the girl's attention

'Now, now, Danny,' said Elisabeth smiling. 'She was only trying to be helpful.'

'But it's none of 'er business what I write about, miss,' replied Danny, his face still red with embarrassment.

'No, it isn't,' agreed Elisabeth.

'I'm only giving him a few ideas,' muttered the girl, pushing her bottom lip forward petulantly.

'Well, I am sure Danny really appreciates your suggestions,' replied the teacher.

'No, I don't,' mumbled the boy.

'But as my mother also used to say, Chardonnay,' continued Elisabeth, '"you get on with your own knitting".'

The girl's brow furrowed with incomprehension. 'I can't knit, miss,' she said.

'Never mind,' said Elisabeth, laughing. 'You just get on with your own poem.'

Later, as she tidied her classroom at the end of school, Elisabeth suddenly had a thought and, leaving things, headed for the school office.

The school secretary was busy putting stamps on envelopes ready to be taken to the post.

'Mrs Scrimshaw,' said Elisabeth, 'could you find me the address of the local football team please?'

'Football team?' repeated the school secretary, peering over her spectacles.

'That's right,' said Elisabeth. 'I want to write a letter.'

At morning break the following day, Oscar arrived at the staff-room door accompanied by Mr Gribbon, who gripped the back of the boy's jacket, very nearly lifting the child off the ground. The caretaker blew air out of his mouth noisily like a weary carthorse.

'I'm sorry to disturb your break, Mrs Devine,' he said, his voice sounding choked, 'but I would like you to have a word with this lad.'

'Oh dear, Oscar,' said Elisabeth, 'whatever have you been up to?'

'Actually nothing, Mrs Devine,' he replied pertly. 'I think Mr Gribbon has got the wrong end of the stick.'

'Oh, no, I haven't!' snapped the caretaker angrily. 'And if I did have a stick I would know what to do with it! It was you what did it!' He stressed every word through gritted teeth.

'Did what?' asked Elisabeth.

'Blocked the toilets, that's what, Mrs Devine,' he told her, bristling with anger, 'by putting foreign objects down the toilet bowls. Three toilets won't flush because of obstructions and I've got all manner of stuff coming out. The water's brought all the varnish off of my polished parquet floor and—'

'Thank you, Mr Gribbon,' said Elisabeth. 'I've got the idea.' She turned to the boy. 'Perhaps you had better explain yourself, Oscar,' she said, putting on her most serious expression.

Oscar sighed. 'I have been trying to do that, Mrs Devine,' he replied, 'but Mr Gribbon, I'm afraid, won't believe me. You see the thing is, the boys' toilets are rather smelly.'

'Now look here—' began the caretaker.

'Please let him finish, Mr Gribbon,' said Elisabeth, 'and then we might get to the bottom of this.' The caretaker grimaced.

'As I was saying, Mrs Devine,' continued Oscar, seemingly unperturbed, 'the boys' toilets are rather smelly and I suggested to Mr Gribbon that if some ping-pong balls were put down the bowls for boys to aim at, then they wouldn't pee all over the floor. Anyway, I found some old ping-pong balls and put them down the toilets and it seemed to work very well but I'm afraid some other boys must have put some old tennis balls down and they blocked the pipes. You see, ping-pong balls float but tennis balls can fill up with water and do not.'

'I see,' said Elisabeth. 'Well, Oscar, I am sure Mr Gribbon was grateful for your suggestions, but he is in charge of the premises and he decides what should be done and what should not be done in the boys' toilets. You had no business taking it on yourself to put ping-pong balls down the toilet bowls, however well-meaning that was.'

'And now I've got blockages and floods and a damaged floor!' cried the caretaker, tense with indignation and thrusting out his jaw.

The boy looked undaunted. 'Well, if I have any other ideas,

perhaps I should run them past you first, Mrs Devine,' announced Oscar.

'Other ideas!' repeated the caretaker angrily. 'We don't want any other ideas.'

'Mr Gribbon is quite right, Oscar,' said the head teacher. 'Let him deal with the boys' toilets.'

'It was just that I read,' said the boy, 'that if you place a brick in the cistern above the toilets it will conserve water.'

The caretaker looked apoplectic. 'You see what I mean, Mrs Devine,' he groaned. 'I really can't be doing with this. You will have to stop him. He's driving me to distraction.'

'No more suggestions, Oscar,' said Elisabeth firmly. 'No more ping-pong balls and forget about the brick. Is that understood?'

'Very well, Mrs Devine,' said the boy.

'Now you go and have a run around in the playground and get some fresh air,' said the head teacher, 'and leave Mr Gribbon to get on with his work.'

'Actually, I'm not that keen on running, Mrs Devine,' he told her, ambling off.

Later in the day when Elisabeth passed the boys' toilets she could not contain her smile. The caretaker had pinned a large sign to the door: 'ATTENTION WET FLOOR! THIS IS NOT AN INSTRUCTION!'

'May I come in?' Elisabeth stood on the steps at Clumber Lodge that evening.

'Well, hello stranger,' said Dr Stirling, kissing her lightly on the cheek. 'I thought you had gone off me.'

'I'm sorry,' replied Elisabeth. 'I just seem to have been so very busy. Start of term and all that. I did mean to phone.'

'Well, it's good to see you. Come on through.'

He led the way into the sitting-room, where a fire blazed and crackled in the hearth. When Elisabeth had first visited the house this room had been cold and unwelcoming with its heavy fawn-coloured curtains, earth-brown rug, dark cushions and dusty furniture. The bookshelf was crammed with books, journals and papers, and on a large oak desk were an old-fashioned blotter, a mug holding an assortment of pens and broken pencils and more papers stacked untidily. On the walls were a few dull prints and an insipid watercolour of a mountain and a lake.

Just before Danny had come to live at Clumber Lodge, Dr Stirling had arranged for one of the musty and unused bedrooms to be redecorated. Elisabeth and Mrs O'Connor had seen their opportunity – they had prevailed upon the doctor to give other parts of the house greatly in need of some refurbishment an overhaul, and the sitting-room had been transformed. It now looked homely and bright. The walls were painted, the wood shone, the prints and watercolours had been replaced by large bright paintings, the faded curtains had given way to long plum-coloured Dralon drapes and a thick-pile beige carpet had been fitted. The desk had been moved out and replaced by a deep-cushioned sofa. Even the large pot plant in the corner gleamed with well-being.

The only item remaining from the old decor was the delicate inlaid walnut table, on which several photographs in small silver frames had been arranged: one showing Dr Stirling with his arm around a striking-looking woman, his wife who had been killed in the riding accident; another a more formal portrait of the same woman posing in front of a horse; and several photographs of a serious-faced James.

'You look just about done in,' said Dr Stirling. 'Come over by the fire and I'll get you a drink. You look as if you need a whisky.'

Elisabeth warmed her hands and then sat on the sofa, stretching back and sighing. 'I *am* done in,' she agreed, 'and I could do with something strong. Where are the boys?'

'Upstairs,' he told her. 'Since you started that chess club at school they've become quite obsessed with the game.' As he poured the drinks Dr Stirling asked, 'Is there something wrong?'

'I just need to talk,' she told him. 'It's been a pretty nerve-racking week.' He passed her a glass and she took a sip.

'You'd better tell me about it,' he said, sitting down next to her. He rested a hand on hers. 'You know what they say, you can trust me, I'm a doctor.' She gave a small smile. 'Is it this proposed merger that's worrying you?' he asked.

'Yes, it's preying on my mind,' she said. 'The term started off so well. Everything seemed to be going fine, the school's future assured, contented teachers, happy children, new furniture and then this comes out of the blue. There'll be all this uncertainty and upheaval, changes of staff, two premises to manage and I just don't think I could work with that irritating man at Urebank.' He let her talk. 'I went to see the Director of Education earlier in the week. He virtually offered me a job in the north of the county at a new, purpose-built primary school, but you know I can't leave here. I don't want to be miles away from John, and from you.'

'I'm glad to hear it. You would be greatly missed if you left the village,' he said. 'And I would certainly miss you. I'm sure you know that, Elisabeth.'

She smiled. 'Well, I've no intention of leaving.'

'The thing is, the school isn't going to close,' he reassured her, 'so why would you leave?'

'But suppose this Mr Richardson at Urebank gets the head-ship and I have to work as his deputy? It would be unbearable.'

'That's not on the cards, is it?'

'Well, Mr Preston didn't go into that, but the papers I was given at the Education Office before I left say there will be one head teacher based at one site, probably with the junior children, and the deputy at the other with the infants and there may be staff redeployments and redundancies. Then the term had hardly started and I was savaged by a Rottweiler.'

'You were what?'

'Metaphorically speaking. Miss Sowerbutts cornered me by the school gates and had a go at me.'

'Why?'

'I told a parent I didn't agree with what had been said to her about her son when Miss Sowerbutts was head of the school. I think perhaps it was a bit unprofessional, but I was so angry at what she had said. Do you know, she told the parent—'

Dr Stirling placed a finger gently over her lips. 'No more,' he said, leaning closer to her. He kissed her again.

The door opened and James and Danny rushed in. 'Oh hello, Mrs Devine,' they said in unison. 'Dad,' said James, 'can you tell Danny that a bishop is worth more than a knight?'

Dr Stirling sighed and shook his head. Elisabeth smiled.

''Ello, Mrs Sloughthwaite,' said Danny, coming into the village store on the Sunday morning. He was holding a small bunch of white flowers.

'Hello, love,' replied the shopkeeper. 'Are those for me?'

'No,' he replied.

'For your girlfriend, are they?'

'I 'aven't got no girlfriend,' he told her, colouring up. 'I'm not into lasses. I'm sick of that Chardonnay following me round and making eyes at me. I can't go anywhere without 'er being behind me. And that Chantelle's t'same. I'm sick of it. I'm 'appy wi' mi ferret. Tha know where thy are wi' ferrets. Ya never know where ya are wi' lasses.'

'So who are the flowers for then?' asked the shopkeeper.

'I'm tekkin 'em to purron mi grandad's grave. I want to tidy it up a bit this morning.'

'That's a nice thought, but it's a bit cold for gardening.'

'I don't mind t'cold,' the boy told her. 'I'm used to it.' He waved the flowers. 'These are called Christmas roses but they're not really roses and they don't flower at Christmas either. Mi granddad loved these flowers. 'E planted 'em at t'back o'caravan and they're the first flowers along wi' snowdrops what ya see in January.'

'You'd think the frost would kill them,' remarked the shopkeeper.

'Well, it dunt seem to,' replied the boy.

'They're just right for your granddad's grave,' said Mrs Sloughthwaite, assuming her usual position leaning over the counter. 'Mrs O'Connor was telling me that you've settled in at Clumber Lodge with Dr Stirling,' she said, beginning her interrogation.

'Yeah, I really like it theer,' the boy told her.

'You're a very lucky boy, Danny Stainthorpe, to have found such a good home.'

'I know.'

'And a little bird tells me that Dr Stirling is minded to adopt you?'

The boy's face lit up. 'Yeah, 'e is. I'm really hexcited.'

'I bet you are, living in that lovely big house.'

'I've got a bedroom of mi own and I can keep mi ferret in his cage in t'shed at t'back and Mrs O'Connor's a really good cook.'

'You seem to have fallen on your feet,' observed the shopkeeper.

'I 'ave,' replied the boy, nodding.

'And did you have a nice Christmas?'

'Yeah, it were great.'

'Did you spend it at home with Dr Stirling then?' She recalled Mrs Lloyd telling her that Chardonnay had gone around to Dr Stirling's on Christmas Day when her sister went into labour but found no one at home, so she knew full well that Danny had not spent the day at Clumber Lodge.

'No.'

'So did you go out to a restaurant?'

'No.'

The boy was less than forthcoming so the shopkeeper decided to get straight to the point. 'So, where did you have your Christmas dinner then?'

'At Wisteria Cottage.'

'Oh, at Mrs Devine's.' She raised an eyebrow.

'Yeah, she invited us all round and cooked t'best Christmas dinner I've ever 'ad. She's a really good cook, is Mrs Devine.'

Was there anything this superwoman was not good at? mused the shopkeeper.

'That was kind of her.'

'I really like Mrs Devine,' said the boy.

'And from the sound of it Dr Stirling does as well,' remarked the shopkeeper, probing.

'We had a really great time. I need to get on, Mrs Sloughthwaite, so do ya sell cat food?'

'I do, love. Is it for your ferret?'

'No, it's for a cat.'

'I didn't know you had a cat.'

'It's not mine. It's a stray.'

'Is it a cream colour with a black face and sticky-up ears?'

''Ow did ya know that?'

'Because it's Miss Sowerbutts's cat and she's been looking for it. Last time she saw it, it was running out of her kitchen with a salmon tin stuck on its head.'

'That's 'ow I found it, down by t'millpond. There's a pair of kingfishers down theer and I went to see 'em and I saw this cat. I thowt it were dead at fust, an' then I saw its belly movin' up and down. It couldn't breathe properly. Anyroad, I managed to get t'tin off of its 'ead.'

'And however did you manage to do that?' asked the shopkeeper.

The boy produced a knife from his pocket and placed the flowers on the counter. Then he held the knife with one hand and tapped his nose with the other. 'Swiss army knife,' he told her. 'It's got all sorts o' things on. It were mi granddad's. It 'as a tin oppener.'

'That was handy,' remarked the shopkeeper.

'Well, ya never know, Mrs Sloughthwaite,' said the boy grinning, 'when you might come across a cat wi' a tin on its 'ead. Anyway, I gorrit off and now t'cat won't stop followin' me abaat.'

'A bit like them two lasses you were telling me about,' said Mrs Sloughthwaite, winking.

Danny grimaced. 'So could I 'ave a tin o' cat food please, Mrs Sloughthwaite? It looks dead 'ungry.'

'I wouldn't feed it if I were you, love,' she told him, recalling Miss Sowerbutts's description of the special diet the animal was on. 'You take it round to Mrs Sowerbutts – you never know, you might get a reward.' And pigs might fly, she thought.

The boy gave a small shudder and pulled a face. 'I don't want to go round to 'er house,' said Danny. 'I'll 'ave to see 'er and I can do wi'out that.'

'Well, just put the cat in her garden then,' said the shopkeeper. 'Then it'll know where it is and you won't have to see Miss Sowerbutts.'

'OK, Mrs Sloughthwaite,' said Danny.

She passed a bar of chocolate across the counter. 'And have this on me,' she said.

'Thanks Mrs Sloughthwaite,' he said.

'And you say hello to your granddad for me, will you? I reckon he's up there in heaven looking down on you and feeling happy with how things have turned out.'

'D'ya think 'e is?' asked the boy thoughtfully.

'I'm sure he is, love.' She passed him the flowers. 'Now you run along.'

So, Dr Stirling and the boys spent Christmas at Wisteria Cottage, did they, Mrs Sloughthwaite reflected when the boy had gone. Funny that Mrs O'Connor had never mentioned it when she was in the store. Although she had spent Christmas with her sister in Ireland, she would have known. Of course, Mrs O'Connor was always very circumspect. She gave nothing away. Mrs Sloughthwaite, resting her bosom on the counter, smiled to herself, feeling rather pleased. There was nothing she could not find out – one way or the other.

'Would you mind, Fred!' shouted the landlord of the Blacksmith's Arms.

'Would I mind what?' asked Fred Massey gruffly. He was dressed in his ill-fitting Sunday best suit, a bargain from a charity shop, and was standing with his back to the fire warming himself and shielding any heat from the other three customers in the public house, who sat at a small table by the window.

'Would you mind shifting yourself out from in front of the fire?' said the landlord. 'You're blocking all the heat.'

'I don't hear anyone complaining,' said Fred.

'Well, I am,' the landlord told him. 'Now shift yourself.'

Grumbling, Fred moved away and approached the bar. 'You wants to get this here chimney seen to,' he said. 'Yon fire gives out about as much heat as a frigid polar bear in a snowstorm. It all goes up the chimney.'

'Well, if you don't like it,' retorted the landlord, 'you can always take your custom elsewhere. You're lucky I've let you come back in here after that argument you had with Albert Spearman, attacking him with your crutch.'

'I didn't attack him,' Fred snorted. 'I poked him and he

deserved it, conning our Clarence into buying that duff animal feed soon as my back's turned and me disabled as well.'

Clarence, Fred's long-suffering nephew, had held the fort on the farm while his uncle had been incapacitated after an accident with the sugar beet cutter. His uncle had been taken to hospital and had spent the next month hobbling about the village on crutches, moaning and groaning.

'Albert Spearman must have thought my brains were made of porridge, trying to pull a fast one like that,' he said now. 'Tried to palm him off with a load of rubbish. Didn't think I'd notice. Aye, well I did.'

'I know all about that, Fred,' said the landlord. 'I've heard it often enough, as have most people who come in here. Now, I'm telling you, any more trouble out of you and I shall bar you again.'

'You come into the village pub for a quiet Sunday lunchtime drink,' said Fred loudly to no one in particular, 'and you get harassed. Give us another pint.' He looked around the bar to find someone whom he could engage in conversation and give the benefit of his opinions, but seeing that the few customers were clearly not interested in what he had to say, he turned to the landlord, who began pulling the pint.

'Quiet in here this lunchtime,' he observed. 'Mind you, I'm not surprised, price you charge for the beer.'

'I've told you what you can do if you don't like it,' replied the landlord. 'The Mucky Duck's just down the road.'

Like most in the village, the landlord didn't like the constantly complaining, tight-fisted, bad-tempered Fred Massey, but he put up with him because, unpleasant as the man was, he was a regular after all and custom was custom. 'So how is your Clarence?' he asked, placing the pint on the bar.

'As much use as a lump of stale bread,' Fred replied, counting out coins from an ancient leather purse before placing a mound of silver and copper on the bar.

'Fagin's hoard,' remarked the landlord, collecting up the change. 'I don't know how that lad puts up with you,' he said. 'You're always at him.'

'Always at him!' exclaimed Fred. 'Huh. He's gormless. Only let out yon Texel ram into the field with the yows last September time and now I've got all these bloody lambs all over the shop. Daft ha'peth that he is. He never listens to what I say. Then last week what did he do?'

'I can't guess,' said the landlord, 'but I have an idea you're going to tell me.'

'I said to him, I said don't let the cows into the field until you've filled the troughs with their feed because they'll be hungry, bunch together and make a dash for it. So what did he do?'

'You tell me,' sighed the landlord.

'He lets the beasts into the field and then starts to fill the trough. Cattle stampede, knock him clean over and he ends up face down buried under all the cattle feed with a broken arm and bruising. I mean, what good is he to me now? I'll have to do all the work myself.'

'That'll be a change,' observed the landlord.

'And another thing,' continued Fred.

'Oh, I thought there would be something else,' said the landlord, praying that another customer might come in.

'I've been telling Clarence time and time again to go up to the graveyard and get it fettled. Every time I see that snooty vicar's wife she's at me about it. I goes up there yesterday and find that somebody else has been cutting and a-pruning. I tackled Mrs Atticus but she says she's not asked anybody else to do it and knows nowt about it. Then she bends my ear saying it was about time somebody tidied up the graveyard and she's not complaining if somebody else has had the civic duty to do it. Well, I'll tell you this, when I find out who's taking the bread out of my mouth I shall a have few well-chosen words to say to him.'

'And what will they be?' asked the landlord.

'I don't know, I've not chosen them yet. 'Course it's all Clarence's fault.'

'I guessed as much,' sighed the landlord.

'I told him, I said you should have fettled that graveyard at the back end of last year. Not much chance now is there, what with his broken arm. He's got no common sense that lad.'

'Not like his uncle then,' observed the landlord, smiling, 'who goes and shoves his foot into a sugar beet cutter.'

Fred scowled. 'I don't know what to do with the lad. He should be married and with kids at his age. Twenty-five and he's never had a girlfriend, not as I know of, and there's plenty of likely lasses about at the Young Farmers. I mean I know he's not God's gift to look at, but he's got a steady job and he's in line to take over the farm when I push up the daisies.'

'You never bothered getting married yourself, then?' teased the landlord.

Fred scowled and took his pint to a corner table. 'No chance. In my book marriage is a dull slow meal with the pudding coming first. In olden days women were made for the comfort of men and they knew their place, cooking and cleaning and looking after the home while men earned the brass. Not now. I'm better off on my own.'

'I'll not disagree with you there,' remarked the landlord.

A moment later Major C. J. Neville-Gravitas breezed into the Blacksmith's Arms.

'Good day, landlord,' he said cheerfully.

'Morning, major. Your usual?'

'Just the ticket,' he said, 'and make it one for yourself, my good man.' He stroked his moustache and looked around smiling.

'Thank you kindly, major,' said the landlord.

'And how are you, landlord, on this bright crisp day?' asked Major Neville-Gravitas.

'I'm fine, thank you, major. How about you?'

'Tip-top.'

'What's all this about school joining up with yon school down the road?' came a loud voice from the end of the bar.

'That is the plan, Mr Massey,' replied the major.

'So you're not hell-bent on closing the village school, like what you tried to do before?'

'Mr Massey,' replied the major, 'I did not try to close the school.'

'Well, you didn't vote to keep it open, did you?'

'I have explained to you and indeed to many others in the village,' said the major angrily, 'that I abstained from the vote in the first instance but was most supportive when I saw how successful the school was becoming. Now can we let the matter lie?'

'Bit late in the day,' remarked Fred. 'And you only did it then because you saw the strength of feeling in the village.'

'Don't you tell me what I did and what I didn't do!' exclaimed the major. 'We have had this conversation before and I do not intend to discuss it any further.'

'Well, I'll tell you this—' began Fred mulishly.

'Don't!' exclaimed the landlord. 'You've been warned. Another word out of you, Fred Massey, and you can take your custom elsewhere.'

'I was only saying—' began Fred.

'Well, don't!' snapped the landlord.

Major C. J. Neville-Gravitas placed a five-pound note on the bar, gulped his whisky and strode for the door. 'Thank you, Fred,' said the landlord. 'That's another customer you've got rid of for me.'

9

The morning was cold and bright that Sunday. Elisabeth paused from hanging some nuts up for the birds in her garden to listen for a moment to the bells of St Christopher's ringing out and calling the faithful for morning service. How happy she was in the village in her cosy cottage, with the school thriving, working with supportive colleagues and finding new friends. There was also Michael Stirling, to whom she was becoming more and more attached. She just hoped things could stay like this. Of course, her life might be turned upside down with the prospect of the amalgamation. It was like a heavy weight hanging over her. But it was too nice a day to have such depressing thoughts, so she banished them, breathed in the fresh air and surveyed the swathe of green beyond the cottage, rising to the fell side and dotted with browsing sheep. A fat pheasant strutted along the rutted, tussocky track, and high above in a milky sky the rooks screeched and circled. A rabbit scuttered out from its hole and stared at her for a moment before lolloping away. She was about to head indoors when she caught sight of a large figure in an old tweed skirt, shapeless waxed jacket and heavy green rubber boots striding down the track which ran past the cottage. A small hairy terrier scampered behind her, its tongue lolling and its tail wagging frantically. When the dog saw Elisabeth it ran towards her, yapping.

'Gordon!' came a thunderous voice from the track. 'Get back here immediately, you silly creature!' The dog scurried to his mistress. 'The times I tell him not to run off like that,' said Lady Wadsworth to Elisabeth. 'He takes not a blind bit of notice of me. He's a little rascal.'

'He's a fine dog,' said Elisabeth.

Lady Wadsworth mellowed. 'He is, isn't he,' she agreed. 'I'm on my usual Sunday constitutional,' she said. 'Stop the old knee joints from seizing up. How are you, Elisabeth?'

'I'm very well,' Elisabeth replied. 'Actually, I was meaning to give you a call. I wonder if you could spare me a few minutes. There's something I need to ask you.'

'Nothing untoward, I trust? I cannot cope with any more bad news.'

'No, no,' replied Elisabeth. 'Come on in and we can discuss it over coffee. Then you can tell me about your bad news.'

'So you want me to become a governor?' said Lady Wadsworth, when Elisabeth had explained. She had settled herself in a comfortable chair by the open fire and was warming her hands, the terrier stretched out on the carpet. Elisabeth had placed a cup of steaming coffee and a plate of biscuits before her on the small occasional table.

'Yes, it was a unanimous vote of the governors and we all feel you are the perfect choice.'

'Really?' Lady Wadsworth took a sip of coffee and then crunched noisily on a biscuit. The dog looked up expectantly.

'You were so massively supportive over the proposed closure of the school,' Elisabeth told her, 'and your intervention certainly had an effect.'

'I should like to think so,' said Lady Wadsworth. 'I have to admit I did exert a little pressure over the closure. I do pride myself on having some influence in the county.'

'And after all, it was your grandfather who endowed the village school,' continued Elisabeth, 'and you have provided us with our lovely new library. So you will join us?'

'Yes, I most certainly will. I am flattered to have been asked. Perhaps getting involved in the school might take my mind off the present problems I have.'

'This sounds ominous,' said Elisabeth. 'Is there anything I can do?'

'That's very kind of you, my dear, but I fear not. It is a sad fact that Limebeck House is crumbling around me. It's far too large and draughty and in desperate need of repair. I do not have the necessary resources to do it. In the past there were housekeepers and maids, gamekeepers and chauffeurs, butlers and grooms. Grandfather even had a full-time mole-catcher and somebody to wind up his clocks.' She sighed. 'Times have changed. You can't get the staff now and if you could you couldn't afford to pay them. There's just Watson now. He does his best, of course, but like the rest of us he's getting on. It's such a worry.'

'I'm sure it is,' said Elisabeth. 'Is there nothing you can do?'

'I was to sell one of my most prized possessions – my Stubbs painting – to pay for the restoration, but it turns out it is a fake. I had an expert up from London and he said it was a copy and not a very good one at that. I was devastated, as you might guess. It was like a nail through the heart when he told me. All these years of thinking I had this beautiful original painting by one of the Old Masters and it turns out to be a reproduction. I feel like taking Sir Tristram's portrait off the wall, I really do, for it was he, you can bet, who sold the original. He was the wastrel son of Sir William Wadsworth, who bought the painting. Tristram was the black sheep of the family, a playboy who spent all his time gallivanting around Europe, gambling and womanising and drinking himself into an early grave.'

'Perhaps the person who valued it is mistaken,' suggested Elisabeth.

'Doubtful. Crispin De'Ath is the recognised expert on Stubbs.'

'Experts have been mistaken before. It would do no harm to have a second opinion.'

'No, I guess it wouldn't.'

'You can't lose anything, and you might have everything to gain.'

'Do you know, Elisabeth, I think you might be right. I shall get on to it immediately.'

Mrs Atticus was walking up the path to the rectory on her way back from morning service when she caught sight of a small figure placing some flowers on a grave.

'Hello, Daniel,' she said.

''Ello, miss,' replied the boy.

'You come here quite often, don't you?' she said. 'I've seen how well you look after your grandfather's grave. There're always fresh flowers.'

'Aye, I do come regular, miss.' He pointed to the flowers. 'These are called Christmas roses an' they were one of mi granddad's favourite flowers.'

'Actually they are called hellebores and they are amongst my favourites too,' the vicar's wife told him. 'They bloom very early and they like the shade. You could plant some around your grandfather's grave. There's a legend surrounding the hellebores, you know. My husband mentioned it in one of his sermons. When a small girl went to see Baby Jesus in the stable all those years ago she saw that the shepherds and the kings had taken Him presents. She had nothing to give and began to weep. The tears fell upon the snow and where they had fallen the hellebores grew and the pure white flowers bloomed. It's a lovely story, isn't it?'

Danny was staring open-mouthed. He looked down at the grave, bent and touched the white petals which lay on the top. 'Aye, it is,' he said.

Mrs Atticus noticed a set of trowels, small forks and shears on the ground near the boy. 'You are not the mystery grounds-man by any chance, are you?' she asked.

'I don't know what you mean, miss,' said the boy.

'Someone's been giving the graveyard a good tidy, cutting the grass around the graves and digging up the borders. Mr Massey is supposed to look after the grounds but he's been rather remiss lately. So are you responsible?'

'Well, it's true I 'ave done a bit o' tidyin' up,' the boy replied. 'I don't like to see things get ovvergrown an' I like being outdoors.' He put his hands on his hips and sucked in his bottom lip. 'Ya see, if you don't keep yer weeds down they'll be waist 'igh in t'summer.'

'That's exactly what I have been telling Mr Massey,' said the vicar's wife. 'Seeds blow over into the rectory garden.'

'An' it's t'devil's own job removin' dandelions once they've tekken root,' said Danny.

'Exactly,' agreed Mrs Atticus.

'Aye, and then there's yer couch grass and yer nettles and yer dock leaves and yer ivy. Some o' them rhododendrons 'ave bushed out an' gone wild. They wants cuttin' back.'

'It's a constant battle,' said the archdeacon's wife.

''Tis that,' agreed the boy. He pointed up at the huge oak tree. 'That's a fair old age,' he said. 'That big branch wants comin' off. It's dead an' could come down in a strong wind.'

'I'll ask Mr Massey to take a look,' said Mrs Atticus. 'That is if he stirs himself to come up here.'

'Well, I'd best gerron,' said Danny.

'It is very good of you, Daniel, to do this,' said the vicar's wife. 'I must pay you for your trouble.'

'Nay, it's all right, miss. I like doin' it. It's good to be outdoors.'

'That's very kind of you,' said Mrs Atticus. 'Now don't you stay out here too long. It's very nippy and we don't want you missing school with a cold.'

'I won't,' said Danny, wiping the earth from his hands. 'I'm nearly done.' The boy thought for a moment and then asked, 'Mrs Atticus?'

'Yes?'

'That big grave ovver theer. The one under t'gret big tree.' He pointed to an enormous marble mausoleum with a stooping angel on the top, in the shadow of an ancient oak gnarled with age and with huge spreading branches. 'It must 'ave bin for somebody dead important.'

'I'm sure he would like to think he was,' said the vicar's wife. She frequently referred to what she called 'that vulgar monstrosity' when there was mention of her husband's predecessor and his elaborate tomb. 'He was a rector who lived in the village many years ago.'

'He must 'ave been really liked for someone to build that for 'im,' said Danny.

'Quite the opposite. He was quite an unpleasant man by all accounts and spent most of his time hunting and drinking and gambling. Burnt the rectory to the ground with himself and his dogs inside during the last century. He had the tomb built for himself. He designed it and left enough money in his will to have it erected. If it was up to me, I'd knock the thing down. No one ever visits it.'

'It's sad is that,' said Danny.

'In my experience, Daniel, the bigger the grave the more high and mighty is the person under it. Your grandfather's grave is much better.'

Suddenly a cat appeared and began rubbing its body against the boy's leg. It was one of the most beautiful creatures Mrs Atticus had ever seen, small, slender and lithe, with a silky cream-coloured coat and the most brilliant deep blue almond-shaped eyes. 'Oh 'eck!' exclaimed the boy, 'it's come back.'

'If I am not mistaken that's Miss Sowerbutts's cat, isn't it?' asked the vicar's wife. 'She's put a notice in the church porch saying it has gone missing.'

'Yeah miss, I know. Mrs Sloughthwaite tellèd me. It keeps followin' me round. I've tekken it back twice now but it keeps comin' back an' won't leave me alone.'

'It obviously likes you,' said Mrs Atticus.

Danny stroked the silky fur. 'I'll take it back when I've finished 'ere.'

'I think that would be a good idea, Daniel.'

'An' I'll pop back next Sat'day an' do a bit more in t'churchyard.'

'Well, don't overdo it, and call in at the rectory when you've finished. I insist you will be paid for your labours.'

'No, you're all reight, Mrs Atticus. I've nowt much else to do come the weekend an' as I said, I like being outside.'

'Well, that's very kind of you,' she said. Would that all young people were as polite and helpful as this young man, thought the vicar's wife as she headed for the rectory to prepare lunch.

Danny was halfway down the high street, clutching the cat to his chest, when he heard a shrill voice behind him. 'Daniel Stainthorpe, stop where you are!' He recognised the voice immediately, for he had heard it many times before. His granddad had said it was as strident as a tree full of crows. The boy froze in his tracks. He turned to see an angry-looking figure, muffled up in a thick black coat and sporting a woollen hat, striding towards him.

'What are you doing with my cat?' demanded Miss Sowerbutts.

'I . . . I . . . was—' he spluttered.

She reached over and took the animal from him. 'Where have you been, Tabitha?' she said. Then she turned her steely gaze on Danny. 'I said, what were you doing with my cat?' she asked again.

' I . . . I . . . was bringing it back, miss.'

'Where did you find her?' she asked.

'Down by t'millpond, miss. It 'ad a tin on its 'ead.'

'She had a tin on her head,' articulated Miss Sowerbutts, stressing the first letter of each word.

'That's wor I said, miss.'

Miss Sowerbutts sighed. She had tried hard to eradicate what she considered to be the dreadful accent of these children, but to no avail. 'Had she still got the tin on her head when you found her?'

'Yes, miss, but I gorrit off an' I dint 'urt it. I were dead careful.'

'Well, I hope you didn't. She's very delicate,' said Miss Sowerbutts, stroking the silky head of the cat. 'When did you find her?'

'Abaat a week ago, miss.'

'A week ago!' she exclaimed. 'Why didn't you bring her back before?'

'I din't know it were yer cat, miss.' He decided not to tell her that he had returned the animal to her garden several times.

'I've been at my wits' end,' Miss Sowerbutts said, her voice becoming calmer. She stroked the cat again.

'It's a lovely cat an' it's really affectionate,' said Danny.

'Yes, well, she's a very special cat – a Siamese and with a very fine pedigree. She shouldn't be out. I keep her indoors. The other cats would be very jealous of her and attack her.'

'I reckon it can 'andle itself, miss,' said Danny.

'And what would you know about Siamese cats?' she asked tetchily.

Probably more than you do, thought Danny, but he knew when to keep his mouth closed.

'Have you been feeding her?' asked Miss Sowerbutts.

'Yes, miss.'

She sighed. 'On what?'

'Just scraps o' meat an' stuff.'

'She has a special diet of fish and chicken. She has a very delicate constitution. I shall take her inside out of harm's way.'

The cat, as if it had understood her, suddenly arched its back, hissed and leapt from its mistress's arms, disappearing behind a large laurel bush.

'I hope you haven't made her wild,' said Miss Sowerbutts, scuttling after her.

'There's a meeting about the school amalgamation next week,' announced Mrs Sloughthwaite.

Her only customer, the aged Mrs Widowson, her of the tragic countenance, gave a small shrug. 'Well, I can't say it's got anything to do with me. My children are well past school age and I don't have any grandchildren. And seeing what some of these youngsters these days get up to, like that lass who lives next door to me for instance, I count it a blessing that I don't.'

'From what Mr Atticus told me,' continued the shopkeeper, leaning over the counter, 'there's not much of a chance of changing the minds of them at the Education. He went to the meeting at Urebank last week and said it was all done and dusted, so I don't suppose they'll take much notice of us.'

'I hear Reverend Atticus has got a new job,' remarked the customer.

'Yes, he was telling me about it. He's been promoted to help the bishop and has this fancy new title. He's not a vicar any more, he's what's called an archdeacon and he's not called reverend either, he's venereal.'

'He's what?'

'Evidently that's what they call archdeacons – venereal.'

'Well, it's a new one on me.'

'And me. Anyway, I shall go along to this meeting all the same, if only to see what the galloping major has to say. I wouldn't trust him as far as I could throw him.'

'As I said, it's not really any concern of mine,' replied the customer.

'Oh, but it is, Mrs Widowson, because you live in the village and what happens at the village school is everyone's business. I mean, I've no kiddies at the school but it's part of your civic duty to take an interest. So I hope you come along and give Mrs Devine some moral support.'

'I shall have to see,' replied the customer, who had no intention of giving up her bingo evening to attend the meeting. 'I've not been that right lately.' She rubbed her forehead. 'Terrible banging headaches I've had. I shall have to go and see Dr Stirling.'

'I think it's the insecticide they're putting on the fields,' remarked the shopkeeper. 'I've been getting a touch of nostalgia as well.'

'No, it's not that giving me headaches,' said Mrs Widowson, 'it's that lot next door to me. Arguing all the time they are over Bianca's baby. She won't let on who the father is and they won't leave her alone. I never thought I'd say this but I feel sorry for the lass. Anyway, I'd best be off.'

'Oh, I haven't told you,' said Mrs Sloughthwaite, stopping the customer in her tracks. 'You will never guess who walked in here yesterday.'

'Who?'

'Maisie Proctor, ex-wife of Les Stainthorpe, that's who.'

'No!'

'Yes, and she'd not changed,' said Mrs Sloughthwaite. 'Came in here as large as life and as bold as brass as if nothing had happened, hair all fluffed up like a peroxide bird's nest and make-up that looked as if it had been laid on with a trowel, and she stood standing there where you're stood standing now, as if she'd never been away.'

'Well, what did she want?' asked the customer.

'You don't need to be a brain surgeon to work that one out. Money. That's what she was after. Hard as a witch's thumbnail is that one. She'd heard about her ex-husband's death and came back sniffing about to see if he's left anything for her, I'll warrant. Brazen madam. She spent nearly all of his money when she married Les Stainthorpe and then took the rest when she cleared off.'

'With that carpet salesman from Barnsley,' added Mrs Widowson.

'No, he was a brush salesman from Rotherham, but that's beside the point. Anyway, she walks in here asking after Danny.'

'You don't say.'

'I do. Of course as you well know I can be the very soul of circumspection when I want to be so I told her nothing. Poor lad doesn't want the likes of her turning up like a bad penny, spoiling things for him. I told her that as far as I knew the boy was being fostered and I left it at that. Then she asked me why nobody in the village had let her know that Les had died. I said to her, I said why should anyone let you know, you've had nothing to do with him since you ran off.'

'With the brush salesman from Barnsley,' added Mrs Widowson.

'Rotherham!' Mrs Sloughthwaite snapped. 'Anyway, he dropped dead tying up his shoelaces.'

'Who did?'

'The brush salesman from Rotherham, him who she took up with. Heart attack it was. Evidently he left her everything and she's selling up and moving back up here.'

'What, to Barton?' asked the customer.

'No, thank the Lord, to Clayton. She's bought some fancy flat down by the river in De Courcey Apartments or some such fancy name.'

'Well I never.'

'And I'll tell you who else has one of them flats.'

'Who?'

'Miss Sowerbutts, that's who. I'd love to see her face when she discovers that Maisie Proctor is her neighbour.'

'Well, fancy her coming back after all these years,' remarked Mrs Widowson.

'I know,' said the shopkeeper. 'Then off she flounces out of the shop. Let's hope that's the last we see of her.'

Unfortunately it was not the last the village saw of Danny's grandmother. The following day she presented herself at the children's department at County Hall requesting to see the social worker who was dealing with the fostering of her grandson.

'Will it mean that you'll have to travel to Urebank every day?' asked Mrs Brakespeare.

'No, Mother, it won't,' replied her daughter.

'Well, I don't like the sound of this merger, Miriam. There'll be too many teachers and not enough children. You mark my words, they'll be sacking a few.'

Mrs Brakespeare sat in her large armchair, positioned strategically by the window where she could observe the comings and goings on the village high street. She was a lean, elderly woman with tightly curled, silver-white hair, a small thin-lipped mouth and an amazingly wrinkled indrawn face full of tragic potential.

'There's no one going to be sacked,' her daughter told her. 'The teachers will either be found positions in the newly amalgamated school, redeployed or offered early retirement.'

Mrs Brakespeare sat stern and motionless. She scrutinised her daughter as a judge might when faced with a condemned prisoner in the dock. 'Well, you don't seem unduly concerned.'

'I'm not.'

'I can't see you coming out of it all that well,' said the old lady petulantly.

Ever the pessimist, thought her daughter. 'And why is that, Mother?'

'Because knowing you, you'll just accept what they offer.

You never have been a one to push yourself forward. Always took a back seat, that's you all over, Miriam. You take after your father in that.'

'As you are frequently at pains to remind me,' muttered her daughter.

'What?'

'As you always like to tell me, Mother.'

'Well, it's true. Your father never pushed himself forward. Always happy in the background. Quite content to take orders from other people when he could have been giving them out himself. He could have been a manager if he had had a bit more gumption. And you're the same, Miriam. You let people walk on you. As they say, "Always the bridesmaid and never the bride".'

Miss Brakespeare laughed.

'You might well laugh,' said her mother, 'but you mark my words, you'll be at the back of the queue when they give the jobs out. You need to stand up for yourself or you'll be demoted.'

'I won't be demoted,' her daughter told her. There was a gleam in her eye.

'You can't be too sure,' she said, tight-lipped.

'Yes, I can, Mother, because I shan't be there to be demoted.'

'What do you mean, you won't be there?'

'Just what I said. I shall not be at the school.'

'You won't be at the school?'

'Mother, I do wish you wouldn't repeat everything I say. You sound like an echo. I shall not be at the school because I intend to take early retirement at the end of next term.'

'Take early retirement?'

Miss Brakespeare sighed. This was becoming wearisome. 'Yes, Mother, I intend to accept an offer to leave. I've been in touch with the Education Office and they are giving me a very generous package.'

'You could have taken it last year when that Mrs Devine

arrived, red shoes and silver heels and all. I don't know why you've suddenly decided now. You're forever telling me how much happier you are at the school these days.'

'I am very happy at the school,' replied her daughter. 'I am very happy indeed and I intend to stay there until the end of the summer term, but circumstances do change.'

'What circumstances have changed?'

Her daughter came and sat beside her. 'Last term various people were invited into school to work with the children, run the football team, take an art class and start a chess club.'

'Yes, Miriam, I am well aware of what goes on in the school. You talk of little else.'

'Well, one of the people who has been coming in is Mr Tomlinson. He takes the school choir once a week.'

'What's all this got to do with you taking early retirement?' asked Mrs Brakespeare.

'I shall tell you, Mother, if you will let me finish.'

Mrs Brakespeare scowled. 'Well, go on then, hurry up. It's nearly time for my tea.'

'As I have just said, Mr Tomlinson—'

'George Tomlinson who plays the organ at the chapel?'

'Yes Mother, the very same. Well, the thing is—'

'I remember his mother. She was big in the Soroptomists. Large woman who always wore those fancy hats with feathers in and spoke as if she had a plum in her mouth.'

Miss Brakespeare breathed out nosily. 'Mr Tomlinson's wife,' she continued, 'died a couple of years ago and—'

'She collapsed in the village store as I recall,' said Mrs Brakespeare. 'Went out like a light.'

'Mother!' snapped Miss Brakespeare. 'Will you please let me finish what I want to say.'

'There's no need to be so aggressive, Miriam,' said her mother, pursing her lips.

'Mr Tomlinson,' continued her daughter, 'George, that is,

and I have found that we have a great deal in common and we've been seeing quite a lot of each other over the past few weeks. He's a very gentle and sweet-natured man and we've been getting on really well. Anyway, to cut a long story short he's asked me to marry him.'

Mrs Brakespeare shot up in her chair as if a bucket of icy water had been thrown over her head, and there was a sharp intake of breath. 'Marry!' she exclaimed.

'Yes, Mother. He has asked me to marry him and I've said yes.'

'I don't believe what I'm hearing, Miriam,' gasped her mother, gripping the arms of her chair. 'Marry George Tomlinson?'

'Is it that impossible for you to believe?'

'I'm lost for words,' said her mother, panting. 'I shall have to have my tablets. I'm coming over all peculiar. Marry George Tomlinson. I've never heard the like.'

'So I won't be just the bridesmaid any more, will I?' said her daughter, beaming.

'I can't take in what I've just heard,' said Mrs Brakespeare. 'Get married to George Tomlinson!'

'Well, you will have to get used to it, Mother, because that is what I am going to do. George is selling his house in the village, I'm taking early retirement next July and we intend to move to Scarborough and live in a bungalow near the seafront.'

'Get my tablets,' panted the old lady. 'I can feel one of my turns coming on.'

Miss Brakespeare passed her mother a small brown bottle which was on an occasional table to the side of the chair.

'I have asked George to call around this evening,' said Miss Brakespeare calmly, 'so you can meet him, and he will stay for some supper.'

Her mother posted three coloured tablets into her mouth, swallowed and then began to weep. 'That it should come to this,' she sobbed. She took a small lace handkerchief from her sleeve and blew her nose loudly.

'I hardly expected hearty congratulations, Mother, but neither did I expect you to react like this.'

'It's come as a terrible shock, Miriam,' said Mrs Brakespeare, her voice wobbling. Then she looked up at her daughter and her voice was as dry as sawdust. 'And I suppose while you're enjoying the high life in Scarborough, I shall be institutionalised.'

Miss Brakespeare laughed.

'You can laugh, Miriam, but I know what will become of me. I'll be tucked away with all those old folks in some care home.'

'Don't be silly, Mother. We've been through all this before. You are not going into any care home. George and I would like you to come and live with us. You can have a little granny flat.'

'You're not pregnant, Miriam?' gasped Mrs Brakespeare. 'Not at your time of life.'

'Of course not, Mother,' replied her daughter. 'What I mean is that you could live in an annexe to the bungalow and I could look after you as I always have done. You like Scarborough. Lovely long promenade, bracing sea air, beautiful scenery.'

'You want me to come and live with you?' sniffed her mother.

Miss Brakespeare put her arms around her mother's shoulders. 'Of course I do. You don't think I'd put you in a care home? Now I know it's come as a bit of a shock, but you'll like George. He's a very kind and decent man.'

'I'm finding all this hard to take in,' said her mother.

'Well, why don't you go and have a rest and I'll bring you up a cup of tea,' her daughter told her.

'Yes, I think I will,' replied her mother. 'This has come as a shock, I can tell you.' She rose stiffly from her chair and shuffled towards the door. Then she turned. 'By the way,' she said, 'what are we having for tea?'

10

Major Neville-Gravitas was propping up the bar in the club-house at Gartside Golf Club. Following his altercation with Fred Massey in the Blacksmith's Arms, he had decided he would drink elsewhere. In the corner the major saw Councillor Smout with an extremely thin, big-nosed individual who sported a shock of frizzy ginger hair. They were bent over the table, heads together like a couple of collaborators plotting an act of treason. The councillor's companion sat and listened and occasionally nodded.

Councillor Smout, catching sight of the major, heaved himself up from his chair and shouted. 'Cedric! Ovver 'ere!'

The major was not inclined to spend an evening with Cyril Smout but felt obliged to at least say hello, so he finished his drink and went to join him.

'Good evening,' said the major.

'Evenin', major,' said the councillor. 'Sit tha sen down.' He raised a fat hand and beckoned to the barman. 'Jack, same again for us two and another un for t'major 'ere. Malt whisky, is it?'

'That would be most acceptable,' replied the major, strok-ing his moustache.

'Mek it a double,' shouted Councillor Smout, resuming his seat. 'I don't offen see you t'golf club?'

'Oh, I come in now and then,' replied the major.

'I come in regular,' the councillor told him. He tapped his nose. 'Useful contacts. This 'ere is Wayne Cooper, our newly appointed councillor, by the way.' He placed a fat hand on the young man's shoulder. 'Straight out o' college and he wins a seat on t'Council. Not bad goin' that, is it?' He turned to his companion. 'Got a lot to learn but you're keen, eh, Wayne?' The young councillor gave a weak smile. 'I'm just fillin' t'lad in wi' what' e's hexpected to do and who to watch. It's a minefield, is local politics. I've been in it long enough to know that. Some of 'em would stab you in t'back while lookin' you in t'face.'

'Good evening,' said the major, pumping the young man's hand.

Councillor Smout leaned back expansively on his chair, stretching his fat legs underneath the table and sucking in his teeth.

'I was pleased to hear that your little problem with the expenses has been cleared up,' remarked the major.

'Oh, that? Storm in a teacup,' replied the councillor dismissively. He swiftly changed the subject. 'So looks like we're up for this 'ere amalgamation then.'

'So it would appear,' replied the major. His drink arrived. He took a sip.

'Likely to be a bit contentious,' sniffed the councillor.

'I sincerely hope not!' exclaimed the major. 'I had quite enough contention over the proposed school closure at Barton. I really do not wish to go through all that again.'

'Well, I was speaking to Norbert Clark, who's Chairman on t'Education Committee,' continued Councillor Smout. 'I was telling young Wayne 'ere. 'E were sayin' that there's got to be new governing bodies for all these amalgamated schools, what means that some of thy governors at Barton will 'ave to join wi' some of us at Urebank and then they'll 'ave to add an extra one.'

'Why is that?' asked the major.

'Why is what?'

'Why does there need to be an extra governor?'

'Because when it comes to t'vote it could be 'ung.'

'I don't follow your drift,' said the major.

'Well, there'll likely be four of your lot and four of ours, so if one lot votes one way and t'other lot votes t'other way, which I' ave to say is not unlikely, then it'll be 'ung, won't it, so you 'ave to 'ave a chairman who 'as t'castin' vote.'

'Ah, yes, I see,' said the major. 'And who is this chairman likely to be?'

'Either you or me,' said Councillor Smout, 'that is until a new one is appointed by t'new governing body.'

'Well, I certainly don't wish to do it,' the major told him. 'It's a thankless job and as the Chairman of Governors at Barton-in-the-Dale School, all I seem to get is criticism and unpleasant comments from those in the village.'

'Well, in that case I shall 'ave to take it on,' said Councillor Smout.

'Well, I'm certainly not interested,' said the major, before sipping his whisky.

'Now let me put mi cards on t'able 'ere Cedric,' said the councillor, leaning forward. 'I want Mester Richardson for t'job, not that Mrs Devine, and I reckon I 'ave t'backin' of all mi governors at Urebank.'

The major frowned. 'Mrs Devine it has to be said has done a very commendable job since she took over at Barton,' he said.

'That's as may be,' said the councillor, 'but she's just too full of 'erself for my likin' an' wants 'er own way all t'time. I never took to her when she was appointed. I felt she were a bit on t'forceful side when we interviewed 'er, and as you well know, major, I did 'ave mi reservations.'

The major could not recall anything of the sort, for all the governors, with the exception of Dr Stirling, had been strongly in favour of the appointment of Mrs Devine, but he remained silent on the matter.

'And another thing,' said the councillor. He took a gulp of his beer and wiped the froth from his upper lip with the back of his hand. 'There's been complaints about 'er. Norbert Clark got this letter saying she 'ad been unprofessional.'

'Really?' muttered the major, staring unseeingly across the table.

'T'former head teacher, Miss Sowerbutts, 'as written to 'im sayin' Mrs Devine 'as been runnin' 'er down behind 'er back, telling parents t'advice what she 'ad given was rubbish.'

'Yes, I have received a letter to that effect,' replied the major. 'I have to say, it doesn't sound like Mrs Devine to me, and as to Miss Sowerbutts's comments I take those with a pinch of salt. As you are well aware, when you served on the governors when she was head teacher, Miss Sowerbutts is the most critical, embittered and thoroughly disagreeable person I have ever met and I take no cognisance of what she has to say.'

'Well, yes, I 'ave to admit,' agreed Councillor Smout, 'she's a rum-un, but there might be summat in what she says.'

'Nonsense,' said the major.

'Anyroad, that apart,' said the councillor, 'Mester Richardson 'as been in t'county longer than she 'as, 'e runs a tight ship and I reckon 'e's right for t'job an' I've said as much to 'im.'

'Was that wise, councillor?' enquired the major before taking another sip of his drink.

'Was what wise?'

'Promising Mr Richardson the job before the interviews have taken place?'

'I 'aven't actually promised 'im t'job,' replied the councillor, 'just that Urebank governors will be reight behind 'im and that there will be some on t'Barton governors who'll be votin' for' im an' all.' He winked at his young companion and then smiled at the major. 'No names, no pack drills.'

The councillor sucked in his teeth and leaned back

expansively in the chair. His stomach pushed forcefully against his waistcoat, revealing a show of white shirt and the top of his trousers. 'I think it's your round, major, isn't it?' he said.

The great black door to Limebeck House was opened by the butler. The visitor was a short, thick-necked individual with a curiously flat face and dark hair greying at the temples. He removed his plain brown woollen scarf and kid gloves, which he handed to the butler, and took off his camel-hair coat, beneath which he wore a finely-cut brown herringbone suit, a mustard waistcoat draped with a gold chain and fob and a yellow silk tie. The cuffs of his pristine white shirt emerged from below the sleeves of his coat and revealed large gold cufflinks.

'Would you be so kind as to inform her ladyship that I have arrived, my good man?' he said without a trace of a smile. 'I am expected.'

'May I take your name, sir?'

'Mr Thomas Markington, of the Markington and Makepeace Fine Arts Auction House.'

The butler disappeared into a small adjacent room to deposit the coat, scarf and gloves and, on returning, closed the heavy front door with a thud and rearranged the draught-excluder in front of it.

'If you would follow me, sir,' he said.

Suddenly Gordon the border terrier appeared around the corner. He eyed the visitor for a moment and then skittered across the wooden floor toward him, his nails clicking noisily, his tail wagging wildly. The visitor gave him a look that would freeze soup in pans, and the dog came to an abrupt halt and flopped on to his stomach, burying his head between his legs.

'I dislike dogs,' the visitor told the butler.

'And I don't think the dog has altogether taken to you either, sir,' replied Watson drily.

As he walked down the decidedly chilly corridor to the library in the footsteps of the butler, his expensive chestnut-brown brogues making a dull sound on the wooden floor, Mr Markington glanced this way and that, taking everything in but with seemingly scant interest. He paused occasionally to examine a gilt-framed portrait of some ancestor or an item of furniture. He picked up a cracked china vase and ran a finger around the rim. His face was expressionless.

The visitor did not have to wait long for the arrival of Lady Wadsworth.

He stood as she breezed into the library, and gave a short bow.

'It's very good of you to come, Mr Markington,' said Lady Wadsworth. 'Do take a seat.'

'I am travelling north,' he told her, 'so it was of little inconvenience for me to break my journey here.'

'Tea?' she asked.

'Thank you, no,' he replied. 'Time is of the essence and I must be away. May I see the picture in question?'

'Yes, of course,' she replied. 'I should tell you that I have already had an art specialist look at the painting and he is of the opinion that it is not an authentic work of art by George Stubbs.'

'So mine will be a second opinion,' replied Mr Markington coldly.

'Indeed,' replied Lady Wadsworth.

The fine art expert adjusted his cuffs and gave a thin smile. 'Shall we take a look?' he said.

He was shown into the drawing-room. It was a cheerless, ill-lit and draughty chamber full of furniture draped in white dust-sheets. They approached the great white marble fire-place, before which was a small stool. Mr Markington stared up at the picture for an inordinate amount of time, all the while sucking his upper lip in a portentous manner. It was a shrewd, considering gaze which gave nothing away. The expression on his flat face was impassive. He then climbed up on the stool, took a small eyeglass from his pocket and examined the picture, occasionally touching the canvas with the tip of a finger.

Lady Wadsworth watched intently, a quiver briefly distending her mouth.

The fine art expert descended, put his eyeglass back in his pocket, straightened his suit and breathed in deeply through his nose. Then he gave a dismissive grunt.

'It's a copy,' he said simply. His face was as blank as a figurehead on the front of a ship.

Lady Wadsworth tried to control her emotions but her voice betrayed the extent of her disappointment. 'Are you sure?' she asked.

'Unquestionably,' he replied in a flat tone of voice.

'And the value?'

The man shrugged. 'A few hundred guineas at most.'

'Well, Mr Markington,' said Lady Wadsworth, 'I am, of course, very saddened to hear that. I am very much obliged to you for making this visit. I shall bid you good day. Watson will see you out.' She swept from the room.

The man nodded dully, his face still expressionless.

'I had some kid gloves,' the visitor told the butler as he put on his coat and scarf in the hall.

'Ah, yes sir,' replied the butler. 'I must have left them in the anteroom. I shall get them.'

Mr Markington stared up at the ornate ceiling, noticing where bits of plaster had crumbled away; he saw the damp patches on the walls, the scuffed floor, the chipped tiles and the old knitted draft-excluder like a fat grey snake beneath the door. How many times had he been called upon by some impoverished Lord this or Lady that to value a supposed painting or antique thought by them to be worth a small fortune, and how many times had he had to inform them the item in question was virtually worthless? It would not be long, he thought, before this cold, neglected mausoleum of a place was turned into a fancy five-star hotel.

'I appear to have mislaid your gloves, sir,' said the butler, emerging from the small room.

The visitor sighed and rubbed his forehead. 'I'll help you look,' he said.

It was a cluttered room with an ornate carved oak bench underneath the window, various walking canes and brollies in an elephant's-foot stand, a stack of coloured prints, an ancient black bicycle resting against a wall, a huge pram with a torn hood and various cardboard boxes crammed with all manner of bric-a-brac. Along the walls was a row of brass coat-hooks.

'They're here,' said Mr Markington, discovering the gloves on the floor behind a crate. 'They must have fallen out of the coat pocket.' As he stooped to retrieve them he froze when behind the crate he caught sight of a shapely white marble foot poking out from under a dust-sheet. He stood and, leaning over, slowly uncovered the figure beneath the sheet like a mortician gently uncovering a corpse. When all was revealed he staggered back to the door and steadied himself on the architrave. 'I think I am about to swoon,' he murmured.

'I'll get a glass of water, sir,' said the butler.

'Fetch Lady Wadsworth immediately!' cried Mr Markington.

'Begging your pardon, sir?' said the butler.

'Now, man! Fetch her now!'

'Really sir, I—'

'Quickly, man! Quickly!' ordered the visitor.

Watson hurried off.

When Lady Wadsworth arrived at the anteroom she found her visitor on his knees like a supplicant. He was stroking the reclining statue.

'Are you not well, Mr Markington?' she enquired, startled by the scene before her.

'I'm lost for words,' he told her.

'Perhaps you might like to rest somewhere a little more comfortable?'

'The sculpture, Lady Wadsworth,' he whispered, getting to his feet. 'From where did you acquire the sculpture?'

'Oh, it was brought back by that rascally forebear of mine, the one who probably sold the Stubbs,' she told him, 'that young Tristram Wadsworth. He gallivanted around the Continent on the Grand European Tour that so many idle young men with more money than sense went on in the past and brought it back. My grandmother refused to have it on show. It's disgracefully revealing and leaves little to the imagination.'

'It is a nude study,' pronounced Mr Markington haughtily. 'Nude sculptures are perforce revealing.'

'Well, my grandmother had it removed to where it is now, out of sight and covered up. She felt it might corrupt the servants. As a child I was never allowed to view it, although as most curious children would have done I did occasionally take a peep.'

'Lady Wadsworth,' said Mr Markington in measured tones, 'what you have in your possession is Hermaphrodite.'

'Who?'

'This is one of the most beautiful sculptures it has been my pleasure to behold. It is probably a sixteenth- or seventeenth-century study of the reclining Hermaphrodite, executed in the finest Carrara marble. The sculptor captures the very essence of her beauty with dramatic naturalistic realism. It's a masterpiece.' He caressed the figure.

'That may be, but it is not the sort of thing one displays in the entrance to one's home.'

'Lady Wadsworth, you are right,' he replied, misconstruing her meaning. 'This magnificent piece should be displayed for the entire world to see. I think this might very well be the work of one of Giovanni Lorenzo Bernini's students or indeed be by the master himself. He was one of the greatest sculptors of the sixteenth century. This life-size reproduction of the classical Roman figure—'

'Another copy,' huffed Lady Wadsworth.

'Yes, but not at all like the Stubbs painting. The first-century representation of the reclining Hermaphrodite now in the Museo Nazionale Romano in the Palazzo Massimo alle Terme in Rome was frequently an inspiration for the great sculptors of the sixteenth and seventeenth century. There are many versions, the most famous being the Borghese Hermaphroditus in the Louvre and the one at the Vatican. This, Lady Wadsworth, could be a work of great significance, a lost treasure.'

'And worth something?' she asked.

'Oh yes,' he replied, smiling for the first time and displaying a set of formidable teeth.

'How much?' she asked bluntly.

'It is difficult to put a figure on such an object. Sadly there is some damage, which will affect the price but—'

'How much?'

'As I said, it is very difficult to put a price on such a work of art as this.'

'Try.'

'Certainly several hundred thousand pounds,' he replied. 'Possibly a deal more.'

'You hear that, Watson?' said Lady Wadsworth, showing her own set of formidable teeth.

'Of course, had there not been the damage I could not venture to put a price upon it.'

'I don't think the other one has any damage,' said Lady Wadsworth. 'Does it, Watson?'

'I believe not, your ladyship.'

'The other one?' repeated Mr Markington, steadying himself on a chair. 'You have another one?'

'In the stable block,' Lady Wadsworth told him. 'Would you care to see it?'

Danny, on his way to the graveyard with some flowers for his grandfather's grave, was passing Miss Sowerbutts's cottage when a strident disembodied voice came from behind a large bush.

'Daniel Stainthorpe!'

The boy jumped and dropped the flowers.

The former head teacher of the village school appeared.

'Daniel Stainthorpe,' Miss Sowerbutts repeated. 'Come here. I want a word with you.'

'I 'aven't done owt, miss,' the boy said defensively.

'I didn't say that you had. I would like you to take a message to Mr Massey. Tell him I am still waiting for him to come and deal with the moles on my lawn. I have asked the man umpteen times to get rid of these annoying little creatures. I might as well talk to a brick wall. Tell him I need them dealt with immediately. Is that clear?'

'I can sort out yer moles for ya if you like, miss,' said Danny.

'I think it is best left to those who know what they are doing,' Miss Sowerbutts replied stiffly.

'I know wor I'm doin', miss,' the boy told her. 'I cleared all t'moles from Mrs Devine's garden.'

At the mention of the name, Miss Sowerbutts pursed her thin lips. 'Did you indeed?' she said.

'They 'aven't been back after I set t'traps.'

'Mr Massey poured some bleach down their holes.'

'Dunt work,' said Danny.

'You are quite right, it doesn't. I imagined that this cold weather would put a stop to all their digging and burrowing but it hasn't. The lawn looks worse than it ever has. It's most distressing.'

'Moles don't mind frost an' snow, an' they can swim so it's

no good tryin' to flood 'em out,' said Danny. 'Only way to get rid of 'em is by layin' traps.'

'And you have such traps?' asked Miss Sowerbutts.

'Oh aye,' said the boy. 'They used to be mi granddad's.'

'And you know how to use them, do you?'

'Aye, I do. Mi granddad showed me.'

Miss Sowerbutts thought for a moment. She had arranged for several couples to visit with the estate agent the following week to view the cottage. An unsightly lawn full of molehills would not give a very good impression. And, of course, she could never be certain when Mr Massey might stir himself to visit and rid her of the creatures.

'You won't make a mess of the lawn?' she asked Danny.

'Well, it's in a bit of a mess now, miss, in't it? I can't mek it look much worse.'

'And how much will this cost me?' she asked.

'Nowt.'

'I beg your pardon?'

'Nowt,' repeated the boy. 'It won't cost you owt. Mi grand-dad used to say, "It'd be a sorry world if you din't do somebody a good turn now an' again".'

'Well, Daniel, I suppose I could let you try. When could you set these traps of yours?'

'Later this mornin' if ya want. I've just got to tek these flowers to mi granddad's grave, then I can sooart out yer moles.'

'Very well,' said Miss Sowerbutts, 'but mind you don't make too much of a mess.'

'I'd keep yer cat inside when I'm setting t'traps if I were you, miss. I don't want it gerrin 'urt.'

'I don't let her out,' he was told. 'I keep her in the house all the time.'

A pity, thought the boy, but he said nothing.

★   ★   ★

On his way to the church Danny met Malcolm Stubbins and Ernest Pocock. Malcolm was wearing the red-and-white football strip of Clayton United, with the name of the team captain, DWYER, displayed prominently in large black letters on the back.

'Hey up,' said Malcolm. 'Off to see your girlfriend, are you?'

'No,' replied Danny.

'Who are the flowers for then?'

'I'm purren 'em on mi granddad's grave if you must know.'

'Why?'

'What do ya mean "why"?'

'Well, he's dead, isn't he? He won't know they're there.'

''E might do, an' anyroad it's a sort o' way o' rememberin' 'im when I visit 'is grave.'

'I don't visit my granddad's grave,' Malcolm told him. 'He was a miserable old bugger.'

'Well, mine weren't,' said Danny.

'Do you want to come for a game of footie later?' asked Ernest.

'Naw,' said Danny. 'I said I'd get rid o' some moles in Miss Sowerbutts's lawn after I've been to t'churchyard.'

'Huh!' snorted Malcolm, 'I wouldn't do anything for her. Miserable old bat. She's horrible. She used to make me stand outside her room for ages and shout at me when she was head teacher. I pass her cottage every morning on the way to school and she stands at the window making faces at me. I pull faces back at her. She once came out to tell me off and I told her she couldn't order me about because she wasn't the head teacher up at the school any more. You should have seen her face.'

'I didn't like her either,' agreed Ernest. 'Mrs Devine's a lot better head teacher.'

'She is,' agreed Malcolm.

'Tha din't say that when she first come t'school,' said Danny. 'Yer mam took yer away.'

'That was because my mam and her had a ding-dong and I was moved to Urebank, but it were worse up there and that's why I moved back. Anyway I get on with Mrs Devine now.'

'I hope she's the new head teacher when the two schools join up,' said Ernest. 'My mum reckons that the head teacher at Urebank will be in charge.'

'Richardson!' exclaimed Malcolm. 'He's as bad as old Sowerbutts. He used to make me stand outside his room all day and shout at me as well.'

'My mum went to this meeting about the schools,' Ernest told them, 'and she said everybody there said the head teacher at Urebank would get the job and Mrs Devine would be made his deputy.'

'That's not reight,' said Danny. 'She's a really good 'ead teacher.'

'Well, it won't matter to any of us, will it,' said Malcolm, ''cos we'll be up at the secondary school by then. Anyway, do you want to come and have a game of footie or not?'

'Naw,' said Danny. 'I promised Miss Sowerbutts.'

'Suit yourself,' said Malcolm. 'Come on, Ernie.'

Danny was busy raking up the leaves in the churchyard when a ruddy-complexioned man in a greasy cap and dressed in soiled blue overalls strode between the gravestones.

'What do you think you're doing, Danny Stainthorpe?' asked the man angrily.

'I were just doin' a bit of tidyin' up, Mester Massey,' replied the boy.

'Well, that's my job, so leave off.'

'It needed doin',' Danny told him. 'It's all overgrown.'

'Don't you go telling me what needs doing. I shall do it when I think it should be done and not before.'

'But all these leaves—' began Danny, kicking a pile at his feet.

'Never mind them leaves. Just leave them leaves alone and

take your tools and get off home. Our Clarence will fettle this when I tell him to do so.'

'How can 'e do it wi' a broken arm?' asked Danny.

'He's got another arm, hasn't he? Anyway, it's not your concern, so leave off what you're doing.'

'But t'vicar's wife said—' started Danny.

'I'm not bothered what the vicar's wife said or anyone else for that matter. That's my job and it shall be done when I do it.'

'I don't mind doin' it, Mester Massey,' said Danny.

'Well, I do, so go and dig the doctor's garden if you want something to do. When I get back I don't want to see you here.'

Danny began picking up his tools. He felt it better not to mention that he would be dealing with Miss Sowerbutts's moles when he had finished in the graveyard.

'Go on, look sharpish,' said Mr Massey, making his way to the gate between the grey stone slabs. When he had got to the road Danny shouted after him mischievously, 'How are yer sheep gerrin on, Mester Massey?'

'I'll come back there and give you a thick ear in a minute, you cheeky little devil,' the man shouted back, before walking off grumbling to himself.

Having packed away his tools, Danny was heading for home to get the mole traps when he noticed a figure standing in front of his grandfather's grave. She was a large blonde-haired woman in an olive green coat and long tan-coloured leather boots. A cigarette smouldered in her hand. He went over.

''Ello,' he said.

The woman turned and considered him for a moment. She put the cigarette to her lips and drew upon it, then blew out a cloud of smoke. 'Hello,' she replied without smiling.

'That's mi granddad's grave,' said Danny.

The woman looked at him with a sudden interest. 'Is it?'

''E died last year. I come 'ere every week.'

'So you must be Daniel then,' said the woman.

'Yea, but most people call me Danny.'

The woman looked at the inscription on the tombstone. '"Les Stainthorpe, dearly-loved grandfather",' she said and gave a dry smile. 'He never liked the name Leslie. Always Les. "Call me Les," he would tell people, "never Leslie. I hates the name Leslie," he used to say. "Can't understand for the life of me why my mother called me such a name. Leslie! Sounds like somebody out of a romantic novel".'

Danny cocked his head and looked up at the woman. 'Did ya know mi granddad?' he asked.

'Oh yes, I knew him all right,' she replied. She drew on the cigarette. 'I was married to him.' She looked down at Danny, who had dropped the tools. 'I'm your grandmother.'

'Well, well, well,' said Fred Massey. 'Look what the wind's blown in.'

Maisie Stainthorpe, former barmaid at the Blacksmith's Arms, walked through the door of the village pub like a VIP arriving at some grand reception. She looked around as if she were waiting for someone to greet her.

'Hello Fred,' she replied, laughing. 'I see you're still propping up the public bar, you old reprobate.'

'You're a sight for sore eyes and no mistake,' said Fred.

She looked at the landlord who stood watching her, his arms folded over his chest. 'Hello Harry,' she said with a half-smile.

'Maisie,' he replied, with a small nod of the head.

She perched herself on a stool, crossed her legs and patted her hair. 'Vodka and orange for me,' she said to the landlord, 'and whatever Fred's having.'

'That's very decent of you,' said Fred. 'I'll have a pint.'

'And get one for yourself,' she told the landlord.

'No thanks,' he replied. He gave her a cold look of disapproval.

'So what brings you to Barton then Maisie?' asked Fred.

'I've been to see my husband's grave,' she told him, 'to pay my last respects.'

The landlord began pulling a pint. He shook his head but said nothing. The last time he had seen the woman she had flounced out of the Blacksmith's Arms having been sacked for stealing. He was surprised she had the effrontery to sweep into the pub as if nothing had happened. He was not inclined to enter into pleasantries with her.

'I was a bit put out,' she said, 'that nobody bothered to tell me that Les had died.'

'Why should anyone?' asked the landlord. He stopped what he was doing and leaned over the bar. 'No one thought you'd be interested or bothered enough to come to the funeral.'

'He was my husband, Harry,' she told him.

'Before you ran off with the carpet fitter from Halifax,' said the landlord. He resumed pulling the pint.

'Frank was a senior sales executive for household appliances and he was from Rotherham, if you must know. Anyway, now that he's passed on—'

'He's dead?' interrupted Fred.

'Frank had a serious heart condition. Coronary thrombosis it was that finished him off. Bent down to tie up his shoelaces and collapsed,' she explained. 'It was a blessing that he went so quickly. He didn't feel anything, just keeled over. Left me comfortably off. I have his pension, he was insured, and he'd put a bit aside.' She sniffed. 'I've bought a new apartment in Clayton. It's got everything – all the mod cons, double balcony, three bedrooms and a lovely view of the river and the cathedral.'

'Bully for you,' muttered the landlord, placing the pint of beer on the bar.

She ignored the comment. 'And I want my grandson to come and live with me.'

'Danny!' he exclaimed.

'I've only got the one as far as I know,' she replied.

'I've heard you've not seen the lad since he was a baby,' said the landlord.

'You're wrong there. For your information, I've just seen him. It's true I've not kept in touch, but that was because Frank didn't want me to have anything to do with Les,' she explained. 'He was very particular about it. Course, I wanted to see Danny but what with us both working we couldn't look after a small child. And besides, Frank wasn't keen on kids.' She looked suddenly indignant. 'Anyway, I don't see why I should explain myself to you. And how long am I supposed to wait for my vodka and orange?'

'Well it's good to see you, Maisie,' said Fred as the landlord got her drink. He lowered his voice. 'This place has not been the same since you left. It's like a morgue, and him behind the bar has a face like the back end of a bus on a wet weekday.'

She chuckled. 'I reckon you're the only one in the village who is pleased to see me. You should have seen the reception I got in the village shop. Old Ma Sloughthwaite doesn't change, does she?'

'Your drink,' said the landlord, placing a glass before her.

'I've been down the social services,' she told Fred, 'and explained that I want to look after my grandson.'

'Well, you've not got much chance of that,' said the landlord. 'The lad doesn't know you for a start and he's happy where he is. They're not likely to uproot him, particularly if he doesn't want to go.'

'Since when have you been an expert on adoptions?' asked Maisie sharply. 'I told the social worker that I'll take it to court if I have to. I'm the boy's nearest relation and it's only right that he should come and live with me.'

'I'm with you there Maisie,' agreed Fred. 'Blood's thicker

than water in my book. I mean, when my sister died, didn't I take Clarence in?'

'He was twenty-three,' observed the landlord. 'And I don't think you did him any favours either.'

'Anyway,' continued Fred, ignoring the remark, 'they'll probably not think Dr Stirling is suitable to look after the lad.'

'How do you mean?' asked Maisie.

'Well, he's never at home is he? Always out seeing his patients. He leaves that son of his in the house by himself all the time. You can imagine if he adopts young Danny what two lads can get up to when they're left unsupervised. And of course, Dr Stirling's had his problems with his own son.'

'Has he?' asked Maisie, leaning forward.

'Ran away from home, didn't he?' said Fred. 'Police were called out and there was a big search in the village before the lad turned up late at night all cold and wet and crying his eyes out in the head teacher's garden.'

'You don't say.'

'Now, you're not telling me that things are right at home when your son runs off like that.'

'Thank you Fred,' said Maisie, finishing her drink in one great gulp and easing herself off the bar stool. 'That's very interesting to know.' She glanced at her flashy watch. 'I must be making tracks. Things to do.'

When she had left, the landlord leaned over the bar and thrust his face into Fred's. 'Why don't you keep your big nose out of other people's business?' he barked. 'See what you've stirred up now with your interfering.'

'I was only saying—' began Fred, getting up from the stool. 'Anyway, I shall have to go as well. I've got things to be getting on with.'

'Well don't let me keep you,' said the landlord, 'but before you do, Fred Massey, you can dig into that purse of yours and pay for the drinks. She left without settling up.'

I I

'Well, Danny,' said Dr Stirling at breakfast the following Thursday, 'I have received a letter this morning from Miss Parsons at the Social Services.' Danny stopped chewing and looked up apprehensively. James, who was sitting at the other side of the breakfast table, stopped eating too and looked up. The doctor passed Danny the official-looking letter. 'You can see your name is at the top. You remember Miss Parsons, don't you? She's the social worker we met who arranged for you to be fostered here.'

'Yes, Dr Stirling,' the boy replied, staring at the letter. He bit his lip.

'Well, as you can see, she wants us to go down to see her in her office tomorrow morning. I'll give Mrs Devine a ring and say you won't be in school and explain where you'll be.'

Danny nodded. He managed a smile but the doctor could see it was an effort. The boy could feel his heart beating in slow thumps. 'Why does she want to see us?' he asked.

'Well, I guess she wants to make sure that you are getting on all right here and if you're happy staying with me and James.'

'I am,' said Danny quickly. 'I'm really 'appy.' The boy didn't sound it. He looked anxious.

The doctor smiled. 'That's good to hear. We're happy having you here, aren't we, James?'

His son nodded. 'You bet.'

'I don't want to go anywhere else,' said Danny.

'There's not much chance of that,' said the doctor.

'Are ya sure?'

'Yes, I'm sure. The meeting will be just what's called a formality, to make sure everything is as it should be.'

'So I won't 'ave to move?' asked Danny.

'No, you won't have to move,' Dr Stirling replied. 'Don't look so worried. Everything will be fine, I promise you.'

Danny swallowed nervously. He didn't look convinced. 'Mi granddad din't like letters what came in brown envelopes,' he said. ''E reckoned that they allus spelled trouble.'

'Well, I wouldn't worry your head about this one. It may be that Miss Parsons wants me to sign some papers to make everything legal, so that you can stay here for good.'

'So I can be adopted,' asked Danny, 'an' stay 'ere for ever?'

'Could be,' said Dr Stirling, 'and once those papers are signed, Danny, you're stuck with me and James for good and we're stuck with you and this will officially be your home.'

'That's great,' said James. 'Can I come as well when you go and see Miss Parsons?'

'No,' said his father, 'she just wants to see Danny and me, and anyway you can't go missing school.'

'Please may I come with you?' pleaded James.

'You have had my answer, young man,' said his father, putting on a mock-serious face.

'Ahhh,' sighed his son.

'Did I hear it's a special day for a certain wee fella tomorrow?' said Mrs O'Connor, coming into the kitchen to brew a fresh pot of tea.

'Danny's going to be adopted tomorrow,' said James.

'Let's not count our chickens,' said the doctor. 'Adoption takes a very long time.'

'Well now,' said the housekeeper, 'isn't that just grand. I'll make one of my special coffee and walnut cakes this morning, so I will, and we can celebrate when you get back.' She looked over to the doctor. 'Sure, wouldn't it be a nice thing to ask Mrs Devine around to join us for tea after school?'

'It may be a little premature, Mrs O'Connor,' he told her. 'Let's just wait and see what Miss Parsons has got to say before we crack open the champagne.'

Danny looked up at the doctor. There was sadness and perplexity on the boy's face, something the doctor could not fathom. He would have thought the boy would look really happy at the prospect of staying at Clumber Lodge, rather than seeming sad and thoughtful, but he dismissed any misgivings and ruffled the boy's hair affectionately. 'Come along, Danny, don't look so down in the dumps. There's really nothing to worry about.'

'Miss, where's Danny?' asked Chardonnay.

Elisabeth had just finished marking the register on the Friday morning Dr Stirling and Danny were at the Social Services when the girl, waving her hand in the air, asked the question.

'He's not in today,' the teacher replied.

'Is he ill, miss?'

'No, he's not ill.'

'Because if he is ill,' persisted the girl, 'we could send him a get-well-soon card.'

'No, Chardonnay, Danny is not ill. He just has somewhere important to go to this morning.' She caught sight of James smiling conspiratorially.

'Is he at the dentist's, miss?'

'Chardonnay,' said Elisabeth, 'it's not really anyone's business where Danny is this morning. I am sure he appreciates your concern but we need to get on with the lesson. Now can we all sit up smartly and look this way. This morning we have a very important visitor in school.'

'Miss, we're always having visitors,' said Chardonnay.

'Nobody ever came into school when Miss Sowerbutts was head teacher.'

'I think it's good to have people coming in to see what we are doing,' Elisabeth told her.

'Is it that Mrs Stickleback again?' asked Chantelle.

'No, and her name is Ms Tricklebank,' said Elisabeth. 'This visitor is called Mr Steel and he is a school inspector. He will be coming into our classroom to see what we are doing. He is at present with the infants but he will be joining us before too long. So you all have to be on your very best behaviour, answer his questions clearly and politely and when he leaves he will, I hope, have a really good impression of our school.'

'He's been here before, miss, hasn't he?' asked Eddie Lake.

'Yes, he has.'

'Is it that funny man with squeaky shoes who looks like somebody out of a horror film?' asked Chantelle.

As if on cue, Mr Steel entered the classroom. He was a tall, cadaverous man with sunken cheeks, greyish skin and a mournful countenance, and was dressed in a black suit. He was wonderfully funereal. The HMI carried a black briefcase with a gold crown embossed on the front.

The children stood.

'Good morning,' said the school inspector. His voice had the dark and solemn tones appropriate to a funeral.

'Good morning, inspector,' chanted the children.

'Good morning, Mr Steel,' said Elisabeth. 'There's a chair in the corner of the classroom if you would care to take a seat.'

The school inspector nodded and strode to the back of the room. His shiny black shoes creaked when he walked.

Chardonnay pulled a face and nudged Chantelle, who put her hand over her mouth to stop herself giggling.

'Perhaps, Darren,' said Elisabeth, 'you might like to tell Mr Steel what we are doing today.'

The boy stood, turned to face the inspector and, as if

performing on a stage, took a deep breath and declaimed loudly, 'Today we are finishing off writing our poems, sir.' Elisabeth opened her mouth to explain a little more but the boy continued, as if reciting something rehearsed. 'For the last few weeks we have been looking at a range of poetry and then writing our own. We are going to enter some of them for the School Library Poetry Competition. They can be on any subject we like, they can rhyme but they don't have to and they can be sad or funny, long or short.'

'May I hear some, Mrs Devine?' asked the inspector. He gave a wide smile, like a vampire preparing to sink its teeth into a victim.

'I am sure the children would be delighted to read some of their efforts,' Elisabeth told him.

'Perhaps we might start with this confident young man,' said the inspector, looking at Darren.

'I would prefer someone else reading my poem,' the boy told the inspector. 'It's just that I've got a few problems with my reading.' The inspector raised an eyebrow. 'I've got a kind of dyslexia,' the boy went on to explain, 'which means I find reading and writing quite difficult. It's the spelling and hand-writing which cause me problems. But I'm working on it. Have you heard of dyslexia, sir?'

'I have,' replied the HMI. 'In fact I have a son who has the same difficulty with his writing.'

'Does he?' asked Darren. He took another deep breath. 'It's quite a problem, isn't it?'

'It is,' replied the school inspector.

'Is he getting special help?' asked the boy.

'Come along, Darren,' said Elisabeth. 'Now that you've explained things to Mr Steel' – she smiled and exchanged a glance with the visitor – 'he won't be too worried if you take your time and read it slowly.'

The boy read his poem, 'The Trouble with Words', in a

slow halting voice to a hushed classroom and to the HMI, who leaned forward in his chair and listened intently.

'Excellent,' said Mr Steel when the boy had finished. 'It's very well written. Perhaps you might let me have a copy?'

Darren beamed. 'Yes, sir,' he replied.

'Can I read mine now, miss?' asked Chardonnay, standing up and shouting out excitedly.

Elisabeth looked a little apprehensive, knowing that the girl's poem, which she had not had the chance to read, was about the new baby. She could imagine all the gory details of the birth being put into verse. 'Come along then,' said Elisabeth.

Chardonnay coughed theatrically and announced, 'Bianca's Baby'. She then recited the poem.

> 'Our Bianca's had a baby.
> It's round and red and fat.
> It's got tiny tufts of ginger hair
> Like our neighbour's noisy cat.
>
> Our Bianca's had a baby.
> It's red and fat and round.
> It's like a little sumo wrestler
> And weighs only seven pounds.
>
> Our Bianca's had a baby.
> It's fat and round and red.
> With big green eyes and tiny toes
> And a birthmark on its head.
>
> Our Bianca's had a baby.
> It's round and red and happy.
> And when it's had its dinner
> It always fills its nappy.
>
> Our Bianca's has a baby
> It's red and fat—'

'Thank you very much, Chardonnay,' interrupted Elisabeth. 'That was very good and I thought you did really well getting all those rhymes.'

'I've not finished yet, miss,' the girl told the teacher. 'There're another three verses.'

'Well, I think we will give some of the other children in the class a chance.'

The girl looked at Mr Steel. 'Do you want a copy of my poem as well?' she asked.

'Indeed I do,' replied the school inspector. 'It was most interesting.' He turned to Malcolm Stubbins. 'Would you like to read your poem, young man?' asked the inspector.

'No,' came the blunt reply.

'Come along, Malcolm,' said Elisabeth.

'I don't want to, miss,' he mumbled. 'It's daft.'

'I'm sure it's not,' said Mr Steel.

'It is,' said the boy.

'I would really like to hear it,' said the inspector.

'Please, Malcolm,' said Elisabeth.

The boy sighed and read his poem slowly, head down over the desk and with a finger under each word.

'When I play football
I feel different.
I can't explain it.
I forget about everything around me.
I just go loose.
When I've got the ball
And I'm running down the pitch
And I see the goal
And I hear people cheering.
I can't explain it
But I feel really good inside.'

The class clapped and the boy coloured up.

'Very good,' said Mr Steel. 'Perhaps I might have a copy of your poem too.'

In the head teacher's office at lunchtime, Mr Steel gave Elisabeth the feedback on what he had observed that morning.

'The boy Malcolm who read the poem about football,' said the inspector. 'I remember seeing that young man when I visited the school when Miss Sowerbutts was the head teacher. He was a particularly difficult boy, as I recall.'

'Yes, he has had his moments, has Malcolm,' said Elisabeth, 'but he's settled down now and football has been the making of him. His one ambition is to become a professional player, and the way he's performing I think it's very likely he will achieve it.'

'Well, it seems there's been something of a transformation in the boy,' said the inspector.

Mr Steel went on to tell Elisabeth he had been most impressed with the high standard of the work, the quality of the teaching, the children's behaviour, the range of extra-curricular activities and the bright and cheerful state of the premises. He thanked her for the copies of the poems he had heard that morning, and promised to write to the children to thank them too.

'And where is your next port of call?' Elisabeth asked.

'Just down the road,' Mr Steel replied. 'I have an appointment at Urebank. I have heard it is proposed that it will be amalgamated with this school some time later this year.'

'Yes,' said Elisabeth.

'And do you know Mr Richardson, the head teacher there?' the inspector asked.

'I can't say I know him,' Elisabeth replied, 'but I have spoken to him on a number of occasions.'

'Well, I hope things work out for you, Mrs Devine,' Mr

Steel said. 'I shall of course send a copy of my written report of my visit to yourself, the Chair of Governors and to the Education Office.'

On his way out Mr Steel passed Chardonnay, in her PE kit and bright trainers, heading for the school hall. 'The vicar's in today,' she told the school inspector. 'He's teaching us how to do pole dancing.'

The inspector's mouth dropped open. 'Pole dancing!' he repeated.

'Chardonnay means maypole dancing,' explained Elisabeth.

The school inspector threw back his head and guffawed with laughter.

Elisabeth called a staff meeting after school to discuss the inspector's feedback. It was a good-humoured meeting, since Mr Steel's comments were entirely positive, save for a few minor issues and suggestions. Miss Brakespeare was in an unusually jaunty mood. She was wearing a new outfit which was a fraction too tight for her: a powder-blue, polyester two-piece suit which crackled when she moved. She had also had her hair neatly permed and her nails painted a pale pink. Elisabeth smiled when she recalled again the time she had first met her deputy head teacher, that dowdy, dumpy little woman. How she had changed.

'Although he looks so dark and daunting,' Miss Wilson was saying, 'I found Mr Steel quite nice. Rather more sympathetic than that Ms Tricklebank, who hardly said a word and never smiled. Mr Steel wasn't as stuffy as I first imagined. I have to admit that I was a little wary when he came into the classroom, after what happened the last time he came in and a child was sick all over him.'

'Yes,' said Mrs Robertshaw, 'when he arrived in my room on his previous visit you might guess that it was Oscar who drew everybody's attention to the smell. And I agree with you,

Rebecca, he was a whole lot more encouraging than that Ms Tricklebank. I don't think she was particularly impressed with what she observed in my room.'

'Anyway,' continued the teacher of the infants, 'he was talking to one of the children for quite some time. I could see little Stevie was getting upset but he just stood there looking up at the inspector as if glued to the spot. Then he burst into floods of tears.'

'Well, I suppose he was frightened, a big man like that all in black,' said Miss Brakespeare. 'I know when I first met him he put the fear of God into me.'

'Anyhow,' continued Miss Wilson, 'he told Stevie to go back to his seat but the child just stood there crying his eyes out. So I told him to go and sit down. "I can't, miss," he sobbed, "this big mister is standing on my shoelaces." Well, even Mr Steel had to laugh.'

'In my room,' said Mrs Robertshaw, 'he spent most of his time interviewing Oscar or the other way round. They sat in the reading corner chatting away like old friends.'

'What about?' asked Miss Brakespeare.

'I did happen to overhear,' admitted Mrs Robertshaw. 'He asked Oscar how he felt he was getting on with his studies.'

'And what did Oscar say?' asked the deputy head teacher.

'The boy was very complimentary actually,' replied the teacher of the lower juniors, 'and said he was progressing – and that's the word he used – very well. Then he said that he had suggested certain improvements but they were not being taken up.'

'That sounds like Oscar,' said Elisabeth. 'And what improvements were these?'

'He said he was into conservation at the moment, having read a book on carbon footprints, and thought the school should install double glazing, install a heat pump (I have not the slightest idea what one of those is) and solar panels, fit low-energy light bulbs and place bricks in the cisterns in the boys' toilets to conserve water. He also mentioned that it would be a good idea to have a windmill on the school playing field to utilise wind power.'

Elisabeth smiled and shook her head. 'He's one in a million, is Oscar,' she said.

'He also mentioned something about putting ping-pong balls down the toilet bowls,' added Mrs Robertshaw. 'I don't know what that was all about.'

'I do,' Elisabeth told her, 'but it's a long story and one not to be raised with the caretaker. Well, the school inspector certainly seems to have taken Oscar's words to heart, because he does mention in his report that we might consider being a little more environmentally friendly. Now if there is nothing else—'

'There is, actually,' said Miss Brakespeare, smiling widely. She looked the epitome of happiness.

'Yes, Miriam, what is it?' asked Elisabeth.

'I shall be retiring at the end of next term,' she announced. 'And I'm getting married.'

Dr Stirling could sense that things were not right when Miss Parsons and her colleague came out of the office to greet him that morning. He could see it in their eyes. Miss Parsons's solemn voice confirmed his unease.

'Good morning, Dr Stirling,' she said, shaking his hand. She turned to the boy. 'Hello, Danny.' She gave a weak smile.

''Ello, miss,' he replied cheerfully. His eyes shone like polished glass.

'Dr Stirling,' said Miss Parsons, 'may I have a word with you by yourself? Danny, I'm going to ask you to sit for a moment with Mrs Talbot. You remember Mrs Talbot, you met her the last time you were here?'

'Yes, miss.' A sudden anxiety darkened the boy's face.

'She's going to look after you for a moment in her office next door while I have a word with Dr Stirling. All right?'

'Yes, miss.'

Dr Stirling touched Miss Parsons's arm. 'Is there something wrong?' he asked when Danny had gone.

'I afraid something has come up,' he was told.

'What?'

'If you would like to come into my office, I'll explain.'

There was a woman in the room staring out of the window. She had scarlet lips and startling bright blonde hair that was black at the roots. She wore a coat as red as a pillar-box.

'This is Dr Stirling,' said the social worker. 'Please take a seat, Dr Stirling.'

The woman glanced at him and gave a small nod. It was a momentary look, level and unblinking.

'Good morning,' said the doctor, wondering who this strange-looking woman could be.

The social worker sat at her desk and turned to the woman. 'As I mentioned,' she said, 'Dr Stirling has been taking care of Danny since the boy's grandfather died.' She turned to the doctor. 'This is Mrs Stainthorpe,' she said.

'Stainthorpe?' repeated Dr Stirling.

'That's right,' said the woman. 'I was married to Les Stainthorpe. Daniel's my grandson.'

'I thought that you had remarried and moved away,' said the doctor.

'I moved away but I never got remarried,' the woman told him, with a hard, impenetrable expression on her face. 'As I said, Daniel's my grandson and I'm here—'

'One moment,' interrupted Miss Parsons, 'if I might just come in here and explain the situation to Dr Stirling?'

'Suit yourself,' said the woman, reaching into her handbag and producing a packet of cigarettes.

'This is a non-smoking building,' explained Miss Parsons. 'I'm sorry.'

'Not as sorry as I am,' replied the woman with a faint twist of the lips. 'I'm dying for a ciggie.' She thrust the packet back in her bag.

'Mrs Stainthorpe,' continued Miss Parsons, 'would like Danny to stay with her.'

'To come and live with me,' corrected the woman, seizing on the remark with alacrity. 'Stay with me? Sounds as if he's coming on holiday. I want Daniel to come and live with me for good.'

Dr Stirling bit his bottom lip and was about to reply, but thought better of it and looked down at his feet. The social worker remained silent.

The woman, seizing the opportunity afforded by their silence, continued. 'I'm his only blood relation, after all, and I don't think it's right that he should be brought up by a single man.'

'That is of no consequence, Mrs Stainthorpe,' said the social worker. 'It doesn't matter whether adoptive parents are married, single or gay, just so long as they can provide a child with a safe, secure and loving home.'

The woman sniffed and raised an eyebrow.

'Mrs Stainthorpe has recently moved back into the area,' Miss Parsons told the doctor.

'After Frank – he was my partner – passed on,' explained the woman, 'I decided to come back to my roots.' She smoothed her dyed straw blonde hair and sniffed again. 'I've bought a brand-new, purpose-built property in Clayton, in De Courcey Apartments, state of the ark it is, overlooking the river and the cathedral with all mod cons. Very select. Frank left me well provided for. He was well insured. There's a spare room what Daniel can have.'

'I thought his grandfather's wish was that he should come and live with me and my son?' said the doctor quietly, looking at the social worker.

'Well, it might have been Les's wish,' said Mrs Stainthorpe, 'but he's no longer here, is he? I'm Daniel's grandmother and by rights the lad should be with me.'

'But as I understand it, Mrs Stainthorpe, you haven't seen Danny since he was a baby,' said Dr Stirling.

The woman's face distorted into an expression of chill disapproval. 'There were reasons for that. I wanted to keep in touch and see how the lad was getting on, and many was the time I thought of getting in contact with him, but, as I've said, there were reasons.' There was a silence as both the doctor and the social worker looked at her. 'Not that I have to explain myself to either of you two. If you must know, Frank didn't want kids about the place and anyway there wasn't the room and I had a full-time job. I couldn't take care of Daniel, but now I can. I've retired and I'm in a position to give him a good home and that's what I intend to do.'

'But you have never been part of his life, Mrs Stainthorpe,' said Dr Stirling.

'I've explained why,' she said.

'But the boy doesn't know you,' said Dr Stirling.

'He soon will,' she retorted. 'Frank didn't want kids, as I said, and he was not keen on me keeping contact with Les. Now Frank's dead and Les's dead, the situation is different and I want my grandson to come and live with me.'

'But Mrs Stainthorpe—' began Dr Stirling.

'Anyway, Les Stainthorpe was not his real grandfather,' she interrupted. Her face flushed with a kind of triumph as she played her trump card. 'So he wasn't in any position to say what should happen to the lad. It was Frank who was Tricia's real dad. Les went on the birth certificate for appearances' sake but he never fathered Tricia, not that I ever told him as much. He always thought she was his daughter. 'Course there were those what thought different. That big-mouthed gossip in the village store for a start. Anyway, Frank was Tricia's father and Daniel's grandfather, though he never knew it either.' She turned to Miss Parsons. 'I don't see why we are talking about this. Danny should be with me. End of discussion.'

'Danny is very settled where he is, Mrs Stainthorpe,' said the social worker. 'He took his grandfather's death very badly and is now just about getting over it. He is doing well at school, has a close friend in Dr Stirling's son and is very happy.'

'I'm not as green as I might look,' said the woman. 'I have a right to have my grandson with me. I've taken legal advice and there's no way a court of law will give custody to a single man not related to him, instead of his grandmother.'

'It's not quite as cut and dry as that,' said Miss Parsons. 'The law does not recognise any rights grandparents think they might have. What it does do is take account of the child's wishes and also of my recommendation.'

'Well, we'll see what the court says, won't we, if you try and prevent me from looking after my grandson.'

'What about Danny?' asked the doctor.

'What about him?' she asked.

'He wants to stay where he is.'

'Well, in my book, adults know what's best for children. He'll soon settle in at Clayton and when he gets to know me he'll like it. We'll get on like a house on fire, see if we don't.'

'I am going to suggest that we take things slowly,' said Miss Parsons. 'I think to move Danny from his familiar surroundings at the present time could be very stressful for him. He's been through quite a lot lately and is still grieving for his grandfather. I think we should leave him where he is for the time being and let him get to know you, Mrs Stainthorpe. You could take him out for the day, and perhaps he could stay at your flat overnight and later at weekends.'

'Apartment,' she corrected. 'It's an apartment.'

'Apartment,' repeated Miss Parsons. 'As I said, I think it would be very disruptive for him to move at the moment. In a situation like this,' she said calmly, 'Danny must come first. His interests are paramount. His welfare, his emotional well-being and his happiness are the most important considerations. Dr Stirling has provided for Danny a very stable home and—'

'Has he?' interrupted Mrs Stainthorpe. Her eyes narrowed imperceptibly.

'Yes, of course he has.'

'Well, from what I've heard it's not that stable.'

'And what have you heard?' asked Dr Stirling, bristling.

'I believe your own son ran away because he was unhappy,' said Mrs Stainthorpe levelly.

'James ran away because he didn't want to start his new school,' explained Dr Stirling, his face becoming flushed. 'Everything's fine now. It was just a misunderstanding.'

'Well, he can't have been that happy if he ran off, could he?'

'Look Mrs Stainthorpe—' began Dr Stirling.

'And from what I've heard you're never at home, what with dealing with all the medical emergencies, and the boys are left unsupervised. That's not very satisfactory in my book. Perhaps Miss Parsons wasn't aware of that.'

The senior social worker sighed and shook her head. 'This is getting us nowhere,' she said. 'As I suggested, I think Danny should get to know you, Mrs Stainthorpe, before any decisions are made about his future. Half-term is coming up, and this might be a good time for Danny to spend a few days with you.'

'I can't be shuttling over here taking him out for day trips and getting to know him,' said the woman. 'For a start I can't drive, and I'm not forking out on taxi fares every time I want to see him.'

'Perhaps Dr Stirling might—'

'I should be happy to bring Danny over for visits,' said the doctor, forcing himself to stay calm. 'I do agree with Miss Parsons that it seems sensible for Danny to get to know you, Mrs Stainthorpe.'

'I am sure Mrs Stainthorpe appreciates that, Dr Stirling,' said Miss Parsons. 'I know that she, like you, has the boy's best interests at heart.'

'Do you mind not talking about me as if I'm not here!' snapped Mrs Stainthorpe. 'Of course I want the best for Daniel. I don't need you to tell him that. As I said, I think the best place for him is with his grandmother. Having said that, I'm not unreasonable and I'll agree to a few visits for us to get to know each other if that's what it takes.'

'Shall we get Danny in and see what he thinks?' asked Miss Parsons.

'There's nothing you or any trumped-up social worker can do to stop me having my grandson live with me,' said the woman aggressively when Miss Parsons had left the room.

Dr Stirling listened in helpless anger. He looked out of the window, refusing to meet her eye.

12

Danny came into the office accompanied by the two social workers.

'Now, Danny,' said Miss Parsons cheerfully, resuming her seat behind her desk. 'Sit down over here.' The boy looked confused. 'I think you know this lady?'

'Hello, Daniel,' said the woman.

''Ello,' he mumbled. He sat on the edge of a chair looking lost and bewildered.

'I wasn't aware that you knew your grandmother, Danny,' said Dr Stirling gently.

'We met in the churchyard the other day,' said the woman. 'I went to pay my respects at my husband's grave. We had a nice little chat, didn't we, Daniel?'

The boy didn't answer. His fists were clenched tightly with anxiety, for he knew by the expressions on the faces of Dr Stirling and Miss Parsons that something was clearly wrong.

'Danny,' said Miss Parsons, 'your grandmother would like you to go and stay with her.'

'Live with me,' said the woman sharply.

The boy's head jerked in the direction of Dr Stirling. He looked at the doctor in slow bewilderment, seemingly unable to understand exactly what she was saying.

'Live wi' 'er?' he repeated. He looked dazed, as if he had just woken out of a sleep.

'That's right, Danny,' the doctor replied. 'Your grandmother would like you to go and live with her.'

Danny sat up straight in his chair and pushed the hair out of his eyes. 'I don't want to,' he said determinedly. He looked Dr Stirling in the eye. 'You told me I wouldn't 'ave' to move. You told me.' He sounded desperate. 'You said I could stay wi' you.'

'I know what I said, Danny,' replied the doctor, 'and I thought—'

'Well, Daniel,' his grandmother interrupted, 'what children want isn't always what they get, and—'

'Mrs Stainthorpe,' cut in Miss Parsons, 'if we could just take this slowly. It is very difficult for Danny to take this in. This has come as a shock to him.' She turned to the boy and smiled. 'Now, your grandmother would like you to go and see her and stay with her in Clayton just for a while to get to know her.'

'Well, I don't want to,' said the boy. 'I'm 'appy weer I am.' He looked at the social worker. 'You told me when Dr Stirling wanted to foster me that ya wanted to mek sure that I'd be 'appy an' like it weer I was to stay. You said that. You told me.' His eyes began to fill up. 'Why do people say things they don't mean? I won't be 'appy if I leave.'

His grandmother made a clucking noise with her tongue. 'Just like Les. Stubborn,' she remarked under her breath.

'Mrs Stainthorpe, please,' said Miss Parsons. She looked at Danny. 'Of course we want to make sure that you are happy. I think if you were to give it a try you might like it. Your grandmother has a nice apartment in Clayton over-looking the river—'

'And the cathedral,' added the woman.

'There's a cinema,' continued the social worker, 'a bowling alley, ice rink and swimming pool nearby and there are lots of things for a young man like you to do. You would have your own room and—'

'Why don't grown-ups ever listen to what kids say?' Danny

interrupted, rubbing his eyes. 'I don't want all that! I want to stay 'ere in t'country with Dr Stirling an' James an' stop at t'village school.' He looked appealingly at Dr Stirling. 'Please.'

'You would be able to come back and visit, Danny,' said the doctor feebly.

'You as well,' said Danny in a small voice. 'Ya want me to go?'

'Of course I don't want you to go,' said the doctor vehemently. 'I want you to stay. I want to adopt you.' The sadness and perplexity on the boy's face matched his own.

'Then why 'ave I got to go?' He gripped the arms of the chair. He looked at the social worker. 'Why can't I stay weer I am?'

'Look, Danny,' said Miss Parsons, 'it's not as simple as that. This is your grandmother and—'

'Can I be allowed to say something—' began Mrs Stainthorpe in a combative tone of voice.

'Not at the moment,' said Miss Parsons sharply, keeping her eyes on Danny. 'I think it would be a really good idea if you were to go—'

'No!' exclaimed the boy.

'—If you were go and spend a little time with your grandmother and get to know her and see where she lives. You can remain with Dr Stirling at present and we can see how things go.'

'No!' interrupted the boy again, his voice wobbling.

'Just for a few days, to go on outings with your grandmother and spend a couple of weekends with her and see how you get on,' continued Miss Parsons. 'You might really like living in Clayton, and if you were to go and live there eventually you would still be able to come back and see your friend.'

'Well, I don't want to,' sniffed Danny. 'Ya can't mek me.' Then he looked at the doctor again. 'Can they?'

'I think you should give it a try, Danny,' he said. 'I want you to stay. I'd give anything for you to stay, you know that, and so would James, but I agree with what Miss Parsons says.'

'Yer goin' to let 'em tek me away?' he asked quietly. He wiped a glistening tear from his cheek with the back of his hand.

'You're not going to prison,' his grandmother told him bluntly.

'You will stay with us for the time being and visit your grandmother,' said the doctor, 'and get to know her, and we will see how things go.' He knew what he was saying was unconvincing.

Danny began to cry. They were quick choking sobs.

'Come along, you're a big boy, Daniel,' said his grandmother. 'I think we can well do without the waterworks.'

'The boy is upset!' exclaimed Dr Stirling angrily. 'It's come as a shock to him. He's just got settled and now he has this upheaval.'

'Excuse me, doctor,' retorted Mrs Stainthorpe. 'You're not talking to one of your patients now. I really can't see this upheaval what you're on about. Daniel's coming to live with his grandmother, which is only right and proper, in a nice new apartment with his own room and everything. Most children would be happy as sandboys with that.'

'I would remind you, Mrs Stainthorpe,' replied the doctor, getting heated, 'that—'

'Let's stay calm about this,' said Miss Parsons quickly, realising that the meeting could well deteriorate into a squabbling match. 'We are all concerned with Danny's welfare. Perhaps you might take Danny for a drink, Mrs Talbot.'

When the boy had gone and the door was closed, the social worker clasped her hands together and looked down at the desk. 'It really doesn't help getting worked up about this in front of the boy. Dr Stirling has been good enough to look after him and the boy has been happy. He was to be adopted.'

'Yes, I know all that,' said Mrs Stainthorpe dismissively. 'Now, we can talk about this until the cows come home but it doesn't change those facts. I want Daniel living with me and live with me he will.'

The social worker looked at Dr Stirling. 'What I suggest is that we arrange a few visits. For the moment we will have to put the adoption on hold.'

'There'll be no adoption,' added Mrs Stainthorpe, narrowing her eyes and pursing her mouth.

'Very well,' said Dr Stirling, rising from his chair. 'I can see that anything else I have to say is of no consequence. I will bring Danny over to you next weekend.'

'No, I'll collect him,' she replied. 'I can get a bus from Clayton.' Then she added pointedly, 'I wouldn't want to put you out.'

'Until Saturday, then,' said Dr Stirling coldly.

'I could do with a cigarette,' sighed the woman. 'I'm gagging.' She dug in her handbag and produced a gold powder compact, flicked it open, peered into the small mirror and dabbed her nose. 'I'll see you next weekend,' she told Dr Stirling, as if dismissing him from her presence.

Despite the doctor's efforts to get Danny to talk, the boy was silent all the way back home and stared sadly out of the car window.

'Where is he, Dr Stirling?' asked Mrs O'Connor. It was later that day.

'Danny's gone up to his room,' the doctor told her. 'He said he wanted to be by himself. He wants to think things over.'

'It's a crying shame,' said the housekeeper. 'That's what it is, a crying shame. His grandmother has had nothing to do with the lad all these years, never sent him so much as a present on his birthday or a card, and then she comes swanning back into his life like some distant relative at the reading of the will, just as he gets settled, and wants to whisk him away. It shouldn't be allowed to happen.'

The doctor sighed. 'Yes, it has upset Danny greatly, but I guess your old Irish grandmother would remark that blood is thicker than water.'

'My grandmother, bless her sainted soul, would have said that if the wheel's not broken it doesn't need mending. Danny's happy where he is and he should be allowed to stay here.'

'Yes, Mrs O'Connor,' he said thoughtfully, 'he should.'

The doctor stared out of the window. The garden, with its dead flowers and skeletal trees, looked dark and brooding and reflected his mood.

He had tried to talk to Danny when they had arrived home after their visit to the Social Services, but to no avail. The boy's heart was so full he couldn't bring himself to speak. He had listened, head down, as the doctor tried to reassure him that he could be happy in his new home.

'I'm so sorry, Danny, that things have turned out like this,' said Dr Stirling. He struggled to think of the words to say. 'It's been such a pleasure, more than that, having you stay here, and you know James and I really wanted you to become part of our family. I just wish I could change things but I can't.'

Danny nodded but kept his head lowered.

'You know that you will always be welcome here,' said Dr Stirling, 'to come and visit whenever you want. You know that, Danny, don't you?'

'Yes,' he said almost inaudibly.

They sat there in silence, both feeling wretched.

'Can I go to mi room please?' Danny asked finally.

'Of course you can,' replied the doctor, 'and we will keep it as your room for when you come to visit.'

'I don't think I'll be allowed,' the boy said in a small voice as he got to his feet.

* * *

'I mean,' said the housekeeper that afternoon, 'does Danny not have a say in all this? Do his wishes count for nothing?'

'He's still a minor, Mrs O'Connor,' the doctor told her. 'The social worker listened to what he had to say and I could see she sympathised with him, but she has to do what the law demands, and his grandmother, were she to take the matter to court, would undoubtedly win. If I challenged the decision and lost, that would be another terrible disappointment for the boy. He would have his hopes dashed a second time. I was advised not to pursue the matter. The law's the law.'

'Well, as my grandmother would say, "If that's the law then the law is an ass".'

The doctor smiled. 'I think that was Charles Dickens actually,' he told her, raising a small smile.

'Well, this Dickens must have got it off her,' said the housekeeper.

'The social worker has a job to do. It's difficult and challenging and I guess sometimes heartbreaking, but they have to do what they think is right and what the law demands.'

'And they think this is right, uprooting the lad? I thought social workers had to have the child's best interests at heart. Doesn't sound like that to me.'

'To be fair, Mrs O'Connor, I think Miss Parsons was on my side. I am sure she would have preferred Danny staying where he is. Her hands are tied. It was suggested that for a trial period Danny should go and stay with his grandmother for a few weekends. Miss Parsons will see how he is getting on and make some visits. You never know, Danny may like it in Clayton and when he's got to know his grandmother he could be happy there.'

'He'll feel about as much at home with that woman as the Pope would in a lap-dancing club,' observed the housekeeper. 'Does it sound as if Danny will like it there, stuck in a flat?' she asked bluntly. 'I know Maisie Proctor of old, Dr Stirling, and

Gervase Phinn

she's only bothered about one person – herself. She led poor Les Stainthorpe a merry old dance, so she did. Made eyes at him, courted him, married him, robbed him and then ran off with another man. It's the oldest game in the book, is that. She was a nasty piece of work when she served behind the bar in the Blacksmith's Arms, making eyes at all the men customers until she was sacked for putting her hand in the till. There's nothing you can tell me about Maisie Proctor.'

'She might have changed,' said the doctor.

'Can a crab be taught to walk straight?' said Mrs O'Connor.

Dr Stirling knew that the housekeeper was probably right.

'And I'll tell you something else,' said Mrs O'Connor, her face red with anger, 'she's only in it for the money, so she is. Wants to get her greedy hands on the family allowance and any other benefits she can squeeze out of the system.'

'I really don't think that is the case,' replied Dr Stirling. 'I'd like to think that now she is by herself—'

'By herself?'

'Yes, the man she was living with has died.'

'The brush salesman from Rotherham, the one she ran off with to marry?'

'She never remarried,' the doctor told her.

'Typical.'

'I guess now she is on her own she would like her grandson with her,' said the doctor.

'Well, as I've said, I think it's a crying shame, so I do,' said Mrs O'Connor. She turned, headed for the door and shaking her head, said as a parting shot, 'And you mark my words Dr Stirling, it will end in tears.'

'May I come in?' Dr Stirling stood in the porch at Wisteria Cottage that evening.

'Of course,' said Elisabeth. 'Come through.'

'You've got the place looking lovely,' he said, walking into the snug sitting-room with its heavy burgundy drapes, old oak dresser and cream-coloured sofa and chairs. A fire of logs blazed and crackled in the hearth. 'It's so warm and cosy in here.'

Elisabeth slipped her arm through his and reached up to kiss him on the cheek. 'You look just about done in,' she said. 'Sit down and I'll get you a drink. Something a bit stronger than tea, I think.'

'It's my turn now to burden you with my problems,' he told her, flopping on to the sofa and sighing.

Elisabeth poured a whisky from the decanter on the dresser and placed the glass in his hand, then sat down beside him. She brushed another kiss against his cheek and interlaced her fingers through his. 'So, what is the problem?' she asked.

'Danny,' he told her. He took a sip from the glass.

'Danny?' she repeated. 'I thought you went with him to the Social Services today to sort out the adoption?'

'That's what I thought,' he replied, 'but I am afraid it wasn't to be.'

'Why, what happened?'

'Danny's grandmother was there.'

'His grandmother? She hasn't seen him since he was a baby.'

'Well, she's turned up like the wicked witch at the christening.'

'I gather from that that you were not impressed with her?'

'No, I wasn't.'

'What's she like?' asked Elisabeth.

'Loud, belligerent, bad-tempered. I found her a most unpleasant woman and I could see Danny didn't take to her either. She wants him to go and live with her.'

'Surely she can't just appear out of the blue and whisk him away, can she?'

'I really don't know,' said Dr Stirling, 'but she's a determined woman and looks as if she's spoiling for a fight over custody.'

'What did they say at the Social Services?'

He breathed out noisily. 'Just that Danny ought to get to know her. I guess they'll decide what they think should happen, in due course.'

'Does that mean you won't be adopting Danny?' asked Elisabeth.

'It's been put on hold until things are sorted out,' he told her. He finished the whisky.

'Poor Michael,' she said, squeezing his hand.

'Poor Danny,' he said quietly.

'What are you going to do?'

'Following the meeting with the social worker and Danny's grandmother, I made a few enquiries and spoke to a solicitor friend of mine. Stephen Smith works in the family court and is one of the best lawyers around. It seems that a court of law might very well grant his grandmother custody, if it was taken that far. She can provide a good stable home for the boy and, of course, she is his closest relative. I just feel so low and helpless.'

'And how is Danny taking all this?' asked Elisabeth.

'He's devastated, poor lad,' replied the doctor. 'He's gone quiet, just like he did when his grandfather died. He went up to his room and wouldn't come down for his tea. James couldn't get a word out of him either and he rarely spoke to Mrs O'Connor. I think he feels I have let him down.'

'No, Michael, he can't think that,' she said. 'You were so good to take him in.' She snuggled up to him and rested her head on his shoulder. 'You're the most caring person I know. Danny doesn't think you let him down.'

'I'm afraid he does,' said Dr Stirling. 'You see, I promised the boy only this morning that he had nothing to worry about and that he would be staying with us at Clumber Lodge. I could see he was troubled about something. I just thought it was nerves but now I know why he was worried. I think he sensed things might not work out. He'd met his grandmother in the graveyard. I didn't know anything about this, he never told me. I think Danny had an idea she might cause trouble for him. You should have seen the look in his eyes, wide and frightened like a caged animal. As I said, the boy is devastated and I am afraid there is nothing I can do.'

Elisabeth stroked his hair and touched the curl at the back of his neck.

'A few more grey hairs in there,' he said, raising a smile.

'It makes you look very distinguished,' she replied.

There was a comfortable quiet between them. They sat holding hands, staring at the fire and thinking.

'James will be upset too,' said Elisabeth finally.

'Yes, he is. He just doesn't know what to say or do.'

'You never know,' she said reassuringly. 'Danny might be able to stay with you, and if he does go to live with his grand-mother he might settle.'

'You haven't met her.'

'I do hope that things work out for Danny,' said Elisabeth. 'I promised his grandfather that I would look out for him. I guess he may feel that if anyone has let him down it's me.'

'Not at all. Anyway, I thought you ought to know the situation.'

'Thank you for letting me know,' said Elisabeth.

'How are things at school?' asked Dr Stirling, changing the subject.

'We had a short inspection today that went off very well, thank goodness,' Elisabeth told him. 'It was the inspector who visited before, the one who looks like an undertaker. One of the pupils said he looked as he had walked out of a horror film. She wasn't far wrong. Looks of course can be deceptive and he turned out to be really positive and supportive.'

'That's good to hear,' said the doctor. 'His report should go very much in your favour when they come to decide on the headship of the new set-up. Any news on the proposed amalgamation, by the way?'

'Yes. I received a letter from the Education Office yesterday,' said Elisabeth. 'They are going to convene further meetings for the staff of Barton and Urebank, to explain their plans for the merger of the two schools.'

'So they are definitely going ahead with it then?' asked the doctor.

'It appears so,' Elisabeth replied. 'The Director of Education says that a newly constituted governing body will be appointed, with representatives from the two schools. I hope you will agree to be on it.'

'I don't think I can,' he replied.

'But you must!' exclaimed Elisabeth.

'James will be at secondary school next September,' Dr Stirling told her, 'so as a parent governor I won't be eligible and neither will Mrs Pocock.'

'That's a bit of a blow. I hope the Reverend Atticus – Archdeacon Atticus, I mean – will be on it. He has been a great ally.'

'And then there's the formidable Lady Wadsworth,' added the doctor. 'I wouldn't like her as an adversary.'

'I just hope the major comes up trumps this time,' said Elisabeth.

'I had better go,' said Dr Stirling. 'The boys will be wondering where I am. Mrs O'Connor's looking after them and she'll want to be away.'

'Can't you stay a while longer?' asked Elisabeth.

'Not really,' he replied, 'much as I would like to.' He turned her face to his and kissed her gently on the lips. 'Thank you for listening. What would I do without you, Elisabeth Devine?'

★ ★ ★

John, wrapped up in his thick coat, scarf and gloves and wearing wellington boots, held Elisabeth's hand tightly as they walked slowly down the small gravel path that skirted Forest View. It had started to drizzle, and both mother and son were getting wet. Elisabeth had suggested to John's teacher that she should use an umbrella, but he had advised against it. Her son, like many autistic people, was a person of strict routine and got upset if those routines were broken in any way. Umbrellas frightened the boy and anyway, he liked walking in the rain.

As they walked, Elisabeth kept up a stream of conversation, telling her son about the events of the week, the children at the school, her hopes and concerns. She told him about Danny and how upset the boy must feel with the prospect of going to live somewhere else.

'He's been through such a difficult time,' she told her son, 'losing his grandfather, not knowing what would happen to him, then getting settled only to be uprooted. He's been so quiet and distant at school. It's so sad to see him like this. He's usually such a bubbly, friendly little boy.'

When she paused John looked down and cocked his head to one side as if waiting for her to continue. Clearly, she thought, he was listening. Occasionally he stopped to stare at a puddle before stamping in the water. He then stared in fascination at the effect, his face expressionless, his brow furrowed as if in deep thought.

The discussion Elisabeth had had with the head teacher that morning had been more reassuring than the last one. There had been no repeat of John's outburst, and Mr Williams had reported some positive signs. The speech and language therapist, who had been working closely with John for the past few weeks, was very pleased with the boy's progress. As she told the head teacher, for most children this improvement would be a minuscule step but for John, with his condition, it was a giant's stride. The therapist had been working intensively at the boy's pace and level, taking it slowly step by step in trying to encourage some communication, using what is called picture exchange, showing him images and representations. There had been an encouraging reaction.

That morning John was his usual calm self.

'Mr Williams said I would find you here,' said Dr Stirling, meeting Elisabeth on the path and giving her a peck on the lips. 'You ought to be inside. You're getting soaking wet.'

'Oh, hello, Michael,' she said happily. 'We're going for a walk, aren't we, John, and we like the rain.'

'May I join you?' asked the doctor.

'Of course, if you don't mind getting wet, but don't stand too close. John likes splashing in the puddles.'

The boy continued to stare at the ground but held out his hand in the doctor's direction.

Dr Stirling took his hand.

'You are very honoured,' said Elisabeth. 'It's usually only me and John's teacher who are allowed to hold his hand. So what brings you here this Saturday?'

'To see a couple of the children,' he told her. 'I was called out this morning.'

'Nothing serious, I hope,' she said.

'No, thank goodness,' he replied. 'One little rascal jumped off a table. I think he thought he could fly. No bones broken, just a few bruises and a sprained ankle. The other child reacted to some new medication. She seems all right now.' He looked at John. 'This young man appears to be doing well.'

'He is,' said Elisabeth. 'There's been an improvement in several things. He seems to understand a whole lot more.'

'That's good to hear.'

'And how's Danny?' she asked. 'He's staying with his grandmother this weekend, isn't he?'

'Yes, she's collecting him this afternoon. He looked on the verge of tears when I told him.'

John stopped and stared at a large puddle.

'I suppose those at Social Services thought that the sooner he gets used to her and the new situation the better,' said Elisabeth.

'If he ever gets used to it,' said the doctor. 'He stayed in his room this morning and missed his breakfast, then he fed his ferret and went out. I don't know where, but I have an idea it was to his grandfather's grave. He usually goes there on Saturdays. He didn't want James to go with him. Said he wanted to be by himself. This really upset James so now *he's* in his room, hardly speaking to anyone, with a face, as Mrs O'Connor would say, "like a smacked bottom". I can't say things are very happy at home at the moment. Even the ever-cheerful and garrulous Mrs O'Connor is in a mood, banging pans and grumbling to herself.'

'Well, you know where to come if you want a bit of peace and quiet,' Elisabeth told him.

'Thank you,' he said. 'I might take you up on that. Thank you for the other night, by the way. It's so warm and welcoming at your cottage and it's good to have someone to talk things through with.' He pinched the bridge on his nose. 'I really don't know what to do, Elisabeth. We've all tried to talk to Danny – James, Mrs O'Connor, myself – but he seems to have gone into his shell. I guess he's resigned to the fact that he has to leave, and he looks so down, as he did when his grandfather was ill. I feel so sorry for the boy. It's like watching a condemned man waiting for his execution.'

'Surely it's not that bad,' said Elisabeth.

'You should see him. He's nothing like the boy he was. I did telephone Miss Parsons at the Social Services and told her how unhappy Danny was and, although she sympathised, she felt she shouldn't stand in the way of letting his grandmother make contact and get to know him. She can't say at the moment what will happen, but she said there is a strong possibility that Danny will end up living with her. Mrs Stainthorpe has made the point that the boys are sometimes left alone at Clumber Lodge when I'm out on a call and she brought up the matter of James running away. Goodness knows how she found that out. I'm afraid it didn't look that good. She made it appear that mine is not the most stable place for a child to grow up in.'

'Michael!' exclaimed Elisabeth, 'that is such nonsense. There couldn't be a better home.'

'Anyway, Miss Parsons said she'd make some visits to see how he is getting on.'

'It seems so wrong,' said Elisabeth, 'disrupting his life like this.'

John suddenly shook both the hands which held him and vigorously stamped his foot into the large muddy puddle, drenching both Elisabeth and the doctor. They both laughed.

'Anyway, someone seems happy enough,' said Dr Stirling.

Over the next couple of weeks Danny spent weekends with his grandmother. He would leave the house on the Saturday and catch the bus to Clayton, refusing to let his grandmother collect him from Clumber Lodge or let Dr Stirling drive him there on the Sunday afternoon. He was quiet and polite when he was with his grandmother but said very little, despite the woman's efforts. Mrs Stainthorpe did try to make the boy feel at home, and took him to the cinema and the bowling alley, but it was clear he wasn't interested. Back at Clumber Lodge, he said little to Dr Stirling and James about the flat or about his grandmother, merely saying if he was asked, 'It's all right.' At school he got on with his work and kept very much to himself.

Danny knew as soon as he saw the apartment where he was to live and his bedroom that he would never like living in Clayton. The block of flats was a large shiny red-brick building with small balconies clinging to the side. It overlooked a murky brown river and a busy main road. There was no garden – just a paved area and few newly planted saplings. His bedroom was small, with plain white walls, a single bed, a table and a small wardrobe.

One evening after he had returned from Clayton he asked if he could speak to Dr Stirling.

'Now, Danny,' said the doctor, 'what is it you wanted to see me about?'

'I think it's time for me to go now,' said the boy sadly.

'Go where?'

'Go an' live wi' mi grandmother.'

'I see.'

'It's just purrin it off, 'avin' these visits. I know as 'ow I'll 'ave to live theer in t'end. It only meks me un'appy 'avin' to come back 'ere. I might as well gerrit ovver an' done wi'. I'll tell mi' grandmother tomorrow.'

'I'm so sorry things have turned out this way, Danny,' said Dr Stirling. 'I really am.'

The boy shrugged. 'Aye, so am I,' he said.

13

'He sounds rather stuffy, this Dr Underwood,' said Mrs Atticus to her husband at breakfast.

The Venerable Archdeacon of Clayton surveyed his usual Saturday breakfast, which had been placed before him: two insipid-looking, undercooked poached eggs on a square of burnt toast. 'I beg your pardon, my dear?'

'I was saying that this new curate of yours sounds rather stuffy,' said his wife. 'The bishop is probably putting some crusty old cleric out to pasture.'

'I think that is a trifle unkind, my dear,' replied the archdeacon, cutting a corner from the burnt toast and popping it in his mouth. He crunched noisily.

'I fear he will be of little help to you, Charles,' continued his wife. 'He'll be bookish and serious and far too old, and I can't see some doctor of divinity from Oxford relating to the people in the village. His sermons will be endless and way over their heads. What you need is some enthusiastic young man who can take some of the burden off your shoulders.'

'Shall we reserve our judgement, Marcia, until we have at least met the man?' said her husband, poking a watery egg. 'He may be quite different from that which you imagine. I gather that like your father and myself he was a scholar at All Souls. I assume you would not describe us as some stuffy, crusty old clerics.' The archdeacon stared out of the rectory window and became pensive. '*Bene nati, bene vestiti, et mediocriter dicti*,' he murmured.

'I beg your pardon?' said his wife.

'I was recalling the qualifications of a fellow of All Souls at Oxford,' the archdeacon told her. 'Well born, well dressed, and moderately learned.'

'Well, let us hope he lives up to that,' said Mrs Atticus. She glanced out of the dining-room window. 'And I guess he will have to stay here at the rectory?'

'I think so,' said the archdeacon. 'Of course he may wish to find a place of his own in the village. However, I think in the first instance we will have to accommodate him.'

'Well, I hope Dr Underwood will not be expecting me to cook and wash for him and clean his room.'

'Perhaps we could get someone in to help with that,' suggested her husband.

'That might be the answer, Charles,' replied his wife, 'because I can't be taking on these domestic duties, what with all my other commitments. I have a very busy term at the school, as you well know, and then I have my dissertation to complete.'

'I am sure Dr Underwood will not be expecting you to cook and clean for him, my dear.'

'I hope not. And what time is he coming?' asked his wife.

'At ten o'clock,' replied her husband. 'I had a call from the diocesan office. Before that I have a prospective bride and groom to see me and then later this morning the Methodist minister and Father Daly to discuss the ecumenical service next week.'

'I think at least the bishop could have let you meet this Dr Underwood instead of foisting him upon us sight unseen,' said the archdeacon's wife.

Her husband placed his knife and fork down carefully at the side of his plate and took a deep breath. 'The bishop has been more than accommodating, Marcia,' he said irritably, wearying of his wife's constant carping. 'It was most considerate of him to allow me to stay here at Barton so that you could continue to train at the village school. In normal circumstances archdeacons have to move. The bishop has been more than generous.'

'Yes, I suppose so,' said his wife. 'Nevertheless—'

'If you will excuse me,' said the archdeacon, rising from his chair, 'I have quite a deal of work to do this morning.'

'Oh look,' said his wife, suddenly peering through the rectory window. 'There's young Daniel Stainthorpe in the churchyard again. The boy spends so much time at his grand-father's grave. It's rather unhealthy for a boy of his age, don't you think? He should be out and about with his friends.'

'I guess he's still grieving,' said the archdeacon. 'He was very close to his grandfather. Sometimes it takes a long time to come to terms with the death of a loved one. He's a very personable young man, is young Danny, and a credit to old Mr Stainthorpe.'

'Yes, he is,' said Mrs Atticus, agreeing, on this rare occasion, with her husband.

Danny stood at his grandfather's graveside. The air was cold and a light rain began to fall. He stared forlornly at the small tombstone, biting slightly at his lower lip. He wiped a tear from his cheek.

'I wish tha were 'ere, granddad,' said the boy. 'To tell us what to do. I don't want to go an' live in Clayton. I wants to stay 'ere but they say I've got to go. I remember you used to say when I were worried an' I 'ad summat on mi mind, that it's never as bad as you think. It's pretty bad now though, grand-dad. It really is.' The boy suddenly sensed that someone was watching him and, turning sharply around, found a young woman holding aloft a bright umbrella.

'Hello,' she said cheerfully.

'Oh, 'ello,' replied Danny.

'Come in under my umbrella,' she told him. 'You're getting soaking wet.'

'No, yer all reight,' said Danny. 'I don't mind t'rain an' it's only drizzlin'. I've been out in it offen enough.' He looked up at the grey sky and then back at the gravestone. 'You must think I'm a bit barmy talkin' to missen.'

'Not at all,' she replied. 'I often talk to myself. Anyway you *were* talking to someone, weren't you?'

'Mi granddad,' replied the boy. 'He died last year. Bit daft in't it, talkin' to someone who's dead?' He sniffed.

'I don't think so,' she replied. 'I talk to my grandparents all the time and they died when I was small.'

'Do you?'

'I do.'

'An' d' ya think they listen?'

'I'm sure they do.'

'If I got worried abaat anythin',' said Danny, 'I used to talk it through with mi granddad. He allus med me feel better an' told me wor 'e thowt I should do.'

'He sounds like a very special man.'

'Oh, 'e was. I really miss 'im.'

'Are you sure you don't want to come under my umbrella?' asked the young woman.

Danny shook his head. 'I likes t'rain on mi face.'

'And what's your name?' she asked.

'I'm Danny,' he replied. 'Danny Stainthorpe.'

'I'm pleased to meet you, Danny.' She held out a hand, which the boy shook.

''Ave you come to see somebody's grave?' asked the boy.

'No,' replied the young woman. 'I'm coming to live in the village and thought I'd have a walk around.'

'You'll like it here,' said Danny. 'All this country stretchin' for miles an' miles, empty skies, old stone walls, all these birds an' animals an' different trees. I love it 'ere, t'sounds an' t'smells. You'll see t'seasons change. Sun on yer face in summer, rain on yer face in autumn, snow crunchin' under yer feet in winter.'

'You're quite the little poet,' remarked the woman.

He smiled. 'Naw, not really.' He thought for a moment. 'It's funny, you just comin' to Barton an' me 'avin' to leave.'

'You're leaving?'

'I don't want to but I've got to move. I reckon I'll be leavin' for good soon.' He gave a sad, resigned shrug. 'Mi grandmother wants me to go an' live wi' 'er in t'town. I know I won't like it. I'm not bothered about ice rinks an' cinemas an' bowling alleys an' swimming baths. I likes it 'ere in t'country. When mi granddad died I went to live wi' Dr Stirling. 'E's been lookin' after me an' wanted to adopt me. It's wor I wanted too. Can't see it 'appenin' now though. I can't remember mi grandmother. I don't know 'er, you see. She left mi' granddad years ago. It was 'im who brought me up. I don't know why she 'ad to come back now an' I don't know why I 'ave to live with 'er.'

'You might get to like it.'

'I won't.'

'There've been times when I thought I wouldn't like something,' said the young woman, 'and when it came to it I got to quite enjoy it. Perhaps you should give it a chance.'

'I don't 'ave no choice in t'matter,' sighed Danny.

'You're only young, Danny,' said the woman, 'but in a few more years you'll be able to decide what you want to do and where you want to live.'

'Aye, I reckon so,' he murmured.

'And if you don't like it in the town maybe your grandmother might let you come back and stay here.'

'Naw, she won't.'

'You can always come out here and visit.'

'Aye, I suppose I could. Anyroad I've got to "like it and lump it", as mi granddad used to say,' replied the boy. His voice was apprehensive. He gazed, frowning, into the middle distance for a moment, his face wet with rain. 'Are ya goin' to be a teacher at t'school?' he asked.

'No,' replied the young woman, 'although I do hope I'll be able to visit.'

''Ave you got kids?'

'No,' she replied smiling. 'There's just me.'

'Mrs Devine – she's the 'ead teacher – is great. She likes people comin' into school. You'll really like 'er.'

'I'm sure I will if she's as friendly as you.'

'I've got to move schools when I go to live in Clayton,' he said sadly. 'I don't want to leave.' A sudden lump of misery rose in his throat, as hard and tight as a nut. He tried to control his emotions but his voice betrayed the extent of his sadness. 'I'm frightened,' he said quietly.

The woman rested a hand on the boy's shoulder. 'I think your granddad would have told you things might not be as bad as they seem at the moment and that they have a way of turning out for the best.'

Danny rubbed his eyes. 'I reckon he would have said that,' he sniffed. 'Anyroad miss, I'd berrer be mekkin' tracks. They'll be wonderin' where I've got to.'

'It's been nice talking to you, Danny,' said the woman. 'I hope we will meet again.' She held out her hand and he slipped his cold hand into hers.

'I'll mebbe see you around,' he said, walking slowly to the small gate. He looked back and gave a small wave. ''Bye,' he shouted.

What a pleasant young man, thought the woman. She recalled the time when she had been the boy's age and had gone to live with her mother. This was following her parents' acrimonious divorce. She had had to leave the attic bedroom she so loved, her friends and her school. She had felt so lonely and been so unhappy and knew how young Danny must be feeling. She walked up the path to the rectory and rang the bell.

The door opened. 'Good afternoon,' said Mrs Atticus. 'May I help you?'

'Good afternoon,' said the woman. 'I have an appointment to see the archdeacon.'

'Do come in out of the rain,' Mrs Atticus told her. The woman came into the hall. 'Let me take your umbrella. It's dreadful weather isn't it, so cold and wet and depressing. I really do dislike this time of year.'

'But spring is just around the corner,' said the woman brightly.

'Sounds like a song,' said Mrs Atticus smiling. 'Spring is just around the corner. And it's a lovely time for a wedding, is spring. We have just had a wedding and the poor bride looked frozen stiff as she walked up the aisle. Now, my husband usually likes to see both of you. He gives a little homily about the sanctity of marriage and the responsibilities and goes through the order of service. He feels it important that both the prospective bride and groom hear what he has to say. Has your fiancé not been able to make it?'

'Fiancé?'

'To discuss the wedding.'

'I think we have a few crossed wires here,' the young woman told her. 'I'm not about to get married. I have an appointment with your husband.'

'Really? When?'

'Ten o'clock. I'm rather early, I'm afraid.'

'He must have double booked,' said Mrs Atticus. 'My husband is to meet the new curate at ten o'clock.'

The woman smiled. 'Yes,' she replied. 'That's me.'

'You?' exclaimed Mrs Atticus. '*You* are the new curate?'

'I am.'

'We were told it was a Reverend Dr Ashley Underwood.'

'I'm the Reverend Dr Ashley Underwood.'

'You!' exclaimed Mrs Atticus.

'Me,' replied the new curate.

The archdeacon's wife stared for a moment. 'I see,' she said, clearly nonplussed. 'Well, let me take your coat, Reverend Underwood, and I will make a cup of tea and get my husband.'

'Ashley, please,' replied the woman, taking off her coat to reveal a pale blue surplice and white clerical collar.

'Ashley,' replied Mrs Atticus. 'You must call me Marcia. Do come through into the drawing-room. It's a bit of a mess, I'm afraid. I am preparing my lessons for next week.'

'You teach at the school?'

'I'm in training at the moment,' Mrs Atticus told her. 'I have a visit from my college tutor on Monday, so I am a little anxious.' She stared at the visitor for a moment. 'I have to say, you have come as a bit of a surprise.'

'A pleasant one, I hope?'

'We were expecting someone rather older, and a man. Do come through and I will let my husband know that you are here.'

Mrs Atticus scurried down the hall and threw open the door to her husband's study.

'Charles! Charles!' she hissed. 'It's a woman!'

The archdeacon looked up from his desk. 'I beg your pardon, my dear?'

'The new curate,' his wife told him. 'It's a woman.'

'Reverend Underwood is a woman?'

'Yes, yes, it's a woman!'

'A woman?'

'Charles, will you stop repeating everything I say. Yes, it is a woman.'

'Good gracious me.'

'She's in the drawing-room,' continued his wife.

'What is she like?' asked the archdeacon.

'She's very young and extremely attractive,' his wife told him.

'Is she indeed,' said the archdeacon, rising from his chair and rubbing his long hands together. 'Well, I'd better go and introduce myself to the Reverend Dr Ashley Underwood,' he said, smiling widely.

Major Neville-Gravitas poked his head around the shop door.

'It's all right, major,' Mrs Sloughthwaite told him, 'Mrs Pocock's not in.'

'Thank the Lord for that,' said the major, entering the village store. 'The last thing I wanted this morning was another skirmish with Mrs Pocock. She has an extremely sharp tongue. I am heartily sick and tired of being barracked by her every time she sees me. I just wish people would get it into their heads that I was not in favour of the village school closing, indeed I was very supportive of it remaining open.'

Yes, thought Mrs Sloughthwaite, though only when you saw the strength of feeling in the village, but she said nothing. 'And now we've got this amalgamation,' she remarked, leaning over the counter, as was her wont.

'Yes indeed,' replied the major.

'I don't know why they don't leave the school alone,' said the shopkeeper. 'Chopping and changing.'

'The Education Department has to make savings,' the major told her.

'Well, they want to make savings in other places, not here. Anyway, that's what Mrs Pocock was saying.'

'Yes, well, Mrs Pocock has a great deal to say for herself,' observed the major, bristling at the mention of his nemesis. 'She was very vocal at the public meeting.'

'Just giving her point of view as a school governor,' observed the shopkeeper. 'You were very quiet. I should have thought you would have had something to say.'

'Nothing I could have said would have changed anything,' replied the major. 'As far as I can see it's all done and dusted, if you follow my drift.'

At the meeting Mr Preston, with his usual practised aplomb, had outlined the procedures of the proposed amalgamation of the two schools. When the Director of Education assured those present that Barton-in-the-Dale school was not under any threat of closure, that the head teacher and her staff would be retained and extra resources would be allocated, there was little dissent apart from Mrs Pocock's outburst. She was of the opinion that Urebank School should be closed and the children transferred to Barton, but this was seen to be impractical. When the meeting closed it was generally accepted that the amalgamation was not an altogether bad thing.

'And when will this happen?' asked Mrs Sloughthwaite now.

'Beg pardon?' asked the major.

'When will this amalgamation take place?'

'Oh, not for some time,' replied the major. 'I should imagine it will be at the beginning of the autumn term, next September. There has to be a period of consultation. Sundry meetings with interested parties need to take place, then there will be the convening of a new governing body and the appointment of the teaching staff to the various posts, and of course, the head teacher to oversee the two premises.'

'Well, I hope Mrs Devine gets the head teacher's job,' said the shopkeeper. 'That man at Urebank, from what I've heard, is about as much use as an ashtray on a motorbike.'

'Well, I am not in any position to comment upon that,' replied the major. 'I have never met Mr Richardson.'

'Mrs Stubbins sent her lad Malcolm to Urebank. She took him away from Barton after a difference of opinion with Mrs Devine, but she soon wished she hadn't and it wasn't long before he was back.'

'I was aware of that, Mrs Sloughthwaite,' said the major. 'It was raised at the governors' meeting at the time.'

The shopkeeper continued undeterred. 'As I said, she soon sent him back to Barton. Of course, as my mother would say, the grass is always greener, isn't it? He had a dreadful time, had young Malcolm, with that Mr Richardson – picked on him he did. I mean I know Malcolm Stubbins isn't the best behaved lad in the world but he spent all day outside the head teacher's room, from what his mother told me. Then he was suspended, excluded and expelled all in the space of a few weeks. Since he's been back at Barton he's been doing really well, from what I can gather.'

'I'm pleased to hear it,' said the major.

'From what Mrs Stubbins told me, that head teacher at Urebank is a very nasty piece of work and we don't want him throwing his weight about in our village school, so if you're on the governing body in this new set-up I hope that you are after supporting Mrs Devine.'

'Ah, well, the appointment of the new head teacher is not in my bailiwick, if you follow my drift,' the major told her.

'Your what?'

'It does not depend upon me,' replied the major. 'The governors, as a body, will decide.'

'But you have a vote.'

'If I am asked to serve as a governor,' said the major, feeling somewhat under pressure, 'I will indeed have a vote.'

'Well, you know where to stick it, don't you?' said the shop-keeper bluntly.

The major sighed. He could see that the next episode in the saga of Barton-in-the-Dale village school was likely to be as contentious as the last one. Councillor Smout would expect him to vote for his candidate and Mrs Sloughthwaite and the villagers would expect him to vote for Mrs Devine. He was between a rock and a hard place. 'May I have a packet of panatellas, please, Mrs Sloughthwaite?' he said.

'Because I'll tell you this, Major Neville-Gravitas,' said the shopkeeper, ignoring his request, 'if Mrs Devine doesn't get the job there will be all hell to pay.'

'I will bear that in mind,' said the major, sighing.

'Miss, I sang in the chapel again on Sunday,' said Chardonnay, approaching the teacher's desk on Monday morning as the children in Elisabeth's class were filing into the classroom.

'Yes, I heard from Miss Brakespeare,' replied Elisabeth. 'I believe she was at the service yesterday and she said you sang beautifully.'

'She turns the pages for Mr Tomlinson when he's playing the organ,' the girl told her. 'Then after the service they go and have a coffee at the Rumbling Tum café. I've seen them.'

'Have you really,' said Elisabeth.

The girl giggled. 'Miss, they were holding hands.'

'Really.' Elisabeth quickly changed the subject. 'And how are your sister and the baby?'

'They're OK, miss. It's a bit crowded in the house and there are nappies everywhere, but he doesn't cry much and he sleeps a lot.'

'Well, I'm pleased to hear that they are doing well,' said Elisabeth.

'Miss, I have to practise this new hymn for Easter,' said the girl.

'Yes,' said Elisabeth, smiling to herself. 'Miss Brakespeare told me.'

The deputy head teacher had entertained the staff earlier that day with her account of Chardonnay's attempt at singing the hymn chosen by the minister at the chapel.

'She started to sing about this old ragged cloth,' Miss Brakespeare told her colleagues.

'A what?' asked Miss Wilson, intrigued.

'An old ragged cloth,' repeated the deputy head teacher.

'"On a hill far away," sang the girl, "there's an old ragged cloth".'

'Oh, "The Old Rugged Cross",' said Elisabeth, smiling.

'I remember one Easter at my last school,' said Mrs Robertshaw, 'I was told by a child that she was to sing in assembly about a cross-eyed bear. I couldn't think for the life of me of a hymn of that title. 'It's called "Gladly This Bear",' said the girl. '"Gladly, the Cross-eyed Bear".'

'"Gladly, the Cross I Bear",' laughed Miss Brakespeare.

It was during the marking of the afternoon register that Chardonnay asked about Danny.

'Miss, do you know why Danny is away?'

'Just put your pens and pencils down,' said Elisabeth to her class. 'There is something I need to tell you all.'

The children did as they were told and sat up smartly at their tables.

'Danny has left,' she said.

'He's left, miss?' exclaimed Chardonnay.

'That's right. Danny has gone to live with his grandmother in Clayton.' Elisabeth glanced in the direction of James as she spoke and saw the look of despondency on the boy's face.

'I didn't know he had a grandmother,' muttered Chardonnay.

'Well, he has,' Elisabeth told her, 'and he is going to live with her.'

'But miss, I thought—' began the girl.

'That's quite enough about Danny, Chardonnay,' said Elisabeth. 'I am sure we will all miss him but he will soon be at another school. Now let's get on with our work.'

'Well, he could have said goodbye, miss,' grumbled Chardonnay, pouting.

At morning break James stayed behind.

'Mrs Devine,' he said. 'Is there nothing you can do to get Danny to come back and stay with us?'

'I'm afraid not, James,' she replied. 'Your father has tried his very best but, as you know, he's not had any success. Perhaps your friend will be happy with his grandmother.'

The boy shook his head. 'He won't. I know he won't. He loves the country, going down by the beck, fishing in the mill-pond, running across the fields, building dens, spotting birds, setting traps. He won't like it in the town, I know he won't.'

'There's nothing I can do,' said Elisabeth. 'I only wish I could.'

She had tried. When she had learned that it had been decided that Danny was to live in Clayton, she had telephoned the Social Services department and spoken to Miss Parsons. Elisabeth had explained she was Danny's head teacher and how happy and settled the boy was. 'I have the utmost respect for social workers,' she had continued. 'You do an almost impossible job out of the very best possible motives, receive little recognition and are paid a pittance for doing so. I know how difficult this must be for you but I do urge you to do everything possible so that Danny can stay where he is. Dr Stirling is a hero. He took Danny in after the boy's grand-father had died so he would not have to go into care, and he gave him permanence, security and love. I know you listen to what the child says and always have to put him first so he can have a happy and successful life, so I do hope on this occasion—'

'I hear what you say, Mrs Devine,' Miss Parsons had inter-rupted, 'and I do sympathise, but in this situation I am trying to do the best for Danny, to make sure he goes to the very best home. I admire Dr Stirling and all he has done for the boy and I have listened to what Danny says, but I feel we need at least to give this a chance.'

'Miss Parsons,' Elisabeth had replied, 'surely Danny's wishes should carry the greatest weight. Shouldn't he decide where he wants to live?'

'Were it as simple as that,' the senior social worker had replied. It would be unprofessional, she had thought, to raise the matter of Dr Stirling's son running away and the fact that his work as a doctor meant he was frequently away from home. These were factors which she had to take into consideration. 'If it doesn't work out,' she had told Elisabeth, 'we can review the case. Let's see how Danny gets on at his grandmother's, and let me assure you that I shall monitor the situation.'

The day he was to leave Clumber Lodge to go and live with his grandmother, Danny sat on the end of his bed, staring at the carpet.

There was a knock at the bedroom door. 'May I come in?' asked Dr Stirling.

'Yes,' replied Danny.

The boy looked up and gave a weak smile when Dr Stirling walked in.

'Have you packed?'

'Yes,' he said quietly.

The doctor sat next to him and put an arm around his shoulder.

'You know, it might not be too bad living with your grandmother.'

'Naw,' Danny nodded.

'You never know, you might really like life in the town. There's lots more to do there than in sleepy old Barton. You'll make new friends at the school and soon forget about us.'

'I won't. I never will.'

'You know you can always come and visit any time. We'd all love to see you. You're not a hundred miles away and there's the bus from Clayton. Maybe you could stay over some time. I know James would really like to keep in touch.'

Danny nodded.

'You know, Danny,' said Dr Stirling gently, 'sometimes in life decisions are made for us, things we find hard to accept at the time, things which might seem pretty bad now but they somehow, sometimes have a way of turning out for the best.'

'That's what t'woman in t'churchyard said,' Danny told him.

'Woman in the churchyard?'

'Yea, she were really nice. She looked a bit like that hangel on that big tomb, an' she said she thought mi granddad would 'ave told me that things might not be as bad as they seem at t'moment an' that they 'ave a way of turning out for t'best.'

'Sounds pretty good advice to me.'

'I just wish I could believe it.'

They sat there in silence for a moment.

'Dr Stirling,' said Danny at last.

'Yes?'

'Thanks for all you've done for me.'

'It's been a pleasure.'

'I din't know what to do when mi granddad died. If it 'adn't been for you an' Mrs Devine—'

'There's no need to say anything, Danny,' said the doctor. 'We were happy to do it. You know—' The doorbell rang. The boy got up from the bed and picked up his small case.

'That must be mi grandmother now,' he said.

'Yes, it probably is,' said the doctor.

'Best not keep 'er waitin'.'

At the sight of Mrs Stainthorpe on the doorstep, Mrs O'Connor's face took on a stony expression. If looks could maim, the woman standing before her would be on crutches.

'Oh, it's you,' she said.

'Yes, it's me and you don't need to look at me like that, Bridget O'Connor. Anybody would think I was kidnapping the boy.'

'Some would say you are,' replied the housekeeper sharply. 'He was happy here before you showed up after all these years.'

'You've never liked me, have you?' asked Mrs Stainthorpe.

'No, I haven't,' replied the housekeeper tartly. 'I never liked you when you lived in the village and I've not changed my mind. Only out for what you can get, that's you.'

'And tell me what am I getting out of this?' she asked.

'Family allowance and any money Danny's grandfather might have left,' replied Mrs O'Connor bluntly.

Mrs Stainthorpe gave a dismissive grunt. 'I was left very well provided for if you must know. Frank left me a tidy sum and he was insured, so you're wrong on that count. Well, am I coming in or am I stopping out here taking root on the door-step?' she asked. Mrs O'Connor moved out of the way to let the woman enter. 'Is he ready?'

'As he'll ever be.'

Dr Stirling came down the stairs accompanied by Danny.

'Good morning, Mrs Stainthorpe,' said the doctor.

'Morning,' she replied sharply. 'Hello, Daniel.'

''Ello,' said the boy almost inaudibly.

'Don't look so miserable,' she said. 'Take your case out to the taxi. I'll be with you in a minute.'

'There's mi ferret,' said Danny.

'Your what?'

'Mi ferret. Can I tek 'im wi' me?'

'A ferret!' exclaimed the woman. 'Certainly not. There's no room for a ferret at the apartment, dirty smelly creature.'

'But I've—' began the boy.

'Anyway, they don't allow pets,' he was told sternly.

'Don't worry, Danny,' said the doctor, 'we'll take good care of Ferdy.'

'Well, go on,' said his grandmother, 'don't just stand there. Put the case in the taxi.'

''Bye, Mrs O'Connor,' said the boy, his eyes filling with tears.

''Bye darlin'.' She gave him a hug. 'You come and see us, won't you?'

''Bye, Dr Stirling,' said Danny.

'Goodbye Danny,' said Dr Stirling. He put both hands on the boy's shoulders and looked into his eyes. 'You be a good boy, won't you?'

'Oh, he will,' said Mrs Stainthorpe.

When Danny had set off down the path his grandmother turned to Dr Stirling. 'I know you don't think much of me,' she said, 'and I know them social workers didn't either and that all of you didn't want him to come with me. You made me out to be the wicked fairy at the christening, but I know what's right for my grandson and what I'm doing is best for the boy.'

'I hope so, Mrs Stainthorpe,' replied Dr Stirling calmly. 'I do hope so.'

14

It was a cold, crisp Saturday morning. Elisabeth braved the chilly weather to put food out for the birds. She was thinking of Danny. Every Saturday morning bright and early he would arrive at her cottage and she would watch him from the kitchen window, filling the trays and the feeders with nuts, seeds and currants, and on seeing her he would smile that broad smile of his and wave. He was such a sunny, good-natured boy, full of life and so at home in the country. She wondered what he would be doing now, cooped up in his grandmother's flat in Clayton. She recalled his grandfather's words when she'd gone to visit him in hospital a few days before his death.

'I'm not feared o' dying,' he told her. 'I've known that there's been summat up wi' me for a while. What does worry me is what'll 'appen to Danny.' The old man's eyes began to fill with tears. ''E's a bit of a free spirit, is Danny, likes t'sun on 'is face, rain in 'is 'air. 'E lives for t'outdoors. 'E's a country lad. Tek 'im away from t'country and 'e'll be like a caged bird beating its wings agin t'bars to try an' get out.'

Elisabeth looked up now to see the sparrows squabbling and chattering in the bare branches of the trees, the shy thrush waiting for his breakfast and the blackbird sweeping down on to the dark earth in search of worms. All free spirits.

She remembered when she had first met Danny the previous summer, the day when she had seen for the first time the cottage she was to buy. Beyond the five-barred gate at the end of the track she'd seen a small boy lifting a dry cowpat with a stick and disturbing a buzzing cloud of yellow horseflies. He stopped when he caught sight of her and, having watched her for a moment, came over.

''Ello,' he said cheerfully, climbing up on to the gate, sitting on the top and letting his spindly legs dangle down. He was about ten or eleven, with large low-set ears, a mop of dusty blond hair and the bright brown eyes of a fox, and was dressed in a faded T-shirt, baggy khaki shorts and wellington boots that looked sizes too big for him. The child's face and knees were innocent of soap and water.

As she made her way back to the cottage now, shivering a little in the cold, she jumped as she caught sight of a figure leaning over the gate. He was a tall broad-shouldered young man with a mass of unruly black curls and a wide-boned weathered face the colour of a russet apple.

'Sorry,' he said. 'Did I startle you?'

'I was daydreaming,' replied Elisabeth.

'It's good to dream,' he replied.

She smiled. 'Yes, it is,' she said.

The young man breathed in deeply. ''Tis a lovely cottage,' he said, 'with a beautiful view.'

'It is,' she replied. 'The garden's a bit of a mess at the moment, I'm afraid. The trees need pruning and the dead plants want cutting back. I did have a young man who looked after it for me.' She thought of Danny again. 'Anyway, may I help you at all?' As she approached the man Elisabeth noticed his striking eyes, the fine high nose and the shining hair as black as jet.

'Hope so,' he replied. 'I'm after looking for a Fred Massey. The woman at the village store told me he lived somewhere over here.'

'Come through,' said Elisabeth. 'I'll point out his farm-house. It's a bit of a walk but you can cut across the fields from here.'

The man was wearing a heavy, thick close-fitting jacket, shapeless corduroy trousers worn at the knees and black boots which had seen better days. Around his neck was wound a colourful kerchief. A heavy earring was fastened to his ear like a small gold manacle.

Elisabeth pointed across the fields. 'If you go through the paddock at the side of the cottage and take the path, it will bring you to Tanfield Farm, Mr Massey's place. Go carefully; he has two rather lively dogs.'

'I guess you'll be knowing Mr Massey,' said the young man.

'He's my nearest neighbour, but I see little of him.'

'And what sort of man is he?' she was asked bluntly.

Elisabeth was non-committal. 'Interesting,' she replied. She recalled the words of Danny's grandfather, who had described the old farmer as 'a tight-fisted old so-and-so and allus on t'make'. She had had one or two skirmishes with the curmudgeonly Fred Massey, and the less she saw of him the better.

'Do you think he might be letting me park my caravan in his paddock?' asked the young man.

'Actually the paddock belongs to me,' Elisabeth told him.

'Belongs to you?' repeated the young man. 'Well, there's a stroke of luck. You're the very person I wish to speak to.'

Elisabeth shook her head. 'If you are looking for somewhere to put your caravan,' she said, 'I'm afraid I can't help you.'

'No?'

'No. I really value my privacy.'

'I'd be no trouble at all.' He looked appealingly at her.

'I'm sorry, but I have to say no,' replied Elisabeth. 'I am sure Mr Massey will let you put it on one of his fields.' And at a price, she thought to herself.

The young man smiled and tilted his head to one side. 'And I can't persuade you?' He had a soft, strangely compelling voice.

'No, I'm afraid not.'

The young man persevered. 'It wouldn't be for too long. Just a few weeks and then I'll be travelling on. I never stay for too long in one place. And I would be no trouble, no trouble at all.'

'I do like my privacy,' Elisabeth told him.

'So do I,' said the man. 'I'd keep well out of your way.'

'I really must say no.'

'But sure, isn't there a caravan there already?' said the man, speaking softly and insistently.

'Ah yes. I was doing a favour for a friend. He lived there with his grandson. Sadly the old man died last year. The caravan's empty now.'

'I'd be as quiet as a mouse and invisible as a ghost,' said the man.

'I'm sorry,' said Elisabeth.

He smiled and placed his hands on his hips. 'Now you don't look like the kind of woman who would turn a poor, cold and weary traveller away on such a bitter miserable day as this,' said the young man. 'Sure don't you have the kind face and the shining eyes of the Good Samaritan himself?'

'And you sound as if you could charm the birds off the trees,' replied Elizabeth, amused by the man's doggedness, 'but I really think you need to talk to Mr Massey.'

'Ah well,' he chuckled. 'No harm in asking. I will bid you good day. Goodbye now. Take care.'

A small girl with large wide-set eyes and long rust-coloured hair, curly and shining, appeared at the gate. She was wrapped up in a thick coat too large for her and wore yellow rubber boots.

'Now didn't I tell you to wait for me in the van?' said the young man in a gentle voice.

'But you've been gone for ages and ages,' she replied. 'I was getting worried.'

'This is my daughter,' the man told Elisabeth. 'A young lady who doesn't do as she is bid.' His voice was soft and kindly.

'Hello,' said Elisabeth brightly.

The child's smile was wary and uncertain. 'Hello,' she replied quietly.

'And what's your name?'

'Roisin.'

'A lovely name.'

The child gave a small smile. 'It means rosebud,' the child told her. 'It's Irish.' She looked at her father. 'Have we found somewhere, Daddy?' she asked.

'Not yet,' he replied, 'but we soon will. Now come along and say goodbye to the nice lady. We have a short walk across the fields to the old farmhouse you can see.'

Elisabeth watched as they set off, the child skipping and swinging her small arms.

'Wait!' she called. 'Just a moment.' She followed them into the paddock. 'I don't suppose it would do any harm to let you put your caravan here for a short while.'

'Aren't you a saint,' the man said, smiling widely. 'We will be no trouble at all and keep ourselves to ourselves, and any odd jobs you want doing, I'm the man to ask.'

'You had better come into the cottage and out of the cold,' Elisabeth told him, 'and I'll tell you where things are.'

'And the rent?' asked the young man with a twinkle in his dark eyes.

'We'll talk about that later,' said Elisabeth, smiling and wondering what she had let herself in for this time.

'It's nice in here,' said the little girl as she followed her father and Elisabeth into the cottage. She took off her boots in the hall and placed them outside the door. Her father did the same. Elisabeth noticed the child's woollen socks were heavily darned, as were her father's. Roisin stared wide-eyed at the long-case clock ticking loudly and rhythmically. 'You've a grandfather clock!' she cried. 'I love grandfather clocks.'

'It was my grandmother's,' Elisabeth told her. 'It stood in the sitting-room in her house and when I was little I liked to listen to it ticking away and look at the coloured figures on the clock face. I used to imagine when I was in bed at night that they came to life and danced on the carpet when we were all asleep. One day the clock stopped. My younger brother Giles used to put his cricket bat inside and I don't think it liked that too much and the pendulum stopped swinging. When I moved here it started working again. It was like magic. I think it felt at home.'

'If we ever stopped travelling,' said the child thoughtfully, 'I think I would like a cottage like this one. It's nice and cosy. I'd have a big grandfather clock like yours with little dancing figures and a fat cat and I'd grow lots of flowers and I'd feed the birds like you.'

'She's one for the words, is Roisin,' said her father, gently touching the child's head.

'Well, come into the kitchen,' said Elisabeth. 'I'll put the kettle on. I'm sure you could both do with a warm drink.'

As they sat around the old pine table drinking tea, Elisabeth asked about the girl's schooling.

'If we stop in a place,' her father told her, 'Roisin goes to the local school, that's if we like the look of it. It's sometimes not that easy for her settling in, meeting new people and making friends and then having to move on again, but she's used to it. Of course, there have been a few unkind comments about the sort of life we lead, and some head teachers are not all that welcoming. We are quite used to that as well. I'm not your conventional traveller, of course, more of an itinerant. I'm not a gypsy or a tinker and I have no Romany blood and I don't travel around with others. It's just that I've never been a one to settle. I like to be on the road. I'd feel cooped up in a house. I like the open spaces, the changing countryside, the freedom to go where I want and stop where I want and move on when I want.'

Elisabeth nodded and thought again of Danny.

'I teach Roisin myself,' said the man. 'She's a good little reader and writer, she plays the flute and can sing and she has a good general knowledge. There's no child who knows more about the animals and birds or the countryside.'

There is one child, thought Elisabeth, picturing Danny striding across the fields. 'And will you send her to the village school in Barton while you are here?' she asked.

'I will have to see it first,' the man replied, 'but I think I will. It has a good reputation.'

'Really?'

'I was speaking to the woman in the village store and she told me it's a very good school. The head teacher is quite a formidable woman, I believe, but is good-natured and knows what she's about.'

'Is she?' said Elisabeth, giving a wry smile.

'Pretty strong-minded by all accounts and a bit out of the ordinary. She's evidently turned the school around. Do you know her at all?'

'Oh yes, I know her,' said Elisabeth.

'And she seems all right?'

'Oh yes. I think you could say that.'

'Well, thank you for the tea,' he said, getting to his feet. 'We'll get settled in. I'll park the caravan well out of sight so as not to spoil your view.'

'Will you be warm enough?' Elisabeth asked. 'It's going to freeze tonight.'

'Sure we will,' he told her. 'We have a paraffin heater, a bit smelly but it keeps us warm, and we have a small stove. All a person could want.'

'Well, if you do need anything you know where I am.'

'Thank you,' he said, shaking her hand. 'I really do appreciate your kindness. Come along now, Roisin. Say thank you and goodbye to the lady.'

'Thank you,' said the child. 'Goodbye.'

'I'm called Elisabeth, by the way.'

'I'm pleased to meet you, Elisabeth,' said the young man, smiling and showing a set of remarkably white even teeth. 'I'm Emmet, Emmet O'Malley.'

'Gypsies!' exclaimed Mrs Pocock. She was standing, arms folded tightly over her chest, before the counter in the village store with Mrs O'Connor.

'Well, he looked like a gypsy,' said Mrs Sloughthwaite. 'He had long black curly hair and shiny white teeth and a big gold earring in his ear.'

'Sounds like more like a pirate to me,' said Mrs O'Connor.

'Came in here looking for somewhere to park his caravan,' the shopkeeper told them. 'He was very polite and very good-looking. Reminded me of Errol Flynn, he did. He had one of those smiles that would melt snow. We had quite a conversation.'

'I hope there's not more of them,' said Mrs Pocock, her eyes narrowing. 'We can't be doing with an encampment of gypsies in Barton. There'll be all that mess and they're such a nuisance.'

'I sent him up to Fred Massey's,' said the shopkeeper.

'You did what!' cried Mrs Pocock.

'I sent him up to Fred Massey's,' she repeated. 'He's got that many fields he doesn't know what to do with them. I didn't want him putting his caravan on the village green or on that glebe pasture by the church. I mean, they're pieces of common land and if he sets his caravan up there he can't be shifted.'

'I never thought of that,' said Mrs Pocock.

'By the sound of it I don't think this man will be any trouble,' said Mrs O'Connor.

'You should have told him to move on,' said Mrs Pocock to the shopkeeper.

'It's not up to me to tell people what they should or shouldn't do,' said Mrs Sloughthwaite in a peevish voice and with a heave of her bosom. 'Anyway, as I said he was a likeable sort of chap and he had a little girl with him. Bright as a button she was and well-behaved with it.'

'And light-fingered as well, I shouldn't wonder,' added the customer. 'I don't hold with having gypsies in the village. Things will go missing, you mark my words, and not just from the village store.'

'I once had my tea leaves read by a gypsy fortune-teller, so I did,' announced Mrs O'Connor. 'Everything she said would happen, did.'

'Nonsense!' snapped Mrs Pocock.

'It did, as true as I'm standing here.'

'I mean, it's all nonsense this fortune-telling lark, all hocus-pocus,' said Mrs Pocock dismissively.

'Well, I think there's something in it,' said the shopkeeper. 'They have what's called second sight, do gypsies. I have a bit of it myself. I had my hands read by a fortune-teller once in Whitby.' She placed her chubby hands on the counter, palms upwards. 'She told me that the left hand showed my destiny in the stars and my right hand showed what I was making of it. She said I was a very kind-hearted woman and that I could look forward to a long and happy life.'

Mrs Pocock shook her head. 'They always say that,' she remarked. 'They tell you what you want to hear. It's not likely she'd tell you that you were mean and obnoxious and that you'd be dead before the week was out.'

'And I always read my horoscope in the Gazette,' continued the shopkeeper. 'Here,' she said, opening the paper on the counter, 'listen to what it says is in store for me this month: "The presence of Saturn, your planetary ruler, indicates that this is a time of challenge and excitement for you".' She lifted her bosom from the counter where it had been resting. '"You need to be upfront and not give in to compromise. Magnetic Mars reveals that January will go with a bang and not a whimper. A young stranger will be a potent influence in your life before the month is out, but one who needs to be watched with caution for he could spell danger".'

'They always go on about meeting a stranger,' said Mrs Pocock. 'You being a shopkeeper it's very likely you'll meet lots of strangers in your line of work.'

'Does it say this stranger will be tall, dark and handsome?' asked Mrs O'Connor.

'No, it doesn't, more's the pity,' replied the shopkeeper. 'I can't say as how I like the sound of this potent stranger so I shall be keeping my eyes peeled.'

'I don't like the sound of him either,' said Mrs O'Connor, putting a hand to her throat. 'What sort of danger?'

'It doesn't say,' replied Mrs Sloughthwaite.

'Huh!' snorted Mrs Pocock. 'Anybody could have told you you would meet some stranger. They pluck things out of the air, these horoscope writers. It's all vague and airy-fairy. You weren't told anything pacific.'

'That's as may be,' said the shopkeeper, 'but it's keeping me on my toes all the same.'

The tinkle of the doorbell made the two customers jump. They turned sharply, almost expecting to see the troublesome stranger who had been predicted in the horoscope walk through the door.

A young woman entered, carrying a baby. She was a large, healthy-looking girl with lank mousy brown hair, large watery blue eyes and prominent front teeth. A dewdrop sparkled at the end of her nose like a diamond.

'Hello, Bianca,' said the shopkeeper in a cheerful voice.

'Hello, Mrs Sloughthwaite,' replied the young woman, her voice doleful and plodding.

'It's quite a while since you've been in.'

'I've had the baby to look after,' she said, approaching the counter.

'Well, let's have a look at the little lad,' said the shopkeeper, reaching out and taking the baby from his mother's arms. She moved the bit of blanket which covered half the child and beamed widely, two great dimples appearing on her round rosy cheeks. The baby's little face peered up at her. 'Why, he's a bobby-dazzler and no mistake.' Bianca smiled and sniffed. The two customers came over to have a look.

Mrs O'Connor stroked the baby's cheek. 'He's a bonny-looking wee baby, so he is,' she said. Mrs Pocock turned her small wrinkled eyes upon the child and looked closely down her nose and said nothing.

'He's no trouble,' Bianca said. 'Sleeps right through the night, takes his feeds and hardly ever cries.'

'Well, you're very lucky, that's all I can say,' remarked Mrs Pocock. 'The trouble I had with my Ernest. He wouldn't sleep, cried from morning till night with colic and filled his nappy as soon as I changed it. I said to my husband, that's the last baby I'm having.'

'So what's the little fella called?' Mrs O'Connor asked Bianca.

'Brandon.'

'Brandon!' repeated Mrs Pocock. 'Wherever did you get that name from?'

'Perhaps it's named after the baby's father,' suggested Mrs Sloughthwaite, hoping she might uncover the secret of the child's paternity.

'No,' replied Bianca. 'We just like the name.' She chewed a strand of her long stringy hair.

'And how are you in yourself?' asked Mrs Sloughthwaite in a solicitous and kindly manner.

'Oh, I'm not too bad but I've got cracked nipples.'

'I had them,' said Mrs Pocock. 'Talk about agony. I tried one of those breast pumps the health visitor gave me when I had my Ernest, but gave it up as a bad job after a week. You'd best get it on bottled milk.'

'Dr Stirling says that breast milk is best for the baby,' said Bianca, 'so I'm keeping going. Anyway I don't have to buy bottled milk so I save money.'

'Things are a bit tight are they, love?' asked the shopkeeper.

'A bit.' Her voice trembled a little.

'You want to get the child's father to do his bit and fork out,' said Mrs Pocock aggressively. 'Typical of lads these days. They get a lass into trouble and then you never see hide nor hair of them again. No responsibility.'

'His dad does what he can,' said Bianca sadly. 'He gives me money when he's able.'

The shopkeeper couldn't resist. 'So do I know the father?' she asked.

'I'm not telling no one, Mrs Sloughthwaite,' she said. 'My dad says if he finds out who it is he'll punch his lights out.'

The shopkeeper rocked the baby in her chubby arms and stared down at the little elfin-faced child with the pale brown eyes set in an oval face, the large ears, sandy lashes and tufts of ginger hair. There was little doubt in her mind as to who the father was. She smiled and determined that for the time being she would hold her superior knowledge like a dog with a bone.

'Excuse me, Mrs Devine,' said the school secretary the following Monday morning, 'there's a parent with a little girl wishing to see you.' She paused and pushed a stray strand of hair from her face. 'He's – how shall I put it? – a bit out of the ordinary.'

'In what way?' asked Elisabeth, intrigued.

'I think he's a gypsy,' whispered Mrs Scrimshaw.

'Thank you, Mrs Scrimshaw,' said Elisabeth. 'I'll come down. I have been expecting him.'

Her visitor, observed suspiciously by the caretaker from the school hall, was staring intently at the children's writing which had been mounted on the wall in the entrance hall when Elisabeth turned the corridor. His daughter, swinging her small legs backwards and forwards, sat on a chair, reading.

'Good morning,' said Elisabeth.

The man drew a huge slow intake of breath, shook his head and then smiled. 'You!' he exclaimed.

'Me,' Elisabeth replied stolidly, coming over and shaking his hand. 'It's good to see you again, Mr O'Malley.' She crouched in front of the little girl and patted her hand. 'Hello, Roisin.'

'Hello,' replied the child. She looked mystified.

Elisabeth stood, smoothed the creases out of her skirt and said in a pleasant voice, 'If you would like to follow me, Mr O'Malley, and you too, Roisin, we can have a little look around the school before the children arrive and then sort out a few details.'

'You didn't say you were a teacher at the school,' whispered the child's father as he followed Elisabeth down the corridor.

'Actually, I'm the head teacher,' she told him, 'the formidable but good-humoured head teacher who, I hope, knows what she's about.'

'Oh dear,' he said stopping in his tracks, 'about our conversation—'

'I perhaps should have told you who I was,' said Elisabeth, 'but I have to admit I was interested in what was being said about me in the village. Now if you like what you see and want Roisin to stay, I should be delighted to have her. She would be in the lower junior class with Mrs Robertshaw, who is a very good teacher, and I know, should you decide to send her here, your daughter will be happy and settle in.'

On the tour of the school they came across Oscar, early as usual, sitting quietly reading in the corner of the small school library. The boy looked up when he caught sight of them, took off his glasses and pinched the bridge of his nose. He stared for a moment at the little girl. It was a studying look, neither friendly nor unfriendly.

'Hello, Oscar,' said Elisabeth. 'Here bright and early again.'

'Good morning, Mrs Devine,' replied the boy, closing his book. 'I see there's another new pupil.'

'I hope so, Oscar,' replied Elisabeth.

'We'll be bursting at the seams at this rate.' He looked at Roisin. 'Hello,' he said.

'Hello,' she replied uncertainly.

'What are you reading?' he asked, noticing the book the girl was carrying.

She showed him the cover. 'Peter Dixon!' he cried. 'You like Peter Dixon?'

The girl nodded. 'He's my favourite poet.'

'And mine,' enthused the boy. He dug into his bag and produced a thin glossy-backed paperback with a colourful cover. 'Have you read this one? It's his latest. It's a signed copy. I wrote to him.'

'No!' replied Roisin, moving closer and examining the book.

'You can borrow it if you like,' said the boy.

'Why don't we leave Roisin here with Oscar for a moment?' said Elisabeth to the girl's father. 'Then we can talk about whether or not you wish her to come to Barton-in the-Dale.'

The man smiled. 'I think I've decided,' he said.

The following week a tall gangly lad with long thin arms and long thin legs and wild, woolly red hair appeared at Mrs Sloughthwaite's counter. His arm was in a sling.

'Hello, Clarence,' said the shopkeeper cheerfully.

'Hello, Mrs Sloughthwaite,' he mumbled.

'And how are you?'

'Not too bad.'

'And how's your arm?'

'On the mend.'

'And how's your Uncle Fred?'

He grimaced. 'Much the same.'

'He works you too hard.'

'Aye, happen he does.'

'You ought to tell him, you know.'

'He won't take too kindly to me doing that,' said Clarence. 'Says I make a pig's ear of everything I do. I never seem to do anything what's right for my Uncle Fred. I'm keeping out of his way at the moment.'

'I meant you ought to tell him about the other business,' said the shopkeeper.

'I don't know what you mean.'

'Oh, I think you do.'

Colour flushed the young man's face. 'I don't know what you're on about, Mrs Sloughthwaite.'

'My brains aren't made of porridge, Clarence,' said the shopkeeper. 'I'm talking about Bianca.'

'She's told you!' he exclaimed.

'No, she hasn't told me but I've got eyes in my head. That baby couldn't be anyone else's. He's the spitting image of his father.'

The boy gave a great grin. 'Do you think so?'

'Oh yes, there's no mistaking it.'

'We were keeping it a secret,' said Clarence. 'Do other people know?'

'No, they don't and I don't mean to tell anyone either. One thing you can say about me is that I'm the soul of indiscretion. I shan't say a word but I think you ought to tell your Uncle

Fred. He's got a fair bit of money stashed away up there at Tanfield Farm and nothing to spend it on except ale. It wouldn't hurt him to part with a bob or two. Your Bianca's a bit strapped for cash from what I hear.'

'I do what I can, Mrs Sloughthwaite,' the young man told her unhappily.

'I know you do, love, but you and Bianca need help. That little Brandon is your Uncle Fred's great-nephew after all. He's family. That baby is his flesh and blood. He should help out.'

'He wouldn't,' said Clarence sadly. 'He'll say that it's something else I've got wrong.'

'Do you think you've got it wrong, having such a little treasure?' she asked.

'No, I don't,' replied the young man. 'It's the best thing I've ever done. I'm going to be a good dad, Mrs Sloughthwaite. I'm going to try my best.'

'And despite what other people might say, I don't think you got it wrong,' said the shopkeeper. 'These things happen. You've got a lovely little boy and his mum's a nice enough lass and you're well suited.' The young man looked down and nodded. 'You like Bianca, don't you, Clarence?'

'I love her, Mrs Sloughthwaite,' he said, looking up. 'She's the only one I feel I can talk to. I'd do anything for her.'

'Well, you ought to go and see her father then, and tell your uncle.'

'I don't think I dare.'

'Neither of them is as hard as you think,' said the shopkeeper. 'Their barks are far worse than their bites. You need to sit down with Bianca and her parents and with your Uncle Fred and sort things out for the sake of the baby.'

'You think?'

'I do. That kiddie needs a father and you need to be there to help bring him up. Bianca's parents and your uncle are sure to find out one of these days, probably from some nosy gossip in the Blacksmith's Arms who has seen you with Bianca. It's best coming from you.'

'Aye, I guess you're right.'

'I know I am,' said the shopkeeper. 'Now what is it you want?'

'Do you sell disposable nappies, Mrs Sloughthwaite?' he asked.

15

'So how do you like Barton-in-the-Dale?' asked Archdeacon Atticus, as he stacked the plates and dishes at the dining table.

Archdeacon Atticus, his wife and the new curate had just finished a deeply unappetising dinner of unidentifiable, pale stringy meat, watery potatoes and undercooked cabbage followed by lumpy lukewarm tapioca pudding.

'I like it very much so far,' Ashley replied. 'It's a very friendly place. Everyone has been very kind. St Christopher's is a lovely old church. It has so much character.'

'Indeed,' agreed the archdeacon. 'A fine example of Norman architecture. Lamentably the church was despoiled at the Reformation, statues were smashed, saints beheaded, magnificent stained-glass windows destroyed and lovingly crafted marble tombs desecrated.'

'Somebody ought to desecrate that dreadfully vulgar marble tomb in the churchyard,' observed Mrs Atticus. 'You will have seen it of course, Ashley. They ought to take a sledgehammer to it.'

'My wife, as you might ascertain, Ashley,' said her husband, smiling weakly, 'is not at all enamoured of the Reverend Steerum-Slack's mausoleum.'

'It is a little bit over the top,' agreed the young curate.

'That is an understatement if ever I heard one,' said Mrs Atticus. 'I mean, what sort of person pays to have that monstrosity erected? He should have left his money to the poor. He was very well off by all accounts. It must have cost an arm and a leg. It takes up half the churchyard and I have to look upon it every morning from our bedroom window. Perhaps now you are in a senior position in the Church, Charles, you could authorise its removal.'

'I think not, my dear,' replied her husband.

'It is so good of you and your wife to let me stay at the rectory,' said the new curate, keen to change the subject. It sounded to her like the beginnings of a domestic dispute.

'Oh, there's plenty of room here,' replied the cleric. 'It is a pleasure to have you. I trust your room is satisfactory?'

'Oh yes, it's fine.'

'Well, all I can say is that you are easily pleased,' said Mrs Atticus. 'I find this rectory a draughty old place at the best of times and in need of urgent refurbishment. It's cold and musty and full of noises. The heating is temperamental with its grumbling radiators and gurgling pipes, the stairs, which are far too steep and precarious, creak so much one wonders if the very floorboards are ready to give way beneath one. And as for the kitchen, it's virtually medieval.'

'Well, it suits me,' said the new curate amiably.

'Really?'

'It has character.'

Mrs Atticus opened her mouth to reply, but her husband was quick to take the opportunity of interposing. 'It's a very pleasant little village, is Barton-in-the Dale,' he said, changing the subject. 'Perhaps a little quiet for some people. Marcia, I know, finds it very sleepy and uneventful, do you not, my dear?'

'Insular would be the word that springs to mind, Charles,' replied his wife. 'A gossipy and claustrophobic place where everyone knows everyone else's business. If you wish to have a private life, Barton-in-the-Dale is not somewhere you would choose.'

'You are being a trifle hard on the village,' remarked the

archdeacon, smiling somewhat uncomfortably. He certainly did not wish his new assistant to change her mind and ask the bishop for a move to somewhere more lively and interesting. Admittedly he had been surprised to find a young woman as the new curate, but she was proving most satisfactory, very satisfactory indeed.

'You will find, Ashley,' Mrs Atticus told the new curate, ignoring her husband's comment, 'that you will not be able to walk down the high street without a curtain twitching, say anything in the doctor's surgery without it being broadcast around the whole neighbourhood, or purchase an item from the village shop without all and sundry knowing what you are having for tea. You will be waylaid by parishioners all the time, asking about church functions and services and what are we doing about the Harvest Festival and the summer fête and when is the next meeting of the Mothers' Union. I have endured this since we moved here.'

'It's not been too bad for you, my dear, since you have started teaching at the school,' observed the archdeacon. He tapped his knife against his plate in irritation. 'Things have been a deal better for you, have they not, and you have been much happier in yourself?'

'Yes, there is some truth in that,' agreed Mrs Atticus. 'Although I still get pestered – by parents now rather than parishioners – but I don't mind as much. Still, I mustn't grumble. I suppose it was good of the bishop to let us stay here so I could finish my training at the village school.'

'Indeed it was very good of him,' agreed her husband, turning to the new curate. 'As I explained to Marcia, it is most unusual, indeed I believe unprecedented in this diocese, for an archdeacon to stay in the church where he has been the vicar. I am most grateful to his lordship for making an exception in my case. He has been most accommodating. Initially, he did suggest that we should move to Clayton, but Marcia wished to remain here and he very kindly assented.'

'It was because of the travelling,' Mrs Atticus explained. 'I couldn't possibly have remained at the village school if I had had to travel out here from Clayton to Barton. The buses are terribly unpredictable and in winter the roads are virtually impassable. And then there is all the equipment, books and materials I should have to carry. It was quite out of the question.'

'And that is why we can remain here for the time being and we have Ashley to help,' said Archdeacon Atticus.

'And I shall be more than happy to be of help,' said the new curate. 'Perhaps I might organise the Harvest Festival and the summer fête and take on the Mothers' Union that was mentioned. I can see how very busy you are, Marcia, with all the preparation you have to do as a teacher, and, after all, it is church business and not something people should expect you to take on.'

'Well, that is kind of you,' said Mrs Atticus. 'It certainly would take a great deal off my shoulders. You are quite right, of course, everyone seems to assume that it is the job of the vicar's wife to take on all these extra responsibilities to do with the church.'

'And might I suggest something else?' said the new curate.

'Yes?'

'Of course, you may not feel you wish to delegate it.'

'Well, what is it?' asked the archdeacon's wife.

'I should be more than happy to take on my share of the cooking. I really do not expect you to come home from school and start in the kitchen. Actually, cooking is a hobby of mine. I find it very therapeutic.'

'Take on the cooking!' exclaimed the archdeacon's wife. 'You mean you would prepare the meals?'

Archdeacon Atticus tried hard to contain his excitement at such a suggestion.

'Of course you may not wish me—' began the new curate.

'I should be delighted if you did,' trilled Mrs Atticus. 'I hate the kitchen and I find cooking a terrible chore. Furthermore, I can't claim to be very good at it.' She smiled.

'You are a trifle hard on yourself, my dear,' said the archdeacon, thinking the very opposite. 'However, I think Ashley's suggestion is an excellent one and it will enable you to concentrate on your school work.'

He said a silent prayer, thanking the Lord that he would no longer have to endure his wife's cooking.

'And how did your first funeral service go?' asked Mrs Atticus.

'Very well, I think,' replied the new curate. 'It was a full church. It appeared that the whole of the village turned out. Mr Fish must have been a very well-loved man.'

'Well, don't expect such a large congregation at the Sunday services,' observed Mrs Atticus. 'I think most of them will have turned out to have a look at you. They are a most curious lot in the village and certainly don't like to miss anything.'

'That's what Dr Stirling said,' replied the new curate. 'He gave a very moving address.'

'Oh, you have met our local GP then?' asked the archdeacon.

'Yes, he seemed charming.'

Mrs Atticus raised an eyebrow. 'Yes, he's a very pleasant man. Not a great deal to say for himself, but he is an excellent doctor.'

'I was asking about the boy I met in the churchyard, young Danny, who has gone to live with his grandmother.'

'Ah yes,' said the archdeacon. 'A very sad case. The child was terribly upset, as one might imagine, when he lost his grandfather and really didn't know what would happen to him. Then Dr Stirling fostered him and he was all set to adopt the boy.'

'And then his grandmother, a harridan of a woman, turned up like the proverbial bad penny,' added Mrs Atticus, 'and whisked him away. It amazes me that she was allowed to do it.'

'I didn't meet Dr Stirling's wife at the funeral service,' said the new curate.

'No, he is a widower,' explained the archdeacon. 'His wife, a charming woman and a doctor herself, was tragically killed in a riding accident. Poor Dr Stirling went through a terrible time coming to terms with it, but time is great healer and he seems more himself these days.'

'So he lives alone?' asked the new curate.

'No, he has a son, James.'

'Perhaps we might invite him around for a meal some time,' suggested the new curate. 'I could try out one of my new recipes on him.'

The archdeacon's wife exchanged a glance with her husband. Mrs Atticus had heard rumours, of course, that Dr Stirling and Elisabeth were, in common parlance, 'an item', but nothing seemed to be happening on that score. When they were together in school their relationship seemed to her to be strictly professional, even a little formal. Dr Stirling reminded her of her own husband when he was a young priest. He too was rather serious and intense, a man with a warm, attentive manner and kindly eyes, but shy. It was she who had made the first move in their relationship. Perhaps Elisabeth needs a bit of a push, she thought, and a bit of healthy competition in the form of the attractive curate might just do the trick.

'Yes, I think that would be a splendid idea,' she said with a small smile.

The three women, with suitably cheerless expressions, sat in the parlour at the rear of the village store.

'Well, that's another one gone,' observed the shopkeeper,

prior to taking a sip of tea and helping herself to a sliver of cake.

'Sure doesn't it come to us all, Mrs Sloughthwaite,' observed Mrs O'Connor, sighing dramatically. 'None of us can escape when the celestial trumpets sound and we shuffle off this mortal coil to be summoned to join the great majority on Time's winged chariot. In darkness we come into this world and into darkness we return.'

The shopkeeper gave a quizzical smile. Mrs O'Connor, she thought, was not a woman to use one word when several would suffice.

'No,' agreed Mrs Pocock, helping herself to her third salmon-paste sandwich and taking a huge bite. 'We all have to die. It's a fact of life. It comes to all of us in the end.'

'It does indeed,' added Mrs O'Connor, nodding gravely. 'Life is just a journey to death. As my grandmother used to say: "Make the most of every day, for life is short and wears away."'

''Course, in this weather the old folk are dropping like flies,' observed Mrs Pocock, 'what with the cold and damp. I've never known it so bitter. You can hear your bones rattling.'

'He was a good age, was Mr Fish,' observed Mrs Sloughthwaite, 'and of course he'd been on his last legs for a good few years.'

'It was a godsend that he lasted out to see his granddaughter get wed,' observed Mrs Pocock. 'Nice sandwiches, these.'

'I used to see him sitting on the bench on the village green looking like a lost soul,' remarked Mrs O'Connor. 'He certainly had the smell of clay upon him, God rest his soul.'

'I thought that Chardonnay sang the hymns beautifully,' said the shopkeeper. 'Who would have thought that such a big ungainly lass like that could have such a lovely voice?'

'And the first hymn was very appropriate,' added Mrs Pocock.

'In what way?' asked the doctor's housekeeper.

'Well, it was "Shall we Gather by the River".'

'And?'

'River – Fish.'

'Oh, I see,' chuckled Mrs O'Connor.

'I've never seen the church so packed out with people,' observed Mrs Pocock.

'Well, let's be honest,' said the shopkeeper, giving a faint snort, 'they were all there to give the new curate a good once-over rather than being there for Albert Fish's funeral. I don't wish to be unkind, but it wasn't as if he was that well known or indeed well liked.'

'He was a grumpy old man at the best of times,' added Mrs Pocock scathingly.

'New curate!' exclaimed Mrs O'Connor, with an expression of frowning surprise. 'There's a new curate at St Christopher's?'

'Just started,' Mrs Sloughthwaite informed her. 'Reverend Atticus has been given this fancy title of archdeacon and he's now not a reverend but a venereal.'

'Fancy,' said Mrs O'Connor. 'I don't think we have venereals in the Catholic Church.'

'He now works for that trendy happy-clappy bishop in Clayton,' continued the shopkeeper. 'The one who opened the church fête last July wearing that T-shirt with "JESUS SAVES!" on the front.'

'And do you remember,' said Mrs Pocock, 'Malcolm Stubbins, cheeky monkey, going up to him and saying that Jesus ought to be put in goal if he was so good at saving.'

'He's better off behind a desk, is Mr Atticus,' said the shopkeeper. 'I mean he's a nice enough man and never says a bad word about anybody but he could send an insomaniac to sleep with his sermons. He's far too academical for St Christopher's. Considering the new curate had never met Mr Fish, I thought what she had to say about him was very touching.'

'Yes,' agreed Mrs Pocock, 'there were few wet eyes in the church. Mrs Fish looked gutted.'

Mrs Sloughthwaite raised an eyebrow.

'Did you say "she"?' asked Mrs O'Connor.

'That's right,' said the shopkeeper, 'the new curate is a woman and she seems very nice. She christened Bianca's baby, and Mrs Lloyd who was godmother was in the shop the other day and she was telling me—'

'A woman!' interrupted Mrs O'Connor. 'The new curate is a woman?'

'They do have women priests now, Mrs O'Connor,' the shopkeeper told her. 'Your lot might not hold with having them but they're taking over in the C. of E. and good luck to them, that's what I say. Women give the best advice in my experience, they're more sympathetic and they are better listeners and that's what you need in a vicar.'

'Well I never,' said Mrs O'Connor, 'a woman priest in Barton. And what is she like, this new curate?'

'She seems very nice,' replied the shopkeeper, shuffling into a more comfortable position. The chair creaked under her prodigious bulk. 'Young, blonde, slim and very attractive.' She smiled. 'I would like to have seen the expression on Mrs Atticus's face when she turned up on her doorstep like one of them models out of a glossy magazine. I bet she was expecting some doddery old clergyman well past his sell-by date.'

'And did you see Fred Massey sitting there in the front pew with a face like a bag of rusty spanners ogling her?' remarked Mrs Pocock. She gave a small cold laugh. 'His eyeballs were out on stalks.'

'To be honest, I couldn't take my eyes off Miss Sowerbutts,' said Mrs Sloughthwaite, 'straight-backed and with a face like a death mask. They ought to hire her out for funerals, she looks that miserable – as grim as the corpse in the coffin.'

'I don't know why she was there anyway,' scoffed Mrs Pocock, reaching for a slice of Battenberg cake. 'She never sets foot in the church normally, not as far as I know.'

'She was there,' explained the shopkeeper, 'because Mr Fish used to be the caretaker at the school before Mr Gribbon. He worked there for donkey's years, until he fell off the ladder and broke his collarbone. Miss Sowerbutts was looking daggers at Dr Stirling when he got up to speak.'

'Why should she be cross with Dr Stirling?' asked Mrs O'Connor.

'Because she fully expected to have been asked to do it herself, that's why. She showed up at Joyce Fish's cottage before the body was cold and said she'd be happy to say a few words at the funeral, but went away with a flea in her ear when the widow told her that it had all been arranged and she wasn't required. Mrs Fish told me that herself when she came in to order the food for the funeral tea. They had a right old spread by all accounts – ham sandwiches, cheese straws, mushroom volivonts, sherry trifle and fruit cake, by the way. She was going to have sausages on sticks but she opted for black pudding, it being a funeral and all.'

'It's strange, so it is,' observed Mrs O'Connor, 'how grief can sharpen the appetite.'

'Anyway,' continued the shopkeeper, 'as she told me, there was no way she was asking Miss Sowerbutts to say anything. She said her husband couldn't stand the sight of her when he worked at the school and would be spinning in his grave if she got up in the pulpit and started spouting. She asked Dr Stirling because he had treated her husband for years and she said he's a real gentleman and she likes his voice.'

'He does have a nice voice, so he does,' agreed the doctor's housekeeper, 'and in all the time I've done for him, he's never ever raised it.'

'Speaking of Dr Stirling,' said Mrs Sloughthwaite, looking directly at Mrs O'Connor and starting to fish for information, 'he seemed to get on very well with the new curate.' Then, she added with exaggerated emphasis, 'Very well indeed.'

'Sure, doesn't the man get on famously with everybody,' said the housekeeper non-committally. 'Of course, he's not been quite himself these days since Danny had to leave. He was going to adopt the boy, as you know, and we were all that excited at Clumber Lodge. It's upset us all, and young James has gone quiet again. The house is not the same.'

'Poor lad, having to put up with Maisie Proctor as a grandmother,' said the shopkeeper.

'She has a lot to answer for, that one,' observed Mrs Pocock. 'Fancy turning up again after all these years and taking the lad away. I'll tell you this—'

'So, I was wondering if Dr Stirling knows the new curate, then?' said Mrs Sloughthwaite, still staring at Mrs O'Connor and intimating that the housekeeper might provide her with some juicy bit of gossip. She was determined that the conversation should not deviate from the topic in which she was most interested.

'I wouldn't know,' replied Mrs O'Connor. 'I wasn't aware that there was a new curate, and in any case Dr Stirling isn't likely to tell me if he knows her or not.' Dr Stirling's housekeeper had known Mrs Sloughthwaite long enough to appreciate that anything said to her in the village store would be relayed in quick time around the village. The housekeeper had learned to be very guarded when talking to her.

'Because they were a good ten minutes chatting away after the funeral service,' said the shopkeeper. 'I mean, most of us got a "Good morning" and a handshake from her and that was the extent of it, but they were talking ten to the dozen, like old friends.'

'She might have been consulting the doctor about a medical matter,' suggested Mrs O'Connor.

'Hardly,' retorted the shopkeeper. 'The surgery is the place for that.' The shopkeeper thought for a moment and then with a heave of her bosom she remarked, 'Mrs Devine will have to watch out. She might very well have a rival.'

Mrs Sloughthwaite was nothing if not observant. She missed very little that went on in the village, and had lingered in the churchyard following Mr Fish's service to note who had attended the funeral and to catch up on any gossip. She had observed with interest the long and animated conversation which had taken place between the local GP and the new arrival in the village.

The curate had been standing by the door, greeting members of the congregation as they filed out of the church. She slipped a small hand into Dr Stirling's and shook it warmly. 'Dr Stirling,' she said. 'I am sure your words were a great comfort to Mrs Fish and her family.'

'And I know that yours were,' replied the doctor. 'It was a most moving service.'

'Well, thank you,' she said. 'I have to admit I was a little nervous, this being my first funeral at St Christopher's.'

'Well, it certainly didn't show,' the doctor reassured her, smiling. 'I hope you will be very happy here in Barton-in-the-Dale, Reverend Underwood.'

'Ashley, please,' she said. 'I shall be very happy if we have such a large congregation on Sundays.'

'I think many were here to see you,' the doctor told her. 'You will find that there are a lot of inquisitive people in the village.'

'I do hope I can number you amongst my congregation?' said the new curate.

'I'm not really a churchgoer,' replied the doctor.

'Then I shall have to use my powers of persuasion,' she said. 'How is Danny?'

'You know Danny?' said Dr Stirling, staring at her with surprise.

'He was visiting his grandfather's grave and I met him in the churchyard. We got talking,' she explained. 'He was very upset about having to leave the village and spoke very highly of you and all you had done for him.'

'Ah,' laughed the doctor, 'so you are the mystery woman in the churchyard. Danny said you were really nice and gave him some very good advice. He said you looked like the angel on the big tomb.'

She coloured a little. 'Don't mention the tomb, it's a bone of contention in the Atticus household. Anyway, young Danny is a very pleasant boy, very friendly. I do hope things work out for him.'

'Yes, so do I,' replied the doctor.

'I'm sure he will settle in time,' she said, trying to put the best aspect on a miserable situation.

'I hope so,' he said. 'Well, I guess I had better be making tracks. It was good to meet you.'

'And maybe I will see you at morning service next Sunday,' she said, giving a disarming smile.

'Maybe,' replied the doctor.

'I have some very good news, children,' said Elisabeth one morning in assembly. 'But before I tell you about it I have asked Mr Gribbon to have a word about the boys' toilets.'

The caretaker strode to the front of the hall. 'Some of the boys here, and you know who you are,' he said, stabbing the air with a bony finger, 'have been putting foreign objects down the toilet bowls and blocking the pipes. Now, this all started when one particular pupil, and he knows who he is, put ping-pong balls down the toilets and then others started depositing other things. Whoever is responsible wants to stop it off because if I find out who the culprits are—'

'Thank you, Mr Gribbon,' interrupted Elisabeth. 'I think all the boys here have got the message.' She looked at the faces before her. 'This will stop. Is that clear?'

'Yes, Mrs Devine,' chorused the children.

The caretaker walked to the back of the hall where he remained, arms folded and scowling.

'Now the good news,' said Elisabeth. 'I am delighted to say that several of the poems we sent in for the School Library Poetry Competition have been accepted for the anthology. Three have been shortlisted for one of the prizes: Oscar's poem, "My Dog Daisy", Darren's poem, "The Trouble with Words", and Chardonnay's poem, "My Sister's Baby", have been selected.'

Chardonnay could not contain herself. 'Mine!' she shouted out.

'Yes, yours, Chardonnay,' said the head teacher.

The girl puffed out her cheeks and breathed out noisily.

'Let's congratulate our three talented poets, shall we?' said Elisabeth. The children clapped and cheered. Several girls near Chardonnay prodded her or patted her on the back. 'These three shortlisted poems,' continued Elisabeth, 'go through to the final, and the three young poets and Miss Brakespeare shall next week be going to the public library in Clayton for the award ceremony. So we all need to keep our fingers crossed.

'Now it occurred to me that you might all like to hear the poems which were selected, so I am going to ask each of the lucky three to read out their poem.'

Following the readings by Chardonnay and Darren, it was Oscar's turn. The boy came to the front of the hall, cleared his throat several times, and then, tilting his colourful glasses slightly on the bridge of his nose, announced, 'My poem is called "My Dog Daisy".' Then he read his verse:

'When my dog Daisy was a puppy,
She would leap and bound,
Run and race,
Jump and chase,
Spring and scamper,
Like all young dogs tend to do.

Now my dog Daisy is older,
She growls and grumbles,
Snaps and snarls,
Scratches and smells,
Sleeps and snores,
Like all old dogs tend to do.

Puppies and children,
Old dogs and old people,
They have a lot in common.'

Resuming his place, Oscar glanced in the direction of the caretaker, who was glowering at him from the back of the hall.

At the end of school, Elisabeth sat with Mrs Robertshaw in her classroom. She was interested to hear how Roisin was getting on.

'Well, it's early days,' said the teacher, 'but she seems to be settling in nicely. She's a delightful child, very quick on the uptake and interested, and a very good reader.'

'Her father will be pleased to hear it,' said Elisabeth.

'Oscar has taken quite a shine to her,' said Mrs Robertshaw. 'He seems to have taken her under his wing. You should see them in the playground, chattering away like some old married couple.'

'And how are the other children treating her?' asked Elisabeth.

'Very well, as far as I can tell.'

'Evidently there've been a few unpleasant comments from some children in her previous schools. As you know, children can be a delight but sometimes they can be cruel, particularly to someone who is a bit different.'

'About her being a gypsy you mean?'

'Well, she's not really a gypsy,' Elisabeth told her. 'Her father describes himself as an itinerant. She travels with him and they don't stay in the same place for too long. I don't expect that Roisin will be with us for much longer.'

'Pity, she's a nice little girl,' said Mrs Robertshaw, 'and very pretty. Her father looks too young to have a child of her age, don't you think? He looks more like a brother.'

'Oh, he must be in his early thirties,' said Elisabeth.

'Do you think?' asked the teacher. 'He looks a lot younger to me.' Then she added, 'I must say, he's very dishy.'

'Yes, he is very striking looking,' agreed Elisabeth.

'Do you know what happened to the mother?'

'No, he's not said.'

A face appeared around the door.

'Miss, can I have the key to the games cupboard, please?' asked Malcolm. He was wearing a red and white football strip.

'Come in, Malcolm,' said Elisabeth. 'I want to have a word with you.'

The boy looked worried. He was used to being told off. 'What about, miss?' he asked.

'To say how pleased I have been with you lately.'

The boy shifted uneasily. He was clearly embarrassed by praise, something he rarely received at home.

'Since you have returned to this school you have kept out of trouble and—'

'Miss, I've got to go. I've got a football match,' the boy interrupted. 'They'll be starting.'

'I've nearly finished,' said Elisabeth. 'Now as you have seen, we have had some new pupils starting here at Barton this term and you know yourself how difficult it can be for new pupils to settle in.'

'Yes, miss,' said the boy impatiently.

'I think you had quite a difficult time when you started at Urebank.'

The boy nodded. 'Yes, it was horrible, miss. I was picked on.'

'So you know what it can be like starting at another school. Well, I want you to keep an eye on the new children and make sure nobody picks on them. I want you to be a sort of monitor. Will you do that for me?'

'What do I have to do?' asked the boy.

'Just make sure that no one is unkind to them. Can you do that?'

'OK.' The boy looked at his watch. 'Can I go now, miss?'

'Yes, off you go, and remember I'm relying on you.'

The boy ran off.

Mrs Robertshaw turned to Elisabeth. 'Poacher turned gamekeeper,' she said. 'Clever.'

16

Elisabeth arrived home from school later that afternoon to find her garden had been transformed. The previous month Danny had tidied everything: he had cut back the dead flowers, dug up the weeds, pruned the bushes and trimmed the hedges, but since he had gone the lawn had gathered a fresh carpet of dead leaves, part of the paddock fence had blown down, and the gate leading to the track by the side of the cottage had come off its hinges. Elisabeth had meant to do something about these things but had been so busy she just had not had the time. She had been minded to ask Fred Massey to take on the task, but he could not be relied upon, and anyway she did not like the grouchy old man, who was forever complaining and out for what he could get.

Now, she looked at her neat and tidy garden with satisfaction. During the day someone had been very busy. The lawn had been raked clean, the fence repaired and painted an olive-green and the gate to the track repaired. Even the porch had been swept. She had an idea who was responsible.

She tapped on the door of the caravan.

'Hello, Mrs Devine,' said Roisin, poking out her head.

'Hello, Roisin,' said Elisabeth. 'May I speak to your father?'

'Come in, come in,' came a voice from inside.

The caravan was warm and comfortable and there wasn't a thing out of place.

Elisabeth was surprised to see how clean and tidy

everything was. Something that smelled very tasty was simmering in a pan on the small stove.

'I hope I'm not disturbing you,' she said.

'Not at all,' he replied.

'I guess it was you who has been busy in my garden,' she said.

'Well, I like to keep busy,' he told her, 'and it did need sorting.'

'You really shouldn't have bothered, but thank you all the same. It looks a whole lot better.'

'There's a big branch on the horse chestnut tree that wants coming off,' he said. 'It's been hit by lightning by the looks of it, it's split and charred, and in a strong wind you might be in bed one night and find it comes crashing through your roof. I'll get it sorted tomorrow.'

'Yes, I know it needs doing,' said Elisabeth. 'Danny, the young man who used to live in the caravan and look after my garden for me, kept mentioning that the branch was dangerous and wanted cutting off. But I really don't expect you to do that.'

'It'll be a pleasure,' he replied.

Elisabeth looked over to where Roisin was curled up on the bed, her nose buried in a book. 'I hear from her teacher that your daughter is settling in well at Barton-in-the-Dale?' she asked.

'Yes, very well,' the girl's father replied. 'I can't remember when she has taken so well to a new school.'

'Mrs Robertshaw tells me she's very bright, a very good reader and clever with numbers, and Mr Tomlinson, who comes in to teach music, says she is a talented flautist. I sometimes hear her in the evening.'

'It doesn't disturb you, I hope.'

'Not at all,' said Elisabeth. 'She plays beautifully. Is it you who plays the violin?'

'I try,' he replied.

'I'm very pleased Roisin is happy at the school. You mentioned to me when we first met that it is sometimes not that easy for her settling in, meeting new people and making friends.'

'Touch wood, she's fine.'

'That's good.'

'She has a boyfriend, you know,' he said in a hushed voice, 'a little boy called Oscar. She's been invited for tea next Sunday. He's going to show her his fossil collection.'

'Are you talking about me, Daddy?' asked Roisin, looking up from her book.

'And why in the world would I be doing that?' replied her father.

Elisabeth shook her head and smiled.

'The thing is, Mrs Devine,' said the man quietly. 'I've a mind to stay on here a bit longer than planned. It's a lovely part of the country, Roisin seems settled and tells me she'd like to stay, I couldn't get a better place to put the caravan and people seem really friendly hereabouts. Would that be all right with you?'

'You are welcome to stay as long as you like, Mr O'Malley,' Elisabeth told him. 'I said to you when we first met that I do value my privacy, and as you promised you have not disturbed me at all. I hardly know that you are there.'

'Except for the music,' he said.

'Which I like,' she replied. 'You know, one of the reasons why I bought this cottage was that it is off the beaten track. In winter I like to go out into the garden at night, crunch through the snow, look at the stars and feel the cold air on my cheeks. Then in summer I love to sit on the old bench and hear the leaves rustling and smell the scents. I might see the white bobtail of a rabbit in the bushes or the sly fox watching from the footpath. One March I saw two hares in the field. They had these long, lean bodies and great erect ears, and they squared up to each other. I watched fascinated as they punched and pummelled. I had never seen anything like that before.' Roisin had stopped reading to listen, her head on one side. 'I just love the peace and quiet of this place,' said Elisabeth.

'You're a romantic, Mrs Devine,' he told her.

She smiled. 'Maybe I am. Anyway, yes, you may stay. Oh, and I think it's about time you called me Elisabeth – out of school anyway.'

'We are very happy here,' he told her, 'so we would love to stay. I just need to find a bit of work to keep the wolf from the door and I'll be as content as I'll ever be.' He looked over to his daughter. 'Did you hear that, Roisin?' he said, 'We can stay.'

The girl clapped her hands gleefully and beamed. 'Thank you, Mrs Devine,' she said.

'I suppose the word which comes to mind would be dramatic,' said Miss Brakespeare. She was sitting with her colleagues in the staffroom the following lunchtime, regaling them with an account of the award ceremony of the School Library Poetry Competition, which had taken place that morning. Elisabeth was, as usual, supervising the school dinners before patrolling the school.

'Go on,' urged Mrs Robertshaw. 'This sounds interesting.'

'Well,' said the deputy head teacher, becoming quite animated, 'we arrived at the public library and everything went really smoothly at first. The chief librarian, Mrs Twiddle, introduced the judges: Philomena Phillpots, "the Dales poetess", a strange-looking woman in a sort of flowered smock and purple lipstick, the editor of the *Gazette* and the mayor of Clayton. The children from the different schools in the area took it in turns to read out their entries. Chardonnay gave a most dramatic rendering of her poem about the baby, illustrating it with various actions which left the judges open-mouthed, and of course Oscar delivered his poem like a seasoned actor taking centre stage.'

'What about Darren?' asked Mrs Robertshaw.

'He really surprised me,' said Miss Brakespeare. 'He had learned his poem off by heart and recited it beautifully. I could see the judges were much moved. Anyway, the last to stand up was a boy from Urebank and he read this poem called "The Colour of My Dreams". It was very good, and I thought to myself at the time that it was a bit too sophisticated to have been written by a child of ten. Anyway, this boy had no sooner finished than Oscar came over to me and said it wasn't his poem. I said, "How do you mean, Oscar?" and he said, "He didn't write it," and I said, "How do you know?" and he said, "Because I've seen it in a poetry book," and I said, "You must be mistaken," and he said he wasn't. "Actually, it's a poem by Peter Dixon," he said.'

'He's his favourite poet,' interposed Mrs Robertshaw.

'Well, anyway, I said, "Maybe the boy has based his poem on the one written by Mr Dixon," and he said, "No, he hasn't." Then he reached into that big leather briefcase he always carries around with him and produced this book of verse. There it was – the very same poem, word for word, which the boy from Urebank had read out as his own.'

'So what did you do?' asked Miss Wilson.

'What could I do?' replied the deputy head teacher. 'I went with Oscar and we informed Mrs Twiddle, who told the judges.'

'Good for you, Miriam,' said Mrs Robertshaw.

'At first they were not inclined to believe me. The poetess in the floral tent pulled a face and pointed at Oscar and said, "I think he must be mistaken," and, "How old is this child?" and Oscar piped up, "Old enough to talk!" Well, you should have seen her face. Then he told her he was surprised she hadn't heard of such a famous poet as Peter Dixon and showed her the poetry book and the poem published in it. The judges couldn't do anything other than disqualify the boy from Urebank.'

'Good grief!' exclaimed Mrs Robertshaw. 'The boy's teacher won't have been best pleased.'

'Oh no, he wasn't,' said Miss Brakespeare. 'He glowered at me and then, as I was leaving, he came over and said, "I suppose you're satisfied." I said that it wasn't me who had copied out someone else's poem and if he was angry with anyone it should be his pupil.'

'You did right,' said Mrs Robertshaw.

'Then this teacher said that things would change at Barton when his head teacher was in charge.'

'He said what?'

'That Mr Richardson would be taking over.'

'Do you think he knows something we don't?' asked Miss Wilson.

'I've no idea,' said Miss Brakespeare, 'and Mrs Devine has not said anything to me. Anyway I have to admit I did feel a tad smug on the way home. After all, Darren won the first prize.'

That afternoon the school secretary arrived at Elisabeth's classroom door. She was red in the face and flustered and started gesticulating outside the classroom window.

'Get on with your work quietly, children,' said Elisabeth. 'I need to speak to Mrs Scrimshaw about something.'

In the corridor the school secretary could barely get out the words. 'He's in the entrance,' she spluttered.

'Who?' asked Elisabeth.

'You had better come and see for yourself,' said Mrs Scrimshaw, striding off down the corridor.

In the entrance was a young man in a smart blue suit. The secretary stood back, her hands clasped before her. 'It's him,' she whispered as the head teacher passed her.

'May I help you?' asked Elisabeth.

'Mrs Devine?'

'That's right.'

'I'm Tom Dwyer,' he told her.

Elisabeth looked puzzled. 'Tom Dwyer?'

'You wrote to me,' said the young man. 'It was about one of your pupils, some lad in your class who is keen on football. Malcolm. You asked me to drop him a line and tell him how important it is to read.'

'Oh, Mr Dwyer!' cried Elisabeth. 'Of course. You're the captain of Clayton United. I never expected you to call into school.'

'Well, I'm not one for writing letters,' he replied. 'Anyway, I was in Barton today. My Auntie Bridget lives in the village and my mother's always on at me to call in and see her. You might know her. She works for the local doctor.'

'Mrs O'Connor?' said Elisabeth.

'That's right,' said the footballer. 'So, shall we go and see this young man and put him right about reading?'

It was a memorable occasion for the children that afternoon and especially for Malcolm Stubbins, who sat wide-eyed as he listened to the footballer telling the class about his life. The man turned to Elisabeth and winked before stressing to the children how important it was to read books and work hard at school.

'Thank you so much for coming in, Mr Dwyer,' said Elisabeth as she walked with him to the school exit at afternoon break. 'You have made a young man very happy, and your visit might get Malcolm, who is one of my most reluctant readers, to pick up a book.'

'A pleasure,' he replied, 'although I have to admit that I wasn't a very good reader myself when I was at school. The only thing I really cared about was football.'

Mrs Scrimshaw rushed out of the office. 'Excuse me, Mr

Dwyer,' she said, 'might I have your autograph for my young nephew? He's a great fan of yours.'

'I didn't know you had a nephew, Mrs Scrimshaw,' said Elisabeth after the visitor had gone.

'I don't,' said the school secretary, her face rather flushed.

Clarence stood on Miss Sowerbutts's doorstep. He was carrying a garden fork, an old sack and a bottle of bleach. He remembered his former head teacher, for he had been a pupil at the village school. He had been frightened of her as a boy and still was, and had not been looking forward to the visit. Taking a deep breath, he rang the bell.

'Oh, it's you,' said Miss Sowerbutts, opening the door a fraction and peering out.

'I . . . I . . . I've come about your m . . . moles, Miss Sowerbutts,' he stuttered.

'M . . . my Uncle Fred asked me t . . . to come. He said they've come b . . . back.'

'Well, you are too late,' she told him.

'P . . . pardon?'

'You can tell your Uncle Fred I don't have a mole problem any more – no thanks to him.'

'P . . . pardon?'

'I will not be requiring his or your services in future because the moles have gone. Daniel Stainthorpe dealt with the problem, and you can tell your Uncle Fred from me that his efforts in putting bleach down the runs were a total and utter waste of time and only succeeded in killing the grass and not the moles.'

'M . . . my Uncle Fred said it's the b . . . best way of getting rid of them,' stammered Clarence.

'Well, if that is what your Uncle Fred thinks then he has less intelligence than I credited him with – which I have to say was never very much in the first place. You have to lay traps for moles and that's what will get rid of them, not a bottle of bleach. In any case, how do you think you can be of any help to me with your arm in a sling?'

'I . . . I can dig with one hand,' said Clarence, 'and I just need to pour some bleach down the runs.'

'Did you not hear what I said?' snapped Miss Sowerbutts. 'I have just told you that putting bleach down the holes is of no use!'

'B . . . but m . . . my Uncle Fred told me to do it.' He swallowed nervously, his gullet moving up and down like a frog's.

'Well, you can tell that uncle of yours that he is incompetent, ineffectual and unreliable and that I am most displeased with him. I have lost count of the number of times I have rung him up to come again and deal with these wretched creatures, and I have not seen hide nor hair of him since he ruined my lawn with his bleach. He is most untrustworthy. I shall of course not be paying for his services – such as they were.'

'H . . . he'll not be h . . . happy, Miss Sowerbutts,' said Clarence.

'I couldn't care less whether he is happy or not, he won't get a penny out of me.'

'Well, is there anything else you want doing?' he asked uncertainly. 'My Uncle Fred asked me to ask you.'

'Anything else!' exclaimed Miss Sowerbutts. 'If the cottage fell down around my ears the very last person I should ask for help is your Uncle Fred, and you can tell him that from me. Now, be on your way and take your bottle of bleach with you.'

A moment later, as Miss Sowerbutts had settled down in an easy chair with a glass of dry sherry and the crossword, there was another ring on the doorbell. 'For goodness' sake,' she said to herself. 'You can't have a minute's peace and quiet.'

On the doorstep stood Ashley Underwood, muffled up in a thick winter coat and with a woollen hat pulled down over her head. Miss Sowerbutts clearly did not recognise her.

'If you are selling anything, I do not require it,' said Miss Sowerbutts crossly, 'and if you are canvassing for a vote I know for whom I shall vote, and if you are in the hope of converting me you are wasting your time.'

'I'm the new curate at St Christopher's,' explained the visitor, rather taken aback by the brusque manner of the woman. 'I just came to introduce myself.'

'The new curate? Oh yes, I saw you at Mr Fish's funeral. I didn't recognise you.'

'I'm doing the rounds of the village to get to know people,' said Ashley. 'I didn't have much of a chance to speak to you after the service.'

'No, I had to rush away,' said Miss Sowerbutts. She had indeed made a quick exit, angry that she had not been invited to speak at the funeral. 'I am not a member of your congregation, Reverend Underwood,' Miss Sowerbutts informed her, 'and to be quite frank I don't agree with organised religion.'

'Well, if there is anything I can do for you,' said the new curate. 'If I can be of any help—'

'No, thank you. I am quite self-sufficient,' she was told. 'Anyway, I shall be moving to Clayton in the near future.'

When the Reverend Underwood had departed, Miss Sowerbutts returned to her easy chair, her glass of dry sherry and her crossword, only, a moment later, to be disturbed again.

There was an elderly couple on her doorstep, accompanied by a young man in a smart grey suit, highly polished shoes and designer glasses. 'Good afternoon, Miss Sowerbutts,' said the young man cheerily. 'I'm Paul from the estate agents. We've come to view the cottage.'

On his way back from Miss Sowerbutts', Clarence was accosted by Mrs Atticus.

'Will you ask that uncle of yours,' she said sharply, 'to come and tidy up the graveyard? How many times does he need asking?'

'I'm doing it tomorrow, Mrs Atticus,' Clarence told her.

'*You* are doing it?'

'Yes, I'll be there first thing.'

'With your arm in a sling? And pray tell me how you intend to cut and prune and dig and rake with your arm in a sling?'

'Well, my Uncle Fred—' began the boy.

'Look,' said Mrs Atticus. 'Tell that uncle of yours to get off his backside and sort the graveyard out himself. And tell him there is a big dead branch on the oak tree that wants cutting off. And you can also tell him that should he not have it all done by the end of the week, I shall be dispensing with his services.'

'I'll tell him,' said Clarence, thinking of what his uncle would say.

Elisabeth called into the village shop on Saturday morning to find Mrs Sloughthwaite and Mrs O'Connor in earnest conversation.

'Oh, hello, Mrs Devine,' said the two of them in unison.

'Good morning,' replied Elisabeth. 'Another cold day, isn't it?'

'I don't mind the weather,' said Mrs O'Connor, 'so long as it's dry.'

'We were just looking at Mrs O'Connor's horoscope in the *Gazette*,' Mrs Sloughthwaite told her. She glanced down at the newspaper on the counter. 'It says, "Jupiter's friendly location heralds a period of optimism. Your relationship with someone younger will assume a greater impotence over the coming weeks—"'

'Impotence?' repeated Mrs O'Connor.

'Sorry,' said the shopkeeper, 'importance. I'm wearing the

wrong glasses.' She continued reading. '"Your relationship with someone younger will assume a greater importance over the coming weeks and you should not be afraid of giving sound advice to someone you love".'

'I am afraid I take this sort of thing with a pinch of salt,' said Elisabeth.

'Come on, Mrs Devine,' said the shopkeeper, 'it's only a bit of fun. Let me read your horoscope. I bet you're a Libra.'

Elisabeth laughed. 'Yes, I am as a matter of fact.'

'Let's have a look,' said Mrs Sloughthwaite, poring over the newspaper. 'Now then, it says, "The new moon refreshes your energy and recharges your batteries. An opportunity arises which you least expect and that you should grasp with both hands. There will be a drastic change in a relationship and this will bring emotional prizes and romantic rewards. Something from your past will reappear and you will have to make a serious choice. Your planetary pattern is thoroughly supportive and—"'

'I think I've heard quite enough, thank you, Mrs Sloughthwaite,' said Elisabeth smiling. 'It would be a dreadful thing if we could all see what was in store for us.'

'Well, what can I get you?' asked the shopkeeper, folding the newspaper.

'I just called in for some paper tissues,' said Elisabeth. 'I think I'm coming down with a cold.'

'There's a terrible catching flu about at the moment, so there is,' said Mrs O'Connor. 'You'll have to mention it to the doctor when you see him. He'll give you something for it.'

'Yes, I will. I'm glad to have bumped into you, Mrs O'Connor,' said Elisabeth, not wishing to discuss Michael in the presence of Mrs Sloughthwaite. 'I had your nephew in school earlier this week. He caused quite a stir, and not only with the children. Mrs Scrimshaw has not quite got over it yet. I never knew you had a famous footballer in the family.'

'He's my sister Peggy's boy,' Mrs O'Connor told her. 'He's a good lad is young Tommy.'

'It was thoughtful of him to call into the school and speak to the children,' said Elisabeth.

'Yes, he said he'd been. I had to smile, so I did, when he said you asked him to talk to the kiddies about reading. He never picked up a book when he was at school. Football mad he was. That was the only thing that interested him. Mind you, he said if he had had a teacher like you when he was a lad he might have taken to reading a bit more.'

'I think your nephew has a touch of the blarney, Mrs O'Connor,' said Elisabeth.

'I gather from Mrs O'Connor,' said the shopkeeper, 'that Dr Stirling hasn't heard from Danny since he went to live with his grandmother?'

'So I believe,' said Elisabeth.

'No, the doctor's not heard a word,' said Mrs O'Connor. 'Young James has been pestering his father to give Danny a ring, but Dr Stirling felt it better to leave things as they are for the time being and let the lad settle in with his grandmother.'

'Yes, he was telling me,' said Elisabeth.

'But I'll tell you what, Mrs Devine,' said Mrs O'Connor, 'I can't see the lad ever settling in there. He'll never be content where he is. The boy's lived here all his life and was so happy at the doctor's. It was a crying shame when they made him go and live in Clayton with his grandmother. Fancy her turning up after all these years and dragging the poor wee lad away. I've never liked that woman – hard-faced she is and selfish as they come.'

'Yes, I think many of us felt that Danny should have been allowed to stay,' agreed Elisabeth. 'It would be good to know how he is getting on, though. I think I might give the head teacher of Clayton Juniors a ring next week and see how Danny is doing.'

'You will let us know?' said Mrs Sloughthwaite. 'He's a nice lad, is Danny.'

'Of course,' said Elisabeth. 'Now I must be making tracks.'

Mrs Sloughthwaite slid a box of tissues over the counter. 'I'll put these on the slate,' she said. 'You're off to Forest View this morning then, are you, to see your son?'

Was there nothing this woman didn't know? thought Elisabeth. 'Yes, I am,' she replied.

'And how is he doing?'

'He's making steady progress. He's very happy there. Well, I must rush. I've been invited for lunch up at Limebeck House after I've been to Forest View.'

'Mixing with the aristocracy, eh?' observed Mrs Sloughthwaite.

'I think Lady Wadsworth wants to see me about school matters. She's recently been co-opted on to the governors and I guess she wants to speak to me about the various duties and responsibilities that the role involves.'

It was later that morning that Major Neville-Gravitas made his appearance at the village store.

'Good morning,' he said breezily. 'Just a packet of my usual panatellas please, Mrs Sloughthwaite.'

'So when is it the interviews for the head teacher's job are taking place, major?' the shopkeeper asked. She turned and plucked a packet of cigars from the shelf and slid them across the counter.

'Oh, not for a while yet,' he replied.

'And from what I gather, Mrs Pocock and Dr Stirling won't be on the interview panel?'

'That is correct.'

'Why is that then? They are governors at the school, after all.'

'They are governors at present, but their children will have left Barton by the time the two schools are amalgamated next September, so they will not be eligible as parent governors of the consortium. I have been asked, of course, to be on the new governing body.'

'Well, I hope you know where your loyalties lie when you come to vote,' said the shopkeeper. 'You will not be very popular in the village if Mrs Devine doesn't get the job, I can tell you that for nothing.'

'So you have been at great pains to tell me repeatedly, Mrs Sloughthwaite,' replied the major, 'and as I have pointed out to you and to everybody who has waylaid me on the high street, mine is but one vote amongst many. I shall have to judge both candidates on their merits and cannot be seen to favour one, however good she may be, prior to the interviews. It would be unfair to dismiss the other candidate without even hearing what he has to say. Having said that, I shall certainly acquaint my fellow governors on the interview panel with the excellent work Mrs Devine has done since she has been head teacher here at Barton. I am sure that Councillor Smout, the Chairman of Governors at Urebank, will do the same for Mr Richardson, who I believe—'

'Are you going to pay for these cigars?' interrupted Mrs Sloughthwaite, wishing she had never raised the matter.

As the major dug into his pockets to pay for the cigars, the door to the village store was thrown open with a loud bang, shaking the glass and rattling the bell. A hooded individual, his face save for his eyes covered with a thick scarf, slammed the door shut, locked it, turned the 'Open' sign to 'Closed' and pulled down the blind.

'Hey,' shouted Mrs Sloughthwaite, 'what do you think you're doing?'

The man threw a dirty rucksack on the counter, pulled a vicious-looking knife from his pocket and took hold of the major's arm. He held the weapon to the major's throat.

'I say!' protested Major Neville-Gravitas.

'Shut it, granddad!' he was told. The man turned to the shopkeeper. 'Fill it up, missis!' he shouted. 'Empty your till and put in any cash and t'stamps from t'post office or t'old bloke 'ere gets it.' He held the knife closer to the major's throat.

'The post office doesn't open until nine-thirty,' the shopkeeper told him coolly, pressing a fat fist firmly on the top of the cash register.

'Well, oppen it!'

'I can't be doing that,' Mrs Sloughthwaite told him. She had the dull glare of a defiant child. 'It's against regulations, and anyway the safe's on a time lock.'

'I'm warning thee, missis,' growled the man, 'either tha does as I say or this old bloke gets it.'

'I don't think you'll be so stupid as to add murder to robbery,' she said evenly. The shopkeeper stood four-square and sturdy, her fist still pressed on the cash register.

'I think it might be a good idea, Mrs Sloughthwaite,' said the major in a frail, trembling voice, 'if you did as he asks.'

Mrs Sloughthwaite, stone-jawed, stood impressively behind her counter like a large and solid Eastern statue. She folded her arms over her substantial bosom. 'I've already told you,' she told the thief calmly, 'that the post office safe is on a timer and doesn't open until nine-thirty, so you'll get no money or stamps from there.'

'I can wait,' snarled the thief.

'And by then there will be a queue of people outside wanting their pensions and you'll have to run the gauntlet through them. Many are equipped with Zimmers, walking sticks, crutches and wheelchairs, so it won't be easy getting past them.'

'Will you shurrup!' the man ordered. 'Just fill t'bag from the till, will ya, and stop yer rabbitin' on!' From the tone of his voice the thief was getting desperate. The point of the knife hovered at the major's neck. 'Do it or granddad 'ere will get it!'

'There's not much in my till,' said Mrs Sloughthwaite, remaining surprisingly unruffled. 'I've only just opened, and I cashed up yesterday and took the money to the bank.'

'I'm warnin' you, missis—' began the robber.

'Perhaps it might be better not to argue with him,' said the major weakly.

'Just put t'money in t'bag an' stop your bloody arguing!' shouted the thief. 'You're doing mi 'ead in!'

Mrs Sloughthwaite opened the cash register and, taking out a few notes and some change, put the contents in the rucksack. The thief let go of the major's arm, stretched out, and plucked the rucksack from the counter at the same moment as the shopkeeper reached down and snatched up a large spray can of oven cleaner. She sprayed it liberally in the thief's face. Screaming in agony, the man dropped the rucksack and the knife and began rubbing his eyes frantically. 'You daft old bat!' he shrieked. 'You've blinded me!'

Mrs Sloughthwaite, despite her inelegant gait, moved with impressive speed and, skirting the counter, sprayed again. 'Stop! Stop it!' the man yelled.

'Well, just keep your mouth closed or you'll get another dose,' said Mrs Sloughthwaite. She turned to the major, who stood transfixed and open-mouthed, as if caught in amber. 'Move yourself, major,' he was ordered. 'Get that washing line and tie him up.'

'Perhaps we should seek help,' the major replied feebly. He stretched his collar from his throat and rubbed his neck.

'Major, get the washing line and wrap it around him,' Mrs Sloughthwaite commanded him. 'Do as I say.'

Major Neville-Gravitas did as he was told and wrapped the washing line around the writhing figure until the man was well and truly trussed up.

'Now sit,' the shopkeeper ordered the thief, as if talking to a dog. 'And one more peep out of you and you'll get another eyeful of oven cleaner.'

'Mi eyes,' moaned the man, falling on his knees. 'I can't see. You've blinded me, yer vicious old hatchet.'

'You should have thought of that,' said Mrs Sloughthwaite, 'before you tried to rob the post office.' She pulled down the man's hood, removed the scarf and wiped his eyes with a handkerchief which she produced from her overall pocket. 'Brainless lump, that's what you are.'

The thief, a hulking big-boned lad with jug ears and blood-shot, streaming eyes, suddenly broke into fulsome sobs beyond his control. 'It's the first time I've done this,' he howled.

'Well, let's hope it's the last,' said the shopkeeper.

There was a rap at the door. 'Are you open?' came a strident voice from outside.

'That's Mrs Fish wanting her pension,' she told the major. 'Let her in, will you, while I telephone the police.'

17

Lady Wadsworth did not wish to speak to Elisabeth about being the new school governor; she was far too excited and wanted to share her good fortune.

'The Stubbs was indeed a fake,' she said, 'but Mr Markington, the fine art dealer I asked to call, discovered these two marble sculptures. They've been tucked away out of sight for I don't know how long gathering dust, because, well – not to put too fine a point on it – they are rather revealing. My grandmother did not care to have two life-sized naked figures reclining in the entrance to the hall. She thought they might give the servants ideas and corrupt the young. Anyhow, these sculptures, so Mr Markington informed me, are really rather special and collectable and he reckons they could fetch serious money at auction.'

'That's wonderful news,' said Elisabeth. 'Now you will be able to do all the repairs that need doing.'

'One hopes so,' said Lady Wadsworth. 'Should they fetch a good price I intend to have all the stonework on the exterior of the house repaired and then start on the refurbishment of the interior. After that it's the garden and grounds. I shall have to employ someone to help Watson. He is getting a little long in the tooth these days and things are getting too much for him.'

At this point the butler entered with a tray of tea, which he set down on an occasional table. 'If that will be all, your ladyship,' he said.

'Yes, thank you Watson,' replied his mistress.

'It's just that I have to visit the dentist in Clayton this afternoon,' he told her, his face betraying no emotion. 'I need to have a couple of fangs out.'

'Oh dear, he heard,' whispered Lady Wadsworth as Elisabeth tried to hide her amusement. 'Anyway, as I was saying, now that I am in a position to do so, I need to get him some help. Of course it's so difficult to get good staff these days, and one has to spend all the time and trouble finding someone.'

'I think I may be able to help you there,' said Elisabeth. 'I know a man who might just suit.'

The following day Emmet O'Malley called at Limebeck House to see Lady Wadsworth and was employed as her handyman-cum-gardener.

'It must have been quite traumatic for poor Mrs Sloughthwaite,' remarked Archdeacon Atticus, 'confronted with an armed robber as she was.'

It was the evening when Dr Stirling had been invited for dinner at the rectory. The four diners sat around the table having enjoyed a sumptuous meal, cooked by the new curate, of roast pheasant with onion gravy, roast potatoes done to a turn and buttered parsnips, followed by lemon tart and fresh cream.

'From what I heard it was far more traumatic for the robber,' replied his wife. 'Evidently she covered the man in oven cleaner and trussed him up like a Christmas turkey before the police arrived.'

'And I was told this was a very sleepy, uneventful place,' said the new curate.

'It usually is, Ashley,' said the archdeacon's wife. 'The only event of any consequence was last century when the notorious Dean Steerum-Slack, he of the outlandish mausoleum in the churchyard which wants knocking down, burnt the original rectory to the ground with himself and his dogs inside.'

'A very courageous act on her part,' observed the archdeacon, not wishing to hear again about the tomb of his notorious predecessor. 'Do you not think so, Dr Stirling?'

'Yes indeed,' replied the doctor. 'A very brave act.'

'Well, let us not dwell on the matter,' said the archdeacon, 'and thank the good Lord that no one was hurt.'

'Except the armed robber,' added Mrs Atticus, 'who deserved everything he got.'

'Maybe,' said her husband. 'Well, this is most pleasant, is it not?' he continued, rubbing his long clerical hands together and keen to change the subject. 'I have to say you have done us proud, Ashley. We have had an excellent sufficiency.'

'Well, you certainly have, Charles,' remarked his wife. 'You've put on a good few pounds since Ashley arrived and took over in the kitchen.'

'Oh dear,' said the new curate, 'perhaps I should prepare something less fattening in future.'

'Oh, it's not your fault,' said Mrs Atticus. 'The increase in the archdeacon's waistline is entirely due to his over-indulgence in having second portions of everything.' She looked at her husband. 'I can never recall you having second helpings when I did the cooking.'

The archdeacon felt it politic not to reply, but thought for a moment of the last meal his wife had placed before him: a slab of gristly dry ham, watery overcooked cabbage, charred roast potatoes and lukewarm lumpy gravy.

Mrs Atticus turned back to Dr Stirling, who had been very quiet throughout the meal. 'It's all about healthy eating, isn't it?' she said.

'It is,' he agreed.

The archdeacon's wife continued. 'It's about cutting the fat intake, getting some daily exercise, eating plenty of fruit and vegetables and watching the alcohol consumption. Is it not?'

'Mrs Atticus,' said Dr Stirling, 'you should give talks on leading a healthy lifestyle.'

'Since my wife has started training as a teacher,' remarked the archdeacon, 'Marcia has become very pedagogical.'

'Meaning?' asked his wife with a note of pique in her voice.

'Just that you have become very practised in teaching others, my dear,' replied the archdeacon pleasantly.

'I am sure that Dr Stirling is much better qualified than I to lecture on healthy eating,' said Mrs Atticus.

'I'm afraid I'm not too good as a speaker,' confessed the doctor.

'Nonsense! You are far too modest,' said the archdeacon's wife. 'Perhaps you could persuade Dr Stirling to speak to the Mothers' Union, Ashley?'

'Yes,' agreed the new curate, 'I am sure they would find a talk from Dr Stirling most interesting and informative.'

'I fear not,' replied the doctor, recalling the last time he had given a talk to a group of women. It had been to the Barton-in-the-Dale Women's Institute just before Christmas and it had not been a great success. Most of his audience had looked bored from the start, some had shuffled in their seats, and when the doctor had showed a series of slides and turned off the lights, several elderly members had fallen asleep and snored audibly throughout.

Mrs Pocock, who had been present, had reported back to Mrs Sloughthwaite that it had not been one of the most riveting talks she had heard. 'To be honest,' she said, 'the Reverend Atticus's sermons are more interesting, and that's saying something. Of course,' she went on to divulge, 'it's always fatal to put the lights off after we've eaten. It puts most of us to sleep.'

After Dr Stirling's talk the president, Mrs Bullock, whose hearing aid had whined throughout his lecture, had asked those present to show their appreciation in the usual way. Following a ripple of applause, she continued. 'And I would ask you ladies,' she said, 'to have a word with Mrs Scrimshaw, our speaker finder, if you have any suggestions for future speakers.' Then she added, 'Because we tend to be scraping the barrel these days.'

'She's quite a catch,' observed the archdeacon to his wife as he poked the coals in the sitting-room fire to bring them to life.

Dr Stirling had gone, Ashley was busy washing the dishes in the kitchen and Mrs Atticus had settled into her favourite armchair.

'To whom are you referring?' asked the archdeacon's wife.

'Why, the new curate,' replied her husband.

'She is not a trout, Charles,' said his wife. 'Quite a catch, indeed. What a strange expression to use.'

The archdeacon sighed. 'Let me then rephrase it, Marcia,' he said wearily. 'The Reverend Dr Underwood has proved to be most suitable.'

'Now you sound as if you're giving her a reference,' remarked his wife. 'Put some more coal on the fire, it's like an igloo in here.' The archdeacon did as he was asked and settled down into *his* favourite armchair.

'Ashley has indeed proved to be a great asset,' remarked Mrs Atticus eventually. 'I really do not know what I should have done without her, what with all my school work and you shooting backwards and forwards to Clayton every day.'

'I will not disagree with you there, my dear,' concurred her husband.

'One wonders why she isn't married,' said Mrs Atticus. 'She's attractive, clever, has a good sense of humour and is most personable. She would make someone a splendid wife.'

The archdeacon remained silent. He had an idea where this was leading.

'She seemed to get on very well with Dr Stirling,' continued Mrs Atticus. 'Don't you think?'

'Yes indeed,' replied her husband.

'They make quite a couple.'

'Oh dear, Marcia,' said the archdeacon, 'I do earnestly hope that you are not setting yourself up as some sort of matchmaker. It was a trifle obvious you suggesting he speak to the Mothers' Union.'

'Nonsense, Charles! You know the man. He's nice enough and a very good doctor, but probably very lonely. He needs a wife to take him in hand, but he's inordinately shy. He hardly had a word to say for himself this evening. What he needs is a bit of a push.'

Well, if there is any pushing to do, thought the archdeacon, his wife was admirably qualified in that respect.

The following week the village was buzzing with talk of the attempted robbery. The *Gazette* devoted the front page to the incident, with the headline: 'PLUCKY PAIR FOIL ARMED ROBBER', including a photograph of Mrs Sloughthwaite holding aloft the spray can of oven cleaner and standing next to the major, who struck an appropriately military pose with the washing line draped over his arm like a lasso.

The village store had never been busier. The salesman who sold the oven cleaner presented Mrs Sloughthwaite with a great bouquet of flowers, and a representative of the Post Office called to congratulate her on her outstanding actions. It went without saying that Mrs Sloughthwaite's customers were royally entertained as they listened to the graphic account.

'Of course I was told something like this would happen,' she told the clutch of women gathered around her counter. 'My horoscope said that I would be meeting a stranger who would bring trouble. I know you were very septical, Mrs Pocock, but it was written in my stars.'

'It was fortunate you had the oven cleaner to hand,' remarked Mrs Widowson.

Mrs Sloughthwaite reached under the counter and produced a rolling-pin, which she held up like a club. 'And if he had succeeded in getting over my counter,' she said, 'he'd have had a dose of this.'

'It must have been a terrible ordeal,' remarked Mrs O'Connor, 'confronted as you were by an armed robber like that.'

Mrs Sloughthwaite placed the rolling-pin down on the counter and folded her chubby arms across her impressive chest. 'Well, I'll admit it's not something you welcome, but he was such a big useless lump of a lad and he hadn't the first idea of how to go about a robbery.'

'And poor Major Neville-Gravitas having a knife at his throat,' said Mrs Widowson. She touched her neck and gave a small shudder.

'Huh,' scoffed Mrs Pocock, 'knowing him he'd have talked his way out of it. Slippery as an eel in a barrel of oil, is that one.'

Mrs Sloughthwaite smiled to herself. She resisted the temptation of telling her audience exactly how the major had reacted. She would save that for another time.

The locals in the village pub were also treated to a blow-by-blow account of the incident, although with a rather different slant. The major, looking every inch the retired army officer in his blue blazer with brash gold buttons, pressed grey trousers, crisp white shirt and regimental tie, was giving his version of events.

'So my army training stood me in very good stead,' he told the landlord at the Blacksmith's Arms. He had decided to return to his former drinking haunt, not wishing to get into another conversation with Councillor Smout at the golf club.

'Since when did soldiers in the Catering Corps have commando training?' asked Fred Massey from the end of the bar.

'For your information, Mr Massey, I was in the Royal Engineers and I went through rigorous military training. Of course you never did National Service, did you, so you wouldn't know anything about the armed forces.' He turned to the landlord. 'Anyway, as I was saying, I managed to keep calm, disarm the blighter and tie him up before the police arrived.'

'Well, you deserve your whisky, major,' said the landlord. 'It was a mighty brave thing to have done. This one's on the house.'

There was a smattering of applause from one or two customers.

'Thank you kindly,' said the major, stroking his moustache and basking in the praise.

'We don't often get a hero in here,' said the landlord, and then, turning to Fred, added, 'it's usually grumblers and grousers that I have to put up with.'

'Hero? Huh,' huffed Fred. 'From what I heard it was old Ma Sloughthwaite who tackled the robber.'

'I hardly think that a defenceless woman would be able to disarm a lunatic with a knife, wrestle him to the ground and subdue him,' said the major.

'Defenceless woman!' he exclaimed. 'She could take on the SAS single-handed, that one.'

'Well, major,' said the landlord, 'you are to be congratulated. A lot of people in the village have much to thank you for.'

'That's good of you to say,' said the major. 'I have to admit I have been very surprised and quite overwhelmed by the goodwill messages I have received. Why, only this morning I received a card from Mrs Devine—'

'Don't mention Mrs Devine to me,' said Fred glumly. 'She's not in my good books at the moment.'

'And why is that?' asked the landlord.

'Because I usually do the jobs in this village,' Fred told him.

'When you can get your Clarence to get around to it,' said the landlord under his breath.

'And Mrs Devine,' continued Fred, undeterred by the comment, 'has got some gypsy fellow repairing her fence, fixing things for her and cutting down branches on her trees. Now Miss Sowerbutts is going elsewhere as well. She got Danny Stainthorpe to get rid of her moles and the vicar's wife had the lad doing the churchyard until I put a stop to that. Taking bread out of my mouth, is this.'

'Well, Mr Massey,' said the major, finishing his whisky in one great gulp, 'if you were more amiable, industrious and dependable, then people might ask you.' And with that he bid the landlord, 'Good day,' and left Fred Massey seething at the end of the bar.

'Well, it was on my desk this morning, I know that, and it's not there now.'

The school secretary was looking red and flustered, having searched the office for the missing money.

'And you've had a good look?' asked the caretaker.

'Of course I've had a good look, Mr Gribbon,' she said irritably. 'I've spent half the morning having a good look.'

'In your drawers?'

'I beg your pardon?'

'Have you looked in your drawers?'

'It's not in my drawers.'

'Do you want me to have a look?'

'No, I do not. The money was on the top of the desk, right there in front of the typewriter. I didn't put it in a drawer.'

'Well, someone must have took it then,' said the caretaker.

'There's been nobody in the office this morning,' said the secretary, 'apart from you and that new little girl.'

'Ah well, there you have it,' said the caretaker.

'What do you mean, there I have it?'

'That gypsy kiddie. She'll have took it.'

'Don't be ridiculous,' retorted Mrs Scrimshaw.

'Light-fingered, that's what they are, these travellers. Not only are they a damn nuisance, they can't keep their hands off of anything. As my dad used to say about gypsies, "If it moves they kick it, if it doesn't they nick it".'

'I'm not interested in what your father used to say, Mr Gribbon,' replied Mrs Scrimshaw, 'I just need to find the money. There was over a hundred pounds in the envelope, money for the school trip. I'd just totalled it up and I was to take it to the bank at lunchtime. I shall have to see Mrs Devine if it doesn't turn up before morning break.'

'She'll not be best pleased,' remarked the caretaker, jangling his keys.

'Well, thank you for the reassurance,' replied Mrs Scrimshaw. 'Why don't you get back to buffing your floors?'

'Mrs Pugh, the new part-time cleaner, is doing them this morning,' the caretaker told her. 'I've hurt my foot. It's agony when I walk.'

'It makes a change,' said the secretary.

'What does?'

'It's usually your back you complain about. So how did you hurt your foot?'

'It was that bloody plaque Lady Whatshername has had made for the library what did it,' said the caretaker, pulling a pained face. 'It weighed a ton and I dropped it on my foot. I can't buff my floors, the state I'm in. Incapacitated, that's what I am. Mrs Pugh's doing them. I've showed her how to do it and she's taken to it like a fish to water. She's a godsend, that woman. There's nothing what she can't turn her hand to.'

'Well, go and supervise her then. I've got to find this wretched money.'

The caretaker ambled off. 'You mark my words,' he said before departing, 'it's that little gypsy kid. The money will be in the bottom of her bag as we speak.'

'And you've made a thorough search?' asked Elisabeth later that morning when the secretary reluctantly informed her of the missing money.

'Everywhere, Mrs Devine,' she replied.

'Well, it's a real mystery.'

Mrs Scrimshaw decided to tell the head teacher of Mr Gribbon's suspicions.

'I'm sure Roisin would not have taken it,' she said, 'but she was the only pupil to come into the office this morning, so I have to admit it's got me wondering.'

'I cannot believe that she took it either,' agreed Elisabeth.

'Do you think we should perhaps have a word with her?' asked the secretary.

'Not for the moment,' said Elisabeth. 'Just keep on looking. I am sure it will turn up. And don't get upset, Mrs Scrimshaw, these things happen.'

The school secretary sniffed and blew her nose when the head teacher had left. She recalled the time before the arrival of Mrs Devine when she had mislaid the school cheque-book. It had eventually turned up under a pile of reports that cluttered the small, stuffy school office in which she used to work. Miss Sowerbutts had reacted in her usual sharp and unsympathetic manner. How very different was her successor.

At the end of the day, when the money had not turned up, Elisabeth considered what she should do. Perhaps, she thought, as had been suggested, she ought to have a word with Roisin the next morning, but then she thought better of it. She decided on another, more subtle plan when she discovered the girl in the small library with Oscar.

'And what are you two doing here?' asked Elisabeth.

'The thing is, Mrs Devine,' explained Oscar, 'my mother's got a counselling session today and said she would be a bit delayed, and Roisin's father is picking her up later. He's working up at Limebeck House. We're looking at this very interesting book on fossils. I was explaining to Roisin that ammonites were once thought to be coiled-up snakes turned to stone by St Hilda of Whitby. Sometimes people carved little heads on the front and sold them. I have three at home that I found in Port Mulgrave when we were on holiday in Scarborough. Now the thing about ammonites—'

'I'm sorry to interrupt, Oscar,' said Mrs Devine, 'but I wonder if you two could do a small job for me?'

'Of course,' replied the boy.

'The thing is,' explained the head teacher, 'Mrs Scrimshaw has mislaid some money in the school office. It was for the school trip. I'm afraid if she doesn't find it there will be a lot of very disappointed children. I wonder if you two might help her to look for it?'

'Mrs Scrimshaw,' said Elisabeth, when she arrived at the school office with the two children, 'I have a couple of little helpers here.' The secretary looked surprised, particularly when she caught sight of Roisin. 'They are going to help us look for the missing money. Now,' she said, turning to Oscar, 'Mrs Scrimshaw is sure she put the money here, just in front of her typewriter.' She tapped the desk. 'But, as if by magic, it has disappeared.'

'I don't think it's anything to do with magic, Mrs Devine,' observed the boy. 'There's always a simple explanation.'

'Was it in a brown envelope?' asked Roisin.

'It was,' replied Mrs Scrimshaw.

'I remember seeing it there,' said the girl, 'when I brought the class register back this morning.' The secretary raised an eyebrow and glanced at Elisabeth.

'Perhaps you put it somewhere safe, Mrs Scrimshaw,' said Oscar. 'I know my mother frequently does this and then forgets where the safe place is. She's quite scatty at times.'

'No, Oscar,' said Mrs Scrimshaw, not at all pleased to be compared with the boy's scatty mother. 'I didn't move it. It was there, right in front of the typewriter.'

Oscar crouched down and peered at the space beneath the machine. Then, taking a ruler from the desk, he slid it underneath and the brown envelope appeared.

'Well I never,' said Mrs Scrimshaw.

The boy nodded sagely. 'It must have slid under there,' he told her. 'As I said, there's always a logical explanation. Oh, I can see your father waiting outside, Roisin, talking to my mother. We had better be making tracks.'

'Thank you, Oscar,' said Elisabeth. 'Thank you very much.'

'Any time,' said the boy, taking Roisin's hand in his as he left the office.

'Have you time for a coffee?' the new curate asked.

She had met Dr Stirling coming out of the chemist's the day following his talk to the Mothers' Union.

He glanced at his wristwatch. 'Well, I do have one more patient to visit this morning, but— '

She rested a hand on his arm. 'It's just that I wanted to have a word with you about something,' she said. 'I won't keep you long, I promise. I meant to mention it yesterday and didn't get the chance with all those doting elderly ladies surrounding you.'

He smiled. 'Hardly "doting",' he said. 'They were keen to tell me about all their ailments and medical conditions. That's one of the disadvantages of being a doctor, I'm afraid.'

'So can you spare ten minutes?' she asked.

'Well, I guess Miss Sowerbutts can wait a while longer. I was just calling in to see how she's getting on. She's been having a few dizzy spells lately.'

'She's a bit of a dragon, isn't she?' Ashley said. 'She was very sharp with me when I called round to her cottage to introduce myself.'

'Her bark is worse than her bite,' Dr Stirling told her. 'She's just a lonely old woman who hasn't got much in her life. She seems to feel all the world is against her. Anyway, let's go and have that coffee.'

In the small café at the end of the high street they sat at a corner table. The waitress, a large, morose-looking girl with lank mousy brown hair tied back untidily into a ponytail, approached the table.

'Hello, Dr Stirling,' she said.

'Hello, Bianca,' he replied. 'How's that baby of yours?'

The girl's face brightened. 'Oh, he's doing fine, doctor, and I'm trying real hard with the breastfeeding.'

'I'm glad to hear it,' he replied.

'And I've given up the ciggies as well.'

'Good.'

'I've still got them cracked nipples though, doctor.'

Ashley smiled.

'Well, you call into the surgery and we'll sort it out,' he told her.

'And I still haven't got the hang of that breast pump the health visitor gave me.'

'A lot of new mothers find it hard at first, Bianca,' Dr Stirling told her. 'You pop in and see me next week. Now, we'd like two coffees, please.'

'This is my treat,' said Ashley when Bianca had left to place the order. The café owner observed the couple at the corner table with more than a little interest.

'No, no,' said Dr Stirling, 'let me get them.'

'It's the least I can do,' said the new curate, 'after you spoke to the Mothers' Union for me.'

'I think the less said about that the better,' said Dr Stirling. 'I don't think it was a great success, but then I did warn you that I am not a very good speaker.'

Ashley laughed. 'You're too modest,' she said. 'It was very interesting, although I thought it was a little ironic that after your suggestions on healthy eating they all tucked into the buffet of pork pies and sausage rolls, cream cakes and meringues.'

'I think my words fell upon deaf ears,' said Dr Stirling.

'Well, not on mine,' she said. 'I'm very grateful that you found the time to do it.'

Bianca arrived with the coffee and placed the cups on the table. Then she stood there as if waiting for something.

Ashley dipped into her handbag to find her purse.

'Thank you, Dr Stirling,' said Bianca, 'for all you've done, with the baby and that, and for talking to mi mam and dad.' Her eyes started to fill up. 'You were really nice.'

'A pleasure,' he replied.

'And I don't want you to pay for the coffees. I'd like to do that.'

'Thank you, that's very kind of you,' he replied.

When Bianca had gone, the new curate squeezed Dr Stirling's hand as it rested on the table. 'You're a good man,' she said.

'I don't know about that,' he said, looking embarrassed. 'She's a simple soul is Bianca and she's had a lot to put up with lately.' He took a sip of the coffee. 'Anyway, how may I be of help?'

'Be of help?'

'You said you wanted a word with me about something.'

'Ah yes. Well, I thought I'd visit some of the patients in the hospital,' she told him.

'I think they would welcome that,' he replied.

'But I don't want to tread on the chaplain's toes. Sometimes hospital chaplains tend to be a bit protective of their role and don't take too kindly to other clerics pushing their noses in.'

'I am sure Father Daly would be more than happy to have an assistant,' he told her. 'He's a lovely man, but overworked and getting a bit long in the tooth now. I'm certain he would jump at the chance of having a bit of help. I'll have a word with him if you like. I'm visiting the hospital next week.'

'Perhaps I could come with you,' suggested Ashley, 'then you could introduce me.'

'Yes, of course. It's next Wednesday.'

'It's a date,' she said.

The policeman stood on the doorstep at Clumber Lodge. He was an unusual-looking man, with his dark eyes, colourful acne and greasy black hair. He looked too young to be a police officer. Next to him, his colleague, a pale-faced woman with her blonde hair scraped back savagely on her scalp and into a tight little bun at the back, had an earnest and unsettling expression on her face. They brought the chill of the morning with them.

'Dr Stirling?' said the young policeman.

'Yes, that's right.'

'Police Constable Thomas,' he said. 'We have met before.'

'In similar circumstances,' added his colleague.

'Yes,' replied Dr Stirling, 'you called when my son went missing. I remember. Is there something the matter?'

'May we come in?' asked the policeman.

'Yes, of course,' said the doctor. 'Come through into the sitting-room. Would you like a cup of tea?'

'Thank you, no,' said the young policeman. His colleague sat down on the edge of a chair and stared ahead of her with a blank expression.

'How may I be of help?' asked Dr Stirling, standing by the

fireplace. He was rather apprehensive, recalling the last visit of the police when James had gone missing. The young police-woman had said then that she would need to speak to his son on his return. It had sounded to Dr Stirling as though she was of the opinion that the boy might have run away because he was being maltreated. Dr Stirling guessed that the reason for their visit was to check up that this was not the case.

'It appears that history is repeating itself,' said the young policeman.

'I'm sorry,' said the doctor, 'I don't quite understand.'

'You will recall that last time we were here it was concerning a runaway child,' said the woman.

'Yes, that's right. As I have just said, you called when my son went missing. I do remember.' He sounded irritated. 'Is there something the matter?'

'Well, we are here on the same business,' said the young policeman.

'James is upstairs in his room,' the doctor told him. 'He's fine now. There will be no running away again, I can assure you of that. Perhaps you would like to speak to him?'

'It's not your son that we are here about,' said the young policeman. He took a small black notebook from his pocket, moistened his index finger with his tongue and began flicking through the pages. 'It's concerning a Daniel Stainthorpe.'

'Danny!' exclaimed Dr Stirling.

'We are conducting another missing person enquiry,' said the policewoman.

'The boy has run away,' said the young policeman. 'I think you are aware that he is now living with his grandmother in Clayton?'

'Yes.'

'Well, he didn't return home from school yesterday after-noon. He's been out all night and, of course, his grandmother is understandably very worried about him.'

The doctor sighed.

'It seems to be quite an occurrence,' said the policewoman.

'What does?' asked the doctor. He felt a sudden flash of irritation.

'Children running away.'

Two small, red angry spots appeared on the doctor's cheeks. 'I really am not sure what you mean by that comment!' he exclaimed. 'I would remind you that Danny was not in my care. Had he been, he would most certainly not have run away. He was settled and happy when he was here, and what he wanted most was to remain with me and James. It is his grandmother from whom he has run away, probably because he was unhappy. That is not what I call a recurrence. It's an entirely different situation.'

The policewoman gave a thin, condescending smile.

'Please don't upset yourself, doctor,' said the young policeman. 'My colleague was merely stating a fact. I am sure it is just a coincidence.'

'Danny was to come and live with us as my adopted son,' continued Dr Stirling, 'but then his grandmother turned up out of the blue and wanted the boy to live with her, something he did not want.'

The doctor's impassioned speech seemed to fall on deaf ears, for the two police officers looked at him impassively.

'Have you seen him?' the young policeman asked, in a voice which made it clear he wasn't at all interested in Dr Stirling's opinion.

'No,' replied the doctor. 'I haven't.'

'Have you any idea where he might have gone?' asked the woman.

'No.'

'Do you know anyone who might know where he might be?'

'No, I don't.'

'Perhaps we might speak to your son now,' said the police-woman. 'He's the boy's friend, isn't he?'

'Yes.'

'So, he may have an idea where the boy has gone to.'

'I'll get him in a moment,' said Dr Stirling.

'We will soon find the boy,' said the young policeman, snapping his notebook shut. 'Children run away all the time. As I said to you when we were last here, I've known a number of cases when kids have had a bit of a tiff with their mums and dads and run off.'

'Has he had some sort of argument with his grandmother, then?' asked Dr Stirling.

'Not that we are aware of,' the policewoman told him. 'His grandmother does find him a bit of a handful. Evidently he can be quite a wayward and rather sulky child by all accounts.'

'Danny?' cried Dr Stirling. 'Nonsense! He's nothing of the sort. He's a pleasant and very polite young man.'

'Anyway, we will keep our eyes open,' said the young police-man, easing back his cuff surreptitiously to check the time on his watch. 'As I've said, youngsters do sometimes run away for one reason or another, mainly to get some attention or after an argument, but they usually return when they are hungry and it starts getting dark.'

'But you say Danny was out all last night?' asked the doctor.

'Yes.'

'It was freezing cold. Wherever could the boy have been in this weather?'

The young policeman shrugged. 'Bus shelter, railway station, barn, outbuilding, somewhere warm. There are lots of places.'

'I'll get my son,' said Dr Stirling.

James was of little help but suggested Danny might be down by the mill dam, where he had made a den. It was agreed that

Dr Stirling and his son would search down there that morning and in any other haunts the boy might have gone to.

'And contact us if he turns up,' said the young policeman.

'Yes, of course I will,' said the doctor. 'That goes without saying, and could you keep me informed if you hear anything?'

'We will be in touch,' the young policeman said. His colleague rose from the chair and smoothed the creases out in her skirt. 'Good morning, Dr Stirling,' she said.

18

Dr Stirling and James searched in all the places where they thought Danny might be. They started at the den the boy had built, but it was empty, then they looked in the small copse and beneath hedgerows, and in the deserted barns and outbuildings. They trudged down the rutted track in the wood which led to the mill dam, on ground like iron and dusted with a light snow that even the rays of the morning sun could not melt. Tired and cold, they walked on past tall black-trunked trees, the branches silvered with hoar frost, and past spindly misshapen saplings, sparkling holly hedges, tangled undergrowth and green-covered boulders, but there was no sign of the missing boy. Eventually they arrived at the mill-pond. The huge waterwheel, rotten and rusted, was silent, and the stone building a crumbling roofless ruin. Beneath, the water was black and thick as oil.

'Danny!' shouted Dr Stirling. 'Danny, are you here?' The fresh coolness of the air hit the back of his throat. 'Danny!' he shouted again. 'Danny, are you here?' The wood remained silent.

'He might be at the churchyard,' suggested James. 'Danny often used to go there, to his granddad's grave.'

But at St Christopher's there was no sign of the boy.

'Maybe he's at Mrs Devine's,' said James. 'He spent a lot of time there digging the garden and feeding the birds.'

'Well, let's go and have a look,' said his father, 'and pray that he's there.'

But the garden at Wisteria Cottage was empty.

'I saw you two trespassers from the kitchen,' said Elisabeth good-humouredly as she came out to meet them. She had a broad smile on her face. 'You look mightily suspicious you two, creeping around in my garden. Whatever are you up to?'

'Danny's missing,' Dr Stirling told her.

The smile left Elisabeth's face. 'Missing?' she repeated.

'We thought he might be here.'

'Well, no, he's not here.'

'He's run away, Mrs Devine,' said James. 'The police are looking for him. We've looked everywhere but we can't find him.'

'Oh dear,' sighed Elisabeth. She shook her head. 'You know, I thought this might happen.'

'You have no idea where he might be, have you?' asked Dr Stirling.

She thought for a moment. 'Do you know, I think I might,' she replied.

'You do?' cried the doctor.

'I think he's in the caravan where he used to live. I was look-ing out of the bedroom window last night and I thought I saw something flickering in the caravan. I put it down to a trick of the light or the moonlight reflecting off a window, but I think it must have been Danny. Poor boy must be frozen to death.'

'Thank God for that,' said Dr Stirling. 'Well done, Elisabeth.' He looked at his son. 'Mrs Devine to the rescue again, eh, James?'

'Come along,' said Elisabeth, 'we had better take a look.'

'Don't be angry with him, Dad,' James said.

The boy's father placed his hand on his son's shoulder and smiled. 'I won't,' he said gently.

Les Stainthorpe's caravan had remained in the small paddock next to the cottage since the old man's death. Before going to live with Dr Stirling, Danny had been through his grandfather's few possessions, taken what he wanted, then locked the door and put the key under a stone. Elisabeth found the stone and lifted it. The key had gone.

'He's inside,' she said.

Dr Stirling tapped on the door of the caravan. 'Danny,' he said. 'Danny, are you in there?' No sound came from inside. 'Danny, it's Dr Stirling. Open the door, there's a good lad.' There was still no response. He was about to knock again when Elisabeth stayed his hand.

'Leave it a moment, Michael,' she said. 'He needs a little time to think. He'll open the door in his own time.'

She was right, for a few minutes later the door of the caravan creaked open and Danny stood in the doorway, his face flushed with distress and his eyes full of tears.

''Ello, Dr Stirling,' he said, biting his bottom lip so he wouldn't cry.

'Hello, Danny,' said the doctor quietly. 'We've been looking all over for you.'

'I'm sorry I've put you to all this trouble.' The boy had misery written all over his face. 'I 'ad to come 'ome. I'm sorry.'

'Don't worry your head about that,' the doctor replied. 'The main thing is that we have found you safe and well. Here's Mrs Devine and James. They've been worried about you too.'

''Ello, Mrs Devine,' said the boy, his voice strained with tears. 'Hi, James.'

Elisabeth smiled and nodded.

'Hello, Danny,' said James. He looked pale and nervous.

'I think we'll get you back to Clumber Lodge, Danny, for a hot drink and some breakfast.'

The boy stared forlornly at the floor and didn't move. 'Will I have to go back?' he asked, gnawing his lip.

Dr Stirling and Elisabeth exchanged glances. 'We'll talk about that later,' said the doctor. 'Now come along, it's too cold to stay outside in this weather.'

Danny looked up. There was sadness and resignation in his face. He knew that he would be returned to his grandmother.

Dr Stirling left the house early. It was the following morning, and Mrs Stainthorpe was due to collect her grandson. The doctor had really wanted to be there when Danny left, but he had received an emergency call to which he had to attend. The night before, he had telephoned the police, cooked Danny a meal and put the boy to bed.

'Please would you ask Mrs Stainthorpe to stay until I get back?' he asked Mrs O'Connor. 'Put her in the sitting-room and get her a cup of tea.'

The housekeeper huffed. She could think of a drink she would like to give to that woman and it wasn't tea. Prussic acid, more like. 'Very well, Dr Stirling,' she replied. Poor man, she thought. The last time she had seen him so quiet and dejected was after his wife had died.

'I shouldn't be long,' he said. 'I should like to say goodbye to Danny before he leaves.' When Dr Stirling had left, Mrs O'Connor shouted up the stairs. 'Danny, will you come down here a minute, I'd like to have a wee word with you.'

A moment later the boy came into the kitchen. He had an expression of grim forbearance on his face, like a condemned man being dragged off to his execution.

'Sit down for a minute,' the housekeeper told him. 'I've made some scones – your favourites. You can take a few with you when you go.'

The boy sat in miserable silence at the kitchen table, cupped his head in his hands and stared vacantly though the window at the gloomy grey sky. Rain snaked down the windowpanes. It was a cold miserable day which reflected his mood. At the rear of Clumber Lodge the garden was neglected. Beneath ancient oaks and tall sycamores, with their thick, shiny black trunks and intricate mesh of smaller branches, was a tangle of overgrown roses, buddleia and thorns, dense holly thickets and laurel bushes. The wind blew fretfully at the window frames and the rain continued to patter on the glass.

'I were gunna fettle t'back garden when t'weather eased up,' said Danny sadly.

'You made a grand job of the front garden, so you did,' the housekeeper told him. 'Maybe you can come over some time and sort out the back.'

'Mebbe,' muttered the boy.

The housekeeper placed a liberally buttered scone on a plate and slid it across the table. 'Now get that down you,' she said. 'You've had no breakfast and you can't start the day without something inside you. That's what my owld grandmother used to say.'

The very last thing Danny wanted to do that morning was to eat. His stomach churned and his throat felt dry. 'I'm not that 'ungry, Mrs O'Connor,' the boy replied, miserably pushing the plate away. 'Thanks anyroad.'

'Well, I was wanting to have a wee chat with you,' she said, 'before your grandmother arrives.'

'I don't really feel like talkin',' Danny told her. He was on the verge of tears.

'Maybe so,' she said, 'but there's one or two things I want to say to you before she comes. Now, first things first. Have you got everything?'

'I think so.'

'Have you fed that ferret of yours?'

'Yeah.'

'And did you say goodbye to James before he left for school?'

Danny nodded.

'And did you write a note to Dr Stirling thanking him for having you?'

'Yeah,' he mumbled. There was a tremble in his voice. 'I left it on t'chair in mi . . . in t'back bedroom.'

Danny suddenly began to shake with crying, then he burst into quick choking sobs. 'I don't want to go, Mrs O'Connor. I don't want to go back. I don't like it theer. I likes it 'ere.'

'I know that, darlin',' said the housekeeper, sniffing. She plucked a handkerchief from her apron pocket and blew her nose noisily. Her face was soft with concern. She moved around the table and, sitting next to the boy, put her arm around him.

'You know, your grandmother is a very lucky woman, so she is,' she said.

Danny looked up, his cheeks wet with tears. He looked genuinely puzzled. 'Lucky?' he repeated. ''Ow is she lucky?'

'Having a grandson like you, that's why. You could have been a real tearaway like some of the youngsters these days. You could have been moody and rude and bad-tempered, a lad who didn't do as he was told, who leaves his room as if a bomb has hit it.'

Danny stared at her blankly.

'You could have been like that Malcolm Stubbins,' she continued, 'who, from what I hear, leads his poor mother a merry old dance.'

'He's not that bad these days,' said Danny. 'Anyroad, I'm not like Malcolm Stubbins, Mrs O'Connor.'

'I know you're not, darlin', and that's why your grand-mother is a lucky woman. I mean, you're a well-behaved and polite boy and you do as you're told and you always left your room here nice and tidy.'

'I promised Dr Stirling that I'd be a good boy,' said Danny.

'Yes, well, doctors don't know everything,' said the house-keeper, more to herself than to the boy. 'What I'm getting at is that if you *had* turned out to be a real handful, I reckon your grandmother wouldn't be all that keen to have you living with her.'

'I suppose not.'

'She wouldn't have wanted one of these moody and badly-behaved children, now would she?'

Incomprehension crept across Danny's face. 'I don't know what you mean, Mrs O'Connor,' he said.

'I don't mean anything,' said the housekeeper. 'I'm just remarking that had you been a difficult and disobedient boy, she would have waltzed you back to the Social Services in no time at all.'

Danny thought for moment and let what Mrs O'Connor had said sink in. Then a flash of understanding lit up his face. 'Are ya sayin' that I should—' he began.

'I'm just making an observation, that's all,' she told him. 'Your grandmother couldn't have put up with that sort of boy, so as I say, she's very lucky to have such a nice, well-behaved young man living with her.' She winked. 'Close your mouth, Danny, and eat your scone.'

The doorbell rang.

'Now you run along upstairs to your room for a wee while,' she said, rising from the table and smoothing her hands down the front of her apron. 'That will be your grandmother and I want a word with her.'

A woman with badly dyed blonde hair and alarming eyebrows stood on the doorstep in a cloud of cheap scent. A cigarette smouldered between her fingers. Her face, bright with blotchy rouge and heavy black eyeshadow, looked pinched and sullen. The scarlet lips drooped in distaste.

Mrs O'Connor, her face distorting into an expression of chill disapproval, stared at the visitor for a moment. 'You had better come in,' she said, 'but before you do, will you extinguish the cigarette. Dr Stirling doesn't allow smoking in the house.'

Mrs Stainthorpe gave the housekeeper a dismissive look of barely suppressed animosity. 'You don't say,' she said casually, flicking the cigarette into the garden. 'Well, I wouldn't want to pollute the atmosphere in the house, would I?' She pushed past the housekeeper. 'Is he ready?' she asked.

'Danny will be down in a minute,' Mrs O'Connor told her. 'He's upstairs getting his things together.'

'Well, I hope he hurries up. I've got a taxi waiting. He's costing me an arm and a leg, that lad.'

'Dr Stirling told me to ask you to wait until he got back.'

'Is he out?'

'On an emergency.'

'Well, I haven't got all day and the meter's running in the taxi,' said Mrs Stainthorpe, giving a superior little sniff. She fingered one of the heavy earrings fastened to her ear. 'I've got things to do, and the last thing I wanted this morning was chasing after him upstairs.'

'You can wait in the sitting-room,' said Mrs O'Connor with meticulous coldness. She pointed to a door. 'Through there.'

The visitor moved at a leisurely pace into the sitting-room. Her small appraising eyes took in everything: the bright paintings, the long plum-coloured drapes, the thick-pile beige carpet and a deep cushioned sofa and chairs.

Mrs O'Connor remained at the door of the room, her arms folded across her chest.

'Nice in here,' said the visitor. 'He's not short of a bob or two is Dr Stirling, by the looks of it. I can't understand why he wants to adopt somebody.'

'Danny isn't just somebody,' Mrs O'Connor told her brusquely, 'and Dr Stirling is a kind and caring man and wanted to give the boy a good home.'

'You don't say,' remarked Mrs Stainthorpe, running a finger over the windowsill and examining it as if to find dust. 'This could do with a good clean by the looks of it.'

The housekeeper could hear a lack of interest in the woman's voice. Her lips twitched as if she was about to say something, but she remained silent and stared at the woman with a mixture of distaste and annoyance.

Mrs Stainthorpe glanced out of the window and over the garden. 'Bloody awful weather,' she remarked, reaching out and picking up a photograph of a woman in a silver frame from a small occasional table.

'Is this his wife?' she asked.

'Yes, it's Mrs Stirling,' replied Mrs O'Connor.

'The one what had the accident?'

'Dr Stirling has only had the one wife,' she was told.

'She should have had more sense riding a horse down a country lane. They're a bloody nuisance, horses on the roads. They ought to stick to the fields.'

It was with difficulty that the housekeeper controlled herself.

'Will you tell him to hurry up?' said Mrs Stainthorpe impatiently, glancing at a showy gold wristwatch. 'As I said, I've got things to do and there's a taxi waiting. He's been nothing but trouble, running off like that. I don't know what got into him. He's got everything he needs at the apartment – his own room, lovely view of the river, plenty to eat, new set of clothes.'

'There must have been a reason,' replied Mrs O'Connor, giving the woman a baleful look. 'Children don't run off for no good reason.'

'He doesn't know when he's well off, that's his trouble. Like a lot of kids these days. I never had it so easy when I was young. 'Course he's been allowed to have his own way. Les spoilt him rotten and since he's been living here—'

'He's better off living here,' interrupted the housekeeper sharply.

Mrs Stainthorpe looked around sourly. 'So you say.' She gave a self-satisfied smile. 'Well, I can't stop here all day on the off-chance that Dr Stirling will grace us with his presence.' Then in a sweetly sarcastic voice she asked, 'If it's not too much trouble, will you tell Daniel his grandmother is here to collect him?'

Danny came into the room. 'I'm ready,' he said.

Mrs Stainthorpe's painted eyebrows arched with disapproval. 'So I see,' she said. 'Now then, young man, what's all this running off? You've put me to no end of trouble.'

'I'm sorry,' he mumbled. 'I won't do it again.'

'I should think not. Go on, get in the taxi.'

'Could we wait until Dr Stirling gets back?' asked Danny. 'I'd like to say goodbye to 'im.'

'No, we can't!' she snapped. 'I've wasted enough time as it is. Go on, do as you're told.'

Mrs O'Connor bent and gave Danny a lingering hug and whispered in his ear. 'I shall not tell you to be a good boy, Danny,' she said. 'Just remember what my owld grandmother used to say: "There's more than one way to skin a rabbit".'

'Danny got off all right then?' Dr Stirling asked his housekeeper later that morning.

'He got off but he wasn't all right,' Mrs O'Connor told him dourly. 'Poor wee fella, he looked distraught. I did ask madam to wait but she said she had things to do. I'd like to know what things. She's a selfish piece of work is Maisie Proctor, so she is, and she could cut an iceberg in half with that sharp tongue of hers. Only out for what she can get.'

'Perhaps we're being a little hard on the woman, Mrs O'Connor,' said the doctor. 'I guess that behind that bluster and sharpness there's a rather sad and lonely woman.'

'Knowing her, she won't be sad and lonely for long. She'll be sharpening those red nails of hers to dig them into another unsuspecting dupe. Always had her eyes for the main chance, did Maisie Proctor. Anyway what was the emergency, Dr Stirling? You rushed out of the house like a cat with its tail on fire, so you did.'

'It was Miss Sowerbutts,' he replied.

'She's had an accident?'

'I'm afraid so,' the doctor replied. 'Quite a nasty fall. She's in Clayton Royal Infirmary. They're keeping her in for observation.'

Dr Stirling then related the events and why he had been called out that morning. Miss Sowerbutts, negotiating the narrow and steep stairs in her cottage with a tray of morning coffee, had not seen her cat stretched out on the top step. She had tripped and fallen headlong down the stairs, banging her head and breaking her arm in the process. She had lain there dazed and in pain. It was fortunate that Malcolm Stubbins, on his way to school, had heard the woman's cries for help. Staring through the letterbox, the boy had seen the prone figure at the foot of the stairs and, finding the door unlocked, had gone to her assistance. With great presence of mind the boy had placed a cushion under her head, put a blanket over her, dialled 999 for an ambulance and then, having looked in the address book on the hall table, had phoned Dr Stirling.

'And how is Miss Sowerbutts?' asked Mrs O'Connor now.

'She's a very lucky woman. If young Malcolm hadn't heard her shouting for help or ignored it she could very well have been there for quite some time. I gather she doesn't have many visitors, and in this weather she could have developed hypothermia. The boy kept calm and did exactly the right thing. He may have saved her life.'

'Well I never,' said the housekeeper, shaking her head. 'I must say I take back what I said to Danny about Malcolm Stubbins.'

'What did you say to Danny about Malcolm Stubbins?' asked the doctor.

'Oh, something and nothing,' she replied evasively.

'Anyway, as I said, had it not been for the boy's quick thinking and the way he kept calm and stayed with Miss Sowerbutts until I arrived, it could have been a lot worse. Sometimes this kind of sudden emotional stress can send people into shock.'

'I can't say that I like the woman and although I wouldn't wish an accident like that upon my worst enemy, as my owld grandmother used to say, "Pride comes before a fall," and there's none prouder than Miss Sowerbutts. How long will she be in hospital?'

'I can't say,' the doctor told her. 'I think she suffered some concussion and her arm is broken. She's certainly been in the wars lately.'

'Well, she won't be claiming compensation for *this* accident,' remarked Mrs O'Connor, 'not like the last time when she slipped in the supermarket and got that big payout. Of course, knowing her it won't be her fault. Probably blames the cat.'

'I think you are being a little harsh, Mrs O'Connor,' said the doctor. 'She's another rather sad and lonely woman and has become rather sour and embittered in her old age.'

'Well, as my grandmother used to say,' replied the house-keeper, '"When the milk turns sour, make cheese".'

'There really is no answer to that,' replied Dr Stirling, having not the slightest idea what she meant.

Mrs O'Connor headed for the door. 'I'll put the kettle on. I'm sure you would enjoy a cup of tea.'

'There is something else,' said Dr Stirling.

'Yes?'

'I said I would do something for Miss Sowerbutts.'

'Do something, doctor?'

'I said I would look after her cat.'

'Her cat?'

'Evidently it's a rare breed,' said the doctor, 'some strange sort of Siamese cat, and Miss Sowerbutts asked me to look after it.'

'You're too soft-hearted, Dr Stirling, that's your trouble. People put on your good nature, so they do. However, I suppose we could look after it until she's out of hospital.'

'She was insistent that it has to have a special diet of fish and chicken,' the doctor told her.

Mrs O'Connor sniffed. 'Well, Miss Sowerbutts isn't in any position to insist on anything at the moment, is she, Dr Stirling?' she replied. 'So it'll get what it's given.'

'May I come in?' At first Dr Stirling didn't recognise the muffled figure on the doorstep, encased in a dark-red duffel coat with a scarf wrapped around the lower half of her face. 'It's Miss Parsons from the Social Services,' she explained.

'Come in, come in,' said the doctor.

The visitor came into the hall and shivered. 'It's so cold out there this evening,' she said, removing her scarf and rubbing her gloved hands together.

'Do go through into the sitting-room,' he said, 'and warm yourself by the fire. Here, let me take your coat.'

The social worker removed the duffel coat. She was wearing a thick, shapeless grey jumper, a long patterned skirt and the sort of heavy boots a hiker might wear.

'Well now,' said Dr Stirling, 'I hope you are not the bringer of bad news?'

'No, no.'

'I assume it's about Danny that you have called to see me?'

'Yes, and I'm sorry for the late hour, but I was passing through the village on the way back to Clayton after a conference and thought I'd call in. I am sorry it's unannounced. I hope it's not inconvenient.'

'No, not at all. It's fine,' the doctor told her. 'Do sit down.' He picked up a pile of papers and magazines from a chair.

Miss Parsons was a handsome woman with a wide intelligent face and large bright eyes. Small rectangular spectacles dangled on a cord around her neck. She sat by the fire and warmed her hands.

'May I offer you a coffee?' asked Dr Stirling.

'No, thank you,' she replied. 'I've had a surfeit of coffee today. I'm afraid if I drink more than four cups in a day I suffer some ill-effects. I get palpitations, so I try to ration my intake of caffeine.'

'Very sensible,' said the doctor. 'Now what is it you wished to see me about?'

'Firstly I want to say how very sorry I am that things did not work out with the adoption. I am sure it's been an upsetting time for Danny and I guess an anxious time for you too.'

Dr Stirling nodded. 'It has,' he replied.

'Of course I heard about Danny running away,' said Miss Parsons. 'It's our policy to follow things up and to see why.'

'I'm pleased to hear it.'

'Did he say anything to you as to why he ran off like that?'

'Actually he said very little.'

'I called to see his grandmother yesterday,' said Miss Parsons, 'and then I visited Danny at his new school to talk to him.'

'I see.'

'His grandmother claims he is not an easy child and—'

'Nonsense!' snapped the doctor. 'He's the easiest child in the world. He's no trouble at all and—'

'If I might finish, Dr Stirling,' said Miss Parsons. 'His grandmother, as I have said, finds Danny not an easy child. He's not misbehaved or disobedient but he is very quiet and only speaks to her when he has to, and he spends most of his time, according to her, sulking in his room.'

'Danny does not sulk.'

'I'm merely telling you what his grandmother told me. She says she is doing her very best but she's not finding it easy. The boy has his own bedroom, has plenty to eat and is not neglected.'

'It's not about that,' said the doctor. 'Danny loves the country. He'll be like a caged animal in a small apartment. He wants to be out in the open air. And it's not like the boy to sulk,' said the doctor. 'He's a bright, good-humoured and chatty little boy.'

'Well, he doesn't appear to be like that for his grandmother.'

'That's because he's probably very unhappy,' the doctor told her. 'He's still grieving for his grandfather and misses everything he's familiar with. He's homesick for the countryside.'

'Yes, I think he is,' she agreed. 'I spoke to Danny and it is clear he doesn't like living in Clayton. I think you are right that it's more to do with the change in his environment than anything else. He loves the freedom which I'm afraid he doesn't have in Clayton. I can see that. When he got to talking about the countryside he got quite animated – how he liked to roam in the woods, build hiding-places and hidden dens, climb trees, hunt, fish, pick flowers, watch birds, set traps. Of course, he misses you and James and his friends at the village school too. I did say to him that I thought he had to give this a chance, to try a bit harder to get on with his grandmother.'

'Mrs Devine was telling me that she had contacted his school in Clayton,' said Dr Stirling. 'She was not very happy with what she heard.'

'No, I too had a word with the head teacher,' Miss Parsons told him. 'I'm afraid Danny doesn't seem to like that either. The head teacher described him as a sad and quiet boy who doesn't mix with the other children. He's no trouble and does what is asked of him but, despite his teacher's efforts, Danny seems distracted and not interested in his work. Of course it's always a bit stressful for a child starting a new school. He may well settle in time.'

'So Danny is not happy at home or at school,' remarked the doctor.

'No, not at the moment,' replied Miss Parsons.

'So what is there to be done?' asked Dr Stirling.

'As I have been at pains to point out, the boy's welfare comes first in all things. Now I appreciate that at the moment Danny is unhappy, but I am pretty certain that he is not neglected or ill-treated, and his grandmother, despite what people might think, is doing her best. I know she might not be the easiest person, but she would not have wanted Danny to live with her if she didn't love him. He is well fed and clothed and looked after. He is certainly far better off than some of the children I have to deal with who have very little, some of whom lead quite desperate lives. In my experience children are very resilient, and I think for the time being we should see how things go. I therefore think that Danny should remain with his grandmother.'

'I see,' said Dr Stirling. 'For the time being.'

'Yes. We assess all cases on their merits, and running away is not sufficient reason for Danny to be taken away from his grandmother and put into care. We will, of course, monitor the situation, make more visits and see how he is getting on and we will keep you fully up to speed. Maybe after a few weeks he will settle there.' She got up. 'Thank you for seeing me at this late hour. Now, I really must go. It's been a long day. I am afraid I'm not a very good delegate on these courses. All the lectures and discussion groups and plenary sessions make my head swim.'

'I appreciate you calling round, Miss Parsons,' said Dr Stirling. 'It was good of you to keep me informed. Please keep in touch and let me know how Danny is getting on.'

'I will indeed.'

When the social worker had gone Dr Stirling poured himself a large brandy. He cradled the glass in his hand, took a gulp and then opened the letter Danny had left on the bedside table and read it again.

Dear Doctor Stirling

I'm sorry to have caused all this trouble. I shouldn't have run off like that. I won't do it again. It's not that bad in Clayton though I do miss the village and the country and you and James and Mrs O'Connor and Mrs Devine and school and Ferdy. I hope Ferdy is OK by the way. I'd like to see him sometime. Maybe I could get a bus one Saturday and come and see you all. I know I should be glad that I'm not in a children's home and I know that there are a lot of kids worse off than me. Don't worry about me.

From Danny.

19

'And what are you looking so pleased with yourself about?' asked the school secretary.

Mr Gribbon, standing at the office door, certainly appeared in a better frame of mind than usual.

'To be honest, Mrs Scrimshaw, I am pleased,' he replied. 'Mrs Pugh, the part-time cleaner, has turned out to be most satisfactory. She's gone through them toilets like a dose of salts.'

'I'm very happy to hear it,' replied Mrs Scrimshaw. 'And no more foreign objects down the toilet bowls?'

'No, touch wood,' the caretaker replied. 'But I'm keeping my eye on that Oscar. He's a pain in the neck, that lad, and has far too much to say for himself.'

'Perhaps now you have Mrs Pugh we can look forward to less comment about all the work you have to do and how your back is always playing you up. How's your foot?'

'Not too bad,' replied the caretaker. 'You found the money then?'

'I beg your pardon?'

'The money you lost. You found it?'

'Yes, it had been pushed under the typewriter,' she told him. 'So you were wrong about little Roisin. The trouble with you, Mr Gribbon, is you jump to conclusions. It's a good job the girl wasn't accused of taking it.'

'I never said she'd took it,' replied the caretaker. 'I said she might have. Anyway, I called in to tell you something which concerns both of us about this amalgamation.'

'Well, make it quick because I've lots to do,' said the secretary.

'Mrs Pugh told me something very interesting,' said the caretaker, sitting on the corner of the desk. 'You know she works part-time at Urebank as well as here? Well, she told me that the caretaker there is intending to pack it in before this amalgamation. He's going for early retirement or redundancy. This means it leaves the field open for me for the job in the new set-up.'

'Really,' said Mrs Scrimshaw looking down at the letters on her desk. 'And how does this affect me?'

'Mrs Pugh said that the school secretary down there at Urebank, a very competent woman by all accounts, she said, and who virtually runs the place, has no intention of going.'

'You don't say.'

'And that should Mr Richardson get the job and move up here, she wants to come with him.'

'Who, Mrs Pugh?'

'No, the school secretary.'

Mrs Scrimshaw shot up like a puppet which has had its strings suddenly pulled. 'Move up here!' she exclaimed. 'Become secretary at Barton? Over my dead body, she will.'

'Well, it's to be expected,' said the caretaker, rubbing salt into the wound. 'It stands to reason that if Mr Richardson takes over the juniors, which I gather will be on this site, he will want to bring his own secretary with him. That means that you'll have to move down to Urebank, or at worst be redeployed or out of a job.'

'Who will have to move down to Urebank?' Elisabeth had come up behind the caretaker and could not help but overhear.

'Oh, I was just speculating, Mrs Devine,' he replied, feeling awkward and jumping up from the desk. He rubbed his jaw. 'Of course none of us want that to happen. I mean for him to take over . . . well . . . to come up here . . . if you see what I mean. I'll get on with buffing my floors.' He scurried off.

'I wouldn't worry your head about that, Mrs Scrimshaw,' said Elisabeth. 'I can't see that happening.'

'I hope not,' said the school secretary. She picked up an official-looking brown envelope. 'I didn't open this one, Mrs Devine,' she said, 'because it has "Personal and Confidential" on it and it's from the Education Department.' She was intrigued as to the contents. 'Would you like to reply to the sender? I could type out the letter before I leave.'

'No, I'll open it later, thank you,' said Elisabeth. She had a good idea what it would be about.

Later at home Elisabeth read the enclosed letter. As she had expected, it was from the Director of Education inviting her for interview at eleven o'clock in the Council Chamber at County Hall the following Friday.

20

Miss Sowerbutts, her hair wild and wiry, sat up stiffly in her hospital bed. She looked as if she had survived ten rounds in the ring with the heavyweight boxing champion. Her pale face, moulded into a permanent expression of discontent, sported a gash across the forehead, a huge purple bruise circling her black eye, a cut lip and a swollen mouth. Her arm was in a plaster cast. On the bedside table were an uneaten, congealed plate of macaroni cheese and cup of cold, insipid-looking tea. A teabag floated in the milky liquid like a dead mouse.

'And how are we today, Miss Sackbutts?' asked the young doctor, putting on his cheerful bedside manner.

'It's Sowerbutts,' she corrected him sharply, 'and how do you imagine we feel this morning?' She did not expect an answer.

The doctor smiled weakly. 'We have had the results back from all the tests,' he told her, 'and I am very pleased to tell you that they show there is nothing to worry about, nothing untoward.' The patient nodded slightly. 'You have had a nasty shock, but in time things will heal and you'll be back to your old self.' The young doctor tried to imagine what the old self would look like. It was not a pleasant picture which came to mind. He had been told by the nurses what a cantankerous old woman she was and that they would be glad to see the back of her.

'When can I be discharged?' asked Miss Sowerbutts dourly.

'Soon,' the young doctor replied. 'We would like to keep you in for a couple more days to be on the safe side, just to make sure that you are fit enough to go. Do you have someone to look after you when you get home?'

'No, I don't.'

'I see. Well, it might be a good idea to get someone in to help you. I could arrange for a carer if you wish.'

'That won't be necessary. I am quite capable of looking after myself.'

'Well, just so long as you take things easy,' said the young doctor.

'There is something wrong with my teeth,' said Miss Sowerbutts, moving her mouth from side to side.

'Your teeth?'

'My false teeth. They were taken away when I was admitted and now they've been returned to me they don't seem to fit.' She gave a twisted and rather alarming smile, displaying a set of large and ugly yellow teeth.

'Probably because your mouth is still very swollen,' explained the young doctor. 'I am sure that when the swelling goes down they will be all right. Anyway, I will have a word with the sister.' He glanced at his wristwatch, eager to be away.

'I have already had a word with the sister and I can't say she has been all that helpful.'

'I shall speak to her after I have finished my rounds,' said the young doctor. 'And now, if there is nothing else . . .'

'There is,' said Miss Sowerbutts. 'I should be in a private room. I did mention this to the sister but she has not seen fit to do anything about it. I have a private patients' plan and should not be in a general ward.'

'I believe that the private rooms are fully occupied,' the doctor told her.

'Well, it is just not good enough!' snapped Miss Sowerbutts. 'I pay through the nose for private medical care and should not be put in a general ward next to some destitute who clearly has mental problems. I had to endure the moaning and wheezing and coughing of the woman in the next bed all night.'

'I will have a word with the sister about that too,' the doctor assured her. 'And now if you will excuse me—'

'And the food is execrable.' She gestured to the plate beside her.

'I beg your pardon?' The young doctor tried to hide his irritation.

'Inedible. Not fit to be eaten.' The young doctor sighed and scratched his forehead. He had thought when he was on Accident and Emergency that times were stressful, but at that moment wished he was back with the cuts and bruises and broken noses.

'And am I to see a specialist?' demanded Miss Sowerbutts.

'There is really no need for that,' he told her with an edge to his voice. 'But I have no doubt that Mr Pennington will see you before you are discharged. You have suffered some bruising and a broken arm, which will heal given time. Now I really must get on. I do have other patients to see.' She opened her mouth to respond but he hastened away.

Later that morning the ward sister approached the bed with a frosty expression. 'Doctor tells me you have a series of complaints,' she said coldly.

'Yes,' said Miss Sowerbutts. 'I should be in a private room. I am not an NHS patient, which I explained to you. I am a private patient. I had a most disagreeable night having to listen to the woman in the next bed coughing and spluttering and shouting out.'

'You won't have to put up with that tonight,' the ward sister assured her stiffly.

'Good.'

'The poor woman died this morning.'

'Oh, well, I'm sorry to hear that, but nevertheless—'

'You will be moved into a private room when one becomes available,' said the ward sister. 'Anything else?'

'The food is inedible.'

'It's simple and nutritious and quite adequate,' said the ward sister. 'Should you wish, your relatives or friends can supplement it with something more.' She made an effort to hide her irritation.

'And then there's the question of my teeth, which I have mentioned to you before.'

'Your teeth?'

'Yes, my teeth. They are most uncomfortable and have turned a most unpleasant colour.' She showed a mouth full of yellow teeth.

The ward sister was quite taken aback by the ugly set of dentures she now looked upon and realised what had happened. The woman had the wrong teeth. She was sure that the set she was viewing were originally in the woman who had occupied the next bed and was now stretched out in the morgue, probably in possession of Miss Sowerbutts's teeth. The two sets of dentures must have been mixed up when they were taken to be cleaned. The ward sister did not lose her composure but asked a nurse to bring a bowl. 'If you would place your teeth in here,' she said to Miss Sowerbutts, holding out the receptacle, 'I shall ask the orthodontist to take a look.'

In the corridor the sister asked the nurse to retrieve Miss Sowerbutts's teeth from the poor woman in the morgue and replace them with the ones in the bowl.

'And give them a good scrub,' she told her.

It was much later that day when Miss Sowerbutts finally got her own teeth back. It had been a difficult task extracting the false teeth from the corpse, for rigor mortis had set in and the mouth of the deceased had been firmly clamped shut.

At visiting time Miss Brakespeare appeared. She was dressed in a smart camel-hair coat, red scarf and matching beret.

'I thought I would call in and see how you are,' she told her former colleague.

'"Bearing up", as my mother would say,' replied Miss Sowerbutts.

'So how are you feeling?'

'About as well as I look: sore, bruised, aching and desperate to get out of this place.'

'I've brought you some biscuits and a bunch of grapes.'

'Thank goodness for something edible. The food in here is unfit for human consumption. Put them in the bedside cabinet, will you.'

'Well, we've had a right carry-on in the village,' Miss Brakespeare told her.

'Really.' Miss Sowerbutts nodded and gave a thin smile that conveyed little more than feigned interest.

'Someone tried to rob the village store and post office,' she said. 'He threatened Major Neville-Gravitas with a knife, so Mrs Sloughthwaite sprayed him in the face with oven cleaner.'

'Who, the major?'

'No, the robber. They trussed him up. Thankfully nobody was hurt – well, apart from the robber, who was nearly blinded. Fancy though, such a thing happening in Barton. We've never had anything like it before in the village. Everybody's talking about it and we've had newspaper reporters and television cameras. It's been really exciting.'

Miss Sowerbutts laughed in a mirthless way. 'Well, that's one more reason for me to go and live elsewhere,' she remarked. 'Fortunately De Courcey Apartments have a very sophisticated security system.'

'Then, you know Mr Massey's nephew, young Clarence? I

taught him some years ago. He's not the shiniest apple in the orchard but he's a nice enough lad, well—'

'Don't mention that foolish young man to me,' interrupted Miss Sowerbutts. 'I have never met anyone so lacking in common sense, and that useless uncle of his is a most idle and unreliable individual. Only covered my lawn in bleach to kill those moles I had, and the only thing he succeeded in killing was the grass.'

'Well, his nephew has up and gone with that Bianca, the young woman who had the baby. Evidently the child is his. They've got themselves a council flat in Clayton – actually it's not too far from where you're going to live – and Clarence is working at the bread factory—'

'Miriam,' said Miss Sowerbutts, with a faint twist of the thin lips, 'might I stop you. I am not really interested in the carryings-on of an unmarried girl who has managed to secure a council flat by dint of having a child and who is no doubt receiving every state benefit she can get her hands on.'

'I see,' said Miss Brakespeare. 'I just thought you might be interested.' She breathed in and glanced at her watch. 'Is there anything you want?' she asked her former colleague eventually.

'I want a private room, that's what I want,' said Miss Sowerbutts crossly, 'but they've put me in this general ward with all manner of unsavoury people. There was a down-and-out in the bed next to me last night shouting out and making all manner of noises. I didn't get a wink of sleep.'

'So, there's nothing I can get you?' asked Miss Brakespeare, wishing to escape.

'Well, you could stock up on a few provisions for me – milk, bread, butter, that sort of thing – for when I get out. I've made a list. It's in the drawer on my bedside cabinet. Go to the supermarket, not the village store. I don't patronise that establishment. I find the proprietor very sharp and offhand.'

'She did very well tackling the robber as she did,' said Miss Brakespeare.

Miss Sowerbutts made no comment. 'And you could call into the chemist's for my prescription and pop in at my cottage to make sure everything is all right. I'll give you the keys before you go. If it's cold turn up the heating. While you are there give the plants a water. If I think of anything else, I'll give you a ring.'

'Well, I'd like to be of help,' said Miss Brakespeare, smiling awkwardly, 'but I'm off to Scarborough for the weekend. I just popped in before we set off. We're going straight on from the hospital.'

'You're going to Scarborough in this weather? Sooner you than me.'

'We like it at this time of year. It's very bracing, and we've booked to see a Gilbert and Sullivan at the Spa. Mother is quite excited.'

'Oh, I see,' said Miss Sowerbutts with a hard stern expression on her face.

There was an embarrassed silence. 'It must have been a terrible shock for you.'

'What was?'

'Falling down the stairs like that. One has to be very careful at your age.'

Miss Sowerbutts pressed her lips together in a tight thin line. 'I am not senile, Miriam. It was the stupid cat, stretched out like that. I could have broken my neck.'

'Where is the cat, by the way?'

'Dr Stirling is looking after it until I get home, so you don't need to worry. I'll not be asking you to look after it.'

'I couldn't anyway. Mother's allergic to cats,' said Miss Brakespeare meekly. They sat in silence for a while. 'And fancy Malcolm Stubbins of all people coming to your rescue.'

'Yes, for once in his life he acted very sensibly,' admitted

Miss Sowerbutts. 'I shall send him a book token when I get out of here, though I very much doubt he will ever use it. I always found that boy to be a wayward child, self-willed and perverse, but I have to confess that what he did was commendable.'

'He seems to have settled down lately,' said her former colleague. 'I think the starting of a football team at the school was the making of the boy. He heard last week that he'd been spotted at one of the matches by a talent scout who works for the football club in Clayton, and he will be attending some sort of sports academy one evening a week. And you remember Chardonnày, well—'

'Miriam, may I stop you there? I am not really interested any more in matters related to the village school,' said Miss Sowerbutts. 'I am now moving on to pastures new and a life in Clayton.'

'And are you looking forward to your move?' asked Miss Brakespeare. 'I believe you've sold the cottage.'

'Yes, and they're supposed to be moving in next month. I am certainly not looking forward to the upheaval,' replied Miss Sowerbutts. 'However I am going to manage on my own, the state I am in at the moment, I do not know.' Miss Brakespeare resisted the temptation to say she would help. 'I shall just have to delay moving until I am good and ready.'

'So will Dr Stirling have the cat when you move into your flat?'

'Apartment,' she corrected. 'No, he won't. It's merely a temporary measure until I get out of hospital.'

'Well, I don't think they allow pets in the flats – apartments, I mean.'

'Of course they allow pets, Miriam. Whatever gave you that idea?'

'Well, Mrs Sloughthwaite was saying that Danny Stainthorpe, who's gone to live with his grandmother, wasn't allowed to take his pet ferret with him.'

'What have Daniel Stainthorpe and his grandmother got to do with me?'

'His grandmother's living in the same block of flats – apartments – as you.'

Miss Sowerbutts jolted up in her bed as if she had been bitten. 'Don't be ridiculous! The apartments are part of the prestigious waterfront development and are well out of her league.'

'De Courcey Apartments, overlooking the river and the cathedral,' said Miss Brakespeare. 'She was telling Mrs Sloughthwaite in the village store and post office that she's moved in.'

'That dreadful woman who served behind the bar at the Blacksmith's Arms and ran off with the salesman, her with the peroxide hair and the cigarette dangling from her mouth, a neighbour of mine?'

'That's what Mrs Sloughthwaite told me, and she said they don't allow pets.'

Miss Sowerbutts leaned back on her pillow and closed her eyes. 'This is just too much,' she moaned.

'Well, I'm only telling you what I heard,' said Miss Brakespeare.

'Does it give you some perverse pleasure, Miriam,' said Miss Sowerbutts, 'to tell me such depressing news?'

'Of course not, I just thought you ought to know, that's all,' she said. After a few silent and uncomfortable moments Miss Brakespeare glanced at her watch. 'Well, I must be off,' she said cheerfully, getting to her feet. 'We want to get to Scarborough and check into the hotel before it gets dark. Then we've got a meal booked before the theatre. I'll call in to see you again when I get back and you're out of hospital.'

'I really wouldn't bother,' whispered the patient in the bed, who had been thoroughly depressed by the visit.

'Oh, and a bit of news,' said her former colleague. 'I'm retiring at the end of next term.'

Miss Sowerbutts opened her eyes. 'Retiring?' she repeated.

'Well, what with all this amalgamation and such I thought it was time. I've looked into it and I get full enhancement on my salary, a lump sum and my full pension, so I'll not be badly off. I shall be moving to Scarborough. Mother's always liked that part of the coast. And, of course, George likes it there too.'

'George?'

'George Tomlinson. He plays the organ at the Bethesda Chapel. Didn't I say? We're getting married.'

'All I'm saying, Mrs Scrimshaw,' said the caretaker as he stood at the door of the school office, 'is that it looks as if there's another woman on the scene.'

'And where did you hear this nugget of gossip?' asked the school secretary, peering over her glasses.

'René Holroyd who runs the café in the high street was telling Mrs Sloughthwaite and she told Mrs Widowson, who mentioned it to my wife.'

'The jungle telegraph *has* been busy,' remarked Mrs Scrimshaw.

'They were seen in the café very lovey-dovey by all accounts,' related the caretaker. 'Holding his hand she was. So it looks as if something's going on with Dr Stirling and that new vicar.'

'And what is your point?' asked the school secretary.

'I'm just saying that they seem to be getting on very well together,' said the caretaker. 'Mrs Widowson, who's big in the Mothers' Union, told my wife that Dr Stirling has been giving talks down at the church for her.'

'And?'

'And that they've been seen in his car together, so perhaps the good doctor's affections are elsewhere now, or he's playing fast and loose with Mrs Devine.'

'And what's it got to do with me?' she asked, 'Or with anyone else for that matter, where Dr Stirling's affections are?'

'Nothing,' said the caretaker. 'I'm just saying.'

'Is Dr Stirling married to Mrs Devine?' she asked.

'No.'

'Engaged?'

'No.'

'Are they going out together?'

'Not as I know of.'

'Then why shouldn't Dr Stirling be in a café with the new curate?'

'If you put it like that—' began the caretaker.

'Really, Mr Gribbon,' she sighed. 'You're worse than the woman in the post office when it comes to tittle-tattle. Now I've got better things to do than listen to what Dr Stirling might or might not be getting up to, and I'm sure Mrs Pugh could do with a helping hand buffing the floors.'

Elisabeth, who had heard the conversation from outside, walked slowly down the corridor to her classroom.

As soon as she arrived back at her cottage Miss Sowerbutts was on the telephone to the estate agents. The dapper young man in the smart grey suit, slicked-back hair and designer glasses arrived the following day as she had requested. He sat on the edge of a chair clutching a sheaf of papers, with one foot masking the other to hide the hole in his sock. The visitor had been asked to leave his shoes in the hall so as not to mark the pale cream carpet in the lounge. He had not been offered a drink.

'So, it's just a matter of your signature, Miss Sowerbutts,' he said, 'and then we can proceed.'

'I did not ask you here for me to sign anything, Mr Raddison,' said Miss Sowerbutts, 'I asked you here to inform you that I do not intend to move, that the cottage is no longer for sale.'

'Not move!' exclaimed the young man. 'I don't understand.'

'After careful consideration,' she told him, 'I have decided to stay in Barton-in-the-Dale, certainly for the foreseeable future.'

'But Miss Sowerbutts, the price was agreed, the contracts have been drawn up and the purchasers are ready to move in. They have sold their house and are just waiting now for you to complete.'

'Well, I don't intend to "complete", as you put it,' she replied.

'But everything is arranged,' he pleaded. 'You accepted their offer. It was agreed.'

'I have signed nothing, and until I append my name to the contract of sale nothing can proceed.'

'But Miss Sowerbutts—'

She held up a hand. 'Young man, let me repeat myself. I am not selling the cottage.'

'But why?'

'Because I have changed my mind,' she told him.

'May I ask the reason?'

'Because I was unaware that pets are not allowed in the De Courcey Apartments, and as you can see' – she gestured to the lazy Siamese cat stretched out on the carpet – 'I have a cat.'

Of course the principal reason for the change of mind was not the cat. Following her fall down the stairs the creature was not in her best books, and the idea of finding another home for it was not so unthinkable. It was the thought of having a neighbour of the ilk of that dreadfully common Mrs Stainthorpe that made her shudder. She had been led to believe that the residents of the state-of-the-art apartments would be of the educated, professional, genteel class, like herself.

'It was clearly stated in the contract, which you have had

sight of, that no pets are allowed,' the young estate agent reminded her.

'No, Mr Raddison, it was not clearly stated,' Miss Sowerbutts retorted. 'It was tucked away in minute print at the bottom of a page. It was only recently pointed out to me by a former colleague of mine.'

'Could you not get someone to look after your cat?' suggested the young man feebly.

'Out of the question!' she snapped.

'But Miss Sowerbutts, the couple who bought – were to buy – your cottage will be bitterly disappointed. They have been looking for somewhere in the village for so long, and—'

'Be that as it may,' she said, rising from her chair to indicate that the discussion was at an end, 'I intend to stay in Barton-in-the-Dale.'

Councillor Smout spread out like some great Eastern potentate in the large ornate chair in which the mayor sat at council meetings. It was the morning of the interviews for the headship of the newly amalgamated schools. On Councillor Smout's right were the four po-faced governor representatives from Urebank and Ms Tricklebank. On his right were the governors from Barton-in-the-Dale: Archdeacon Atticus, Lady Wadsworth, Councillor Cooper and Major Neville-Gravitas. Elisabeth sat at a small table facing them.

'Now then, Mrs Devine,' said Councillor Smout, resting his hands on his stomach and rotating his fat thumbs slowly around one another, 'we all know why we are 'ere, so let's get crackin'. I 'ope you've 'ad a good journey.'

'Yes, thank you,' Elisabeth replied and smiled at the line of faces.

'Dun't seem that long since I was interviewin' you for t'post at Barton, does it?' he asked, smiling.

'No,' Elisabeth replied. 'It doesn't.'

The councillor introduced each of the members of the interview panel and then rubbed his hands together. 'Right then. Now if I could start t'batting, if you was given the post, what problems do you think you'll 'ave to face wi' this merger?'

Elisabeth thought for a moment before replying. 'Well, I would like to start from positives rather than negatives,' she said, 'and there are many advantages which will come with the merger of the two schools.'

'Which are?' asked Councillor Smout.

'Well, it means that neither school will close, which is a good thing, and that both villages will still have premises for their various community activities, and there will be greater expertise on the teaching staff, smaller classes and extra resources. The benefits I should think will be great and will far outweigh the disadvantages.'

'But there will be some disadvantages, won't there?' asked the chairman.

'I guess there will be some teething problems – teachers and pupils from both schools getting to know each other, for example, and, of course, some of the children will have a longer journey to school – but with goodwill and the children's best interests at heart, I think these can be overcome. I think the amalgamation could be a really exciting challenge.'

The remaining questions, which were surprisingly few in number, were of a general nature and Elisabeth felt she had acquitted herself well. Then the chairman turned to the senior education officer. 'Have you anything to ask, Ms Tricklebank?'

'Yes, Mr Chairman,' she replied. 'I have.' Her question was simple and direct. 'What do you think makes a good school, Mrs Devine?'

'A good school,' she said, thinking for a moment. 'I think a good school is a place which is caring, where children and staff are valued, where there are high expectations and lots of encouragement and praise for both teachers and children. It's a peaceful, clean, orderly place, cheerful and welcoming, where there is respect for and tolerance of others, where the curriculum is wide and challenging and tailored to individual needs. It's a school where there are high standards, self-motivated pupils and plenty of enjoyment and laughter. It also needs to have firm, clear, decisive leadership and management.'

'And of course it is first and foremost a place for learning, where there is hard work, good discipline and high academic standards,' added Ms Tricklebank. 'Would you agree?'

'Yes, of course, but in my experience children learn better when they are happy and secure. Their education should not be deprived of all pleasure, playfulness and creativity. Would *you* not agree?'

'I am here to ask the questions, Mrs Devine,' said Ms Tricklebank, 'and not to answer them.'

Elisabeth bit her tongue. She found this woman intimidating, but she did not intend to be cowed by her and met her gaze steadily.

'And these characteristics of the good school which you have outlined,' continued the senior education officer, 'do you think the children judge a school by those same criteria?'

'Probably not,' replied Elisabeth.

'So what do you imagine are the things that they would consider make a good school?'

'Being with their friends, enjoyable lessons, teachers with a sense of humour, an adult they can talk to, lots of clubs and activities, good lunches of course, and decent toilets.'

'Toilets!' interjected Councillor Smout.

'Yes, toilets,' replied Elisabeth. 'Bright, clean, well-maintained toilets. In my experience the environment of a school should be of the standard found in the very best home.'

'An interesting answer,' said Ms Tricklebank, giving a small quizzical smile.

'But pupils and teachers will agree on one thing,' said Elisabeth, 'and that is that in a good school there is no bullying.'

'Thank you, Mr Chairman,' said the senior education officer, writing something on the papers spread out before her. 'I have no more questions for this candidate.'

21

Elisabeth curled up on the sofa in front of the open fire in her cottage later that evening, wondering what she would do if she had been unsuccessful. She felt that the interview had gone well until it came to Ms Tricklebank's grilling, but that after that the atmosphere had become rather strained. Elisabeth had lost her composure when challenged so sharply by the senior education officer. The panel of ten, a rather daunting number for a start, was a disparate group who, apart from the ever-smiling and nodding archdeacon and Lady Wadsworth, appeared to be unimpressed by her answers and maintained its serious countenance throughout. She could count on the votes of both Archdeacon Atticus and Lady Wadsworth, but as to the others, she had strong doubts. At the conclusion of the interview, when she had been asked if she was a serious candidate, and to which she had replied that she was, Elisabeth had sensed by the expressions on some of the governors' faces that she would not be offered the post.

Perhaps her answers had come out as too pat, she thought, and she had appeared overly confident. Perhaps the governors from Urebank had asked few questions because they had made up their minds prior to the interview that their vote would be for Mr Richardson, whom they knew, presumably admired and got on well with. Elisabeth was aware that she would not get the vote of Councillor Smout and the new governor. That young Councillor Cooper would no doubt follow his colleague's lead. She clearly did not impress Ms

Tricklebank in trying to answer the probing questioning which was put to her.

The more she thought about it the more anxious Elisabeth became. If she didn't get the job, what could she do? She couldn't give up her cottage after all the hard work and money she had spent on it. She didn't want to move to another school, away from the village that she had grown to love and further away from Forest View, and yet she might have to. The overheard conversation in the school office troubled her. She knew the caretaker was one for gossip and for exaggerating, but nevertheless it had upset her to hear that Michael was on such good terms with another woman. The new curate was attractive and intelligent and personable. Had Michael now fallen for her, she wondered? So what did the future hold for their relationship? She loved the man but he seemed chary about taking things further, of committing himself. But she knew one thing for certain, and that was she could not work under Robin Richardson.

The phone rang. It was Major Neville-Gravitas. 'Hello, Elisabeth, it's Cedric Neville-Gravitas here. I trust I am not disturbing you?'

Elisabeth felt her heart miss a beat. 'No, no, not at all. Good evening, major.'

'Well, I hope you are sitting down,' he said.

Here it comes, she thought, I haven't got the job.

'Are you still there?' he asked.

'Yes, I'm still here,' she replied before taking a deep breath.

'Well, I thought I'd give you a bell to let you know the outcome of the interview.'

'Yes.'

'Of course, strictly speaking, I shouldn't say anything at all,' he rambled on. 'We were told by Ms Tricklebank that letters informing the candidates of the governors' decision are in the post and it's best not to say anything until everything's official. Anyhow, I thought you ought to be put out of your misery.'

Elisabeth's heart sank. 'I see.'

'You got the job.'

'What?'

'The governors decided to offer you the post,' the major told her.

'They did?' cried Elisabeth.

'Indeed they did, and may I be the first to congratulate you. Excellent interview, very impressive answers. Of course this is strictly off the record, me telling you – hush, hush, and all that, if you follow my drift. But the decision was unanimous.'

It had taken the appointment panel little time to make up its mind. Councillor Smout had listened with increasing unease as each of the governors from Urebank had stated their preference for Elisabeth. Then the four governors from Barton had readily concurred. Councillor Cooper, much to the chairman's surprise, had said that he found Mrs Devine was in every respect the better candidate. Ms Tricklebank had then added her endorsement, referring to her recent visits to the two schools and the observations of Mr Steel, HMI, and herself. Both felt that the leadership and management at Barton-in-the-Dale school were far superior to that at Urebank. The chairman, faced with such a fait accompli, had no option but to endorse the decision to appoint Elisabeth.

'I really got the job?' asked Elisabeth now.

'As I have told you,' said the major, 'you won't officially know until you receive the letter from the Education Department in a couple of days' time, but very well done. Of course I always thought you would get it, you know. Oh, and the other thing is that Councillor Smout is not to take on the chairmanship of the new governing body. I have been asked to do it.'

'I'm very pleased,' said Elisabeth.

'Really? It's very kind of you to say so. I look forward to working with you again.'

'Thank you,' she said. 'Thank you very much.'

When she had placed down the receiver Elisabeth shouted out, 'Yes!' Then, as she reached for the telephone to let Michael Stirling know the good news, it rang again.

'Hello, Elisabeth. It's Marcia Atticus here. I shouldn't strictly be telling you this because Charles is so particular about procedures and protocols, but I just had to let you know the outcome of the interview. You got the job. Charles told me when he came back from County Hall. He said you were wonderful and was so proud of you. Evidently it took barely ten minutes for them to make up their minds and—'

'Marcia, I know,' said Elisabeth excitedly. 'Major Neville-Gravitas has just rung to tell me.'

Mrs Atticus sounded peeved. 'Well, so much for procedures and protocols. According to Charles the governors were told not to say anything. It took me a good half-hour to wheedle it out of him and then he asked me not to tell you because the appointment had to be confirmed by the Education Office. "Fiddlesticks!" I told him. "That's just a formality." Of course in this village news travels like wildfire. I expect Mrs Sloughthwaite will have already placed a poster in the window of her shop announcing the good news. Anyway, isn't it just super? I'm delighted for you. And I have some splendid news too. You know that big marble monstrosity of a tomb in the graveyard which I so dislike? Well, I eventually got Mr Massey to cut down a dead branch on the big oak tree which over-hangs it – evidently his nephew whom he passes all the work on to has finally broken loose and gone to live in Clayton – and the branch came crashing down on top of the tomb. Quite demolished it! The remains are being removed next week. It wasn't quite such good news for Mr Massey. Unfortunately he came crashing down with the branch and is now in Clayton Royal Infirmary with a broken leg. Ashley went to visit him – Dr Stirling has been really good to Ashley and took her to see the chaplain and she's now helping out at the hospital. Anyhow, I must rush as she's cooking something special for dinner – sautéed sea trout in some special sauce. She's an angel, she really is. There is nothing she can't turn her hand to. I shall see you in school on Monday. Congratulations again.'

Elisabeth had no sooner put down the receiver when the telephone rang again. It was Lady Wadsworth. 'Hello Elisabeth. I just wanted to let you know—'

'I'm sorry to interrupt, Helen,' said Elisabeth, 'but you are the third person to let me know I got the job, though it's really kind of you to ring.'

'Well, we were told not to say anything by that severe-looking woman from the Education Office, that Ms Tricklebank, who I don't think is capable of smiling. She said to keep mum until the official offer was made, but I seem not to be the only one who just couldn't wait to tell you. By the way she was most complimentary about your answers.'

'She was?' exclaimed Elisabeth.

'Indeed she was. She said you are the sort of head teacher who sets the standard by which other head teachers should be judged. What about that, then? Anyway, my dear, may I add my heartiest congratulations.'

'My feet haven't touched the ground yet,' admitted Elisabeth.

'Well, I have some excellent news too,' said Lady Wadsworth. 'The statues went to the auction in London yesterday. It was the devil's own job shifting them. They weighed a ton, but Mr O'Malley was most helpful. He's proving quite a find. Anyway, they attracted a great deal of interest and they fetched a figure well in excess of the reserve. I can now go ahead with all the alterations.'

'I'm delighted,' said Elisabeth.

'And I have had a serious word with Mr O'Malley this afternoon. He's an excellent worker and seems to be able to turn his hand to anything. I should be very sorry to lose him, but he strikes me as someone with wanderlust. I should think it won't be too long before he's thinking of going off on his travels again. I did tell him that living in a caravan was no sort of life for a child and he should think of settling down.'

Elisabeth thought of Danny and his happy life with his grandfather in a caravan.

'I suggested,' continued Lady Wadsworth, 'that he should think about staying here in Barton and that he and Roisin could live in the lodge. I could have it done up.'

'And what did he say to that?' asked Elisabeth.

'He said he'd think about it. So we both have to work on him.'

'I'll do my best,' said Elisabeth. 'There's the doorbell. I must go.'

'Probably someone else to tell you the good tidings,' said Lady Wadsworth. 'I'll speak to you again soon.'

Elisabeth hoped it would be Michael as she went to answer the door, but on the doorstep stood a rather dishevelled figure in a shapeless anorak and faded jeans.

'Hello, Elisabeth,' he said.

'You!' she exclaimed.

'May I come in?' asked her ex-husband.

Elisabeth was unable to speak, and stood in the doorway staring at the man she had not seen for six years.

'So, may I come in?' he asked again. 'It's really cold out here.' He was shivering.

'Yes, yes,' she said, opening the door wider. 'Come through into the sitting-room.'

Simon went over to the fire and warmed his hands. He looked drawn and ill at ease. 'I've been outside for a while, summoning up the courage to ring the bell.' Elisabeth didn't answer. 'You're looking well,' he said, trying to sound cheerful.

'Yes, I am very well, thank you,' she replied. She was standing by the door thinking how very different he looked. He was no longer the tall, immaculately dressed man she had married, the self-assured partner in a top accountancy firm. He looked small, he had lost weight and there were threads of grey in his dark hair.

'And you've got this cottage.' He looked around him. 'It's looking lovely, but then you always did have good taste. May I sit down?' Without waiting for an answer he sat in a chair by the fire, placing his hands on his knees. 'Any chance of a drink?'

'A whisky?' Elisabeth asked. 'You still drink whisky, I assume?'

'That's fine.'

As she gave him his drink she asked, 'Simon, why are you here?'

There was a strained, almost puzzled look in his eyes.

'What is it you want?' she asked when he didn't answer.

He avoided looking at her and stared into the fire. 'I wanted to see you,' he said quietly.

'Why?'

He looked up at her with a mixture of sorrow and regret. 'Just to see you and talk to you.' He sipped the drink and swallowed nervously. 'We didn't part on the best of terms.'

'No, we didn't.'

'I'm pleased to see that things have worked out for you,' he said. 'I mean that, I really am.'

'And how does your wife feel about you wanting to see me and talk to me?' she asked.

'Julia left me last year,' he said. 'It didn't work out. I soon discovered that we had very little in common. She had a fiery temper and would fly into tantrums at the slightest thing. Work dominated her life. She was manipulative, too. When we split up she managed to get me edged out of the firm. I lost the partnership and was pushed into resigning. She was a fiercely ambitious woman and if anything or anybody got in her way, well, she—'

'Simon,' interrupted Elisabeth, 'I'm not a marriage guidance counsellor. Your life with Julia is of no interest or concern to me. I've moved on.'

'No, I know that. It's just—'

'I think you should go,' she said.

'I've wanted to see you for a long time, Elisabeth. Please hear me out. What I did—'

'What you did, Simon, was walk out of my life and your son's for another woman,' Elisabeth said angrily. 'I don't feel any pleasure in knowing that it didn't work out for you but I am really not interested to hear all the details.'

'I know that—'

'Let me finish! You have never been in touch, never phoned me up to see how John is, never even sent your son so much as a birthday card and now you walk back into my life and want to talk about things. Well, no thank you.'

'I know, I know,' he said. 'Julia got quite neurotic when I did suggest keeping in touch with John. Honestly, I really did want to see him. She was incredibly jealous, got quite paranoid if I spoke to another woman, imagining all sorts of things.'

'John is not another woman, Simon, he's your son.'

'I promised Julia that—'

'So it was all Julia's fault, was it?' asked Elisabeth. 'How convenient for you.'

'No, of course not,' he replied. 'I should have kept in touch. I know that now.'

'Simon,' said Elisabeth, 'I've had a tiring day. What is it you want?'

'I just wanted to see you,' he said pathetically. 'To talk to you.'

'About what?'

'I've had a lot of time to think about things recently, going over in my mind what happened between us, rehearsing what I would say to you if I got the chance. I wanted to say that I'm sorry, I wanted to say that. I very much regret how I behaved, how I treated you.'

'It's a wonderful thing, is hindsight,' said Elisabeth.

'I know I behaved badly. I suppose I felt trapped, crowded in. I didn't want to hear when you wanted to talk about John's condition.'

'No, you didn't,' Elisabeth conceded dolefully.

'I should have tried harder. I know that now.'

'I know it wasn't all one-sided, Simon,' said Elisabeth. 'I was tense and anxious too, and I know that I could be tetchy and bad-tempered, but I wanted support not recriminations, I wanted us to work through this thing together, not be at each other's throats. We were on opposite sides from the start. I tried so many times to get you to face up and accept John's disability, to get you to come with me to the specialist, visit the school, but you were reluctant even to talk about it. You just shut it out. You wanted a son who would be a clever and sporty boy like the sons of all your colleagues at work, a "normal child", whatever that means. I think you wanted to believe that he was a kind of late bloomer and that he would suddenly emerge as this child of exceptional ability. You would not admit it until it became obvious that there was something wrong, and then you couldn't cope with a little boy who lived in his own closed world and would be dependent upon us all his life.'

After a few silent and uncomfortable moments he replied. 'You're right,' he admitted sadly, looking at his feet. 'I was frightened and I suppose jealous too.'

'Jealous of what?'

'Of John.'

'You were jealous of a severely disabled child? Oh come on, Simon, you can do better than that.'

'Before we had him, Elisabeth, we had such a great life. Didn't we? Friends round for supper, theatre, restaurants, trips abroad. When John came along it changed our lives so completely. Everything was different. We never went out, friends dwindled, we never had a holiday. Your life centred completely on John. I just felt that you didn't love me in the same way when he arrived. He dominated your life. It was John this and John that. It got too much for me. Yes, I was jealous. At the time it seemed your child was a kind of substitute for a husband. You were desperate to throw yourself into the parenting business in a big way and—'

'I don't need to listen to all this, Simon,' interrupted Elisabeth. 'I really don't know where this conversation is going. I'm happy and settled, and you can't just appear out of the blue, say you are sorry and expect—'

'I miss you, Elisabeth,' he said sadly. 'I never realised how much until these last few months.' He rubbed his eyes. 'I want you back in my life. You loved me once and—'

'Stop it, Simon. I really don't want to hear this.'

He wiped his eyes. 'Maybe if we took things slowly at first, got to know each other again . . . I still have feelings for you, Elisabeth. I still love you.'

'This is going nowhere,' she said. 'It's selfish of you to do this to me. You come back and start to turn everything upside down. Simon, I was devastated when you left. I could barely cope, but I did cope because of our son. I now have a terrific job, my dream cottage and good friends, and I am near John so I can see him regularly. After all those years of worry and sometimes desperation I am truly happy, and I think John is too.'

'I know he is.'

'How would you know? You haven't seen him for six years.'

'I have,' Simon replied quietly.

'What do you mean?'

'When Julia left me last year I made contact and I've been seeing John for the last few months.'

'I don't believe you.'

'Why would I lie about something like that? You can ask Mr Williams if you want. Perhaps you are wondering how I found out where he was. Well, I phoned your last school. They wouldn't tell me where you had gone to, just that it was somewhere near a specialist school for autistic students. It didn't take much of an effort – just a few phone calls – to find Forest View. I've been seeing John most Sundays.'

'The head teacher would have mentioned it,' said Elisabeth.

'I told Mr Williams not to say anything to you. I heard how well you were doing and thought that seeing me would have complicated things.'

'You were right there.'

'Whatever you think about me, Elisabeth,' he said, 'I am not that selfish. I've been a bloody fool, I know that now, but I would never want to make things difficult for you.'

'And you say that you have been seeing John on Sundays?' she asked.

'Yes, I have. You might not believe this but I've got attached to the boy and I've learned a great deal about his condition. It's true that when he was born I did have ambitions that he would be clever and sporty, but all fathers hope for that for their sons, don't they? Now it doesn't matter to me.'

'David Williams should have told me,' said Elisabeth, not listening to what he was saying.

'Don't blame him,' said Simon. 'As I said, I asked him not to say anything. He described how well you were doing as the head teacher of a village school, how popular and successful you were. Of course he wouldn't tell me which school it was so I called in at County Hall, where, as you know, there is a list of the county schools and the names of the head teachers. I found your name. I asked at the village store and the large woman who serves there told me where you lived.'

'I see.'

'I shall go on seeing John whatever may happen between us,' he said, 'but I hope to keep seeing you. I want to put the past behind us.' He stood up and approached her. 'We could try again, Elisabeth. Take things slowly at first. I've changed. I just want a second chance.'

There was a loud rapping at the door and a mad ringing of the doorbell.

'Excuse me,' she said.

'Now, Mrs Devine,' said a hearty voice when she opened the door. A bottle of champagne was thrust into Elisabeth's hand. 'I have come to help you celebrate.'

'Michael!' Elisabeth exclaimed.

'And after a toast to your success I am taking a rather exceptional and attractive newly appointed head teacher out for dinner. I have just heard the wonderful news.'

Simon appeared in the hall.

'Oh, I'm sorry,' said Dr Stirling, 'I wasn't aware you had company.'

'This is Simon,' Elisabeth told him flatly. 'My ex-husband.'

Elisabeth called at Clumber Lodge the next morning, keen to see Michael Stirling and to explain the matters of the previous night.

Mrs O'Connor, having congratulated Elisabeth on her becoming the head teacher of the new consortium, explained that Dr Stirling had gone out after receiving a telephone call earlier that morning.

'It must have been important, because he got a locum doctor to take his Saturday morning surgery,' the housekeeper told Elisabeth. 'He shot out of this house like a scalded cat. And speaking of cats, I'll be glad when this madam gets taken back, so I will. She gets under my feet. No wonder people trip over her.' She pointed to the Siamese rubbing its body against her leg. 'She won't leave me alone. Follows me everywhere, so she does. Cupboard love, of course. She likes my steamed fish. Now that Miss Sowerbutts is out of hospital the cat wants taking back, but James won't do it and I'm certainly not. I find it hard work speaking to that woman. She's a face that could have been hacked out of wood with a blunt axe, so she has.' The housekeeper stopped suddenly when she saw Elisabeth's troubled look. 'Are you all right, Mrs Devine?' she said. 'You look quite agitated, so you do.'

'I really do need to see Dr Stirling,' replied Elisabeth. 'You have no idea where he might have gone?'

'No, he didn't say, just up and went. Didn't even have time to put his outdoor coat on. I guess it's another emergency. I hope it's not Miss Sowerbutts again. I've had quite enough of her cat.'

'I'll call back later,' said Elisabeth. 'I really do need to speak to him. I'm off to Forest View now to see John.'

'Well, I don't know what time the doctor will be back,' Mrs O'Connor told her. 'If I were you I'd leave it until this afternoon. I'll tell him you've called.'

At Forest View the head teacher congratulated Elisabeth on her success.

'My goodness, news travels fast,' she told him.

'Ah well, one of my new governors, Councillor Cooper, called in yesterday after the interviews,' said Mr Williams, 'and told me. He said to keep it to myself until it's made official but I pressed him to tell me. He said you gave an outstanding interview. I believe he's just joined your governing body too? He's a sharp young man and very enthusiastic, and I am sure will be a great asset. He's going to come in here each week and help in the classes.'

'So you knew I was up for interview yesterday?' asked Elisabeth.

'You still have a lot to learn about this part of the world,' Mr Williams told her. 'Nothing can be kept secret for too long around here.'

'And yet you kept my ex-husband's visits a secret,' said Elisabeth.

The head teacher looked embarrassed. 'Ah yes, I felt rather uncomfortable about that. How did you find out he has been to see John?'

'Because he called around unexpectedly last night,' Elisabeth said. 'I'd not seen him for six years.'

'I did want to tell you, Elisabeth,' said Mr Williams, 'but he begged me to promise not to say anything. You see, when he asked about you I told him how happy and settled you are, how successful things are at the village school, and I guess he didn't want to spoil it. You know, I think he is genuinely happy for you. I am sure he regrets a great many things he's said and done in the past. He's been coming here for the last few months, always on a Sunday, and I can see he's become close to John. He's not just going through the motions. He's interested in John's condition, is always asking questions and offers help. Perhaps at last he's come to terms with his son's condition.'

'And John likes to see him?' asked Elisabeth.

'Oh yes, I think he likes to see him, as far as I can tell.'

'Well,' said Elisabeth, 'that's all that matters. How is John, by the way?'

'Why don't you come and see for yourself?'

Elisabeth, on her visits, usually found her son sitting at his favourite table by the window, carefully arranging coloured beads in straight lines, but that morning he was busily occupied at a large plastic trough full of water, gently causing ripples and circles with his fingers.

'I told you on your last visit that he's become fascinated with water,' said the head teacher. 'Well, it's become something of an obsession. If it starts to rain he pats the table to tell us he wants to go outside. The thing is, Elisabeth, bearing in mind his condition, John's starting to communicate really well now. If he's happy and he wants something he taps the table. If he's distressed he pats his head. I really think that with this sort of progress it won't be too long before he starts using more sophisticated means of communicating. Eventually I hope he will be able to go out of school for the day with you. Small steps at first of course, but this is most encouraging.'

John was clearly pleased to see his mother and started tapping the side of the trough. Then he clasped her hand. Elisabeth could feel tears springing up behind her eyes.

22

Dr Stirling arrived at the Social Services Department that morning, intrigued as to why Miss Parsons wished to see him so urgently. Her telephone call that morning, despite her reassurance, had alarmed him.

'Dr Stirling,' she said, 'would it be possible for you to come down to my office?'

'When?' he asked.

'This morning, if you are able.'

'Is it about Danny?' he asked quickly.

'It is about Danny, yes.'

'He's not run away again, has he?'

'No, no, nothing like that.'

'Well, what is it then? Is he all right? Has he had an accident? Is he in any trouble?'

'I really would prefer to see you, Dr Stirling,' she said, 'rather than discuss this over the telephone. I would appreciate it if you could come to my office, where everything will be explained. I can assure you that Danny is fine and that he's not in any sort of trouble, but it is important that I see you.'

'Well, I have Saturday morning surgery, but if it is that important I guess I can rearrange things. You are sure the boy is all right?'

'Yes, I'm sure,' she replied.

In Miss Parsons's office Dr Stirling looked out of breath and anxious. 'What is it, Miss Parsons?' he asked urgently. 'What's happened?'

'Please sit down, Dr Stirling,' said the senior social worker calmly. She sat behind her desk and placed her hands on the top, locking her fingers together. 'There is nothing to get worried about. As I said on the phone, Danny is fine. He's in the other room.'

'May I see him?' asked Dr Stirling.

'All in good time. I wanted to have a word with you before you see him. The thing is, Mrs Stainthorpe called me early this morning. I gave her my private telephone number in case there were any problems. She told me that she can't cope with Danny. She has tried her best but it isn't working out.'

'Not working out. Well, if she—'

'Please let me finish, Dr Stirling,' interrupted Miss Parsons. 'Mrs Stainthorpe said that when Danny came to live with her she found her grandson moody and distant and that he spent most of his time in his room, sulking and rarely saying anything. Since he returned after running away things have not improved, in fact she tells me things have got worse. Danny has become very untidy, plays his music so loudly that other residents in the apartments have complained, and he goes out without telling her when he is coming back. She's had a letter from the school saying Danny is not doing his homework or applying himself.'

'Miss Parsons,' said Dr Stirling, 'this is so completely out of character. The boy is not like that. He's really not.'

'I know that,' agreed the senior social worker. 'I think there is method in what he is doing.'

'I don't follow.'

'He's a bright boy,' said Miss Parsons. 'I think there's reasoning behind his behaviour.'

'You mean he's deliberately being difficult?'

'Yes. I do.'

'So what happens now?'

'Mrs Stainthorpe is of the opinion that Danny might, after

all, be better staying with you. She sees how unhappy he is and she feels you are perhaps better able to deal with him, that the boy "needs a man to sort him out". Her words. Now I want to ask you, Dr Stirling—'

'You don't need to ask me, Miss Parsons,' he said. 'Of course I want him to come back.'

'And Mrs Stainthorpe says she will have no objections if you eventually wish to adopt Danny, but that she would like to see him now and again. She doesn't want to lose contact with him.'

Dr Stirling looked at his hands. 'Danny is right, you know. So often adults just don't listen to children. They don't take any account of their wishes. He never wanted to move in the first place, and if he had been left where he was then none of this would have happened.'

'We do listen to what children have to say,' said Miss Parsons. 'We listen a great deal, but sometimes our hands are tied or our recommendations are overruled. It's not easy, the work we have to do and the decisions we sometimes have to make, but we try our best and we can't do more than that.'

'Yes, I know,' said Dr Stirling. 'I appreciate all that you have done.'

'Would that all endings were like this,' she said smiling ruefully. 'Danny is now back where he wants to be and that's the main thing.'

'May I see him now?' asked the doctor.

'Of course,' she replied. 'You know, Dr Stirling, Mrs Stainthorpe is not quite the hard and selfish woman that people think she is. Talking to her about Danny, I have seen a rather different side to her. He's the only family she has. I think she's lonely and genuinely hoped things would work out. I do hope Danny will keep in contact with her.'

'I'll make sure he does,' Dr Stirling told her.

'Shall we get the young man in?' asked Miss Parsons.

Danny came into the room, his head down. He couldn't meet Dr Stirling's eye and twisted his hands nervously, gnawing his bottom lip.

'Hello, Danny,' said the doctor.

'Hello,' mumbled the boy, finally looking up.

'Come on,' said Dr Stirling, putting an arm around the boy's shoulder. 'Let's go home.'

Back at Clumber Lodge Dr Stirling asked Mrs O'Connor to come into the sitting-room.

'All's well that ends well,' said the housekeeper, bustling into the room.

'As your Grandmother Mullarkey would no doubt say,' added the doctor.

'No, no, it's Shakespeare, Dr Stirling,' Mrs O'Connor told him. 'Fancy you not knowing that.'

The doctor smiled. 'Sit down a moment, will you, Mrs O'Connor. I would like a word with you.'

'Is something wrong?' she asked.

'No, nothing's wrong.'

'Sure it's a wonderful thing, so it is, to have the boy back.'

'Mrs O'Connor,' said the doctor, 'when I went to collect Danny this morning, Miss Parsons told me that when he returned to his grandmother's after running away, Danny I gather became quite difficult.'

'I can't believe that, doctor,' she said.

'Yes, he became very untidy, played his music so loudly the neighbours complained, went out without telling his grandmother when he would be coming back and refused to do his homework or apply himself at school.'

'Sounds like a different boy,' remarked the housekeeper.

'Yes, that's what I thought,' said Dr Stirling. 'Miss Parsons thought that there was method in Danny's behaviour.'

'Method?' she repeated.

'That Danny was deliberately being difficult.'

'Doesn't sound like the lad at all,' said Mrs O'Connor.

'No, it doesn't. That he was intentionally being so unmanageable his grandmother might think again about having him live with her.' Mrs O'Connor patted her hair and said nothing. 'One wonders, of course, whether he was put up to it.'

'Put up to it, Dr Stirling?' said the housekeeper. 'And who in the world would put him up to it?'

Dr Stirling smiled. 'I wouldn't know,' he said.

Elisabeth called at Clumber Lodge later that day.

'Hello, Michael,' she said nervously when he answered the door.

'Hello, Elisabeth,' he replied. He looked gaunt and tired and sounded uneasy.

'I called round this morning to see you.'

'Yes, Mrs O'Connor said. Come in, come in. I wanted to see you. I didn't have much chance to congratulate you yesterday.'

In the sitting-room Elisabeth sat in a chair by the window, next to the inlaid walnut table on which the photographs of the doctor's wife had been arranged. She glanced at them and then looked over to the fireplace where Michael stood. He looked equally ill at ease, not knowing what to do with his hands.

'I wanted to apologise for yesterday,' she said. 'Almost pushing you out of the door like that.'

'There's really no need,' he replied solemnly. 'I guess you had things to talk about and I came at the wrong time.'

'Well, Simon turning up as he did came as quite a shock. I've not seen him for six years and he arrives on my doorstep.'

'Quite a surprise.'

'I didn't recognise him at first. He'd changed so much. He had lost so much weight and he looked exhausted and unwell.

Not the Simon I once knew. I never thought I would say this but I felt sorry for him. His marriage has broken down and he's lost his job. He looked so sad and vulnerable. He told me he had been seeing John for the past few months. I never knew that.'

'So . . . what did he want?' asked Dr Stirling. He was desperate to know, but feared what he might hear.

'To talk. He wanted to talk to me.'

'What about?' His voice quavered.

'It was to tell me he was full of regrets and remorse, sorry for the way he'd treated me, how he had reacted to John's disability. He said he'd had time to think about things and wanted to see me and tell me how bad he felt about it.'

'Is that all he wanted – to talk and say he was sorry?' He looked at her wistfully.

'No,' Elisabeth answered quietly. 'He asked me if we could try again, put it behind us and get back together.'

'I see.'

'I really think he's a changed man, Michael. I think he is genuinely sorry for the past.' There was great tenderness in her voice.

'So what did you say?'

'To what?'

He coughed and swallowed nervously. 'When he asked you to take him back. What did you say?'

'I said—'

The door burst open and the two boys rushed in. Danny ran straight to Elisabeth and threw his arms around her neck. 'I'm back, Mrs Devine,' he spluttered. 'I know I shouldn't hug you an' I won't do it when we're in t'school but I'm so made up I just can't stop missen. I'm back wi' Dr Stirling an' James an' Mrs O'Connor an' mi ferret. I'm so made up, I can 'ardly speak.'

'You're not doing too bad a job, Danny,' replied Elisabeth,

her eyes lighting up. She turned to Dr Stirling. He was looking at her intently, as if committing her face to memory, his pale blue eyes shining. 'And when did all this come about?' she asked.

'Danny's grandmother felt, after all, he would be better staying here,' he explained, 'and of course we are delighted to have him back.'

'And I'm comin' back to t'school on Monday!' exclaimed the boy.

'Danny,' said Dr Stirling, 'would you and James go up to your room for a moment please? I need to speak to Mrs Devine.' The boys could tell by the tone of his voice that this was likely to be a serious matter and not for their ears. 'Go on now, off you go both of you.'

The two boys left the room but remained in the hallway, leaving the sitting-room door ajar, the better to hear what was said.

'You were saying,' said Dr Stirling. He looked stiff and tense and his voice had a slight tremor in it.

'Yes, you asked me what my answer to Simon was,' said Elisabeth. 'Well, I told him I have a lovely cottage, that I've made many wonderful new friends, that I have just heard that I am to be offered a really exciting and challenging job, that I can see John every week and—'

'And?'

'And that I was in love. He is not the best-dressed man in the world and he can be stubborn at times and he's very untidy and he's a bit overweight and he's quite shy and doesn't say an awful lot, but he's the sweetest, kindest man in the world and I love him.'

'Oh!' he said. 'I think I need a drink.' He poured himself a large whisky and downed it in one great gulp. 'You love him, you really love him?'

'Yes, I do,' she replied, her eyes filling with tears.

He drew a huge intake of breath. 'I don't know what to say.' He laughed with relief.

'Say something, for goodness' sake,' said Elisabeth.

'I wrote you a letter when I got home last night,' he said, reaching into his pocket. 'You know I'm not that good at communicating my feelings, showing my emotions – I never have been. My mouth just won't seem to form the words I wish to say and I have wanted to say this to you, Elisabeth, so many, many times. I suppose it was the fear of rejection. I can't count the occasions I have cursed myself for my incurable reticence. But seeing you with your ex-husband . . . well, you'd better read it.' He held out the letter.

'Will you read it?' she asked.

'I know it by heart,' he said. He put the letter back in his pocket. 'I say that I love you not only for what you are and what you have achieved in life but for putting up with the thoughtless things I sometimes say and do. I say that I love you for the good things you have brought out in me, as you do with all those who know you, that you've made me feel a better person. When my wife died I had never felt such black despair, but you have drawn me out into the light. I say that I hoped that one day you could love me, but if not, then I wished you a happy life.'

'Michael,' she said, 'I've loved you for so long.'

'I think I've loved you longer,' he said. 'Ever since you shouted at me in the surgery when you first came to Barton.'

'I didn't shout,' she sniffed. 'I never shout.'

'Well, when you ticked me off for being so pig-headed,' he said good-humouredly.

He sat next to her, curled his arm around her shoulder and kissed her gently on the lips. 'I think it is customary in these circumstances,' he said, 'to go down on one knee.' He knelt before her and covered her hand gently with his own. 'And to ask you, my dear, dear Elisabeth, will you marry me?'

The voices of the two boys who had been eavesdropping could be heard in the hall. 'Say yes!' they shouted. 'Say yes!'

'Yes,' Elisabeth replied, beginning to cry. 'Of course I'll marry you.'

''Course, I knew it would happen,' said Mrs Sloughthwaite to her customer, as she rested her plump arms on the counter of the village store and post office. 'I predicted it from the beginning.'

'Psychic now, are you?' asked Mrs Pocock.

'It is true that I have a touch of the sixth sense,' replied the shop-keeper with a heave of the formidable bosom. 'I mean it was bound to come about. Anyway, it was forecasted here.' She tapped the horoscope page in the newspaper open before her. 'Oh yes, it was all in here if you care to read it. It was written in the stars.'

ACKNOWLEDGEMENTS

I owe a debt of gratitude to my editor, Francesca Best, ever-patient, good-humoured and encouraging, my publicist Kerry Hood for her tireless support and my literary agent Luigi Bonomi at LBA who has championed my work with great enthusiasm. I should also like to thank Helen Goodwin, social worker; Phil Champion, Principal of the Hesley Group of schools and formerly head teacher of Fullerton House Special School; and The Venerable Clive Mansell, Archdeacon of Rochester, for their invaluable advice.

About the author

Gervase Phinn is a teacher, freelance lecturer, author, poet, former schools inspector, educational consultant, and visiting professor of education. For fourteen years he taught in a range of schools, then acted as General Adviser for Language Development in Rotherham before moving on to North Yorkshire, where he spent ten years as a school inspector – time that has provided much source material for his books.

He is a Doctor of Letters of the University of Leicester and the University of Hull, a Doctor of the University of Sheffield Hallam, a Fellow of the Royal Society of Arts and an Honorary Fellow of York St John University and Leeds Trinity University. He is also President of the Society of Teachers of Speech and Drama and former President of the School Library Association.

Gervase lives with his family near Doncaster.

You can find out more on his website, www.gervase-phinn.com.

Read on for an extract from the hilarious and moving
new book in the Little Village School series . . .

The School Inspector Calls!

Gervase Phinn

Summer has arrived in Barton-in-the-Dale and as a new
term begins at the little primary school, it's not just the
warm weather that's getting people hot under the collar.

Meetings with the teachers from Urebank School to
discuss the merger are producing more than a few
fireworks, a disruptive new pupil arrives, set to cause
trouble, and a surprising staff love affair is exposed.
There's also a big school production of *The Wizard of
Oz* to organise as well as an impending visit from the
Minister of Education. Head teacher Elisabeth Devine
certainly has her work cut out for her.

And that's just some of the drama set to shake up
the village. Throw in a sprinkling of secrets, shocking
revelations, old flames, new liaisons, psychics, weddings
and misfortune . . . There's plenty to gossip about this term.

Coming out November 2013

HODDER &
STOUGHTON

I

Elisabeth Devine, head teacher of Barton-in-the Dale village school, stared down at the letters on her desk and sighed. She had been expecting this first piece of correspondence from the Education Office but now, as she read the contents, she felt her chest tighten with apprehension. She looked out of the classroom window at the vast panorama of fields, criss-crossed by silvered limestone walls which swept upwards to a belt of dark green woodland, the distant purple peaks and an empty azure sky. She dropped her eyes, reread the contents of the letter and sighed again.

She had been invited to a meeting with Ms Tricklebank, the Director of Education, to discuss the forthcoming merger of Barton-in-the-Dale village school with the neighbouring primary school at Urebank. The Education Committee, in an effort to save money, had decided to close some small schools in the county and amalgamate less successful ones and those which were losing pupils. The number of children at Urebank had decreased and it had been decided that the school would become part of a consortium with Barton-in-the-Dale.

The 'one-to-one consultation', the letter informed Elisabeth, would be for Ms Tricklebank to outline plans for the amalgamation which would take place the following term and would give Elisabeth the opportunity to 'talk things through' with the Director. Then a series of meetings involving both sets of the schools' staff would be arranged.

Elisabeth welcomed the opportunity of discussing the arrangements with the Director but did not look forward to the meetings with Mr Richardson, the headmaster (as he liked to style himself) at Urebank, and his team which would follow. She knew however that as the newly-appointed head teacher of the integrated schools, this was one very large nettle she would have to grasp – and pretty firmly, too.

Elisabeth's appointment had not been without its difficulties. She had been in competition for the post of head teacher with Robin Richardson, a self-important and condescending man who had subsequently been offered the post as her deputy, which he had grudgingly accepted. It would be a real challenge, thought Elisabeth, to get the teachers of both schools to work as a team and an even greater challenge to get the man who had been in competition for the head teacher's post and therefore felt angry and embittered, to accept the situation and work *with* her rather than against her.

The second letter did nothing to lighten her mood. It was from Mr Steel, Her Majesty's Inspector of Schools, informing her of an intended visit some time later that term. He said he would inform her of the date in due course.

A head appeared around the classroom door, a face as large and round as a full moon.

'Is it all right if I come in, miss?' asked the pupil cheerfully. She was a plump girl with bright ginger hair tied in bunches by two large bows. Smiling widely, she displayed an impressive set of shiny silver braces clamped on her teeth.

'Yes, of course, Chardonnay,' said Elisabeth, her face brightening at seeing one of her most good-humoured and enthusiastic pupils. 'My goodness, you're here bright and early at the start of term.'

'To tell the truth, I'm right glad to get back to school, miss,' replied the girl. She scowled and wrinkled her nose as if an unpleasant smell had wafted her way. 'I just had to get out of the house. There's been nothing but moaning and groaning and shouting and squabbling all the holidays. My dad's as grumpy as a bear with a sore bum. He's been in a right rotten mood since his van got nicked with all his tools in. And my gran's been just as bad complaining after being taken to hospital when she fell over line dancing and broke her ankle. My dad said it was her own fault because she'd had too many lager and limes. My mam said they were both doing her head in and she had enough trouble of her own having had a right old ding-dong with the manager at work. Now that our Bianca with the baby has gone to live in Clayton with her boyfriend, I've had no one to speak to.'

Elisabeth shook her head and laughed. 'Quite a time, by all accounts,' she said.

'Did you have a nice Easter, miss?' asked the girl.

'I did, thank you, but like you I'm glad to get back to school. There are a lot of things to do this term.'

The girl grinned. 'You're getting married soon aren't you, miss?' she announced.

Elisabeth smiled. 'I am, yes.'

'He's dead nice is Dr Stirling, isn't he, miss?'

'I think so.'

'It's right romantic,' said the girl, sighing heavily. 'Just like in the book what I'm reading. It's called *Sweet Dreams are Made of This* and there's this right dishy doctor and—'

Elisabeth changed the subject. 'How are your sister and baby, by the way?'

Chardonnay's sister Bianca had given birth unexpectedly on Christmas Day. The sixteen-year-old girl, barely out of school and fearful of how her parents would react, had managed to keep her condition a secret. She had taken to wearing a large shapeless coat, baggy jumpers and smocks – putting off the inevitable. Little Brandon had arrived, kicking and screaming lustily, delivered on the living room floor by Mrs Lloyd, a retired midwife who had been dragged from her festive dinner. Bianca, pleased at leaving home and getting away from all the recriminations and complaints, now lived with her partner Clarence and their child in a council flat in Clayton.

'They're doing right well, miss,' the girl told her. 'Bianca's still got her part-time job at the Rumbling Tum café in the village and her boyfriend is working at the bread factory in Clayton. He's on the Farmhouse Crusties at the moment but he hopes to be promoted to the slicers next month.'

'I'm really pleased to hear that things have worked out for them,' said Elisabeth. 'Though I guess that Clarence's Uncle Fred is missing him on the farm?'

'He is, miss. He wants him to go back but our Bianca won't have it. She said Clarence was taken advantage of and his uncle's a mean-minded old bugg— so-and-so.'

Of course, Bianca was quite right. Mr Massey, Clarence's uncle, was a tight-fisted, grasping and curmudgeonly old man and not well liked in the village.

'Well, I'd better put the kettle on in the staffroom, miss,' said the girl. 'The teachers will want a cup of tea when they arrive.'

Chardonnay and her friend Chantelle had volunteered to be tea monitors the previous term and they took the job seriously. They were charged with washing the cups and saucers in the staffroom, emptying the teapot and putting on the kettle for the teachers' morning and afternoon tea. The health and safety regulations precluded them from actually brewing the tea, something which the girls thought to be 'just plain daft,' accustomed as they were to doing it all the time at home.

'By the way, miss,' said the girl, 'we need a new rubber what-do-you-call-it on the teapot.'

Elisabeth looked at her quizzically.

'You know, miss, that rubber nozzle thing what goes on the end of the spout to stop the tea from dribbling. I was emptying the tea leaves down the lavvy this morning and it came off and got flushed away.'

'We'll get another,' Elisabeth told her. 'I don't think, however, that it is a very good idea to get rid of the tea leaves down the lavatory bowl. You remember what trouble we had last term when the toilets got blocked.'

'We've always done it, miss,' replied the girl. 'Anyway, I couldn't get it out before it got flushed away.'

'I see.'

'I've always managed to get it out in the past,' the girl told Elisabeth casually, 'and put it back on the spout, but this time I wasn't able to fish it out.'

Elisabeth stiffened and her mouth drooped with revulsion. Perhaps, she thought to herself, the teachers should make their own tea in future.

Mrs Scrimshaw, the school secretary, sat behind the desk in her office, her unfashionable horn-rimmed spectacles dangling on a cord around her neck. She stared wide-eyed and anxious at the screen and keyboard before her.

During the Easter holidays, when she had called in to school to deal with the post, she had discovered, to her consternation, two large cardboard boxes in her office. She knew what they contained, for the head teacher had fore-warned her. The new computer and printer had arrived. Reluctantly she had unpacked the contents and gazed in bewilderment at the assortment of wires, plugs and discs.

The caretaker had arrived at the office to see what she was up to. Mr Gribbon was a tall gaunt man with a hard beak of a nose and the glassy protuberant eyes of a large fish. He spent a great deal of his time regaling anyone willing to listen about the excessive amount of work he was expected to do and how he was a martyr to his bad back.

'Computer, eh?' he remarked, jangling his keys. He perched on the corner of the desk.

'Yes,' replied the secretary irritably, 'a computer.'

'I didn't know you were *au fait* with computers, Mrs Scrimshaw,' he said.

'I'm not!' she snapped.

'Well what are you doing with one, then?' asked the caretaker.

'Mrs Devine's got it into her head that I should use it instead of my electric typewriter.' She picked up a long black wire and held it as she might a venomous snake, her face screwed up in distaste. 'I've no idea where this goes,' she said.

'Well, there'll be a socket for it somewhere,' said the caretaker.

'Mr Gribbon,' retorted the school secretary, scowling, 'I am not entirely unaware of the strikingly obvious. Of course there'll be a socket. The machine is full of sockets and there are all these wires and plugs. I shall never get the hang of it. I'm supposed to be going on a course at the Teachers' Centre when school starts next week to learn how to use it and I'm dreading it. I'll feel such a fool with all these clever people who will know what to do. I don't know why I just can't use my typewriter.'

'We have to move with the times, Mrs Scrimshaw,' the caretaker told her unhelpfully.

'Is that so? And since when have you moved with the times?' she asked crossly, thrusting the tangle of wires back in the box. 'You're still using that old sweeping brush and you've been wearing that threadbare overall for as long as I can recall. You're not exactly *au fait*, as you put it, with all things modern.'

The caretaker made to speak but Mrs Scrimshaw hadn't finished.

'And as for moving with the times, in my view, if the wheel isn't broken it doesn't need fixing. I was perfectly happy with my typewriter and I have had no complaints.'

'The thing is, Mrs Scrimshaw,' said the caretaker, who should have had the common sense to let things lie, 'everybody's into word-processing these days. I mean from what Mrs Pugh was telling me, the secretary down at Urebank School is very clued-up on the computer.' Mrs Pugh was the part-time cleaner who spent two days at Barton-in-the Dale and the remainder of the week at the neighbouring school of Urebank. 'Mrs Pugh,' continued Mr Gribbon, jangling his keys, 'says the secretary down there rattles the letters off in no time.'

'Does she really. Well bully for her,' said the secretary.

'Mrs Pugh was telling me that the secretary down at Urebank—'

'Mr Gribbon!' interrupted Mrs Scrimshaw, 'I am not interested in what Mrs Pugh has to say, or anyone else for that matter. Now, did you want something?'

'I just popped in to say "hello" and to see if you wanted anything.'

'What I want is for this wretched machine to work,' she replied. 'You can make yourself useful and see if you can find out where all these wires go.'

'Oh no!' snorted the caretaker, sliding off the desk. 'Not my province. Anyway, I've got things to do. My floors need buffing.'

'Then I suggest you get on with buffing them,' she told him tersely.

The caretaker departed, leaving the school secretary staring in dismay at the computer.

★   ★   ★

Now, on the following Monday morning, the first day of the summer term, Mrs Scrimshaw sat staring at the machine on her desk. She had tried to get the computer to work but to no avail and wondered just how she was going to cope.

A small boy entered the office. He was a rosy-cheeked child of about eight or nine with bright brown eyes and hair cut in the short-back-and-sides variety, with a neat parting. He could have been a schoolboy of the 1950s, dressed as he was in short grey trousers, a crisp white shirt and striped tie, a hand-knitted grey pullover, long grey stockings and sensible shoes.

'Hello, Mrs Scrimshaw,' he said cheerfully.

'Oh hello, Oscar,' she replied glumly. 'You're here nice and early.'

'I was keen to get back to school,' he told her brightly. 'To be honest, I've been pretty bored over the holidays. "At a loose end," as my mother would say. I think she's quite glad that I'm back at school.'

Yes, I can well believe that, thought the school secretary. The boy could be annoying at times.

Oscar's eyes lit up when he caught sight of the machine. 'Wow!' he cried. 'A computer.'

'Yes,' she replied, weariness in her voice.

'It's a really top-notch one,' said the boy excitedly as he ran his fingers across the machine.

'Really?' the school secretary said with little enthusiasm.

'I have a computer,' Oscar continued. 'I got it last Christmas but it's not as hi-tech as yours. Pretty basic, actually. I'm hoping my parents will upgrade it for my next birthday.'

Mrs Scrimshaw lifted her head sharply like a dog picking up a scent.

'You know how this thing works then do you, Oscar?' she asked.

'Oh yes.'

'And you know where all these wires go?'

'Actually, they are called leads,' the boy told her, 'and each fits into a socket. All the sockets are different so it's impossible to put a lead in the wrong one. It's quite simple really. Would you like me to show you?'

'Thank you, Oscar,' said Mrs Scrimshaw. 'I would.'

She watched fascinatedly as the boy plugged in one lead after another and brought the computer to life.

'It's easy when you know how,' he explained, his small fingers tapping away on the keys. 'Shall I show you how to get on to the word-processor so you can write your letters?'

'If you could,' said the secretary, leaning over him.

When Mrs Devine put her head around the office door a moment later she found the school secretary and Oscar scrutinising the text on the screen in earnest discussion.

'Hello, Mrs Devine,' said the boy. 'Mrs Scrimshaw is just showing me how her new computer works.'

At the staff meeting that morning, before the start of school, Elisabeth welcomed her colleagues back and mentioned the proposed visit of the HMI and the forthcoming meetings with the teachers of Urebank which would take place later that term.

Mrs Robertshaw, the teacher of the lower juniors, was a large woman with a broad, red but friendly face and steely-grey hair twisted up untidily on her head. She was dressed in a brightly-coloured floral dress and shapeless lavender cardigan and sported a string of hefty glass beads around her neck. She folded her arms, narrowed her eyes and said tartly, 'Well, all I will say is that I cannot see that we will ever be able to work with the teachers at Urebank. I'm sorry to be so negative, Elisabeth, but it has to be said. As you know, I went to look around the school when I was minded to apply for a post there. I've been in this business long enough to smell a happy school and Urebank is not a happy school. The older children looked subdued and bored and the infants were disorganised and overexcited. Mind you, the teacher of the infants was at least friendly, which is more than can be said for the po-faced teacher of the upper juniors, the deputy head, who looked as if he'd been dug up. They should have closed the school when they had the chance.'

'Surely it's not that bad, Elsie?' volunteered Miss Brakespeare, the deputy head teacher, who sat crossed-legged in a stylish navy-blue suit and lemon blouse. She was aware that her colleague was prone to exaggeration.

'Oh, but it is, Miriam,' continued Mrs Robertshaw. She turned to Elisabeth. 'You may use all your charm, diplomacy and powers of persuasion but you've as much chance of getting them to work with you as getting the pope to visit a lap-dancing club. The head teacher at Urebank, that dreadful Mr Richardson, is a cold, disagreeable, humourless, ill-tempered and pompous individual who will do everything to undermine what you attempt to do.'

'Really, Elsie,' said Miss Brakespeare with a wry smile, 'why don't you tell us what you truly think about the man.'

Miss Wilson, teacher of the infants, could not help but chuckle. She was a slim young woman with short raven-black hair, a pale, delicately boned face and great blue eyes.

'You can laugh, Rebecca,' said Mrs Robertshaw, 'but you'll not be laughing when you have to work with him. He has the personality of a lump of petrified wood.'

'The deputy head teacher doesn't seem a whole lot better, by the sound of it,' remarked Miss Wilson.

'A pea out of the same pod, is Mr Jolly,' Mrs Robertshaw told her, 'and that's a paradox if ever there was one. He's about as jolly as a funeral bell. I think he's of the belief that he is doing the children a favour just by turning up for school. I mean, you've met him haven't you, Miriam?' she asked the deputy head teacher. 'It was that time when you went with our pupils to the poetry competition and his nose was put out of joint when one of our children won first prize and one of his was disqualified for copying out somebody else's poem?'

'Well, yes,' agreed the deputy head teacher, 'he wasn't the most agreeable person, I have to admit.'

'Well at least the infant teacher sounds nice enough,' said Miss Wilson.

'She's all right I suppose but a bit wishy-washy, as is the teacher of the lower juniors. They've probably become disillusioned and who can blame them, having to work for Mr Richardson and his sidekick.'

Elisabeth, who had been quiet but acutely attentive during this tirade, with her hands clasped on her lap, at last spoke.

'Well, we have little choice in the matter,' she said. 'The amalgamation is to take place so we will have to work with them come what may.'

'I'd be the first to put a bomb behind the teachers at Urebank,' remarked Mrs Robertshaw.

The staffroom became silent as the teachers contemplated what had been said and what lay ahead of them.

'I guess there will be difficulties,' said Elisabeth, 'but we have to make it work for the good of the children. I am, of course, looking for your full support.'

'That goes without question,' said Miss Brakespeare.

'Hear, hear,' chorused the others.

'Now, to more pleasant things,' said Elisabeth. 'We need to be thinking about the end-of-year school production. Any ideas?'

'What about *Oliver!*' said Miss Brakespeare. 'It's such a lovely heart-warming story and has some very catchy melodies.'

'They put on *Oliver!* at one of the schools where I was a supply teacher,' said Mrs Robertshaw, 'and it was a disaster. They had a nasty-tempered bull terrier called Butch for Bill Sikes's dog. Ugly beast it was, with teeth like tank traps and a fat round face. It attacked the Artful Dodger and then disgraced itself on stage by lifting its leg—'

'I don't think we need to go down that road, Elsie,' interrupted Elisabeth, smiling.

'What about an adaptation of one of Oscar Wilde's stories?' suggested Mrs Robertshaw. 'We've been reading them in class and the children have really liked them. Perhaps an adaptation of *The Selfish Giant* or *The Happy Prince*?'

'It's certainly worth considering,' replied Elisabeth, 'but they are rather sad stories. I was thinking of something a bit more cheerful. It needs to be a production that has a strong storyline, which involves a lot of children, has some memorable tunes, bright costumes and with some humour and maybe a little sadness.'

'What about *The Wizard of Oz*?' suggested Miss Wilson.

'Of course!' said Elisabeth.

'Excellent idea,' trilled Miss Brakespeare.

'An inspired suggestion,' agreed Mrs Robertshaw. 'I know just the children to take the leads.'

'Well, we all seem agreed,' said Elisabeth. 'So *The Wizard of Oz* it is. We'll send for the play version straight away.'

'And as soon as it arrives we will start auditions at the drama club,' added Mrs Robertshaw.

There was a sharp knock at the door and the caretaker entered.

'Yes, Mr Gribbon?' said Elisabeth.

He held up, between finger and thumb, the rubber spout from the teapot. 'Guess where I found this, Mrs Devine?' he asked, grimacing.

*　　*　　*

At morning break, Elisabeth called into the school office to find Mrs Scrimshaw tapping away happily on the keyboard of her new machine.

'You seem to have got to grips with the computer,' she said. 'I'm very impressed.'

'Actually, Mrs Devine,' replied Mrs Scrimshaw, looking up, 'it's relatively easy once you know how.' She was feeling quite smug.

'It's a wonder you managed to sort out all those wires.'

'Actually, they are called leads,' the secretary told her, sharing her new-found knowledge, 'and each fits into a socket. All the sockets are different so it's impossible to put a lead in the wrong one. It's quite simple really.'

'I hope young Oscar wasn't being too much of a nuisance? He's a very inquisitive child and can sometimes be a bit meddlesome.'

'No,' replied the school secretary, 'he was just interested. He likes to know what's going on in the school, does Oscar.' The boy in question had given Mrs Scrimshaw a crash course that morning and offered to continue with the lesson after school during the time he waited for his mother to collect him.

'I really didn't expect you to be using the computer until you had been on the course this Friday,' disclosed the head teacher. 'I imagined that you would still want to use your typewriter until you were *au fait* with the new machine.'

Mrs Scrimshaw gave a little smile at hearing the use of the phrase *au fait*. 'Oh no, Mrs Devine,' she said, 'I thought I'd make a start. In my book, the sooner one becomes conversant with the new technology, the better.'

'I am very pleased you feel that way. I have to admit when I first broached the matter of you using a computer, I did have an inkling that you were not all that keen on parting with your typewriter.'

'One has to move with the times, Mrs Devine,' the school secretary told her.

'Actually,' said Elisabeth, 'I called in to say that I'm expecting a couple of parents – a Mr and Mrs Banks. They are coming in to see me after school this coming Friday, if you could put that in your diary. When they arrive, could you show them down to my classroom please? They want their son to start here. Evidently things haven't worked out for Robin at his last school.'

'Robin Banks!' exclaimed Mrs Scrimshaw. 'The child's called Robin Banks?'

'Yes,' replied the head teacher.

'Well how ridiculous. Fancy inflicting a name like Robin Banks on a child.'

'I am afraid that sometimes parents do not think things through when they come to naming their children,' Elisabeth told her.

'I'm sure some do it deliberately,' remarked the school secretary, sniffing. 'I remember we've had at the school a Sunny Day and a Sandi Beech, Hazel Nutt and Daisy Chain, twins called Armani and Chanel and one poor child was burdened with Terry Bull.' She paused and shook her head. 'And once we had a girl named Jenny Taylor.'

'Jenny Taylor?' repeated Elisabeth, looking puzzled.

'I shan't explain, Mrs Devine,' said the secretary. 'I shall leave you in blissful ignorance.'

Mr Gribbon, having alerted the head teacher to the fact that 'some of the kids have started putting foreign bodies down the toilets again,' strode off to his small storeroom near the boiler, his keys jangling in his overall pocket. There he found Mrs Pugh, the part-time cleaner, waiting for him with a mug of steaming tea in her hand.

'I've just made a pot, Mr Gribbon,' she said chirpily.

The caretaker's face brightened. 'Oh hello, Mrs Pugh. All done have we?'

'All done, Mr Gribbon,' she repeated, handing him a mug. 'Shelves dusted, tables wiped down, toilets cleaned, carpets swept and the floors buffed just as you like them. You can see your face in the floors.'

'I was going to buff them myself,' he told her.

'Well I've saved you the trouble. "Everything's tidy," as my sainted Welsh grandmother would say.'

'She'd not be saying that if she could see the classrooms at the end of the day after the kids have been let loose,' complained the caretaker. He exhaled noisily through his teeth. 'And the teachers are just as bad. It'll look as if a bomb's been dropped on the place.'

'Well it keeps us in a job, Mr Gribbon,' she said cheerfully.

'Aye, I suppose so,' he grumbled, looking down at his tea. Then, after a thoughtful pause, he looked up. 'I can't tell you what a godsend you've been since you started here, Mrs Pugh.' He took a gulp of his tea and flopped into his old armchair.

'That's very kind of you to say so, Mr Gribbon,' replied the part-time cleaner. She gave a small, self-satisfied smile and patted her purple-tinted perm.

'Oh yes, you've lifted a heavy weight from off of my shoulders and no mistake since you started here,' he said.

'Well I'm surprised you managed for so long without any help,' she sympathised.

The caretaker nodded in agreement. 'I'm not one to complain, Mrs Pugh, but it has been hard what with having to do all this rubbing and scouring, polishing and cleaning single-handed.'

'What with your bad back and all the heavy lifting,' she added.

The caretaker put on a martyred expression. 'Yes, I sometimes wonder myself how I ever managed. The last head teacher, Miss Sowerbutts, was a tartar and the present one is not much better, always wanting something or other doing. I was never off my feet.' He stretched out his legs and took another gulp of tea.

'Taken for granted, Mr Gribbon,' observed the part-time cleaner.

'You're not wrong there, Mrs Pugh.'

'Well, you've got me to help now,' she said.

The caretaker leaned back and rested his head on the back of the chair. 'I have indeed, Mrs Pugh, and as I've said, you've been a godsend.'

'I just wish the caretaker down at Urebank was as appreciative as you, Mr Gribbon,' she said. 'Face on him like a wet weekend in Port Talbot and always finding fault with something or other. And the head teacher, well! Don't get me started on him.'

'Taken for granted, Mrs Pugh,' observed the caretaker.

'You're not wrong there, Mr Gribbon.'

'They don't know how lucky they are, Mrs Pugh,' said the caretaker. 'I wish I could have you full time.'

'Beg pardon, Mr Gribbon?'

The caretaker's face flushed. 'W ... w ... what I meant was that I wish you could work here all the time instead of me having to share you with Urebank.'

Mrs Pugh smiled. 'Well, next term when this amalgamation takes place, there's every likelihood you will have me working with you full time.' She patted her purple hair again. 'You'll probably get sick of the sight of me,' she added coyly.

'Never!' protested the caretaker.

'Tea all right?' she asked.

'Champion. Just the way I like it.'

'My sainted Welsh grandmother, God rest her soul, always liked her tea strong,' the part-time cleaner told him. 'Strong enough to stand a spoon up in it, as she was wont to say.'

'I remember if I left a spoon standing up in a cup of tea,' said the caretaker, smiling at the memory, 'my grandmother used to say that that was how Nelson lost his eye.'

'You are a card, Mr Gribbon, and no mistake,' she said, chuckling.

'Well you make a lovely brew, Mrs Pugh,' said the caretaker. 'I bet you're a good cook as well.'

'As a matter of fact I have been told so,' she replied. 'My coffee and walnut cake is the talk of the Townswomen's Guild and in cookery at school, Miss Reece said my spotted dick was the best she had ever tasted.'

'My wife doesn't cook,' said the caretaker gloomily.

'Sadly, I don't get much opportunity to cook cakes and puddings these days,' Mrs Pugh continued. 'My husband is a boiled beef and carrots man. He hasn't got a sweet tooth in his body. He likes his savouries, does Owen.'

They were quiet for a while.

'Kids will be arriving soon,' observed Mr Gribbon, breathing out loudly. 'By the way, I took that rubber spout you found down the toilet to Mrs Devine. I told her she needs to speak to the kids about putting foreign objects down the toilets and nip it in the bud before they all start doing it. Last term this little tyke called Oscar—'

'I've met him this morning,' interrupted Mrs Pugh. 'He has far too much to say for himself, that young man. Only started to tell me that there was still dust on some of the books, just after I'd given the school library a good going-over!'

'He's a pain in the neck is that lad,' barked the caretaker. 'Last term he started putting ping pong balls down the toilet.'

'Ping pong balls!' exclaimed the part-time cleaner.

'Said the boys could aim at them to stop them dribbling on the floor.'

'I've never heard the like,' said Mrs Pugh.

'And it started a craze,' continued the caretaker. 'Soon the other kids started putting things down and the pipes got blocked with tennis balls.'

'Tennis balls!'

'Then I had water and I don't know what else all over my parquet floor.'

'Dear me.'

'It took some buffing, I can tell you.'

'I bet it did.'

'I don't know what gets into kids these days,' sighed the caretaker, blowing out his cheeks.

'They have it too easy,' declared Mrs Pugh. 'Owen and I never had children.'

'Nor us,' said the caretaker, 'but had we had children they wouldn't have turned out like that Oscar, I can tell you that for nothing.'

There was a sharp knock on the door. Outside stood the boy in question.

'Ah there you are, Mr Gribbon,' said the boy cheerily. 'I've been looking all over the school for you. I think you should know that there's a rather unpleasant smell in the boys' toilets and there's a dripping tap.'

We love a happy ending. But, almost more
than that, we love the promise of a new beginning.

Join us at www.hodder.co.uk, or follow us on Twitter
@hodderbooks, and be part of a community of escapists
who enjoy nothing more than curling up with a good book.

Whether you want to find out more about this book,
or a particular author, watch trailers and interviews, have
the chance to win early limited editions, or simply browse
our expert readers' selection of the very best books,
we think you'll find what you're looking for.

And if you don't, that's the place to tell us what's missing.

We love what we do, and we'd love you to be part of it.

www.hodder.co.uk

@hodderbooks

HodderBooks

HodderBooks